Frances Paige acquired ma when the first volume of her family saga, *The Sholtie Burn*, was published in 1986, but she has always been a popular and prolific writer, under a variety of pseudonyms. She has published two previous novels under the name Frances Paige: *Three Girls* and *Lost Time*. *Maeve's Daughter*, the second volume of her saga, will be followed by a third book about the McGraths.

Born in Scotland, the author is married to a psychiatrist whose thinking, she admits, has greatly influenced her approach to characterization. She and her husband live in Lancashire and travel regularly to south-west France, her second love.

By the same author

Three Girls
Lost Time
The Sholtie Burn

FRANCES PAIGE

Maeve's Daughter

GRAFTON BOOKS

A Division of the Collins Publishing Group

LONDON GLASGOW
TORONTO SYDNEY AUCKLAND

Grafton Books
A Division of the Collins Publishing Group
8 Grafton Street, London W1X 3LA

Published by Grafton Books 1989

First published in Great Britain by
Souvenir Press Ltd 1987

Copyright © Frances Paige & Souvenir Press Ltd 1987

ISBN 0-586-20157-2

Printed and bound in Great Britain by
Collins, Glasgow

Set in Times

Acknowledgements

I would like to express my appreciation of the sterling help I've received from two Local Studies Librarians, Anne Escott of the Glasgow Room, the Mitchell Library, and Ethel Goodall of the Public Library, Motherwell. They were both unfailing in their courtesy, and I thank them sincerely.

BOOK ONE

Going Forward
1885–1890

1

No one can wear a hat like mother, Maevy thought, watching the tall elegant figure in full fig coming towards her with her grand-daughter, Lizzie, in tow, a manikin in an identical bottle-green velvet suit, the nipped-in waist, the puffed sleeves, more exaggerated than most Glasgow women or children might wear, the same red hair – in Lizzie's case ringleted where her grandmother's was swept up and partly concealed by the black pill-box hat trimmed with tulle and one green rose. A confection, not a hat, worthy of the Colosseum Millinery Department itself.

The woman and the child each wore a black astrakhan muff on a silver chain. Lizzie's hands were buried in hers – it was a nippy December day with the wind blowing off the Clyde – but Maeve had one hand raised to greet her daughter and namesake. Her blue eyes were brilliant in the paleness of her face, her smile had a richness.

Maevy bent to her small nephew, whose hand she was holding. 'There's your cousin Lizzie, Robert.' She gave her own hat a tug, unwieldy on her head after the trimness of her Sister's cap, moved her body against the blue serge of her suit, feeling her back itch. And her corset was too tight. The Royal Infirmary's diet was meant to sustain, not hone, the figure. 'You look lovely, Mother,' she said as they met and kissed. 'Your perfume will kill the smell of carbolic on me.'

Maeve lowered her voice, glancing at the boy, 'Someone, you know who, said I spent as much on perfume as a Frenchwoman!'

Maevy laughed. 'She'll have you running a brothel at

Braidholme next!' They had always shared the same sense of humour, especially about Catherine, Robert's mother.

'A brothel, is it? Now, that's a grand idea to be sure. Set Sholton by the heels.' Sometimes Maevy imagined that since her father's death the Irish lilt in the voice had intensified. Perhaps it was her mother's way of keeping his memory green. 'Anyhow, it's you who look lovely in your mufti, but, then, a bonny face fits the dishcloth.' She bent to kiss her grandson. 'Well, Robert, are you looking forward to seeing the Christmas Fair?'

He nodded, his face serious. 'Yes, Grandma, but Father says after the new baby arrives, he'll take a box at Hengler's Circus.'

'Oh, you'll enjoy that. There are little monkey jockeys riding the ponies, and a clown called Yorick and a wonderful water spectacle and . . .'

'How do you know all that?' Maevy asked. 'You never took us when we were small.'

'And didn't I often wish we could? But five children on your father's pay . . . No, it was Emily and Victoria, Kate's charges, who described it to me . . . like magic, it sounded.'

'That's what Father says,' Robert put in, 'like magic, with hundreds and hundreds of tons of water flooding the stage and he's going to ask you, and Uncle John and Aunt Isobel, and Uncle Patrick and Aunt Maria with little Sarah and you, Aunt Maevy and . . .'

'You forgot me, you forgot me!' Lizzie, who had been listening open-mouthed, jumped up and down, her curls jumping, too.

He considered, like a little man in his grey Harris tweed coat and voluminous cap to match. 'Yes, you'll be coming. You're the eldest.'

'And what about your other cousins in America?' Maeve said.

'Father didn't say them.' Robert looked worried.

'Well, we'll just have to take lots and lots of boxes.' Lizzie clapped her hands.

'She's just like your brother, Terence,' Maeve laughed at her daughter, 'no penny-pinching.'

'Listen to the pot calling the kettle black.' Maeve shepherded the two children in front of them, 'Come on, then, or we'll be arrested for standing in Jamaica Street for too long.'

The Colosseum had been one of the first Glasgow stores to introduce electricity, and when they went in the place was a blaze of light with Chinese lanterns in their hundreds. The children were speechless.

'Don't stray away from us, mind,' Maevy said to them as they went up the grand staircase. 'If you get lost you won't see all the splendid things when we go through the Grand Arcade.'

It well deserved its name with its bowers of artificial flowers and coloured bead-work, but what enchanted the children even more was Mr Walter Wilson's New French Circus, where a small mechanical pony galloped round the room with a mechanical lady on its back, pirouetting and dipping on one pointed toe. But even that could not be compared with the Wonderland with its quacking geese and stalking cats, and the Italian organ grinder who obligingly played when a penny was dropped in his front.

Maeve said to her daughter, 'Do you remember when you were taken to church when you were small and you shouted out, "Where's your monkey, Joe?" to the new organist?'

'I never did!'

'Terence nearly died of shame because he was trying to impress Catherine.' Maeve's laugh rang out and Maevy had to laugh with her. 'There was an old Italian called Joe who used to come round the village on Sundays with a barrel organ and a monkey sitting on it. You always ran out and danced.'

Across the years Maevy inhabited the dancing figure, skirts held out, even heard in her ears the clackety noise of boots ringing on the metalled road. And felt again the sharp nudge of Terence's elbow as she struggled to stand on the church pew . . . 'You've a great imagination on you to be sure,' she said, mimicking her mother's way of speaking.

At last they had both to admit they were whacked. 'What wouldn't you give for a cup of tea?' Maeve said, although to Maevy she looked as fresh as paint. It was no good telling herself she was a nurse and had no time for fal-de-rals. Her mother had given birth to six children in Colliers' Row and reared them in poverty, no, only five . . . John. Her heart could still miss a beat when she remembered that dearly beloved young brother who had drowned in the Sholtie Burn. She had told Charlie McNab about him once, when they were taking a turn in the Necropolis, handy for the Infirmary.

'And is that why you became a nurse, all that scouring and cleaning, to wash away your guilt?'

'No, it isn't!' She had been stung. 'And how about you slaving away in general practice in Sholton and dashing in here any time you have a minute?'

'It's to see you.' He had laughed at her.

'What a hope!'

'All right, I want to be where great things are happening, not that they don't happen every day in the practice at Sholton, births and deaths, but it's the future. I want to be part of it, just as I want to be part of your future. Go on, Maevy, say you'll marry me . . .'

She had shaken her head, drawn her red-lined cloak closely round her. 'I'm not ready yet.'

* * *

'Good day, Mrs McGrath.' It was one of the shop-walkers, resplendent in frock-coat and pearl pin in his stock. 'Are the children happy with our little display?'

'They're enchanted, Mr McAllister. We're afraid we're never going to be able to drag them away from all these marvels.'

'Yes, the piping bullfinch has been a great success. Have you visited our new afternoon tea salon, by the way?'

'We were just thinking about it . . .' Maeve glanced ruefully at the children.

'Might I presume to detail one of our staff to keep an eye on your daughter's children . . .'

'Oh, they're not mine. They're my nephew and niece,' Maevy interrupted.

'Ah . . .' A natural mistake, the man's look seemed to say. 'They'll be in good hands, I can assure you.'

'Thank you, then, Mr McAllister.' Maeve gave him her brilliant smile. 'We'll take advantage of your kind offer.'

'It's our pleasure.' He bowed. 'And I'll see that you get an invitation to our Fashion Show. They only go to our most valued customers.' He bowed again. 'Good day, Mrs McGrath, good day, Miss McGrath.' Had he empha-sized the 'Miss'?

'Isn't this great?' Maeve squeezed Maevy's arm like a girl as they made their way to the afternoon tea salon. That was Mother, everything was always turned into an adventure. She remembered the blanket houses she had taught them to make in bed, draping them over the bed ends. 'Imagine you're camping in darkest Africa like David Livingstone . . .'

How sad Father must have been to die and leave her. For the first time she saw her through his eyes. How many wives were exciting to live with? She thought of the prim face of her sister-in-law, Catherine, the precise diction

13

when she was speaking at one of her meetings for the Temperance Movement. Poor old Terence. She would be watching him like a hawk at Maria and Patrick's Christmas party tonight.

'So, what's the family news?' she said when they were sipping their tea and nibbling one of the Colosseum's renowned 'fancies'.

'The business is going well, I'm there every day, have been since Lizzie went to Isobel and John.' Maevy saw the momentary sadness. 'Patrick hasn't missed his chance with horse-cars, naturally, but it's only a matter of time before the City Council take them over, so that revenue will go.'

'You still do carting for the railways?'

'Oh, yes, plenty. Short hauls. And plenty of work comes in from the Cleansing Department. But Patrick has no love of horses, unlike your father. It was his love of them that took him into the stables that night . . .' Her eyes glittered with sudden tears but unlike most women she did not dab at them with her handkerchief. They swam luminously in her pale face as she smiled. 'Glasgow's too small for our Patrick. He's desperate to get everything mechanized. Sometimes I think he'll pack up and go to America.'

'I think Maria still suffers from homesickness. She looks so wistful at times.'

'Still . . .' Maeve forked a piece of iced cake with genteel gusto, 'I should have thought she'd have put down her roots by this time. Sarah's two now and little Gaylord's a lovely baby. They're fortunate.' She meant because they were full cousins.

'She's happy with Patrick, isn't she?'

'Oh, yes, she adores him. Of course Bessie Haddow was his great love but that's behind him now. Maria has Bessie's gaiety with more assurance but then she'd been

14

brought up to it. She doesn't come from a butt and ben as Bessie did.'

'As we did.' Her mother nodded. She had never been given to talking about her old home in Ireland which had been so different.

'It was a comedown for you.' Surely I can say that now. I'm nearly twenty-four, a Sister in the Royal, one of Today's Women.

'What do you mean, a comedown?'

'Well . . .' a cake crumb had lodged in her throat, 'you had a different life, hunting . . .' The blue eyes snapping fire in the pale face made her stop.

'Never underestimate the power of love, Maevy.' And then she was saying, coolly, 'How are you getting on with Charlie McNab?'

'Charlie?' She lowered her eyes to the iced cake on her plate. There was an initial 'C' on it in chocolate icing. It could not be . . . no, it was for 'Colosseum', of course. Embarrassment addled one's mind. 'Oh, he's about the Infirmary a lot,' she said airily.

'But is he about *you* a lot?'

'For an Irish lady that's a coarse remark to make. This family of mine is obsessed with Charlie McNab! Maria's even asked him tonight, as if he was one of the family. We're the best of friends, that's all.'

'Och aye. I'll believe you. Thousands wouldn't.' Her smile disappeared. 'He's the best doctor we've ever had at Sholton. I couldn't have got through your father's death without him. I've a good family, but sometimes you need someone outside to put things in perspective. He supplied that, wise beyond his years, and with a touch of gaiety thrown in.'

'Oh, I know all that, Mother.' The serge was making her back itch again. 'But I'm interested in my career. I might even be the Matron some day . . .'

15

'And an old maid into the bargain.'

'Marriage isn't everything.'

'It was to me.' She put her hand on Maevy's hand and looked into her eyes. 'When are you going to forget John Craigie?'

She shook her head, unable to speak. How they probed, mothers . . . if only she could rid her mind of him. What was it about Isobel's husband which had taken her heart at sixteen and kept it? He hadn't an intellect like Charlie McNab's, or a future – a minister in a mining village – he had no dash, no polish, and yet she still could hardly enter a room where he was without trembling. 'How is Isobel?' She forced herself to speak calmly, 'Is she better in health now Lizzie's with them?'

'Still frail, she always will be, Charlie says, but she's making a splendid mother. And John's as fond as she is. I met them the other day when he was escorting Lizzie to the Hall for a birthday party.'

'The son and heir's?'

'Yes, Nigel, he's called. I think he's ages with Lizzie, getting on for eight.'

'Our Lizzie's moving in elevated circles. Of course, you've known his father for a long time, haven't you?' She was bland. Terence had once told her there had been a friendship, more than a friendship, he had hinted, but he had been expansive with drink.

'I had the privilege of riding one of Lord Crawford's horses for a time.' Her eyes were cool. 'Did I ever tell you about that business with Isobel? Three years ago, it'll be. More tea?'

'Yes, please. It's nice.'

'It's China. They know here I prefer China. Involutional melancholia, Charlie called it. He was very worried.'

'I hadn't realized . . .' She listened through the subdued

16

chatter and the tinkle of teacups to her mother's voice, the lilt coming and going like a bright thread woven into it. She had always been able to paint a picture with words, true Irish . . .

Maeve sat up straight in her carved oak chair in the board-room of McGraths. It helped, as did the room itself, lined with the best oak like the staterooms of the Clyde liners, as did the painting of Kieran above the mantelpiece. One of the best artists of the Glasgow School.

'I asked you to stay back to discuss Lizzie.' She saw the two brothers look away from each other, felt the immediate tension. 'Oh, I know it's a painful subject but there's her future to consider. Either of you have a greater claim on her than I have, and I'm getting older. She needs young parents . . .'

Terence was the first to speak. 'I'd have her like a shot, Mother, but Catherine's never forgiven me for . . . Bessie. I've asked her often. She won't have Lizzie. She's adamant.'

'You, Patrick?' She looked at him.

'Yes, we'd like her. Even if we have children of our own. We've discussed it. There's only one thing. Uncle Terence and Kate's husband have been suggesting outlets for the firm for some time. I might have to make quite a few visits. And Maria would want to go with me. After all, she left her own country to marry me.'

'America suits our Patrick's pushing ways,' Terence said.

'Is that so?' They were glaring at each other.

'Will you stop looking at each other like bulls over a gate.' They had given her the reasons she had thought they would. 'It's Lizzie we're talking about, and her happiness. She's left with Susan every day when I'm here . . .'

17

'Why did you raise this today?' Patrick asked. He had always been quicker off the mark than Terence. 'Have you something on your mind?'

'Yes.' You had to be straight with Patrick. 'Isobel. She has John Craigie worried out of his mind, and Charlie McNab who's no fool fears she's going into a decline. Supposing *they* had Lizzie . . .' She saw the two astonished faces raised to her. 'Oh, lads, it would be a sensible thing to do, a young girl eating out her heart in misery, knowing she'll be empty-armed for ever. Lizzie would still be in Sholton where she's at home . . .'

'Would they want to adopt her?' Patrick's voice was sharp.

'It wasn't discussed . . .'

'You go at least, Mother,' Terence's eyes were soft, 'and spy out the land.'

'Yes, go.' Patrick nodded. 'We'll not say any more just now.' She got up.

She found Isobel sitting listless at the fire. Her narrow face was ashen, her usual immaculate hair untidy. 'It's an illness,' Charlie had said to her, 'and yet worse than an illness. The patient feels hopeless, worthless, complete apathy.' His bright black eyes had pierced hers. 'You're not the type to ever know that feeling, even in your deepest sorrow.'

She put an arm round the thin shoulders. 'I was hoping I'd find you a bit better . . .' No answer. 'What can I do or say to comfort you . . .' She looked at the stony face, grey, the deeply-scored eyes. 'Remember I lost your brother, John, in the Sholtie, remember I could have no more children either . . .'

'You had us.' There was a weary impatience in the voice. 'You weren't a failure.'

'*You* a failure,' she hated her own false cheerfulness, 'and you and John the best-loved Reverend and wife since

18

I don't know when! A failure is it when you helped us in the business until you married. No one has ever kept the books like you. And the ladies of the parish are for ever singing your praises . . . although they're disappointed you're not turning up at their sewing meetings.'

'I've nothing to sew for since my baby died.'

'But that's nearly a year ago! What about the poor, then? You were the one who chose to come back with me from America although Kate wanted you to stay on, but, no, nothing would do but that you'd come back to John.'

'You're twisting it, Mother. We came back because we got the telegram about Bessie . . . Maria called today.'

'Did she now? And was she asking you to be sure to come and see that fine house of theirs in Claremont Terrace although it will never be the equal of Catherine's . . .?'

'She's pregnant.' Isobel turned to her, her thin face livid. 'Catherine, now Maria. Do you hear? Pregnant! And a big strong girl like her will have children without any trouble and now that Catherine's had Robert she'll have another one and I'm barren . . .!' Her voice rose in a wail and she flung herself weeping against her mother.

'Hush, hush . . .' She held the girl close, felt her sorrow as if it were her own. 'Hush, hush . . .' Charlie said it was better for her to cry.

She lay exhausted at last, quiet, except when a shuddering kind of moan escaped from her. 'I want to die, die . . .' she repeated the word, again and again.

'I've had a talk with the boys today,' Maeve said, clearly, briskly. She put the girl from her.

'What about?' Her voice was flat.

'Lizzie. I sometimes think she shouldn't be left with Susan so much. No young company.'

'No young company . . .'

'Are you listening to me? Susan's thrawn and set in her

19

ways. Listen to me. You've got a good brain. Maria once wrote to me that sooner or later the boys would have to get together and discuss, not what had happened to them, but what was to happen to Lizzie. It stuck in my memory.' Isobel's head drooped. 'I've had a word with them.'

'So which one's willing to take her?' It was her old sharp tone.

'Neither. Catherine won't have any reminder of Bessie Haddow about the place, and Patrick plans to take Maria with him when he's visiting America.'

'She won't be travelling much now.'

'Maybe not but she won't want Lizzie with a first pregnancy ahead of her. Isobel, the boys have agreed. Would you give Lizzie a home?'

'Us?' There was a flicker in her eyes then she shook her head. 'It's too late. You know I'm not well, not . . . capable. It's this terrible, terrible,' she put her hand to her side, 'load. Night and day. It never leaves me.'

'It would make you well, believe me. You need a child. Lizzie needs a mother, a young mother like you.'

'We love her dearly . . . wee Lizzie. No, it's not possible.' She began to weep again, weak tears, 'But you, Mother, you'd miss her . . .'

'Of course I would. But I've explained to you, have you not been listening, how I worry about leaving her with crotchety Susan all day long, and none of you want me to give up my interest in the business. Besides, I could see her here as much as I like, couldn't I? You wouldn't be able to get rid of me. John would begin to complain about his mother-in-law haunting the place . . .'

'You know he wouldn't.' She looked at Maeve, tear-stained, worn, but with a bit of life in her eyes. 'I can't let you do this, Mother. With the wits I've got left I know you're doing it for me.'

'Dry your eyes, pet. Here's a handkerchief. That's it.

Look, I've had my fiftieth birthday. I want to start gallivanting, go to America again and perhaps go with Kate to Paris to visit her step-daughter. Maybe even go to Ireland, though that'll have to wait until I can bear to go alone . . . Lizzie takes a lot of looking after at my age. She needs young parents who'll run down the Sholtie Brae with her, watch her when she's climbing trees . . . you've got some fine ones in the manse garden. You can have children's parties and ask all her cousins, oh, just think of it, Isobel, it would be a new life for you.'

'The boys will never agree when it comes to it.'

'Didn't I tell you they had. What about John?'

'He loves Lizzie. Next to you.' There was a glimmer of a smile.

'Next to me indeed! But a long way after his Isobel. I even remember him ogling you from the pulpit. Now, go and wash your face and tidy your hair, and put on your prettiest gown – that garnet one sets off your fairness better than anything – and talk it over with John.' She had been too precipitate. The girl still sat, head lowered. Maeve took both her hands.

'Never mind the garnet gown. That'll do for another time. Grief's an illness, but you'll get better from it. Won't you do this for me, for John, for wee Lizzie? For yourself? Just think of the two of you sitting here together and you teaching her fine seaming. I've never been any good at it. And showing her how to bake in the kitchen. Remember the beautiful cake you baked for Patrick's wedding?'

'Would Lizzie *like* to come here?'

'She'd jump at the chance. She'd be running the Sunday School in no time. She's bossy, like me.'

'You're not bossy. Only loving. Well, just a wee bit bossy.' Isobel got up. Her thin fingers tried to tuck in the strands of hair falling about her face. 'I'll go . . . and run a comb through it. Will you stay,' her mouth trembled, 'and speak to John?'

'No, thank you all the same.' It was not a place for her. 'Susan locks up early. She's like a gaoler. And Wally MacDonald's picking me up in the hansom at nine.' She looked at the black marble clock on the mantelpiece with the fluted columns, a monstrosity, a gift from the parishioners on their marriage. Like the tombs in the Necropolis. 'I think I heard it rolling up a little time ago.'

'Oh, Mother . . .' Isobel knelt down and buried her head in Maeve's lap. She stroked the fair hair, blind fair, they used to call it, fair right to the roots and no sign of it darkening. John must like it when it was spread out on the pillow. Kieran had liked hers, had buried his face in it often. Why was she so prone to tears these days? The big grief was over, yet she felt vulnerable, like some shell-less creature in the sand. She would have to cheer herself up and not get the name of a doleful face.

But the tears were still filling her eyes as Wally drove her home, and the sight of the dark front of Braidholme did nothing to dry them. How cheerless the place would be without that little figure dashing to meet her when she came home from Glasgow. 'Gran, Gran! Guess what happened today?' Life for Lizzie was always an adventure. She was like her mother, Bessie. She laughed the same way, open-mouthed.

2

Claremont Terrace, a stone's throw from Charing Cross, was part of a small development designed by John Baird One, a copy of Edinburgh New Town, it was said. Perhaps Mr Baird was not in the same class as 'Greek' Thomson, the architect of Great Western Terrace where Terence and Catherine lived, but the crescent, for that was really what it was, had appealed to Patrick and Maria when they first saw it with its graceful curve, its projecting Ionic porches, and for Maria, at least, its wrought-iron balconies. 'They remind me of Mama's description of her family home at Norfolk, Virginia,' she had said.

She and Patrick had not spent their honeymoon in Virginia as she had hoped. Patrick could not take much time off from the business in Glasgow, and after less than a week in a small country house in Tarrytown loaned to them by one of her father's friends, they had sailed back to Scotland to stay with Maeve at Braidholme, until such times as they could find a house for themselves.

She had found him shy on their first night, uncommunicative, but she had always been outspoken, and lying in the bedroom at Tarrytown with the river light dappling the ceiling, she had said to him, 'I know how you loved Bessie. Your mother told me and how tragic her death must have been to you. I can feel that because I love you, too, so much. Could you accept my love in lieu of what you've lost?' She had touched his arm and he had turned swiftly to her, half-groaning, and took her in his arms. His passion surprised her but did not frighten her. She gave herself fully with more fervour than perhaps the

23

average bride was supposed to show. How could she know? Her mother had been romantically tremulous but discreet during the bridal preparations. It was a relief to be rid of her virginity.

She popped her head round the door of Patrick's dressing-room. 'Are you ready, sweetheart? It's six-thirty. They'll soon be here.'

He turned to face her, smiling as he pushed the pearl pin through his grey silk cravat. 'And you're the one who was worried about having lost your figure after little Gaylord! I could span your waist wi' ma two hauns!' He sometimes relapsed into the vernacular to amuse her.

'Try, then.' She knew she looked well. Some people thought that having a baby cleared your system of all impurities, but there was no doubt that the face she had seen in the mirror earlier had been suffused with health, the dark eyes alive and clear, the cheeks flushed. Flora, the new maid, had been goggle-eyed.

He came towards her, hands outstretched, his lean face relaxed and happy. He spanned her waist at the same time as he drew her towards him. 'You're bonny, wife.'

'That's what Flora said, "gey bonny". She's bonny herself.'

'Is that the new maid?'

'Yes, I went to interview her last week. At the Saltmarket. What a terrible place that is!'

'I told you it wasn't fitting to wander about Glasgow. You might get harmed in those slums.'

'I've seen much worse places in New York when I did Poor Relief work. Poor mother was appalled.' She laughed at him, tapping his shoulder with her fan. 'You don't want me to be like Mama, do you? The single end the girl lived in – is that the proper term? – was scrupulously clean, and the mother, a decent widow woman,

24

pitifully anxious to get her daughter placed in service in the West End.'

'I'll let you off this time.' He kissed her soundly. 'Shall we go and see the children before we go down?'

She flattered herself that his obvious happiness was the result of having been married to her for five years. He would never have the spontaneous gaiety of Terence, but if she were Catherine, she would worry about being married to such a handsome man with an evident eye for the ladies. And no wonder, she thought, remembering Catherine's prissiness and her good works, especially with the Temperance Movement. She smoothed the flounced apron front of the oyster satin as they walked along the upper hall. 'To tell you the truth, I'm more at home in a maternity gown, but are you pleased with me all the same?'

'Very pleased.' Patrick had always been a man of few words.

Later, going downstairs, she said laughingly, 'I'll ask Maevy about happing.' There had been a discussion in the nursery about swaddling new babies in a shawl, and Jeannie and Patrick had assured her it gave them a sense of security. That was one thing about the Scots. They always thought they were right.

'Yes, do that. Little Gee-Gee looked as snug as a bug in a rug, though.' Gaylord Grant, called after her mother's twin brother who had died . . .

'I've invited Charlie McNab. I can't understand why Maevy won't marry him. She'll regret it one day if he goes off with another woman.'

'Maybe the place in her heart is already taken,' he said as they went into the drawing-room. 'Well, look who's here. Terence and Catherine have beaten us to it.'

'How nice to see you, Catherine.' Maria kissed her

25

sister-in-law, thinking how she had the full low bosom suitable for the current fashion, perhaps even fuller because of her pregnancy. But what a sombre dress, although the cut was so impeccable that it was difficult to believe she was six months gone.

'Someone's got to be first,' she said self-righteously. 'If it were left to Terence he'd come in with the pudding.'

'Don't believe a word she says, Maria.' Terence greeted her with a smacking kiss on the cheek. What a handsome man he was with his curly hair and erect figure, although at times his gaiety seemed to be rather a habit he put on with his clothes.

'It gives us a chance to admire your drawing-room at least.' Catherine looked round the large room. 'Oh, you've put your bureau between the two windows!' Maria followed her eyes to the desk topped with the glass cabinet. It contained a full set of Mark Twain's works, her wedding present to Patrick. He had told her that he had fallen in love with her in the garden at Springhill when she had read aloud to him.

'Yes,' she said, 'we like it there.'

'We prefer a cheval-glass. But then our room at Great Western Terrace calls for that. The effect has been greatly admired.'

The maid, Flora, opened the door to announce the arrival of more guests. Maria turned gratefully to them. 'Why, Mr and Mrs Mitchell!' It was their next-door neighbours. 'You've found the way at last!' She noticed that the combination of black lace, green earrings and green feather fan had certainly added to Mrs Mitchell's charms, which were not inconsiderable, and seemed to eclipse her small husband who was of a uniform greyness, grey frock-coat, grey hair, even his face had a grey tinge. Very suitable for a publisher of rare bibles, she thought, which he was. 'Come in, come in! I'd like you to meet my

26

brother- and sister-in-law from the other side of the park. Oh, and here's Maevy, another sister-in-law! Doesn't she look lovely!'

She had taken special pains with her gown, although Mother would have dressed her up as if she was going to a ball at St Andrew's Hall. 'Maria's the one for the grand occasion,' she had said. 'Don't let her outshine you.' There was no one more for the grand occasion than Mother herself.

She shook hands smilingly with Maria's neighbours. The Dorothy bag and the gloves and the fan, the latter one of Mother's took a bit of managing. I could do with Charlie McNab as porter at least . . . was he here? 'How nice to meet you.' How low the woman's dress was at the front. Terence would have a field day.

She could see Isobel and John handing their cloaks to the maid, a new one, very pretty – but then Maria was not the kind to have plain maids like Catherine, who was afraid of Terence's wayward glances.

The sisters kissed. 'I wondered if you'd be able to come.'

'Oh, yes. Those days are over. I'm as fit as a fiddle. Am I not, John?' His glance was loving.

'She runs me off my feet. Don't I get a kiss, too, Maevy?' That fleeting familiarity in his looks which worried her. Was it that his face was constantly in her mind and each meeting reinforced the memory?

'Well you're my brother-in-law.' She laughed. His kiss landed chastely on her cheek. Was it his goodness rather than the man himself she had fallen in love with? But, no, that was not true. What of the heightening of her blood those March evenings as they had walked back from Crannoch, Isobel out of sight, and she had thought out of mind, in America?

27

'I like your gown, Maevy,' Isobel said. 'You and I can't get away from Mother's choice, can we?' She was wearing a delicate green voile trimmed with satin ribbon of the same shade.

'Is this to be a dress talk, ladies?' John said, smiling at them. 'You're making me feel out of my depth.'

'A thing ministers rarely feel,' Maevy said. 'You're so used to a captive audience that you've no patience when others are talking.' She had noticed before this desire to inflict small barbs in him. Was it the first sign of becoming an old maid?

'Oh, no,' Isobel shook her head. 'He spends hours listening to parishioners in his study, not to mention the patience he shows with Lizzie's tales.'

'She's a caution.' His eyes were fond. 'Twists me round her little finger.' Maevy remembered that he had insisted on bringing Lizzie up as their own child, and that Patrick and Terence had agreed, reluctantly.

Maria was there again. 'Oh, the very people I've been waiting for. How well you look, Isobel. Now, you know everyone. The Carters and Johnsons from the firm are here. And young Mr Cranston and his wife. He's very well up in the Trade Unions, Patrick tells me, and an old friend. And his father who has a farm in Crannoch. Yes, you'll know him. I can't remember the others – they're still to come – and guess who's bringing your mother in his carriage?'

'Put us out of our misery!' Maevy said, smiling.

'Lord and Lady Crawford, her neighbours.'

'Do you know them?' She was surprised.

'Slightly. Patrick has had business dealings with Lord Crawford, and I know Lizzie's been to the son's birthday party, isn't that so, Isobel? Lady Crawford and I will have plenty in common. I'm told she's a first-class horsewoman.'

'I can see what you're after, you scheming girl . . .' Maria held up her hand.

'Here they are.'

Maeve came into the room with Lord and Lady Crawford, smiling, at ease. It was when you observed Mother at a distance that you appreciated her aristocratic bearing to its full. She was not haughty like the other woman who was thin, dark, and seemed to look down her long nose, but it was her demeanour, the way she looked around the room, greeted people with her eyes, smiled, waved, lifted her fan when she caught sight of her daughters, a special, loving smile.

'Look at Mother,' Isobel said, 'queening it.'

Maria left them, and Maevy watched her as she spoke animatedly to the three people. Titles did not frighten Maria. They were just another part of this country which had adopted her. She came back again, a hand on the elbow of each of the women, Lord Crawford behind.

'Lord and Lady Crawford, Maevy. I'm sure I don't have to present them to you since they're your mother's neighbours. And your parishioners, John. And Isobel is known to you, I'm sure, Lady Crawford. I believe their daughter, Lizzie, has been to your son's birthday party recently.'

'Good evening.' Lady Crawford extended the tips of her fingers, looking down her long nose.

'Good evening, Lady Crawford.' The woman was English, Maevy thought. It might be possible to mimic her voice later, the way she said, 'Good evening,' drawled it, la-di-da. How we Scots like to make fools of people when they ever so slightly overawe us . . .

'I know Miss McGrath,' Lord Crawford said. He was more handsome than she remembered him at the Sunday School Picnics, perhaps because of the wings of grey hair and the added assurance of his title. 'You created a sensation in church long ago.'

She laughed, taken by surprise. 'Mother was just talking about that this morning! Am I never going to be allowed to live it down? But you couldn't possibly remember so far back. It's over twenty years ago.'

'Yes, I can.' He was smiling at her, his amber eyes teasing. He lowered his voice. 'I was always so bored by old Murdoch that you created a welcome diversion.'

'Careful!' Maeve put a finger to her lips. 'His daughter's here tonight, my daughter-in-law, don't forget.' And then, to Maevy. 'Didn't I forever tell you? Blue's right for you with your fair hair.'

'Yes, Mother, you forever told me.' She kept her face straight. 'I wouldn't dare wear anything else.' Lord Crawford and her mother laughed, his wife smiled thinly.

'Now, I must tear you away and introduce you to some more of my guests,' Maria said. She led them away.

'Maria's a caution,' Maeve said. 'I think she asked the Crawfords to be one up on Catherine.'

'You seem to be on the best of terms with them anyhow. Especially him.'

'They're neighbours.' Her expression was bland. 'I've known them for over thirty years. Lord Crawford's mother was my only woman friend. Annabel. Do you remember her?'

'Vaguely. She used to climb over our fence in Colliers' Row to get to the Sholton Woods. Terence once said the lace on her drawers was all raggedy.'

'Terence would. She was a dear, odd creature, like a creature of the woods she loved. Your father once said that toffs could be careless. He always hit the nail on the head with words . . .' She turned. Charlie McNab was at her side. 'Charlie! You said you might not manage to come.'

'So I thought, because I had to assist the surgeon, Mr McKendrick. And then two of his patients died before getting as far as the operating room. Not unusual . . .' His mouth tightened for a second and then he was smiling at Maevy. 'Hello. My, you must have set the temperatures soaring in your wards tonight.'

'Oh, yes, I paraded up and down for their benefit!' She laughed. 'When are you going to give up tearing between your practice and the Royal?'

'When one or the other throws me out.'

'He has his surgeon's certificate,' her mother said. 'Nobody ever died from hard work.'

'Oh, you have a grand supporter in my mother, I'll give you that! Next to her own sons you're her favourite man.'

'It's a difficult choice, sure enough.' Maeve laughed at him, almost flirting with him, Maevy thought, half-amused, half-annoyed. She could see the special thing in their eyes for each other.

'I wish I could say the same about Maevy here.' He smiled at her, and she saw again the tiredness in his eyes. She knew what the operating room was like, the closeness, the smells, as much as from the dirty alpaca gowns the older surgeons wore as anything else. They were so stiff with blood and pus that they could stand up on their own. She was one of the few nurses who could bear the place without fainting.

'Oh, I'm a hard nut to crack. Working in the Royal does that to you.' She looked round. 'It's nice to be in civilized surroundings for a change.'

'Aye,' Charlie nodded, looking around the high-ceilinged room. 'This Terrace and the Necropolis shared the same architect. Did you know that?'

She burst out laughing. 'Oh, Charlie! You'd please Maria if you told her that. The Necropolis indeed!'

'It's a most romantic place with its mausoleums and

tombs and owls hooting. We could walk there in the moonlight afterwards.'

'Will you listen to him?' Maevy turned and found her mother had slipped away. She saw her across the room talking to Mrs Mitchell who was waving her huge green feather fan, causing her small husband to duck with every downward swoop of it. The next time she went to visit Braidholme they would laugh about it together. It would not have escaped Mother.

'Hello, Dr McNab, hello, Maevy.' It was Arthur Cranston, thin, intense, so different from his father, Bob, who had once been her own father's gaffer at the pit. Arthur's wife, Rita, was in dull brown chenille, her hair scraped back, her face sallow.

'What's taking up your time just now?' Charlie asked him. 'Is it still truck?'

'We've got a representative in Parliament now. We expect the Bill for complete abolition in a year or so. But there's another strike brewing. Never a dull moment.' He smiled at Maevy. 'Your father and mine saw the effects of that damnable system, were the victims of it. By God, Kieran McGrath inspired me when I was a lad. I remember a meeting at the Sholton Parish hall . . .'

Maevy caught the eye of Arthur's wife. She looked worn and tired. Her shoulders went up, her eyes lifted, as if to say, I've heard it all before. What must it be like to be married to a man with an obsession? Did she sometimes wish she was back in Sholton like her sister-in-law, living in a cottage at the farm? But then, was not Charlie McNab the same with his constant talk about antiseptics and the necessity for quick surgery instead of filling up the wards with patients with wounds full of pus?

'Why wait till they burst, for God's sake?' he had said to her once, when he had been watching her dressing a foecal abscess. The offensive smell rising between them

32

had made her sick, had seemed to cling to her for days, despite the scrubbing and the scouring . . .

'I think . . .' she smiled at Mrs Cranston and made a move to go away, but Charlie's hand came out and caught her.

'No, you don't. I'm taking you in to dinner, I've strict instructions from Maria.' His eyes smiled at her and then he was giving Arthur his attention again. 'So it's this man MacDonald is it?' He kept his arm round Maevy's waist, making her boil with rage. Mrs Cranston's tired eyes rested on her. 'Don't you get caught, too,' they seemed to say.

The dinner was over. The table had been beautifully arranged by Maria with American dishes, a country cured ham, a meat loaf, a huge turkey resplendent on its silver chafing dish, stuffed with nuts and flanked with silver boats of cranberry sauce. There had been pumpkin pie, baked butterscotch pie, the whole display centred round a glazed Christmas pudding on a stand, with the flags of Great Britain and America set in the top. Now they were in the drawing room where, while the guests had been eating, the seats had been rearranged round the room and the lid of the grand piano opened.

Charlie was still at Maevy's side. 'Maria will be cross with you,' she said, 'she likes people to circulate.'

'I have a special dispensation from Maria.' He grinned at her and she thought again how thin and tired his face was tonight and how its paleness made his black eyes glow. 'She's on my side. Will you marry me?'

She laughed. 'You're beginning to say that out of habit. You'd get the fright of your life if I said yes.'

'Try me. I'm faint for love of you. I can't go on.' She hardly knew if he were joking or not.

'You've got your practice and your work at the Royal and . . .'

'. . . snooping about the Gallowgate for the book I'm writing . . .Oh, yes, I don't sit in a corner moaning about the fact that the girl I love doesn't love me. And there's music . . . that reminds me, will you come to the Berlioz concert with me in January? I've got tickets. Sir August Manns will be conducting . . . oh, yes, my life's full enough, but it can be full and empty at the same time because you're not there to share it with me.'

'And so you think I should give up my work to marry you?'

'Well, all women do, as a matter of course.'

'There it is, "as a matter of course". But what about *my* vocation? It's only because . . .' she hesitated, then thought, blow it, I might as well be hung for a sheep as for a lamb, '. . . marrying is the only way you can have me.'

Silence, but a beating silence, because of her heart thudding against her ribs. She remembered one summer evening when she had been visiting at Braidholme and Charlie had called and taken her for a walk along the Sholtie Burn. He had seemed on edge, over-tired, his eyes burning in his pale face. He had been up all night with a difficult birth, he had told her. They had climbed a stile into the Sholtie Woods, and there, suddenly, he had surprised her by his ardour.

What had started as a kiss had turned into an embrace which half-frightened, half-excited her. His limbs were trembling against hers, one hand released its grip and slid down between them. It was he who had pulled away before she protested.

'Ach, I'm ashamed of myself! Like a village lad I am, trembling for love of you, trembling to possess you. You'd

34

be quite right to upbraid me. Why don't you, Maevy, why don't you?'

She had not answered. For a second it had not been Charlie she had been thinking of, but John. Why in all her dreaming about him had she never thought of him like *this*? He was a man like any other man, surely. It was not his fault Isobel could not bear children. 'It doesn't matter,' she said at last. 'It doesn't matter.' She had known her voice was shaking.

'I wish to God it did.' He had spoken roughly. She could hardly keep up with him on the way back. His face had been like a dark cloud . . .

She was in Maria's drawing-room again, brought back by his voice breaking the silence. 'That's what you think, then?'

She looked miserably at him. 'Charlie . . .'

'Now, what are you two looking so fierce about?' It was Maria, glowing with the success of her evening. 'Will you play for us, Charlie, while we're settling down?'

He got up. 'I don't mind. Especially when you charm me with that Yankee voice of yours.'

'Oh, you're a dear man, isn't he, Maevy, a dear man?'

'Don't expect her to say "Amen" to that.' He smiled down at Maevy. 'She's got what her mother calls a "stubborn bit".'

Through lack of practice his playing was not flawless, but he had a natural talent and he enjoyed exercising it. While he played some Chopin waltzes people chattered and moved chairs or absented themselves to 'freshen up' as Maria called it, or partook of the sweetmeats which Flora passed round. Maevy saw Terence talking to her, saw the girl laugh, then pull her face straight again, reprovingly.

People were beginning to quieten, and Charlie, without looking up, began playing the old Scottish songs, 'The

Land o' the Leal', 'I Love a Lassie', a medley where one melody ran naturally into the other. Some joined in, and three bolder spirits, frock-coated and flushed-faced, got up, linked arms, and led the singing.

Maria was on her feet. 'Now, ladies and gentlemen, my brother-in-law is willing to render a few Irish songs. Would you oblige again, Charlie, please?' He bowed and smiled, ran his hands over the keys.

They were away, well-matched in ability, a pleasant contrast in appearance, Charlie dark, bold-nosed, Terence handsome and still with the red curls which had always been the bane of his existence. Maevy remembered him as a boy smoothing them down with water at the scullery mirror before he went to meet Catherine. Her eyes sought John, unconsciously comparing him. He was sitting with her mother, but his head raised as if he felt Maevy's glance, and the sweetness of his expression struck her once again. Did a minister put on his face with his clothes? What a strange thought.

Terence was bowing, waving away further requests, and then Maeve's clear voice sounded across the room. 'I'd like to hear "The Kerry Dance", Terence, if you would.' They exchanged smiles.

Once, in the dark days of her grieving, she had told Maevy that she and Kieran sometimes sang the Irish songs they remembered when they were in bed. 'We were closer then than at any other time, even at the height of our loving.' She had never been afraid to speak or admit to love. It could be the Irish in her. Scotswomen were shy to name it.

She heard Terence's pleasing tenor in the hushed room, '"O, to think of it, O, to dream of it, fills my heart with tears . . ."' And the ending, '"O, for one of those hours of gladness, gone alas, like youth too soon . . ."'

Maria was on her feet, flushed and excited, clapping

36

vigorously. 'A rare treat. Thank you, Terence, and you, too, Charlie. And now I have a surprise for you. Mrs Mitchell, our next-door neighbour, has promised to oblige us. She's a celebrated singer, and although she's just moved here from London, she has already been given one of the main parts in the "Messiah" at the St Andrew's Hall.' Everyone applauded respectfully.

Maevy watched the woman, her head bowed in a modest pose, her restless fan half-covering her face. She looks like a *femme fatale*, she thought, not knowing exactly what a *femme fatale* would look like, but the black lace and the bright green feathers seemed appropriate, not to mention the swinging earrings.

'"Come into the garden, Maud . . ."' Mrs Mitchell poured forth rather than sang. Her voice was rich and full, like her figure, the white shoulders gleamed through the black lace, her bosom rose and fell. There was an outburst of surprised applause at the end which she accepted graciously they could recognize professionalism when they heard it. Then, after a whispered consultation with her husband at the piano, he shot back his cuffs and went into a sonorous but impressive overture. '"Ah, Sweet Mystery of Life,"' Mrs Mitchell sang, burying her chin in her neck.

'Mrs Kennedy Fraser reincarnated,' Charlie whispered in Maevy's ear. 'She recognizes her worth, the next-door neighbour.'

'So does Terence, and not only her singing,' she whispered back. He had crossed the room to congratulate the woman. She was animated. So was her feather fan as she listened, presumably, to Terence's compliments. Her husband sat on the duet stool, ignored.

'I think I'll have to go now.' The maids were coming round with drinks and pots of tea and cakes. The evening had suddenly palled for her. 'I'm more at home in the Royal.' She laughed apologetically.

His eyes pierced her. 'Are you more sure of your identity in a ward full of sick people?'

'What nonsense you talk! I'm on duty.'

'Are you sure that's the only reason?'

'Do I have to explain myself to you?' Her tone was as sharp as his eyes. She got up and went to make her apologies to Maria and Patrick.

'But you said you could stay overnight so that you wouldn't miss anything!' Maria said.

'I know, but I have a heavy day tomorrow, up at five. I'm sorry.' She sounded dull, even to herself. 'I don't want to disturb you at that hour.'

'But we're going to have the Lancers later, and then a sing-song round the piano, and Catherine has arranged for a choir to come in from the Temperance Movement. Oh, do stay!'

'Don't press her, Maria,' Patrick said. 'If she's got to get back, that's it. I'll send out for a hansom for you, Maevy.'

'But going through the streets late at night, on her own!'

'She won't be on her own.' Charlie was at her side. 'I'll go with her and see her back safely.'

'That's fine, then. Do you want the cab to take you to Sholton?'

'No, thanks. I can get a bed at the Royal for the night and catch the milk cart at four tomorrow. I'll be in plenty of time for my surgery.'

Maria sounded mollified. 'Well, if you must, you must. I'm happier Charlie will be taking care of you.'

'Oh, Maevy!' Isobel said when she was saying goodbye. 'That old Infirmary!'

'Where would we be without people like Maevy?' John

said. 'But you must come and see us on your next day off. I know you have to spread your presence thinly, but spare us some of your time, won't you? And Lizzie's always asking when Aunt Maevy's coming.'

'I promise.'

He kissed her fondly. 'Bless you,' he said. But then ministers said that to everyone.

3

'This is good of you, Charlie,' she said when they were in the cab. She felt ashamed of her ungraciousness at Claremont Terrace.

'Oh, I was being good to myself, too.' He was cheerful as he peered through the window. 'Glasgow's far from the douce town it's cracked up to be, especially on a Saturday night.'

'Yes, there are plenty of folks about. I think a lot of them are from the Temperance Movement concert. They get drunk on their own self-righteousness.'

He turned to her. 'Do I detect a crabbit note creeping into your voice, Maevy? It's not like you.'

'Isn't it? Christmas can be a sad time. I felt it back there. You think of the far-off days, when you were young. Are you not going home to Fife for Christmas?'

'No, we don't celebrate it much there. Ne'erday's the time. Besides, my mother and father are long since dead. My sisters and my brothers have their families growing up around them. I feel like an outsider now.'

'I know the feeling.' She looked out. Sauchiehall Street was like the bustling Sholtie in spate. She saw a young family, the father carrying the youngest, the mother with several older ones clinging to her skirts, she in turn hanging on to the man's arm. I'm wallowing in self-pity, she thought, time I was in bed and asleep. She felt Charlie's arm slip round her shoulders and had to stop herself leaning against him for comfort only, she told herself.

40

'Did you believe what you said about my reason for wanting to marry you?'

'Oh, it wasn't intended personally!' She heard herself bluster.

'You never could lie. You've got it wrong all the same. I haven't forgotten that evening in the Sholtie Woods. I apologized once and I'm doing it again. It isn't important. But never imagine I want to marry you simply to have you. If it were only for want of a woman there are plenty of opportunities for me in the course of my work. But until I have the woman I love, releases of the spirit will serve me very well . . . and my burning ambitions can keep me warm on a cold night.'

'Well, take account of mine,' she said.

They were going along Cathedral Street now and in a few minutes the cabbie drew up his horse. Charlie handed her out and paid the man who drove off with a flourish of his whip. 'I'll see you to the Nurses' Residence,' he said.

'There's no need.' She drew her chenille cloak round her. A drift of fog was floating up from the Clyde. The street lamps shone dimly through it.

'Now, don't be childish. There might be a bogey man skulking amongst the bushes.'

'Oh, Charlie!' She had to laugh, and yet she was glad. This forlorn feeling was new to her.

They walked in silence. The cathedral reared up in front of them, dark and forbidding, but as they rounded the corner they saw the sky made pale by the sailing moon, and beyond it the hill of the Necropolis with its monuments, ghostly in the fog.

'It's full of ghosties and hobgoblins, this place,' Charlie said, 'and all manner of queer-like creatures. They come out to play when the moon's up.'

'You're trying to frighten me.'

41

'I wish I could. I wish you would coorie into my arms for fear.'

'I've grown beyond that now.' She thought of firelit evenings in the cottage in Colliers' Row where she had played with her rag doll, while Kate, the big sister, brushed out her mother's hair. A clean towel would be spread round her shoulders. 'A rare treat, this is,' Mother would say, looking like a princess with her red tresses catching a golden glitter from the flames. Terence and Patrick would be out somewhere, probably at Tweedie's farm, but Isobel was there, sewing industriously – her fine seaming was faultless, whereas hers was always crumpled, with sometimes a bead of blood on it from a pricked finger.

Father would be down the pit, but John, the beloved young brother, where was he? In all those memories she could never conjure up his face. Were they all of times after he had drowned, or was her mind refusing to imagine him?

'I get nothing but a surge of pride when I'm near this place.' Charlie waved in the direction of the bulk of the Infirmary. 'I long to see more and more improvements till it's the best in the world.'

'What would they be?'

'More operating rooms, and especially a new Pathological Classroom far away from the smell, instead of next door.' His voice quickened. 'Surgeons dressed in white, and consultations between them *before* the cutlers sharpened their knives. What else? No more septic wounds, new operating tables made of steel instead of wood which gets soaked with blood and pus . . .'

'You want a lot, Charlie.'

'Isn't that the way of folks like me. They dream, and then they try to make their dreams come real.'

42

'You'll make yourself unpopular if you try to put them into practice.'

'That's the least of it. But what I'd like to see are less operations, not more, abdominal abscesses of all kinds treated *before* they reach the operating table. You know, Maevy, the state the patient gets into. I remember well that foecal abscess you were dressing last week. How you stood that putrid smell! God knows you're stout-hearted. Look at the length of time those poor souls occupy beds.' He turned to her. 'You're laughing at me again but it will come, mark my words. The older men are like old dogs who refuse to learn new tricks even with such a God-given gift as Lister's teaching, but there are younger ones coming up, never fear. Younger ones who've got tired wiping pus out of their eyes when the surgeon entered the abdominal parietes with his knife.'

'It's not like that.' She only half believed him.

'I've seen it, but, mind you, I've been coming here for five years. In a few years' time the advance in abdominal surgery will be tremendous, quickly dealt with on the table if it's too late for draining in the medical wards.'

'I think you're right.' She felt cheered by his words. And she would be able to help. Skilled nursing was essential. Her earlier depression disappeared. Hadn't Florence Nightingale been her ideal? She would be a worthwhile cog in this new scheme of things which Charlie pictured.

'Oh, it'll come, you'll see. People will stop saying that there's a pestilence in the Royal which kills patients in surgical wards – the pestilence of ignorance. But it's on its way out.' His voice became hurried and she caught his excitement. 'Lister's the man who's done it if they'll only believe in him. He's a benefactor who'll save more lives than all those the wars of the ages have thrown away. I can see it all, Maevy, an operating theatre, a shrine to cleanliness, glittering silver and glass, copious hot water, white antiseptic enamel, snowy towels . . . it's more than a dream. We're on the edge of seeing it . . .'

They were almost at the door of the Nurses' Residence. 'I'll go straight in,' she said, and, jokingly, 'Florence Nightingale might be watching me. I've enjoyed our talk, Charlie, or rather,' she laughed, 'listening to *you* talking. I'll try and get off for that concert you mentioned. What was the date?'

'The Berlioz?' His voice was dull, the fire had gone out of him. In the darkness his face looked pallid. She could not see his eyes. 'It's no good, Maevy.'

'What's no good?'

'Seeing each other. The situation between us is impossible. You've made it clear you have better things to do with your time. So have I.'

'You've convinced me of that.' She was astonished. 'But . . . we can be friends? We've always been friends?'

'It's not good enough for me. Oh, I'm not going to cut you in Sholton if that's what you mean, but, no,' she saw his head move, 'I won't bother you again.' He turned on his heel and left her.

4

Charlie presented himself at the door of Mr Wilcox's substantial house with only a little trepidation. Most of his anxiety had been dissipated in getting from Sholton to Glasgow by horse bus in time. From there he had to find a cab to take him to the cul-de-sac near the Botanic Gardens where the surgeon's house was situated.

He had been called out in the middle of last night to see a child who had 'an awfy nosebleed, soaked his whole bed, doactor,' so said the father panting at Charlie's door, but which had 'stoapt jist a meenit afore ye cam,' he was told at the cottage when he had run there. In the morning he had been held up by Jimmie Burns.

'It's that cratur Jimmie Burns again,' Biddy said, presenting herself at the door of the dining-room where he was hurriedly breakfasting, 'I told him to see Dr Geddes but he says only you can sort things out.'

'Show him in, Biddy,' he said.

'Show him in, is it?' She looked horrified. Her pug nose had gone ceilingwards.

'Aye, do that. And bring another cup and saucer.'

'Who fur?'

'For Jimmie, of course. The poor lad's walked over a couple of miles. You wouldn't deny him a cup from your pot, would you?'

'Only in the kitchen!' she snorted. 'And that at a pinch! I've never heard the like.'

He had sorted out Jimmie quickly, aided by the hot tea. It was a pitiful sight, he had thought, a grown man mortally afraid of his domineering wife, but how could you put spunk into such a creature? He should have remained with his old mother. 'Just keep out of her way till she calms down,' he advised him, 'then woo her.'

'Woo her!' Jimmie looked terrified.

'Aye, give her a cuddle and a kiss.' He looked down at the toast he was spreading with Biddy's marmalade, hiding a smile.

'Doactor, if a got within a yaird o' her, she'd fetch me sich a clout on the jaw that ma ears would be ringin' tae Kingdom come.'

'You'll just have to look slippy, won't you?' He had ushered him out.

Maybe some day men would walk out on aggressive bitches, and women on men who ill-treated them. Maevy would approve of that, he thought, when he was rattling along Glasgow Road in the horse bus. She wanted to be her own mistress, was not prepared to yoke herself onto a man – but, oh, she was if he was the right one! He was sure there was someone who had taken her heart a long time ago.

He had had a long talk with her mother one night. He had been coming home from a late visit to a sick child when he had seen her white dress glimmering in the Braidholme garden and had stopped at the wicket gate. The flower smells wafted sweetly to him on the night air. 'Somebody's out late tonight,' he called.

She came towards him, moving like a ghost through the mist which had risen after the heat of the day from the Sholtie at the bottom of the garden. 'Oh, it's you, Charlie. We must be the only two in Sholton to keep late hours. Come in and have a turn with me.'

He pushed the gate open and joined her. 'Gardens at night are magical,' he said as they started to walk slowly along the flagged path.

'Soothing, they are. If I feel I'm not going to be able to sleep I come out here.'

'Better than a tonic from the doctor.'

'I'm my own doctor. Other people aren't so independent. Who was it this time?'

'Mrs Docherty's in Colliers' Row. The youngest. A poor wee shilpit thing. I doubt if she'll rear him.'

'Children are expendable with the Dochertys, poor souls. I don't know how you do it, the Royal twice a week, and this busy practice.'

'I've Dr Geddes now, don't forget. He's a grand young man.'

'And what are you? An old one?'

'I'm thirty-two,' and without meaning to, added, 'seven years older than Maevy.'

'Is *she* your yardstick?' He heard the smile in her voice, and the trace of good Irish. It gave it a distinction, a charm, but then she was all charm, Maevy's mother.

'Because I love her.' The darkness made it easy. 'But she doesn't love me. I've given up asking her for over six months now. I'm tired of battering my head against a brick wall.'

'And that's a sad tale now. Did she give you her reason, then?'

'Oh, yes, independence, devotion to nursing.' He laughed shortly. 'She accused me of lust.'

'And what's wrong with good healthy lust? No love is complete without it.' No other woman he knew would speak like that.

'If Sholton wives could hear you! It's the idea that people only use marriage to sanctify it that gets her goat, I think. But I know if she loved me nothing would matter.'

'She still feels guilty about several things.' Her voice was calm. 'Nursing is an expiation for that.'

'But not for turning me down.'

47

'Ah, there you're on more difficult ground. Since she was sixteen she's been the victim of an obsession, and you can't break her of that. She'll have to do it herself.'

'It doesn't sound as if there's much hope.'

'Do you believe there's only one person in the world for each person?'

'At this moment I do, yes.'

'I'm not so sure. That must sound strange to you. You know how deeply I loved Kieran. You saw me at my lowest.'

'That's true enough.' He remembered the white face, all charm drained out of it, dead inside.

'And yet after I was married to Kieran I met another man with whom I honestly could have been happy. Not the same kind of happiness – that only comes once to the lucky ones, that tremulous, possessed and possessive loving – all the same, I think there are sometimes two roads you can travel.'

'You're a good woman . . .' He blew out his breath, laughed, 'but you haven't helped me a bit.'

'Only Maevy could, and she doesn't seem to be disposed to yet . . . but you must admit, I've given you something to think about which is better than useless words of comfort.' She laughed with him. 'Come in and have a cup of tea with me before you go. I'll put a good drop of whisky in it to soothe your dreams.'

'What a suggestion!' He pretended to be horrified. 'What would Biddy and Susan say? It would be all round Sholton by tomorrow.' He had a fleeting thought, instantly dismissed, that if he did go in, sit companionably with her, it might lead . . . she was a beautiful woman for her age, ageless . . . he must be tired to think such thoughts.

'I've been the talk of the town before now.' She stopped, facing him, and he could see her face only dimly

48

in the darkness, but the beauty was still there. It was that same beauty he admired in Maevy, although it was not so strongly developed in her as in her mother. A beauty without conscious seductiveness, a kind of . . . sterling quality, unique, given to few women. 'All the same, Charlie,' she said, 'there's no one I'd rather have for a son-in-law. Now get away home to your bed.'

She had been no help and a great help he had thought later, sitting at the piano and playing softly so as not to waken Biddy. He liked Schumann at night for its romantic sadness. She reduced everything to its proper proportions. His natural sense for the dramatic made him inclined to magnify things, see them as wholly black or wholly white. Yes, he told himself, half-listening to the rippling chords, life is not so bad, plenty of work, music when he had time for it. He would stop longing for a girl he could not have.

And yet his last thoughts before he went to sleep were of Maevy, that fair-haired girl with something of her mother in her, but something more, which was her own essence. Some women faded into nothing after they were past their first youth. She would grow and develop into a greater beauty.

It had been at the beginning of last winter that Mr Wilcox, one of the visiting surgeons at the Royal, had approached him. 'My wife is having a small soirée shortly, Dr McNab. I've given her your name as she commissioned me for heaven's sake to ask some young people instead of those old fogeys I seem to like. You'll be hearing from her soon.' He did not say, 'Would you like to come?' the inference being that what young man in his right senses would not?

Still, it did seem that Mr Wilcox was interested in him. He had been assisting him for a year now, and had found him affable, so much so that he had told him of the book he was writing. It transpired that Mr Wilcox was also interested in the relationship between disease and poverty. Ever since he was a boy in Edinburgh he had thought along those same lines as he went about the squalor of the fennels and wynds with a scarf tied round his mouth to avoid infection.

'But, alas,' he said, 'success stopped that kind of introspection. Once you've become fashionable your rich patients claim you.' He had not looked too disappointed.

'Will you please come in, sir.' The neat maid held open the door for him. He walked into a hall which he was sure would impress the richest of Mr Wilcox's patients.

The soirée turned out to be as affable in every way as Mr Wilcox. The numbers were less than at Maria's Christmas party, so long ago it seemed now, and Mrs Wilcox, strangely enough, looked like his Biddy with her pug nose, if one could imagine Biddy in a dress of grey satin ruched in shimmering folds over an ample posterior.

He was placed beside an old friend of Mr Wilcox's from Edinburgh, who quizzed him during the entire dinner about his medical career, but was interrupted frequently by the Wilcox's only daughter, Letitia, who sat across the table from them.

He had never seen anyone like her, small, dark, with a febrile sort of prettiness and a dress which was lower than any he had seen ladies wear, certainly in Sholton. His shrewd eye placed her age as possibly equal to his own, and he thought that might account for her assurance.

'Dr McNab is one of Father's pets,' she informed the elderly gentleman whose name Charlie had not caught. 'Have you any pets in your hospital in Edinburgh, Mr Lamond?'

'Only white mice, my dear Letitia,' he assured her, his

little moustache working busily. 'Not so fascinating as Dr McNab.'

'Would you say he was fascinating, Mr Lamond?' Her brilliant eyes darted a provocative glance at Charlie.

'Now, I'm no judge of fascination in young men. I leave that to you, dear lady, or my wife.'

Her father boomed from the top of the table. 'Don't let Letitia distract you from your plum duff with her non-sense, Lamond. I put Dr McNab beside you because he has some original ideas. Far-sighted. Tell him about your findings in the back streets of Glasgow, young man.'

Although he had never been shy, Charlie was glad that the talk went on around him, but he was aware of the bright eyes on him across the table. He turned to Mr Lamond. 'I'm scarcely past the theoretical stage,' he said. 'Cause and effect.'

'Cause and effect,' the surgeon repeated, chewing his moustache along with his plum duff.

'It's a vicious circle; illness and disease caused by the dreadful conditions these people live under. In they come to the Royal with the results of those conditions, then back they go to have any good undone.'

'We have a young William Morris in our midst,' Mr Lamond nodded across to Letitia Wilcox.

'Do you paint and write poetry as well, Dr McNab?' Her eyes were too limpid.

'No, just admire those who do, like any man of civilized tastes.'

Mr Lamond wiped his moustache on his napkin. 'Excellent plum duff,' he boomed back at his friend at the top of the table. 'My compliments to your cook. My proposition is,' he turned a bushy eyebrow on Charlie, 'that you can't be an educator and a doctor at the same time, especially a surgeon. Divide your interests and you succeed in neither.'

'I'm in general practice as well, Mr Lamond,' Charlie said. 'I deal with problems every day which are more closely related to environment and poverty than anything else. And there are the personal and intimate relationships which cause such distress. Mind and body are more closely related than we'll admit.'

'My dear sir, if you sat down and listened to the long-winded story that every patient wanted to tell you, you'd never get anywhere. No, I say, "if thine eye offends you pluck it out".'

'But you can't pluck out a distressed mind . . .'

'This young man would have us boring through skulls next, or taking out hearts to give them a rub and a polish!' Mr Lamond addressed the table. There was a burst of laughter.

Mrs Wilcox, her pug nose reaching for her corniced ceiling, got up, waving her fan. 'We'll leave the gentlemen to their further discussions, ladies. Really, why they should spoil our dinner with all that talk of those dreadful poor people . . .' There was a twinkle of well-bred laughter. Charlie met her daughter's eyes. They were amused.

She spoke to him later when they were sitting in the conservatory off the drawing-room. This was not a party like Maria McGrath's where everybody had been enjoined to perform. People were sitting in little groups about the various public rooms, drinking tea or coffee, and talking. Mrs Wilcox had whispered coyly to him that they cherished 'good conversation' in their home. 'Now that we've been dragooned out here by Mother, are you really interested in the poor?'

'Isn't everyone?'

'Oh, oh!' She tapped his wrist with her fan, two quick little taps. 'I know what sort of person you are. You answer any questions put to you with another question and so it can go on for ever.'

'Do I?'

She laughed. Her teeth were very white, as if they had been polished with jeweller's rouge. 'I won't let you tease me. Tell me, apart from working yourself to the bone as a general practitioner in some smoky little place on the Clyde, and slaving away with Father in the Royal, what else do you do?'

'There's precious little time for anything else. Read. Write. Sometimes play late into the night.'

'Play what?'

'The piano.'

'Are you good?'

'No. I haven't time to practise properly. It's for my own amusement.'

'Do you know the "Sweetheart's Waltz"? I've just learned it. It's very pretty.'

'No, I prefer classical music.'

'But that *is* classical music, my dear man. It was written by a famous composer . . . I forget his name.'

'Perhaps it wasn't meant to be remembered.'

Her eyes darted at him, full of mischief. 'I can see I shall have to have my wits about me. Do you like to dance?'

'Yes, I must admit I do, when I get time.'

'Well, Mother has arranged to hold a small dance for my birthday next month.' He thought she might be a good dancer, small and light and thin-waisted. Maevy was more . . . womanly, comely, like her mother. Wasn't it she who had asked him if Maevy was his yardstick?

'That sounds delightful,' he said. It was a word he rarely used in Sholton.

'I'll get Mother to send you an invitation.'

'You must ask the orchestra to play the "Sweetheart's Waltz".'

'Oh, you're a tease!' She smiled her little white smile, giving him a further two quick taps on the wrist. Yes, she was very different from Maevy.

It was at the small dance that Mr Wilcox once more drew him aside.

'If I can tear you away from the Terpsichorean delights,' he said, 'I've meant to ask you this for some time. Have you considered that you might be wasting your talents at Sholton? You're the right age to think of setting up in private practice as a surgeon. They tell me you've established quite a reputation in the Royal already. It won't be easy at the beginning, but I could get you enough to live on with teaching students, and I know a sinecure of a job in a medical library which would tide you over. You could be building up your good will much faster than you are at present, and then at the appropriate time move into a suitable house in the West End.'

'That's beyond me completely,' Charlie said.

'Perhaps at the moment, but begin to think about it, to plan for it. You're in the prime of life. And you might marry . . .' Strangely enough, when he was dancing with Letitia that night she did not seem so brittle.

'Is it really only a month or so since we met, Dr McNab?' she asked him. She was so light that it was like dancing with a shadow.

'I beg your pardon?' The banal strains of the 'Sweetheart's Waltz' were drowning her voice.

'I've thought of you quite a lot . . . recently.' She came closer and spoke softly in his ear. 'Have you of me?'

He moved his head, pretending to look away, and not wishing to lie. His mind was always full, of Maevy and his work in equal proportions. But it was of Letitia he was thinking now. There was no reason to believe Maevy had changed her mind since that party two years ago at Claremont Terrace. She was friendly but cool if he met her in the Royal. And she looked different. She was thinner, more beautiful in his eyes, but something in her demeanour made her seem even more unobtainable. He was defeated by it.

He was no fool. It was not difficult to guess the reason for Mr Wilcox's favouritism. When a girl reaches thirty, or it might be more, any young man with reasonable prospects was fair game for a father who wished to see his only daughter settle down.

'From time to time,' he said, holding Letitia just a little closer.

5

Maevy was glad she had this Sunday off. Sometimes the weight of nursing ill patients grew onerous, but she had never wavered from her decision that it was a worthwhile thing to do. She had seen death so many times that she had no longer any fear of it, but the telling and then the consoling of grief-stricken relatives was sometimes as much as she could bear.

True, even in the eight years she had worked at the Royal she had seen many changes, and those only for the better. She had seen the deaths lessen as Lister's methods filtered through from London. She remembered Charlie McNab's anger at the opposition the great man had received from some quarters, even when he had performed his first experiments in Glasgow. 'A prophet has no honour in his own country,' he had said. 'It took Germany to see the sense of what he was advocating, and now, rightly enough, they're ahead of us.'

She still saw him in the wards, and had assisted him in the operating room, but professional protocol had spared them any embarrassment at the beginning. Now even that had disappeared, and all she was left with was a vague feeling of having done something incredibly foolish over which she had no control. The word went about that he was 'bright', that he was Mr Wilcox's 'pet', and although he was reputed to annoy some of the older surgeons with his confidence, he was a favourite with the nursing staff because of his high spirits.

She had watched him at work, had seen him always use strict Listerian methods, surgical cleanliness in dress, towels treated by steam heat, instruments boiled, scissors and scalpels soaked in carbolic, impregnated dressings, hair, mouths and hands of the dressers and nurses covered.

'What a palaver!' one of the older Sisters had said to her. 'It wasn't like this ten years ago.'

'I believe in it,' she said crisply. Mother had told her once that she was 'getting as starchy as her aprons'. She wondered sometimes if she was acquiring that reputation in the Royal as well.

But today she intended to put all thoughts of the Infirmary out of her head. They would sit in the garden at Braidholme and talk, and she would laugh and gossip with Mother the way they always did. 'I'm really still Maevy McGrath underneath,' she had said once when Maeve had reproached her for looking solemn, 'the youngest of the family, the cheeky one.' 'The one with the stubborn bit,' her mother had answered, smiling. She knew she was thinking of Charlie McNab, but give her mother her due, she had never harped on that as Maria had done. 'Oh, Maevy, he's a dream of delight! How could you?'

And Catherine. 'Well, I suppose you know what you're doing. A doctor would have been an asset to the family, lifted its tone.' She had never forgotten that Terence had come up from the pit before she married him.

The smart tartan horse bus she was travelling in was the property of the McGrath Carting Company. And it was crowded with people going on jaunts, or that favourite Sunday expedition in Glasgow, visiting relatives scattered about Glasgow and its neighbouring villages.

She eagerly watched for the first sign of the countryside amongst the sprawl of iron and steel works, rearing bings, huddled cottages of stone wall which enclosed the policies of the Crawford estate. What a vast tract of land they still owned, she thought, and again, if old Lord Crawford were still alive he would have had most of it excavated for coal by this time.

Luckily his son did not seem to be of the same stamp. She remembered him at Maria's party three years ago, his elegance, his strange amber eyes, his plain, haughty wife. A marriage of convenience, she had thought. Whatever it was, she had not been a patch on Mother that night. How close had she and Lord Alastair been?

Soon the bus had turned into the old Sholton Road, the trees so thick and overhanging on either side that they made a leafy arbour as they trundled along. How often she had walked this way from school, scuffing the leaves with her feet, or making slides with the other children when it was frosty. Those winter mornings spelled her childhood, the crisp brightness, the hoar glittering on the bare branches, or sometimes the ghostly mist rising from the river when even their voices had been hushed and someone's red scarf had stood out like a flame.

'Braidholme, Maevy,' Jake Lowther, the conductor, called, grinning at her, 'Ur ye gawn tae see yer Mammy?'

'Aye, that I am,' she said getting up. 'And tell the driver not to shoogle the bus when I'm getting off, if you don't mind.'

And now she was walking along the drive to the long low house where Mother lived in solitary but happy state, and Susan was opening the door and immediately taking up her usual stance, arms crossed on her chest. 'Well, it's yourself, Maevy. Come away in. Your mother's in the gairden.'

She walked through the sitting-room, so like Mother in its elegance and comfort, chairs and tables serving a double function of being in the right place at the right time, big bowls of flowers, even a great one of gowans in the hearth.

Then, after tea and sandwiches in the summer-house they were strolling down the drive and along the road to the tune of the kirk bell. The village folk hurrying by acknowledged them, some calling out a greeting, 'How's the nursing in Glasgow, Maevy?' This was where she belonged.

'Isobel wants us to go to the manse for luncheon,' Maeve said.

'Luncheon, is it?' she laughed. 'My, we're swanky today. You used to call it dinner.'

'Back in Ireland we always said "luncheon".'

'That's put me in my place. It's kind of them to ask us.'

'They're kindness itself. John has taken the tartness out of Isobel, maybe a bit bossy with her but that's the way with ministers. Remember how nebby she was as a wee lass? And, of course, Lizzie has completed the cure.'

'It's thanks to you, then. You handed over Lizzie.'

'Everything's turned out well . . . except that some day she'll have to be told who she really is.'

The ministry suited John. He was like a father and a beloved son with his congregation. He spoke well and simply and goodness shone out of him. He was the same later at table, making her laugh. 'Now, tell me, Sister McGrath, who do you think has saved more souls this week? You or me.'

And Lizzie was lovely, with hair like her grandmother's but Bessie's mouth, a laughing mouth. How did Patrick and Terence feel about John being called 'Daddy' by her? Mother was right. There would have to be a day of reckoning.

'We've had a grand idea,' Isobel said before they left. 'Lizzie hasn't been to the Exhibition yet. How would you both like to come with us? We'll make it to suit you, Maevy. You're the working woman in the family, and maybe Catherine and Maria will join us and bring the children. What do you say?' How fragile and pretty she looked today in her spotted muslin with her flaxen hair. No wonder John adored her.

'I'll let you know. I've only been once and it was raining.'

'We'll order a specially sunny one,' John said.

'And we'll see if your word carries any weight.' She laughed and Lizzie joined in, laughing the way Bessie had, head back.

'Yes, we'll see if your word carries any weight, Daddy,' she said.

'Lizzie,' his face was stern, 'watch your manners.' Maevy saw the girl's crestfallen face.

They met at the gates of the Groveries. The day was gloriously sunny. John must have been in direct communication with God after all. Catherine and Terence had brought Robert, but Maria, who had Sarah with her, made excuses for Patrick. 'But someone has to work for the firm,' she said, smiling at Terence.

'I came along to lend moral support to John.'

'A minister is the last person to need moral support,' Catherine said. Families . . . Maevy caught her mother's eye.

The riverside was crowded with sightseers watching the swimming gala. Was there anything nicer, she thought, than being one of the strolling crowd, the sun on her head, the strange shapes of the towers and minarets around her, the white palaces and domes – the Baghdad of the Kelvin it had been called. We were far too solemn in Glasgow. This was how life should be lived, the cosmopolitan style.

She took Robert and Sarah to the switchback and fun fair while Lizzie was led away, reluctantly, by John to see the archaeological collection in the Bishop's Castle.

'Mama doesn't allow me to do anything,' Robert said. 'You're different, Aunt Maevy.'

'I won't be different if you break your promise.' She had given them permission to cross one bridge while she took the other. They were on their way to the new Lyon's restaurant where Terence was treating them all to a 'slap-up tea'.

People were strolling over the parapeted bridge she had chosen, mostly in couples. There was a particularly pretty parasol coming towards her, she noticed, black and white with white lace ruffles. The young lady holding it was wearing white ruched muslin with a narrow piping of black round the flounces – there were many flounces – and her dark hair was crowned with a frothy little hat of white lace. Her escort was tall, thin, dark also. It was Charlie McNab. Her heart jumped against her ribs and she stopped and stood at the parapet, looking pointedly towards the other bridge.

Where were the children? Ah, there they were. She waved to them but not too vigorously in case they would become excited and clamber up. She could not dawdle here, she would have to go and meet them in case they did anything foolish . . . she turned and found Charlie and the young woman a yard or two from her.

He recognized her immediately, if he had not done so before. 'Maevy, what brings you here?' He raised his hat and stopped.

'The same as you, I expect,' she said, smiling, trying to look at ease.

'We're both fugitives from the Infirmary, then? I want you to meet a friend of mine, Miss Wilcox, Miss McGrath, Sister McGrath.'

The girl smiled and held out her hand. 'Oh, do you know my father?'

'You're . . .? Yes, I've worked with Mr Wilcox.'

'I don't know how you can do nursing!' She shuddered. 'Or anything to do with surgery! All that . . . mess! I tell Charlie it gives me the creeps.'

'It doesn't do that to Maevy, I assure you,' Charlie said. 'She intends to devote her life to it.'

Maevy met his eyes and spoke hurriedly. 'I'm in charge of my nephew and niece.' She looked around. 'I'd better go or I'll find them swimming in the Kelvin. Good-bye, Miss Wilcox.'

'Oh, must you? Well, good-bye. I'll tell my father I was speaking to you.'

'How's your mother?' Charlie asked, leaning on his cane as if he had all day.

'She's well, thank you. She's here with us today. It's a family party.' She looked around again and this time she saw Sarah and Robert climbing on the fence at the end of the parapet. 'Oh, I must go. Good-bye . . .'

Charlie raised his top hat and she saw his eyes, bold, black, smiling, fixed on her. She rushed away, thinking how undignified she must look to his companion, not really a girl she thought with some satisfaction, there had been little lines round her eyes. And why is it I always remember *Charlie*'s eyes . . .? She reached Robert and grabbed him as he was half-way up the fence.

'Come away, now.' She took each child firmly by the hand and walked quickly towards the main pavilion. She was not in the least upset to have seen Charlie McNab with Miss Wilcox, that not-quite-a-girl. She had heard the rumours often enough about her father's predilection for Charlie. No, she was not upset . . . so why was she sweating and her breathing was hurried and . . .

'You look far away,' Catherine said later when they were seated round a table in the restaurant.

'She's dreaming of her lover.' Terence smiled at Maevy.

'She's far too sensible for that,' his wife said.

'I'm never too sensible for that,' and then, without thinking, she said, 'I met Charlie McNab here today.' She could have bitten out her tongue.

'Oh, did you?' Maria looked up from her plate. 'That was wonderful! Why didn't you ask him to join us?'

'Because he was with a young lady.' She saw Maria glance quickly at Maevy's mother, who raised her eyebrows.

'Well, he's an attractive young man,' Maeve said. 'I'm not surprised.'

Terence sat beside her when they were on deck chairs listening to the orchestra. 'Never seem to see you these days, Maevy. I expect yours is a very busy life.'

'It is, but I enjoy it. You'll understand that. You always seem to enjoy yours. We both put a lot into our work.'

He lowered his voice. 'And into our play.'

'It depends where you play.' She remembered Maria telling her that she had seen him calling at the Mitchells' house. He was daft enough for anything.

'Oh, I'm very careful.'

'A little bird tells me you've become quite interested in singing.'

'You don't have to believe everything you hear.' She glanced at him but he was looking straight ahead, humming in unison with the Viennese Waltz the orchestra was playing.

He's a rascal, she thought. Is he or isn't he visiting Mrs Mitchell? No, he wouldn't be so foolish. She looked along the row and saw the proud lift of Catherine's profile, the doyen of Great Western Terrace. Could she blame him?

63

'*Tra*-la, *la*-la, *la* . . . la-*la*,' she sang, swaying against him so that he had to do the same. They both burst out laughing. 'Oh, it's nice to be here,' she said.

'Aye, nice.' He bumped as he swayed. 'Boomps a daisy!'

'Don't do anything foolish, Terence.'

'Nor you. There aren't many like Charlie McNab.'

She tried to think about all she had seen on her way back to the Infirmary, the fairy lights outlining the Kelvin, the rockets exploding like giant flowers, the road outlined by padella lights. A magical spectacle sure enough. She tried not to think of Miss Wilcox, the black and white vision, and how eminently suited she was to be the wife of a rising young surgeon, especially if he was helped up the ladder by her father. The day had been ruined for her.

'Your parasol, Miss Letitia,' Effie said, 'the sun's hot.'

'Thank you, Effie.' She pouted at Charlie, 'Effie tries always to guard my complexion.'

'Won't your hat do that?'

'Silly boy! Neither my hat nor my parasol are intended to *protect* my skin. They're just . . . *bon ton*.'

'Now, what can that mean?'

They strolled amongst the flower beds of the Botanic Gardens and then went into the Kibble Palace whose steamy heat made Charlie wish he had as few clothes on as the startled nymph under the glass dome. And from whom Letitia averted her eyes, but not too quickly. He did not care for formal dress, felt encased as if his new frock coat was a corset. Would that be a disadvantage if he became a full-time surgeon as Mr Wilcox had suggested? 'Are you looking forward to your trip to America?' he asked her.

'In a way. Father is going as visiting professor, and he'll

be much fêted. I hear Scottish girls are much sought after because of their complexions.'

'Is that so?'

'You should say, "I'm not surprised."'

'Should I?'

'What shall you do while I'm away?'

'Work. And your father has kindly arranged for me to pay a visit to Germany and Holland to see the new techniques being used there. I appreciate that.'

'He admires your capacity for hard work.' He knew she was looking at him, and he pretended to be examining an unremarkable fern. 'He could do a lot for you, Charlie.'

'I've never been one for accepting favours.' Why was he here with this strange woman . . .

'Oh, but it wouldn't be a favour. It's in his own interest. He wants to find someone who could share his own busy practice in the future. He and mother would like to spend more time at our house in Shandon.'

The strange thing to him was that he enjoyed Letitia's company. It was like a salve to his *amour propre* which had been badly dented by Maevy's rejection of him. Letitia amused him. She had a sharp, if shallow wit, was a good mimic, and was never dull. She would make an excellent wife to go home to after a busy day as a surgeon.

In a secluded corner of the Botanic Gardens, under a conveniently placed laburnum tree, he kissed her, and found her response as swift as most of her movements. She at least would satisfy that lust in him which was normal. Hadn't Mr Wilcox said he was in his prime?

6

Maeve McGrath was in the office of the McGrath Carting Company early. It was a brisk October morning, and in the train from Sholton to Glasgow she had taken delight in the autumn foliage. In spite of the spoliation of the countryside there were still small oases of trees and fields between them, a huddled farm or two, even a few cows grazing behind the hedges, places which had escaped the ever-greedy maw of industrialization. Thank goodness I've still got Braidholme, she thought. It's still dear to me in spite of losing Kieran and Lizzie.

She sat up straight, remembering who she was: Mrs McGrath, founder with her husband of the McGrath Carting Company. In her day dress of copper brown broadcloth with its subdued bustle, the neat jacket edged with fur, she hoped she looked in her trim velvet toque every inch a businesswoman on her way to their offices in Gallowgate for their weekly board meeting.

I can sympathize with Maevy, she thought, wanting to fulfil herself in nursing, although her reasons are less clearcut than mine were. She's idolized John Craigie for years, a good, kind, ordinary man but not to be compared with Charlie McNab who is extraordinary. She knew they were no longer seeing each other. He no longer 'just happened' to drop in when Maevy was on leave on a Sunday. She herself had missed Charlie coming striding across the garden with that quick smile of his. 'I thought I'd find the head cook and bottle-washer of the Royal Infirmary here today . . .'

Ah, well, she had long given up looking for the

expected in her children, with the exception of Kate, the golden exception, with her goodness, gaiety and warmth. Patrick was all right now with Maria, a safe, happy marriage if not blessed with the ecstasy that had been there with Bessie, but Terence was a worry, always would be. Maybe that was because of Bessie, too, a constant desire to forget her, a constant desire to find her in someone else.

Catherine did not help with her gloomy piety. She got more and more like old Mooly Murdoch, her father, every day, but the children ought to have consoled him for a marriage with no joy in it. Instead he found his compensation in frequenting those new places opening up all over Glasgow, the Waterloo Rooms, the Grosvenor Restaurant, and such like. It was all good for business, but his wayward eye was not. Oh, but he's a handsome lad, she thought, my favourite.

But she was neither soft nor fond later in the Board Room of their offices. Bob Carter and Tom Johnson were there, as reliable as clockwork, although they were both grey-haired now, Patrick and Terence, one as usual solemn-faced, Terence bright and talkative as he always was. 'We can start now that the Queen has arrived. When are *you* having your Golden Jubilee, Mother? Are you holding a ball for it?' This was a reference to the one they had all attended last year in honour of the Queen, representing one of the best-known businesses in the city.

'I'm not as old as the Queen yet,' she said crisply. 'Unless you think I look it.'

'Do you hear her fishing for compliments?' Terence joked.

Tom Johnson, as humourless as he was loyal, answered, 'Mrs McGrath doesn't need to fish for compliments. We're all as proud of her beauty as her brains.'

Maeve smiled. 'Well, well!' She was not in the habit of

67

gazing in the mirror, but it had told her this morning that her skin was still firm, her eyes bright. 'I thank you sincerely, Tom, but shall we get on with the business before my head is completely turned? You said it was bucking up after the depression, Bob. Could we have the figures?'

Bob Carter looked down at the sheaf of papers in front of him. 'Yes, we've picked up all right but at a cost. We pay more than the other carters, so we have to earn more. The railway carters have had their own Union longer than us now, and they don't work as long hours. But against that we've all those crofters being driven off their land by the clearances who're willing to work all the hours God sends them.'

'I don't think we can ever be accused of exploiting them?' She looked round the table.

'No, we've always been fair,' Patrick said. 'That was the rock you and Father built the business on. But there's more unrest now. 'Eighty-six was a bad year, and when men aren't working they start organizing together.'

'Arthur Cranston will be in the middle of all that.' Terence nodded. 'I've fancied he isn't so kindly disposed towards us now that we've gone up in the world. He said to me not so long ago that the upper classes were gibbering with terror at what's ahead of them.'

'You don't meet *him* at the Waterloo Rooms,' Maeve said.

'No, but I get around.' He waved his hand vaguely. Was he drinking in some low tavern now? She dismissed the thought. 'Do you think there's trouble brewing?' she appealed to Bob.

'It's a time of change. I think we're in for a strike that will put the fear of God in everybody. But meantime, since we have to keep the firm going through bad times as

68

well as good, I'll read the balance sheet.' He was happier with figures.

When the meeting was over, Maeve spoke about family matters to Patrick and Terence. They were all well, and Maria had asked Terence to bring Grandmother to tea since Patrick would be late.

'Will Catherine be there?' she asked.

'If she can spare the time. Now that little Terence is off her hands she's added the Band of Hope Union to her charities.' He spoke shortly. 'I'll call back for you at four-thirty. I've a few clients to see first.'

'That suits me,' she told him. 'I'm going to spend an hour or so dictating letters to Miss Mavor.' She smiled at Patrick when he had gone. 'Always a tearaway, your brother. There's no changing him.'

'He brings in the business, Mother. I'm no good at being a front man.'

'You do your own bit here. The business couldn't run without you. You've got a good wife in Maria, son. I appreciate her hospitality. She makes me feel . . . wanted.'

'You'll always be wanted.' His eyes softened.

'I wish I could say the same about Catherine.'

'She fills the house with her meetings. That's what sends Terence out at night. Well, I'd better get on. The Board meeting eats into the day.'

She thought of the unrest all over the country as she made her way to her own room, a sign of the times. She had read in the *Herald* that there had even been processions through the district of the Pall Mall clubs in London.

But who could blame them? She thought of the miserable wage Kieran had earned down the pit, and how his health had been ruined as well. She remembered the time Alastair Crawford had taken her in his carriage to see his dying mother, and how the clip-clop of the horses had stirred again the idea germinating in her, their own business, something to do with horses . . .

But you had to take the rough with the smooth. She got up from her desk and went to the door. She had never liked ringing a bell. It was too peremptory. Once when she had been in a hurry and used it she had seen the look of resentment in Miss Mavor's eyes, quickly veiled. She was a touchy girl, chosen by Patrick because of her ability. But had you to be plain to be able?

'Miss Mavor?' she said. And smiled. 'I'm ready if you are.'

'Right away, Mrs McGrath.' There was no answering smile, but perhaps Miss Mavor thought it did not go with a business-like demeanour.

It was pleasant sitting sipping tea in Maria's cosy drawing-room. Flora had brought in the cake stand and Terence had jumped up to help her, knocking one of the cakes on to the floor in his eagerness. They both bent down to rescue it. Flora was flushed and laughing.

If I'd been Maria I should have reprimanded her, she thought, but then American women were easy-osy with servants. There was not the same gap between those who served and those who were served. She was sure if she had raised the question with Maria she would have said smilingly, openly, 'But Flora's as good as I am!' Which was true, of course.

I was brought up as a lady, she thought regretfully. She remembered the old days at Woodlea when there had been two Miss Muldoons, the one who sat in old Mairi's kitchen when she came in from the hunt, and the haughty Miss Muldoon who was waited upon by the maids she had been chatting with earlier. All wrong, she thought. Arthur Cranston with his single-minded determination to make conditions better for workers can see the inequality of that system.

Terence returned to his seat and beckoned to the children playing on the floor with their wooden bricks. 'Come along, Sarah, Gee-Gee. Who's first for a ride?'

'You go, Sarah,' Maeve said. 'Ladies first.'

'Do you remember when we all had rides on Father's foot, Mother? We must have been heavy, not like this little smout.' Sarah was small and dainty for her age, resembling Maria's mother. Maeve smiled at the recollection of all those ruffles and bows. 'Ride a cock horse, to Banbury Cross,' he sang, 'Now you, Gee-Gee . . .'

'It's time for the children's tea, ma'am.' Jeannie, the children's nurse, was curtseying at the door.

'So it is. Then you must take them away before they kill their poor uncle.'

'How's Maevy?' Terence said when the room was quiet again. 'I haven't seen her since that day we had together at the Exhibition.'

'I don't see her too often myself. She's always busy, and well-respected at the Royal, Charlie McNab tells me.'

'I'm sorry that's broken up,' Maria said. 'What is she thinking of, a splendid young man, bound to go far? Oh, she's being very unwise.'

'It's for her to decide.' Terence took out his watch and looked at it. 'Happiness lies in different places for different people. Would you mind if I leave now, Mother, and let Patrick see you into a cab?'

When he had left, Maria put her finger to her lips. 'Wait a second.' She rose and went to the window and drew aside the curtain. Yes, she was pregnant. That's good, Maeve thought, a quiverful for Patrick. Maria turned and beckoned to her. She got up and stood behind her.

She could see the flight of steps leading up to the door

of the next house. The light from the occluded moon was enough to illuminate them. There was no mistaking the tall erect figure of Terence as he ran lightly up the steps, pressed the bell with his cane, and stood, fortunately without looking around. The door opened and he went in. Maria put her hand on Maeve's arm and let the curtain fall into place. They both took their seats again.

'The Mitchells?' Maeve said. Maria nodded. 'There could be nothing in it. They have a mutual interest in singing.' Her mouth quirked. So did Maria's.

'I have to tell you, Mother, that he's been dropping in here a fair amount on his way home. I thought it was because he was waiting for his house to empty. He's told me of Catherine's endless meetings . . .'

'Perhaps he was slightly embarrassed . . .' Oh, silly lad, she thought, silly . . .

'Terence?' Maria looked dubious. 'Well, only perhaps because Mr Mitchell is away from home a lot.'

'Is he?' She took a deep breath. 'Well, maybe we shouldn't say or think any more about it, Maria. Terence is . . . Terence, and in any case, beyond my control.'

'Yes, of course. I see I shouldn't have mentioned it to you. I've always been frank with you, as you know.'

'You did quite right.' Maeve smiled at her. 'And are you going to be even franker?'

'Franker?' Maria's eyebrows raised. 'Oh, the baby? Don't tell me it shows already! We're so happy about it . . .'

Patrick came into the room, his face brightening when he saw them. He kissed Maria fondly, then said to Maeve, 'Don't tell me your escort has deserted you?'

'Yes, he had to get back, but perhaps you'll fetch me a cab, Patrick.'

'No, we won't hear of you going so soon,' Maria said, 'will we, my darling?' She appealed to Patrick. 'You must

72

stay and have dinner with us. I've just told her about the baby, but she already knew.'

'Mother's very perceptive.' He smiled at her, and unaccountably she felt the tears come into her eyes.

'I'm very glad for you both. And, yes, I would like to stay for dinner, if you'll have me.'

New babies arriving, new lives beginning. Braidholme had nothing like that. She was in no hurry to go home.

7

That evening Terence did not go home, even after his visit next door . . .

'You're a naughty boy,' Cordelia Mitchell told him, reclining on a chaise longue in her elegant drawing room. 'Cuthbert is away and I'd hoped we'd have a little *tête-à-tête* dinner by the fire.' Terence smiled, regretfully, he hoped. Her costume had been a warning to him, seeming to be more appropriate to the bedroom with its diaphanous material and low *décolletage*. She has a singer's bosom, he thought, eyeing it professionally.

'I'd like to, Cordelia,' he said, 'very much. I feel you could teach me a lot . . . about music.' He hesitated long enough to make her arch her neck and draw her plump white hand down her throat. It had creased lines across it because of its plumpness. 'But duty calls. I've to attend a meeting at our business offices. It's most important.'

'Surely you don't have business meetings in the evenings?'

'We have to,' he assured her. 'The man who represents the workers isn't free during the day. We always like to give him a hearing.'

'I'll forgive you this time since it is duty. Perhaps next week when you have the details for the concert worked out? I rely on you, dear boy.'

'Have I ever let you down?' This is not me, he thought, bending over the plump hand, kissing it, the lad who came up from the pit fifteen years ago.

He was still out of sorts with himself as he walked quickly to Charing Cross where he caught a cab. Catherine had known about his visit to the Mitchells, and that had pleased her. 'At least rendering her a favour is better than carousing in eating-houses.'

'It isn't easy to eat at home if the dining-room is constantly in use for your meetings,' he had said. But she did not know about the appointment he was now going to keep.

He looked at the girl across the table, so young, so fresh, so different from Mrs Mitchell. He found it difficult to *think* of her as Cordelia, far less to use the name, an outlandish name in this part of the world any roads. But this was just a child, really, like Maevy when she had been sixteen, bubbling over with the joy of life.

'What age are you, Flora?' he asked.

'Eighteen.'

'You look sixteen. Just like my young sister used to be.'

'Well, we'll split the difference and say seventeen.' She threw back her head and laughed and he thought, not like Maevy, like Bessie. She had laughed like that.

'You're a tease.' He took her hands over the table, smiling into her eyes.

'And so are you. And wicked into the bargain. What would your wife say if she could see you supping with me in this low place?'

'I never waste my time on idle speculation,' he said, and she mimicked him.

'Idle speculation, is it? And what do those fine words mean? I haven't had an education like Mr Terence McGrath of the McGrath Carting Company.'

'You had as good a one as me. I was a miner in Sholton until I got married.'

'I don't believe it.'

'It's true, though. My father and mother started the business, well, my mother had the idea.'

75

'I can believe that about your mother. She has . . . style. You kind of feel her presence when you go into the room, a real lady. And she misses nothing. What would she say if she could see you here with me?'

'I don't know.' He thought she would be disappointed in him, but not half as disappointed as he was in himself. The thought lowered his spirits for a moment. 'She's not given to criticism, much. She's withdrawn herself from our affairs since my father died, but not over the business. All her energy goes into that.'

'And her loving, no doubt. She looks like a passionate woman.' Flora pursed her full red lips judiciously.

'Now, what do you know about passion, little girl?' he said, putting his hand to her cheek.

'Only what you've taught me.' She laughed, leaning against his hand, her eyes provocative.

'I haven't taught you anything you didn't know, or want to know. Don't put the blame on me.'

'Well, maybe that's right, but there's no future in it, is there?'

'What do you mean?'

'Well, you're married and I know you wouldn't leave your wife or your family for me. You talk too much about those two wee lads of yours to do that. And there's your position in Glasgow and in your business. No, I know exactly the place I take in your life, Mr McGrath. Now, in Melrose, at my sister's, it's different. There I'm something of a city girl working in a fine house, smart . . .'

'You take a very special place in my life, Flora, believe me.' At least she was bright, and young, and she did not nag him, nor turn away from him as Catherine did. She had never liked his love-making, right from the early days of their marriage when she had got up out of bed saying he was a beast. That took the heart out of a man. 'If your children could have been born by Immaculate Conception

76

you would have preferred it,' he had said once, and she had flown into one of her rages. 'Blasphemy is it now? Well, I've had to take most things. I've sunk really low for a minister's daughter . . .'

He had known Flora was high-spirited the first time he had seen her at Maria's. He could read the signals in a girl's eyes as well as the next one. But she had a head on her. She 'wasn't going to sell her hen on a rainy day,' he remembered that expression of his mother's. It had been easy enough to chat to her when she was showing him out, after a time to suggest meeting at this place in the Gallowgate. He had recognized her type, a lively girl kept down at home, desperate for experience, to see life, to have fun.

'Your face has gone all sad. What are you thinking of?' She tickled the palm of his hand holding hers, smiling into his eyes.

'Oh, how unlike my wife you are, and how like someone else I knew a long time ago, someone I loved.'

'Well, why didn't you marry her?'

'I was married by the time I realized it.'

'That shouldn't have stopped *you*. So why aren't you with her instead of me?'

'She's dead, that's why.' He felt his face twist, and took his hand away, lifted his glass. 'How did we get on to this topic, for God's sake?' He made a great effort to compose himself. The wine helped. When would this twisting pain ever go whenever he thought of Bessie? Patrick had done the right thing by marrying her, *he* could mourn with dignity. And had done the right thing again by marrying Maria who was more like what a wife should be.

He pushed down his self-pity. It had never done any good, but how in hell's name could you ever rid yourself of remorse? Could John Craigie tell him? But Catherine's father had put him off ministers for good. Holy Willies

77

had never had any attraction for him, although John was all right, and he, come to think of it, had come out of it better, too, with Lizzie living in his house, getting the name of his own daughter . . . By God, he thought, I've made a proper muck-up of things.

He sat with his head sunk for a minute but when he raised it he was smiling. He forced himself to laugh, to lift his glass to Flora. 'Drink up. I get these gloomy spells sometimes. Pay no attention. It doesn't do to look back. Sometimes, do you know, I think I'll clear out of Glasgow altogether and go and live in Ireland.'

'Ireland?' She raised her brows. 'Why in God's name go to Paddy's land?'

'It's the land of my dreams, maybe. My mother and father are Irish, he's dead, and I was brought up on its songs. I have a picture of it in my head, its greenness and its softness. My father always talked about going back but never did. Maybe I could go in place of him. Everybody's got their own Eldorado. What's yours, Flora?'

'Melrose.'

'Why Melrose. That's the other end of the earth, as far away as Ireland, nearly.'

'It's gentle and peaceful. My sister went for service there and she had the luck to marry a farmer. She asked me for my summer holidays this year. Oh, it was lovely, no smoke nor dirt like Glasgow, nor poor folk lying in the gutter, all grass and trees and fields. She's got a farmhouse with a dairy, and hens to look after and two wee lads like you. Oh, it's heaven on earth at Melrose!'

'Why don't you charm one of the farmers, then?'

'I did. He was nice . . .' She looked away but not before he saw the steeliness in her eyes. She wasn't all sugar and spice, Flora.

'I'm a countryman at heart, too. I have my father's love of horses. I'd like to train them or breed them in Ireland,

78

ride most of the day, sit at a crackling log fire at night, two dogs at my feet . . .'

'Quite the country gentleman, eh?'

'And why not, pray, tell me that?'

'Well, if you're anything like your mother,' she looked at him critically, 'there's no reason why not. You can see she's the real thing. You get good at telling ladies from trash when you're in service . . . like that la-di-da fat yin next door.'

'Have I ever shown you my office in the Gallowgate?' He grinned at her, feeling himself go hot with desire for her.

She laughed throwing back her head, and her throat was white and smooth, unlike Cordelia's. 'You know very well you've shown it to me a few times, cheeky thing! Maybe I've had enough of it. But we'll get out of this smoky hole any roads, though the food's good, I'll say that about it . . .' She bent forward to him, 'Do you see that woman going out with the other one? She's been giving us a good dekko all the time we've been in.'

'Where . . .?' He turned carefully, but only saw the backs of two women, one in blue, the other in brown, lumpy-figured, not his style, as they left the inn.

'Maybe they're tarts,' Flora said, 'though they didn't look like it.'

'I doubt it. It's a decent enough place, this. I wouldn't bring you here if it was anything different. Paul Spencer who runs it tells me some of the folks round about come in for their evening meal. And it's the only place in town you can get half pints to suit a lady like you.' He smiled at her. 'We can recommend their steak and kidney pie, can't we?'

'Aye, it's no' bad, but no' as good as they would serve in yon grand Grosvenor restaurant. Maybe you would be

too well-known there, Mr Terence McGrath?' She dim-
pled at him.

'You're an impudent besom,' he grinned at her, 'but I
like it in you. Are you coming to see my office, then?'

'Maybe I could be coaxed.' She had a provocative little
face, fresh and unlined, inviting, not like that old hag next
door to Maria . . . He corrected himself, Mrs Cordelia
Mitchell. Poor old thing, he thought pityingly, forty-five
if she's a day.

And Flora's body was firm and inviting, too. They had
gone in the back door of the stables because old Jock, the
watchman, had a cottage at the front gates, past the
shuttered chaff and grain barns, the harness room, the
rows of stalls for the horses which were never silent, the
poor beasts, tired out and uncomfortable with their carting all day long from warehouse to railway yard, up and
down the city streets, plod, plod. He knew that feeling of
tiredness from his pit days, hardly ever felt it now. Then
up the winding stair above the stables to the suite of
offices which his mother had planned with such care.

His room had a leather sofa in it which had once been
at Braidholme. He remembered Father lying on it when
he was convalescing after his heart attack. She had
replaced it with a covered chintz one some time ago.
Maybe she had seen him still lying there . . . as Flora lay
now. He threw himself down beside her.

'Ah, but you're lovely!' His face was in her hair. This
was what he had waited for all evening, when she was in
his arms and she became Bessie. And the dark room
became the Sholtie Woods at bluebell time, and the
perfume was all her and of the bluebells, too, and the
softness was that of Bessie and the grass underneath, and
the open mouth was Bessie's . . .

'Bessie . . .' he groaned, 'my Bessie . . .' Flora drew
herself away from him.

'Who do you think I am for God's sake?' She sounded frightened.

He caressed her, soothed her. 'I was only mumbling. Lie down again, sweet lass. Oh, your softness, and the length of you against me, and your arms round me, I could be in Heaven, I could be anywhere . . .' I could be in the Sholtie Woods with the love of my life in my arms, loving me because she was for me only, always and for ever if I'd only had the sense to see it. And I would not remember walking back to Bob Cranston's with her afterwards and seeing her white face in the darkness, and asking her, 'Will you regret it, Bessie?' and seeing her shaking her head . . .

8

All winter and the spring of 1889 Maevy worked hard with a pioneering zeal. She studied midwifery, attended extra lectures, and sometimes even toyed with the idea of becoming a doctor. She had heard about Elizabeth Garret Anderson and thrilled to the idea of being in the vanguard with women like her. But she knew that her skills lay in nursing and that she hadn't the necessary education to fit her to become a medical student. Sometimes she longed for a second Crimea.

But because it was a period of peace, Glasgow had never been gayer. She went out with other nurses on their evenings off, and with their escorts dined and wined in city howffs. She went to soirées in private houses. It was impossible to walk along a quiet avenue at night in the suburbs without hearing sounds of music and singing, or see the shadows of dancing figures behind the lit windows. She was by nature a happy girl, and as keen on a 'tare' as the rest of the nurses. 'The Golden Years', the *Glasgow Herald* had called this run-up to the end of the century.

It was only when she thought of Charlie McNab that her spirits faltered, that doubts set in. She had heard he was visiting hospitals in Germany and Holland. No doubt he would marry when he got home. She had turned him down, hadn't she? Was she going to be a dog-in-the-manger as well?

But in April when she heard that Maria had had a little girl, she could not help feeling a pang of jealousy. Three children now, and she herself, at twenty-seven, not even married. Was she the only professional woman who suffered these pangs? What about her beloved Florence Nightingale, or her protégée, Rebecca Armstrong, of the Royal itself? She had to be reminded several times by her mother before she could bring herself to call and see the new arrival.

She found Maria looking, at first sight, blooming, almost too blooming, her professional eye told her, as if she was doing her best to live up to the image of the high-spirited girl who had come from America. She kissed the girl fondly and apologized because she could not stay long.

'Catherine has persuaded me to go to one of her Bursts in St Andrew's Hall for the Temperance Movement,' she said. 'I felt guilty at not having seen her for a long time and so I accepted.'

'She can't get Terence to go anywhere with her. But you've time for a cup of tea, Maevy?'

'Of course I have.' She took off her hat and gloves and laid them on the arm of the sofa. 'I have to see the new baby. You look well, Maria, a little thinner, that's all.'

'That's good.' She appeared uninterested. 'I've always had a struggle with my weight.' She got up to ring the bell.

'Like me.'

'Oh, you've a lovely figure, like your mother's. I can't believe Patrick when he tells me you were a plump little girl.' Her face had no life in it. A maid came in and curtseyed.

'Tea, Bridget, please.' The girl went out, her apron bow almost lost in the broad expanse of her hips.

'Where's that pretty Flora you had?'

'Oh, dear!' Maria sat down. 'She got pregnant and I had to discharge her. But she said she was going to Melrose to be married. I went to see her mother because I felt so upset. After all, she'd been put in my care. She

83

was as tight-lipped as she'd been when I first saw her. "Too much gadding about for my liking. I told her no good would come of it. Anyhow, she's gone to Melrose to be married from her sister's house . . ." That was all she would say.'

'Well, that's that. Don't let it upset you. It's common enough. You've enough to think about with your dear little daughter. When can I see her?' The animation died out of Maria's face.

'Oh, there's no rush. Let's have our tea first in peace. She cries a lot.' Maevy looked at her but Maria had jumped up and was busying herself with the curtains. 'That new girl isn't a patch on Flora. She forgets those curtains although she knows I like them drawn early.'

'How are your next-door neighbours, the Mitchells, wasn't it?'

'They've left. Didn't you know? They went to live in London again.'

'I remember Terence paying the wife some attention at your soirée long ago.'

'There was nothing in that, just Terence. When she came to say good-bye she said he'd been helping her with a charity concert.'

Maevy was scarcely listening. A suspicion, a presentiment like a coldness was stirring in her. Why had the news about Flora made her feel it was a repetition of something which had happened long ago in the family? Mother could explain it, she thought. A servant made pregnant. How could *she* explain it?

'They left last month, April. I wasn't quite recovered, the birth was difficult, I hadn't much time to give her.' She giggled, 'I hadn't noticed it before but she has a little moustache.' She put her hand to her mouth and Maevy saw tears come into her eyes. What was wrong? She was going to get up and go to her but the door opened and

84

the maid appeared with a tray which she dumped down, curtseyed awkwardly, and left. Maevy watched her sister-in-law pouring the tea. Her hand trembled and the cup clinked against the saucer as she passed it.

'Thanks, Maria,' she said. 'What are you calling the baby?'

'Mary. Patrick wanted my name, so that was as near as we could get to it. Family names can be confusing.'

'Yes, you're right.' There was a strain in the conversation.

'Will you have a piece of sultana cake?' Maria said. 'Cook taught me how to make it. Patrick doesn't take to my frosted icing.' She smiled sadly, surely not because of Patrick's dislike of her frosted icing.

'Thanks, just a little piece. Sarah and Gee-Gee must be thrilled with their little sister.'

'No, they don't like her at all.' Maria stirred her tea quickly, nervously, not looking up.

Maevy laughed, hiding her alarm. 'They don't want a usurper in the nursery, I expect.'

'I'm afraid of her, too,' Maria said. She put down her cup and held her handkerchief to her face with both hands. It was an infinitely pathetic gesture. Maevy jumped up and put her arms round the weeping girl.

'You're run down, Maria. Mothers sometimes turn away from the new baby. It's just weakness . . .'

'No, it isn't.' She spoke through her tears. 'I loved Sarah and Gee-Gee immediately. They were so sweet. But this baby . . .' She raised her face to Maevy, the tears running down her face. 'I've asked the doctor but he says, "Give it time . . ." Oh, I wish I'd stuck to Charlie McNab! He would have been frank with me, but Patrick said we must have someone close by. And besides, you and he aren't friends now. It would have been awkward for me.'

'No, it wouldn't.' She wanted to say, 'Rubbish', but

Maria was in no fit state. She drew up a chair and sat down beside her. 'You might be upsetting yourself needlessly. Here's a dry hankie. I've seen the ugliest babies develop into beautiful swans. But if there's anything wrong with Mary, the sooner it's attended to, the better. Would you like to take me upstairs to see her?'

'Yes . . . yes.' Maria wiped her eyes and handed back the handkerchief. 'Thanks. I'm usually strong, like you. But being a mother seems to alter you in some way . . .'

'You're strong underneath. You've just been worrying on your own too much.' She helped Maria up, and kept her arm round her shoulders as they went upstairs together.

At the door of the nursery Maria straightened and patted her hair. 'Thanks, Maevy. I'm sorry . . .'

The young nurse was giving the children their tea, and they were too engrossed in it to pay them much attention. 'How's the baby been, Jeannie?' Maria asked.

'As good as gold, ma'am.' She looked at Maevy. There was something in her eyes.

The bedroom was darkened, but the first sight of the baby was reassuring. She lay on her side, her eyes closed, and the sparse hair covering her small head glinted in the firelight. Mother's hair, Maevy thought, how it persists . . . there was a flatness about the face, even in profile. The nose was short and squat. Maevy felt a sick kind of ache. 'Do you mind if I lift her?' She bent over the cot. 'And put on the light, will you?' The thing had to be faced.

The sudden brilliance of the gas lamp would have frightened most babies. This one did not start as Maevy cradled her in her arms. She still slept, but her breathing was noisy, catarrhal. She tickled the child's bare toes, supported her back and held her upright in her arms. The head lolled back. She did it again. The eyes opened this time and she saw the speckled irises of a mongol. She cradled the baby in her arms while she tried to think what she should say.

'You're seeing the same as I am,' Maria said.

She avoided answering directly. 'If your doctor won't have tests done, you must arrange to have them done yourself. I know the name of a good doctor in the West End, a specialist in children. He comes to the Royal.'

'It's hopeless, isn't it?'

'Nothing's hopeless. I'm not a doctor.'

'But Charlie McNab is. I have faith in him. I could ask him, or you could. Oh, would you, Maevy? He could advise us.'

'I don't know if he's back from the Continent.' She saw Maria's tragic eyes, looked down at the child. 'I tell you what, why don't you and Patrick drive out to Sholton when he comes home? Mother would know. Or you could ask at his house.'

'Oh, do you think I should?'

'Yes, I do. If Charlie's there, he'll give you some good advice, maybe reassure you . . .' She felt terrible saying that, but the hope in Maria's face was worth it.

Catherine was waiting in the drawing room when they went downstairs.

'We've been looking at the baby,' Maevy said.

'What do you think?' Catherine did not mince words. 'She isn't right, is she?'

'I told Maria I'm no doctor.' She tried to smile.

'You're as good as. Doctors always treat you like morons anyhow. I've been going to Dr Wordie for ages with my nerves and all he says is that I've to rest more.' She certainly looked haggard. 'The only one I've ever known who treated you like a human being was Charlie McNab.'

87

'Would you like a cup of tea, Catherine?' Maria was very pale.

'No, thank you, my dear.' Catherine's face softened. 'We all get our crosses to bear. Would you like to come along with us and take your mind off your worries?'

'No, thank you all the same. Patrick will be in soon and we'll be driving out to Sholton after he's had his meal.'

'That'll be nice for you, a drive out. I think we'd better be going, Maevy.' She drew her cloak around her. 'I'm on the Reception Committee. I've reserved a seat at the front for you with my friend, Mrs Nesbit, the minister's wife.'

'That's kind of you.' She kissed Maria. 'Try not to worry. I'll be in again on my next day off.'

In the carriage driving to St Andrew's Hall Catherine said, 'Of course you don't have to be a nurse to see that the baby's an imbecile. I wasn't happy when they got married. Cousins, you know, full cousins . . . the McGrath family have sailed on the crest of a wave for a long time, but it's over now. That's my opinion. Maria isn't the only one who knows unhappiness. Maybe you did the right thing, Maevy, not getting married when you got the chance. Take it from me, there's nothing but sorrow in it.'

'What I like about you, Catherine,' Maevy said, 'is that you're always so cheerful.'

'I try to be.'

Even worse, you have no sense of humour . . .

9

A few days later, when Maevy was hurrying along one of the Infirmary corridors, she came face to face with Charlie. He stopped although he had been going at full tilt, too, his stethoscope dangling from his pocket.

'Hello, Maevy.' His eyes were brilliant in his lean face. He seemed to have aged since they had last met. But that was almost a year ago, she thought, last June.

'Hello, Charlie. I heard you'd been abroad studying.'

'Yes, I'm not long back. How are you?'

'Still the same.'

'Still of the same opinion?'

'What do you mean?'

'Still full of the desire to emulate Miss Florence Nightingale, or is it Miss Rebecca Armstrong nowadays?'

'Indeed I haven't time to emulate anyone!' She was piqued, and the words escaped from her, 'How's Miss Wilcox?'

'Well, thank you.' He bowed slightly.

'I've got to get on. I'm on my way to surgery.'

'So am I. Maevy, could you meet me somewhere? It's about Maria's baby.'

'Oh, I'm glad they got you! What about when I'm changing shifts? At five?'

'Grand. Where?'

'The seat under the first ornamental gas lamp in the Cathedral Gardens.'

He laughed. 'You sound as if it was your favourite *rendezvous*.'

'So it is.' Hurrying away from him she thought how the

seat was almost her own now. Sometimes she sat there and looked up the hill to the Necropolis, across the little Molendinar Glen, and thought how behind her was this building where they worked to save lives, and in front of her was the inevitable outcome. The only certainty. Sometimes she thought she would like to speak to John about things which troubled her, why although she was giving her heart and soul to nursing there seemed to be something missing . . .

He was striding up and down when she rounded the rearing wall of the cathedral. The organist was playing, and the rich chords seemed to seep through the stained glass windows.

'Fauré,' he said when she went up to him.

'Who?'

'Fauré, the French composer.'

'That's too modern for my taste.'

'You should have come more often with me to concerts.'

'Maybe I should.' It was a beautiful day, the sky limpid, the air soft. It disturbed her. And his vitality disturbed her, standing near to him like this. John was soothing, peaceful, he did not agitate the spirit like this one.

'Do you want to sit or walk?'

'Fancy asking a nurse that stupid question!' She laughed and sat down on the seat behind them. He joined her, smiling directly at her.

'You've got a look of your mother today. Your hair's fair, of course, but it's your . . . look. Upright. A no-nonsense look. I saw it on her the last time I called at Braidholme. She'd just had a visit from a lady in her office, she told me, and her face was like yours, even more so.'

'A lady from McGrath's office? I wonder who that could be?'

90

'Naturally my refined susceptibilities didn't allow me to quiz your mother.' He was teasing her, trying to make her laugh. 'But in any case I wouldn't have dared. She had the "look". Back straight. She relaxed when she saw me. I'm a great favourite of hers, did you know?'

She smiled at him. 'Don't flatter yourself.'

'Who else would do it?' His swift answering smile disarmed her.

'By the way,' she said, 'did Patrick and Maria see you? I suggested it, in a way.'

'I'm glad you did. Of course I can't step in between them and their own doctor, but solely as a friend I went back that night with them to have a look at the baby. They were so distressed, poor souls.' He shook his head. 'Well, there's no doubt she's a mongol. No doubt at all. I don't know why their doctor hadn't the courage to tell them.'

'Is it bad?'

'Bad enough. They might rear her, or they might not. A lot of them die early, sometimes from childhood ailments, often from pneumonia. Her bronchial tubes don't appear to be too good.'

'I noticed that. So what did you say to comfort them?'

'That was difficult.' He bent forward, clasping his hands loosely. 'That she's still their child, that she could well bring them joy, but not if they shut her up in an institution. Mongol children can be cheerful and affectionate, often very musical. I advised them to keep her in the family with her brother and sister if they could, and gave them the name of a good child specialist . . .' He turned towards her. 'Secular and medical advice only, I'm afraid. I'm not very good at the other kind. John Craigie would be better at that.' How piercing his eyes were on her. 'You would know.'

'I've never had to ask him for any.'

91

'You're in full command of your fate, is that it?' His eyes were still on her.

'As far as anyone can be.' He was making her uncomfortable. 'I think I'd better be going, Charlie. Is there anything I can do to help? Patrick's a man who fights his own battles inside himself. When his first wife died he stayed in their house alone. Try and help him and he crawls back into his shell.'

'People change. Go when you can. And talk about Mary. Help to make her part of the family.'

'Yes, I'll do that. He's lucky with Maria.'

'Happy the man who has a good wife.' He did not look at her.

'Well, you won't be long till you're acquiring one of your own,' she said, getting up.

'I hope not.' He stood facing her. 'I hope not, Maevy.' It was like being a butterfly on a pin under his gaze. She spoke hurriedly.

'I've really got to go. Don't walk with me to the Infirmary. You never live it down if you're seen with a doctor.'

'Is it a disgrace?'

'No, they just tease the life out of you.' She laughed. 'But I could say you were an old family friend.'

'That's right. Tell them I'm in love with your mother.'

'Well, you couldn't be in love with a better person.' At times she and Charlie got on like a house on fire.

That Sunday she was late in getting to Sholton, and she walked up the Sholton Road in pouring rain, then along the drive to Braidholme, with the trees dripping on her umbrella and soaking her skirts and boots. Sometimes the other nurses teased her about the regularity of her visits, one had even said she was a 'mother's lass'.

But it wasn't a relationship like that. Since the day she

92

had begun work at the Royal, and perhaps before that, her mother had treated her as an equal, as someone who could be talked with but not at. She never interfered, even over the matter of Charlie McNab, though there was no doubt how she felt.

'My, my, fancy coming away frae Glesca on a day like this wi' the rain stottin' in the gutters!' Susan took her dripping umbrella from her. 'I'll just put this in the kitchen sink. Your mither's gone to the kirk without you.'

'She never went on a day like this!' Maevy unpinned her hat. 'Would you give that a good shake in the kitchen, too? The roses in it are fair drookit.' She laughed.

'I'll do that. She wouldn't have gone, but Lord and Lady Crawford stopped by in their carriage and offered to take her.' Susan pressed her lips together. Her look said, 'Beat that if you can.'

'That was nice of them.' She wouldn't give her the satisfaction of looking impressed. 'I'll go and dry myself at the fire.'

'You do that, and I'll bring you a hot cup of tea. We don't want you sneezing all over your patients when you get back.'

'Thanks, Susan.'

What went on in the woman's head, she wondered, as she stood at the crackling sitting-room fire and held out her skirts to dry. Her eyes travelled round as her mind wandered. Mother must be one of the first to use white paint instead of the grained wood which Catherine had everywhere, and, unlike Catherine, she did not go in for elaborately draped curtains but preferred them hung simply like this on brass rods so that they could be easily pushed back.

Susan . . . she had few friends. Her life was built on her single-minded devotion to Mother. Was that enough in anyone's life? Perhaps it was sufficient to feel wanted,

and Mother certainly depended on her. She had given up
her domestic duties with the greatest of ease when their
circumstances improved, but not the making of a home.
Look at this room. Comfort and elegance, and a lightness.
The chandelier sparkled even on this dark day and so did
those crystal girandoles winking on the mantelpiece. And
the rose-coloured lamps were on. Mother preferred oil
because it gave a mellow light, although Susan cooked by
gas in the kitchen.

Susan it was who ran Braidholme while Mother went to
the Gallowgate every day. She could never have become
a card-calling matron nor a lover of good works like
Catherine. She was her own woman . . .

'Maevy!' She was in the room, smelling of the rain and
her own special perfume, light, lemony. That was one of
her secrets. 'It's good of you to come on a terrible day
like this. Has Susan given you tea?'

'Yes, and I'm as warm as toast here. This place is so
cosy. Such a change from the wards.'

'Everybody needs variety. John was good today, talking
about the change in society in the last few years.' She sat
down beside Maevy on the sofa at the fire, took off her
hat and laid it on the arm. Her red hair gleamed in the
firelight, and the dampness had released some tendrils
which lay on her forehead and her neck. She was still a
bobby-dazzler. 'You're looking pale today, lass.' She had
turned to her. 'You're working too hard.'

'Hard work never killed anyone. I can throw your
words back at you now.'

'What a pleasure that must be!' She smiled. 'Yes, we're
feeling the change in the business, too, just as John said.
We've always tried to play fair with the workers, but I
don't think that's going to be enough any more.'

'I've read about the labour disputes in the *Herald*.'

'All winter. I can see trouble ahead.'

'And what do Lord and Lady Crawford think about it? He'll be even more affected than we will.'

'Oh, that wasn't on the agenda at all!' She smiled. 'Lady Crawford has only one topic of conversation, the hunting field. She's never offered me a seat, though.'

'But Lord Crawford did, a long time ago. One of the boys told me.' She spoke airily. 'I think it was Terence.'

'Yes, he did. A long time ago.' She showed no embarrassment. 'He was the Honourable Alastair then. But I gave up going to the Hall when your father was ill, after the pit explosion.' Trust Mother to get her priorities right. Macvy changed the subject.

'I saw Maria's baby. It's a poor wee mongol.'

'Yes, Charlie told me. Poor Patrick. He'll think the heavens have fallen on his head. I hope Charlie will be able to convince him it isn't the end of the world.'

'I think he tried. He told them she could well turn out to be a blessing.'

'If she lives. The danger is that they'll love her too much. There's always an extra dimension in your love for the afflicted one. But Maria's like our Kate. She has a positive approach to life.'

'Kate hasn't had anything like this.'

'Maybe not, but she's had three miscarriages since little Kieran, and a baby recently that only lived a few days.'

'She never said in her letters!'

'She wouldn't, not Kate. James is urging her to take a trip home to us to set her up again, but she's had a better idea. I had a letter from her yesterday.'

'What was that?'

'To meet me in Paris.'

'Paris!'

'What's wrong with Paris? I've always wanted to see it. She knows that. And Emily lives there.'

'Oh, yes, Madame Charles Barthe.'

'That's right. You never met your step-nieces, nor step-nephews, come to that. Victoria's the quiet one, but Emily was always flighty. She met her husband when James sent them for a year to Paris when they were seventeen or thereabouts.'

'Yes, I remember. Where are the sons now?'

'George is with his father in his export firm, he's twenty-four, and Ernest's at Yale, that's a University there. He must be twenty now.'

'Emily's my age and Victoria two years older. Where does Kieran James fit in?'

'He and Lizzie are ages with one another. All those younger ones growing up make me feel ancient.'

'You don't look it so stop fishing.'

'Sure and it's part of me nature.'

'And no Irish blarney either.'

'Isn't my family forever putting me in my place? Anyhow Emily's seemingly anxious for Kate to visit her. She's as fond of her as if she were her own mother.'

'It wouldn't be difficult to be fond of our Kate. She's not thrawn like me.'

'Now who's fishing for compliments?'

'Trust you. But will you go, Mother?'

'I'd like to. Kate suggests September or early October.' A spasm of envy went through Maevy and she spoke gaily to hide it.

'Well, there, that's settled. It's a wonderful chance.'

Her mother touched her hand. 'Mavourneen,' she rarely called her that, 'why don't you come, too? September would give you plenty of time to arrange it.'

'Oh, I wasn't hinting . . .' She turned to her. 'But I'm sorely tempted. Maybe if I looked into it . . .'

'Do that. You need a change with all that nursing. You're looking frail today. I don't want two Isobel's to worry about. Yes, arrange it!' Her mother's face was glowing. 'You want a different smell in your nose than all that carbolic.'

'Paris sewers?'

'Oh, no, where Emily lives is one of the best districts, I'm told, the Monceau Plain, on the Right Bank.'

'But I couldn't dream of imposing on Emily's hospitality.'

'Nor me. We'll stay in a nice hotel near them and be waited on hand and foot. We could see all the sights together, if you wouldn't find it dull with your old mother.'

'Old mother indeed. And I don't even speak a word of French.'

'We could take Charlie McNab along. He's a dab hand with the French.'

'Maybe you'd rather take him with you than me.' She felt tears at the back of her throat of all things.

'Maevy . . .' Her mother stroked her hand softly, then gave it a brisk pat. 'Now sit there and have a wee rest. I'm going to see Susan about something to eat for you before you go back.'

'Just a bite.'

She went to the window when her mother went out. The rain had stopped now and the garden was glittering with reflected light from the sun which was sliding out from time to time between the heavy clouds. At the end of the lawn she could see the summer house where they sat on fine days. The honeysuckle covered it now, and its window-boxes were gay with wallflowers and alyssum. From its windows you could see the rippling Sholtie where John had drowned . . .

Sometimes, like now, life beckoned far from hospital wards, exciting trips abroad, a husband, family, a house in Sholton like this. She was two people, and hadn't she decided long ago that if she couldn't have John Craigie as a husband she would have nobody?

It's my stubborn bit, she thought, trying to smile at herself.

10

He could not get the letter out of his mind all day. He had booked no outside calls since it was the weekly board meeting, but even when that was going on he had wanted to take it out of his pocket and surreptitiously read it again, although the words were burned on his memory.

The terrible thing was that it had been a confirmation of his worst fears. When Maria told him that Flora had left because she was pregnant, after the first shock, he had done everything he could to find her.

When he had called at her address in the Saltmarket, which by a stroke of luck he remembered Flora mentioning, he had found the flat deserted. A gossiping neighbour at the entry had told him that Mrs Paterson had gone to live with her sister. That was all she knew. The mother was a close-mouthed bitch, she volunteered, dour as they came, but the lass always had time for a word with you. She had cleared out, too. Anybody could see she was 'gawn tae hev a wean'. You couldn't have fourteen as she'd had without knowing what was going on under a body's shawl.

He remembered Flora talking about Melrose, but how could he go there and wander about a strange town looking for a girl called Flora Paterson without knowing her address? He pushed it to the back of his mind, saying, if I don't think about it, it'll go away, saying, I haven't changed . . .

As the days and the weeks passed, and he heard nothing, his natural ebullience reasserted itself. Maybe she hadn't been pregnant at all. Maybe if she was, the father of the child lived in Melrose. Hadn't she talked about a farmer who'd been 'nice' to her?

Besides, his mind was full of other things. Catherine was behaving oddly. She had stopped working for the Temperance Movement and the Boys' Brigade Guild, and so he had no excuse not to go straight home. At their evening meal she sat at the table, scarcely speaking, and looking as white as a ghost. When he tried to fondle her in bed she repulsed him, and when he suggested she should see a doctor she looked at him with unfocused eyes which made him afraid. 'My body is all right,' she said, 'he can do nothing for me.'

'Talk to me, Catherine,' he had implored her one night, but she had turned away from him. Her voice came to him, low, expressionless, making him shudder, 'You've ruined my life.'

'Catherine . . .' he had touched her, and it was as if his touch acted as a catalyst. She flung herself round, and hanging over him, her dark hair around her, she shrieked into his face, 'How do you feel about that, Terence McGrath, eh? To have ruined my life? First Bessie Haddow's and now mine?'

'Keep your voice down, for God's sake,' he muttered.

'Where's the Catherine Murdoch I used to be?' She paid no attention to him. 'Where's that quiet girl who lived in the manse, who was happy till you came along with your blandishments . . .?' She had flung herself away from him, weeping.

The only solace he found nowadays was to go up to the nursery and play with the boys. Robert was now a strapping eight and a half, Terence a sensitive child of three, devoted to his elder brother. He had always loved children, like his father, and took the same delight in them. He rolled on the floor with them like a puppy, and they tugged at his curls.

Then there were the labour troubles which they were involved in along with the other carting contractors in the city. They had been brewing since the New Unionism took hold in Scotland, and now that man, Farquhar, in Dundee, was getting behind the carters in their demands for a ten hour day.

Today they had discussed the position at the meeting. Patrick, as usual, was coldly logical. 'We've never been like the Company,' he said, 'some of their men are working sixteen and seventeen hours a day for a miserable twenty shillings a week, and their stablemen and strappers, I've heard tell, get about seventeen.'

'We complied in June to the demand of the Carters Society,' Maeve pointed out. 'We even paid in advance, and we've always been ready to recognize the Union, not like some contractors who turn away delegates from their own stables saying the state of trade doesn't warrant their claims. That's rubbish. Trade's good and it's improved with the railways, not lessened. Look at the short hauls there are, and the parcel offices. They don't play fair with their workers, that's what's wrong. Your father had a rapport with the men because he'd been a worker himself, like you two. He always gave them a fair hearing.'

'We'll be classed along with the other employers when it comes to the push,' Terence said. 'I've had to break up groups of our men muttering around the stables. Maybe I haven't got Father's skill.'

'Of course you have. You understand horses.' She looked at him. 'It's not like you to be pessimistic.'

'Maybe not, but this is nothing to do with logic. I feel it here, in my gut. We're in for it.'

Later she spoke to him when Patrick and the others had left. 'You look down in the mouth, Terence. Is it only the worry about the carters that's getting to you ?'

'I suppose so,' and then looking at her bright eyes he

101

knew it was no good fooling her. She could always see through him. 'I'm worried sick about Catherine,' he said, 'she's not herself.'

'Do you know what's the cause?' Her eyes were on him. He straightened his lips. 'Terence's pout,' she used to say. He even managed to smile. 'I think she can't stand the sight of me.'

'A bonny lad like you.' She smiled back, then, 'Maybe she feels you can't give her the love she wants.'

'She won't let me. I've tried.'

She shook her head at him fondly. 'You're like a horse, lad, you take a bit of handling. I think Catherine has never learned the right way of it. But she's a funny lass at times, I'll give you that. Contentment isn't one of her strong points.'

'I can't think what it is . . . if she would only talk to me . . .' He did not look at her as he spoke. She would see the falseness in his eyes, would say, 'Out with it, Terence. What are you hiding?'

'Maybe she would talk to someone else. Has she no women friends?'

'Just Mrs Nesbit.'

'Oh, her!' Maeve dismissed with a shrug the minister's wife of one of the most important churches in Glasgow. 'She's got a mind as narrow as some of the wynds in the Gallowgate. I tell you what. Maevy goes every week to see Maria. She'll be there tonight. She's worked wonders, talking to them about wee Mary, encouraging them to set up a relationship with the child, as she puts it. Patrick was just saying to me this morning how indebted they are to her. Indeed he was boasting about Mary's antics, and you know our Patrick. He's never exactly fulsome.'

'Do you mean ask Maevy to come and see Catherine?'

'Why not try it? Being a nurse she can ask questions that Catherine might not like coming from a doctor. She's always had delicate susceptibilities. They tell me Maevy's liked well in the Royal for her gentle ways.' She smiled at him. 'Not always the Maevy *we* know, is it. Remember the stubborn wee girl she was?'

'She's a good lass. Straight as a die and a beauty with it. She deserves better than carrying bed pans all her days.' He felt more cheerful. 'I'll do that, Ma.' He came back to his childhood's name for her. 'I'll call at Claremont Terrace and see if she'll come up to our house for half an hour or so.'

He did not go home at lunch time. He could not face Catherine and the gloomy dining-room with its aspidistras and ferns on their mahogany stands, the heavy green rep curtains always half-drawn in case passers-by could see in, and which gave you the feeling of being under water in a green-scummed pool. The iron grate with its black marble fireplace was like a tomb, and the only relief in his opinion, but not in Catherine's, since she thought he had paid far too much for it, was a landscape by James Paterson, the one in the Glasgow Group he most admired. It reminded him of Sholton in the old days.

Instead he took himself off to the howff where he used to meet Flora, ordered a pie and a pint of ale, and took out the letter which he knew by heart already. His eyes devoured it as if for the first time.

Dear Terence,
This is to tell you that I had a wee girl that I've called Flora on the thirteenth of this month. Don't jump out of your skin. It might be yours and again it might not.

But I wasn't born yesterday. I knew who would marry me and who wouldn't and I knew fine it wouldn't be Mr Terence McGrath. So I told Willie Napier it was his – he'd had me once when I stayed with Ellen, encouraged a wee bit, poor lad – and he fell over himself getting us tied up. So here I am, mistress of all I survey, a tidy farm with as good a house and dairy as our Ellen, if not better.

I don't bear you any ill-will. We had some good times together, and I never thought you were really wicked, just unhappy. But that's your affair. I've got what I wanted, a farm in Melrose and a wee wean into the bargain, and only me and you will ever know that her father might not be Willie Napier of Windyridge Farm. Your pal, Flora.

Maevy was nursing Maria's baby when he was shown into the drawing-room, and when he saw the big head on it he had to turn away his head to hide his pity. Maria did not deserve this, nor Patrick, come to that. But Maria's face was untroubled and smiling as she looked up.

'Here's Uncle Terence come to see you, Mary. Say hello to your new little niece, Terence.'

'Hello,' he said feebly, taking the tiny hand. You can't stand things that don't please your eye, he told himself. Pictures, horses, women. The large head lolled, but the eyes seemed more focused than at the christening. 'I've come to steal Maevy from you,' he said. 'Catherine's getting jealous of her spending so much time here.' He looked at his sister. What a picture she made holding that misshapen child, her fair hair more golden than Isobel's, not red like Mother's but with a warmth, and that fair face of hers with more character in it than her frail sister's. She's the best mixture of the family, he thought; Father's sweetness and Mother's strength.

'It's true I haven't been to see her for a time,' she said. 'Maria tells me she hasn't been well.'

'Yes.' He nodded. 'I don't know what it is. She's withdrawn herself from all her good works, sits about the house, just staring . . . Dr Wordie doesn't know what to make of her.'

'Oh, dear, that's not like Catherine. She's always so busy.'

'I thought if you could have a word with her, Maevy . . .'

'She had a difficult time with her father.' Maevy turned to Maria. 'You never knew him.'

'No. Does Catherine resemble him?'

'Well, she never was what you'd call skittish, but . . .'

'. . . but old Mooly Murdoch was enough to put anyone in the doldrums,' Terence said.

Maevy laughed up at him. 'Oh, Terence, he'll turn in his grave, poor soul. Do you remember him at the Broomielaw when Kate was sailing to America, warning her about perishing in the deep? And praying over her? I was afraid to look at you.' And then more seriously. 'She's probably run down. You men don't realize what it's like to run a house and look after children. Half the women I get into the wards are desperate for a good rest away from their husbands . . .'

'Here's Patrick!' He'd just entered the room. Maria got up to kiss him. 'Do you hear what Maevy's saying, my darling. That you men get the easy end of it.' She spoke fondly. Lucky bugger, Terence thought, watching.

'Well,' Patrick was saying, 'someone's got to earn the money to take care of the wife and children.' He patted Maria's cheek.

'I'm quite satisfied with the arrangement.' Terence saw the look which passed between husband and wife and his heart twisted. He got to his feet.

'I'm stealing your nurse from you, Patrick. Catherine's low these days. I want Maevy to cheer her up.'

'Was it your cab outside? Well, she's helped us, I can tell you.'

He had to try. 'I see a difference in . . . Mary, More . . .'

'Normal?' Trust Patrick. He believed in calling a spade a spade.

'Yes,' he said, 'more normal.' He clapped Patrick on the shoulder, feeling his face redden as he did it. 'Good luck.'

'You, too. Will you look at this before you go?' He took the baby from Maevy to Terence's surprise. He had never been one for that bit of it. 'Let's see if she knows me.' His face was tender. He chucked the child under the chin making encouraging noises, and her mouth widened.

'What did I tell you?' Maevy said. 'She's beginning to know her daddy.'

'What did I tell *you*?' It broke your heart, if it was not broken already.

'Aye, she's a wee marvel,' he said to his brother. 'Come on, Florence Nightingale!'

The drawing-room was empty when they arrived, although there was a good fire burning. 'Maybe she's resting,' Terence said. 'Sit down, Maevy. Would you like a glass of sherry?'

'Do you want me to go on duty drunk?' she laughed.

'God knows how you work in a place like that . . . Where's your mistress, Kitty?' An untidy-looking maid had appeared in answer to his summons on the rope bell.

'That's what Cook was just asking, sor. She usually comes into the kitchen around now to give orders for the dinner.'

'Has she gone out?'

'Oh, no, sor, she hasn't gone out.' The girl shook her head. Tenpence to the shilling, Maevy thought. If anything convinced her of Catherine's state of health it was this girl. In her right mind she would never have had anyone like this about the house. In her right mind . . . a spasm of fear went through her.

'What about the nursery?' Terence was saying.

'She's not there, sor. I've just been up there with the

106

tea. She'll be resting, sor. She hasn't been well all day. She turned away everything Cook sent up.'

'Well, why didn't you say so in the first place?'

'You didn't ask me, sor.'

'That'll do, Kitty.' When the girl had curtseyed and gone out, Terence turned to Maevy. 'God preserve us from the Irish!'

'I thought that was your land of heart's desire.' What's wrong with Catherine? she thought, trying to still her fear. Is it a tiff between them? Terence shouldn't inveigle me into that. But she knew it was more. There had been no saving of this marriage from the day he had married Catherine instead of Bessie Haddow. It had to come to a head sometime.

'Aye, maybe. Come up with me.' She looked at his handsome face as they went up the wide staircase with its wrought ironwork in a Greek key pattern. Why was it this brother of hers was always getting into a fix? It had gone on since his schooldays. She remembered how he had led Patrick on and how they had come rolling down Colliers' Row dead drunk, and them only in their teens. Father had been 'black affronted', but Mother had taken it in her stride.

'You go in first and tell her I'm here,' she said when they reached the bedroom door. It's not a hospital, she thought. It's their private room. I can't just barge in.

'All right.' She saw the fear in his face, too. He came out immediately and there was no disguising it. 'She's not there! Her clothes are lying on the bed!'

'Use your head,' she said sharply. 'She felt better. She decided to have a bath before you came home, get herself ready for dinner.'

He thrust his hand through his curls, smiling boyishly at her, still pale, but reassured. 'You're right. I don't know what I was thinking . . .' He smiled, a glimmer of a

107

smile, 'maybe that she was wandering naked down the Terrace giving the neighbours a treat!' He went back into the room and she heard him shaking the handle of the bathroom door. 'Maevy!' The fear was back. She went in.

'Is the door stiff?' She remembered the bathroom well, a room as big as her own in the Nurses' Residence, with a white marble bath and a fireplace where Catherine insisted on a daily fire. Once, using it at a party, Maevy had come out, saying, 'I feel like the Queen of Sheba in there.' And Catherine, looking pleased, had said, 'Well, Greek Thomson never did anything by halves, even private bathrooms.' She liked to remind people of the illustrious builder of the Terrace. Terence was speaking to her, low, strained, not shouting with his usual quick temper.

'The door's jammed. Come over here.'

It seemed to take a long time to go from one end of the bedroom to the other, this bedroom with its elegant furniture and its . . . coldness. Catherine never succeeded in making rooms look as if they were lived in, or in this case, slept in, or maybe loved in . . . She knew the fear in her mind was making her shy away from what Terence had said, from reaching him, and yet now that she was beside him, she heard herself say coolly, the voice she used for anxious patients, 'She'll have locked it from the inside.'

'No, there's no lock.' He was speaking as if he were short of breath. Staccato. 'Once Robert locked himself in and he was too small to know how to turn the key again. We had to knock the door in. We had the lock taken away . . .'

'Call her.' She wouldn't allow herself to become frightened at this stage.

'Catherine!' He raised his voice, still calm, then suddenly he was banging with his fists on the door and

108

shouting, 'Catherine! Catherine! What are you trying to do to me? Open it . . .!'

'There's no point in that.' She heard the sharpness in her voice again. 'Look, we'll push it together. Let me stand beside you. She's probably wedged something under the handle. Now, together, steadily . . .' They both half-fell into the room as the door gave way, knocking the heavy armchair to one side with the force of their entry.

Catherine lay in the bath. Her head lolled over the end, the eyes open, one breast rose like an island from the water, the bloody water, white, scarlet-nippled. She heard Terence moaning behind her, unaware that he was moaning, mechanically, 'Oh, no, no, no. Oh, no . . .'

'Stop that, Terence,' she said, stunned, hardly feeling.

One arm was submerged, the other hung over the edge of the bath. The gash in the wrist was deep, and under it a pool of blood had formed and congealed round something white. No blood dripped from the wrist. She bent down, picked up the piece of blood-stained paper and slipped it into her pocket, then turned to Terence. He was standing at the wall, his face half-turned towards it, as if to ward off the sight of Catherine.

'Help me to get her out,' she said, 'she might still be alive.' He turned obediently, his face distraught, and without a word came towards her.

'Tell me what to do.'

'Hold there.'

Catherine's body slipped in their hands like a fish as they lifted her out and laid her on a rug at the fire. She put her head down and listened at her chest, thinking, I never knew Catherine had such full breasts. Then she felt her pulse. It was hardly necessary. No doctor, nor Sister from the Royal Infirmary, would ever make this girl live. She got a large white towel and enveloped the body, drawing her hand over the staring eyes.

109

'I'm afraid she's gone, Terence.' She could not bear to look at him. She got up and led him back to the bedroom. 'You go and get the doctor. I'll stay here.' He nodded, his face like a mask.

When he had gone she took the letter from her pocket. It was only one sheet. Her eyes had read it before she could drag them away. There was a date. February 10th. This was June, wasn't it?

'I told you he was carrying on with his brother's maid, didn't I? Now that she's pregnant, will you believe me?'

She stood, holding the piece of paper, knowing that she should be horrified at herself, but unable to feel anything, wondering at the same time why in her quick glance the words had leapt out at her, black against white, very clear, very distinct. The immediate clarity must have a significance. She glanced down again and saw the note had been written on a typing machine. Of course, people who sent anonymous letters wouldn't want to be traced . . .

Feeling flooded into her, like a river which had thawed. Her whole body shook. What had she done? Catherine's body lay on a rug a few yards away from her. She could see it as clearly as if she were in the next room, the marble face, the staring eyes which she'd closed, the gashed wrist, the dark hair like seaweed lying across the breasts. The towel which she'd covered her with for Terence's sake had become tinged with pink.

What agony had Catherine suffered for the last four months, a betrayed wife? What had she gone through in her mind, unable to confide in anyone because of her pride. A loveless marriage.

She had to think it out, even try to explain her own action. Her concealment of the letter had been instinctive, in order to save her brother further pain. Later, she had thought, I'll show it to him. But this was later. Soon the

110

doctor would be here, and the police. Her shuddering was like an ague.

Catherine lay there dead, but Terence, her brother was alive. Always too much alive. 'Carrying on with his brother's maid,' the letter had said, Flora, the pretty one. Her mind raced. Images. Flora passing round a plate at Maria's party. The laughing glance passing between him and the girl. Girls had always fallen for Terence, even at Sholton, even that neighbour of Maria's, Mrs Mitchell, who was scarcely a girl. Even that dead girl next door, daughter of the manse. What good would it do anyone to see this note?

He would be back soon. She must decide. It wasn't a suicide note, was it? But it had a bearing on the terrible thing Catherine had done to herself. But then again only someone who was deranged would make it the cause.

She put her hand up to her face. 'Help me . . .' The fire in the little Dutch tiled fireplace next door had been burning with a sullen glow, the fire Catherine always liked in her bathroom. 'I feel like the Queen of Sheba,' she herself had once said.

There was no one to help her, no one. And then she remembered and it was like an answer, or a part expiation. Hadn't Maria said that her cook had told her Flora had made a good marriage to a farmer somewhere? 'So all's well that ends well,' Maria had said, laughing. Being American she did not have the same outlook as the Scots had on sin. Or pregnant girls who were not married.

'That made it all right, didn't it?' She found she was saying the words. Were those footsteps on the stairs? Terence coming back with the doctor? Poor Terence. Maybe he had made a hash of things, but he was her dearly beloved brother.

What would Mother like me to do? The answer came

to her, sweeping aside all doubt. Mother cared about the family. That would always come first.

She walked into the bathroom and skirted the still figure of her sister-in-law shrouded in the towel, the pinkly damp towel. The stains were the only living things, creeping over the surface. She crumpled the sheet of notepaper and threw it on the sullen embers. A brief flame leapt up from them, licking round the new fuel, consuming it, and then there were only black flakes. She stirred them amongst the red embers until there was no trace. Her foot accidentally touched the body as she stepped backwards. 'Oh . . . sorry.' Was that her own voice? She made herself walk, not run, back to the bedroom.

11

Dr Wordie came in with Terence, fussy, almost irritable. Perhaps he had been interrupted at his evening meal. 'This is a terrible business, Miss McGrath, terrible, terrible . . . sit down on that chair, my dear sir.' Terence was still in a state of shock, speechless.

'Wouldn't you like to lie down, Terence?' Maevy went towards him.

'No . . .' He shook his head. He was like a figure of stone.

She sat down beside him, put her arm round his shoulders. 'It will soon be over, this bit, soon be over.' It was like speaking to a child.

The doctor emerged from the bathroom, rolling down his shirt sleeves. 'I'm afraid she has . . . passed on,' he said. 'Passed on' sounded so gentle, not like the way Catherine had chosen. 'Terrible, terrible . . .' He looked as if the whole of his select West End practice had fallen about his ears. He put on his frock-coat, addressed Terence. 'I'll have to report the matter to the Procurator Fiscal right away and he'll instruct the Police.'

Terence nodded, cleared his throat. 'Do . . . do what you have to do.'

'Er . . .' Dr Wordie looked miserable. 'Things . . . must be left as they are for the time being. Come away downstairs now, Mr McGrath. You can't do any good sitting here.' The three of them walked downstairs, one on either side of Terence, supporting him. Once he stumbled like a man drunk.

'Give him a tot of brandy,' the doctor said in the hall.

113

'I'll be back as soon as I've reported the matter.' Maevy nodded. 'Fortunately the Fiscal lives only a few doors away . . . although what he'll say about this . . .' He shook his head, looking as if he thought Great Western Terrace's unsullied reputation for douce gentility had been ruined. 'I'll let myself out.'

Maevy poured out a generous tumblerful of brandy for Terence and put it into his hand. He must have recognized the familiar smell, and almost as a matter of habit, he raised it to his lips and drank. She saw the blood creep back into his cheeks, and the contrast between his red curls and the pallor of his face lessen.

'It isn't true, Maevy,' he said, 'is it? I can't . . . believe it. Catherine up there . . .' He turned away his head, unable to look at her.

'It's true.' She sat beside him on the elegant sofa – what a straight back it had – 'It's terrible, shocking, that she should be . . . dead.' And then the image of that shrouded body upstairs filled her mind and she burst out, 'Oh, why would she do it? Things are never . . . that bad.' Flames licking round the black flakes, consuming, destroying . . . Bad enough.

'I haven't been an angel, you know that, Maevy, but I loved her at the beginning, at Sholton . . .' His voice dropped, 'loved her . . .'

'Don't look back,' she said, 'screw up your courage. There will be things to be done, servants to be told, Patrick, Mother.' The bleak prospect stretched before her, endless, there would be questions . . . her heart jumped about sickeningly in her body. Would she be able to hide what *she* had done? Had *she* the courage? They sat together in the dark room, she didn't know for how long, in the exhaustion of grief.

The doctor was suddenly there, puffing and panting. 'Sit down, Doctor Wordie,' she said, rising.

'Thank you, Miss McGrath.' He parted his frock-coat tails, subsided into a straight-backed chair. 'I was lucky to get the Fiscal in. Just sitting down to his dinner, as I was. He's gone right away to the Police Station. He'll instruct them to call tomorrow morning to make the necessary enquiries . . . Oh, dear, oh, dear, I knew she wasn't her usual self when she called to see me. Wasn't sleeping. I recommended a little more exercise and hot milk to drink at night. I don't believe in pills and potions . . . I'm forgetting. Two constables will be here any moment . . . to arrange . . . Mrs McGrath. The room will be locked.'

She nodded. How quickly the wheels were set in motion. 'Would you have some refreshment, doctor? You must be wearied.'

'Thank you. Perhaps I'll join Mr McGrath. Just a little, if you please.' She poured out a good tot of brandy. He deserved it for missing his dinner, poor soul.

'And then maybe you could accompany your brother to Mr Patrick's house. Better . . .' His eyes went upwards, as if to say police constables tramping about above, servants whispering . . .

She looked at Terence. In her work she had seen many faces ravaged by grief, but never as bad as his. When Bessie Haddow had died she had been busy helping Patrick and had only briefly seen Terence before the funeral when he had his feelings under control. After all, she was his brother's wife.

But this second blow, far more tragic in its circumstances, had crushed him. He must have partly blamed himself for Bessie's death since it was soon after the birth of his child, but how much more must he be blaming himself for Catherine's? And then her heart started hammering against her ribs and she had to breathe deeply. She, too, was culpable. She had destroyed the letter.

When the doctor had gone upstairs with the two constables she turned to Terence. 'Tell me . . . anything I can do to help.' Her heart was full of love and pity for this handsome brother of hers, scarcely recognizable now. The bright curls which had been the bane of his existence lay lank on his brow, his face had the contours of an old man. 'Would you like another brandy?' He shook his head.

'I killed her,' he said.

'You didn't kill her. You mustn't blame yourself. She was an unhappy woman. She took her own life. She didn't know what she was doing . . .'

'I killed her.'

She spoke slowly. 'You didn't kill her. She died by her own hand.' She wanted to say, 'I read the letter written by that evil person, that was what killed her. Its contents ate into her soul.' She held him, weeping for him, for Catherine, that there should have been such misery between them. 'Grieve for her, don't blame her. Or yourself.'

'I blame myself.' His voice sounded hopeless. 'Someone . . . connected with me . . . had a child. But she's married now. It might not have been mine.' His voice broke. 'You see . . . she looked . . . a bit . . . like Bessie.'

'Oh, Terence,' she laid her wet cheek against his. Terence, the lovable one, the vulnerable one of the family. He had never been wicked, only unwise, forever searching for Bessie Haddow. 'None of that matters now.'

The doctor was there again, with a false air of *bon-homie*, the satisfaction of someone in authority who had been able to set the ball rolling. 'That's that. One of the constables will remain.' And then his face changed to concern as he looked at Terence. 'A dreadful ordeal for you, Mr McGrath. Bear up. Shall we go to your brother's now? Claremont Terrace, isn't it? Let me take you in my carriage.' He bent and touched Terence's arm. 'Does that suit you, Mr McGrath?'

'Yes,' Terence looked at him, through him. 'My . . . children?'

'They're better left sleeping tonight,' Maevy said. 'They're in good hands.' She looked at the doctor. 'The staff?'

'Leave that to the constable. He's used to it. Now, come along, my dear fellow.' He turned to Terence. 'Put yourself in our hands. You're lucky to have such a capable sister to take care of you.'

'*You* go and tell them in the kitchen, Maevy.' His voice sounded normal. 'They'll take it better coming from you. And tell Sadie to take care of my two boys, say that their mother's . . . no, don't say . . .'

The cook, the two maids and the children's nurse were sitting round the table and they pushed back their chairs awkwardly when Maevy came into the kitchen. Their faces were anxious. They must have been aware that something had happened.

'Don't rise,' she said. For the first time her spirits faltered and she felt her head swim. Mrs McLeary was on her feet.

'Something's wrong, Miss, isn't it? Oh, you look that white! Here, sit down.' She pushed forward a chair.

'I'm all right, thank you.' She had known the same giddiness when she had done an over-long spell of duty. 'I'm afraid you have to prepare yourselves for a shock.'

'Now, what is it?' The woman's voice rose on a note of alarm.

'Mrs McLeary, I'm sorry to tell you your mistress has . . . died. There has been a fatal accident . . .'

'Oh, my, oh, my!' The woman's hand went to her face. 'I said there was something when we saw the doctor coming and going, and then the policemen.' Mother

117

always said Susan knew more about them than they did themselves. She turned shrewd eyes on Maevy. 'Where *was* the fatal accident, Miss?'

'In the bath . . .' Kitty, the maid, let out a shrill scream and clapped her hand to her mouth.

'Hush yourself,' Mrs McLeary said severely. 'Proper respect, please, and no hysterics. This is terrible, Miss. Sit down, do. You've had a shock.'

'No, no. It's your master who's in a state of shock. I'm taking him to Mr Patrick's at Claremont Terrace . . . Sadie, Mr McGrath said to tell you to take particular care of Robert and Terence till we come back tomorrow morning, if not before.'

'He can rely on me, Miss. And nothing to be said to them?'

'No, their father will do that.' She turned to the cook. 'I'd be obliged if you'd send a message to the Royal Infirmary for me, Mrs McLeary. Say there's been a sudden . . . bereavement in the family and I'll be back as soon as I can.'

'Jenny'll go right away.' The other maid, although frightened, looked more reliable than Kitty who was sniffing loudly into her apron.

'There will be a constable in the house so you have no cause for anxiety. Perhaps you'd see to his needs.'

She could see the unspoken questions in all their faces. Catherine had always been a fair employer, if pernickety, and Terence was a favourite with all of them.

She met Dr Wordie and Terence in the hall. He had found Terence's overcoat for him. 'We'll get on, then, Miss McGrath.'

The speed of his carriage after he had dropped them at Claremont Terrace was perhaps a sign of relief. I know how he feels, she thought. If only we could put the clock

118

back. If only . . . she still could not grieve for Catherine. There was too much to be done.

Patrick and Maria were sitting companionably at the fire with a tray of evening drinks between them. What a contrast with what they'd left, she thought. It was a shame to disturb them. Maria looked becoming in a flounced tea-gown, her hair loose, Patrick's face was relaxed and happy.

It changed when he saw them. There was hardly any need for words. 'What's happened?' He was on his feet immediately.

'It's terrible, Patrick . . .' Maevy glanced at Terence. 'Catherine has . . . died.'

'She killed herself,' Terence said. 'We found her in the bath. It was full of blood . . .'

'Oh, poor Terence!' Maria went to him and did what Maevy had been afraid to do in case he would break down, took him in her arms. 'Oh, poor Catherine. It's terrible for you. Oh, my dear . . .'

'You must stay here.' Patrick was beside his brother, practical as always. 'We'll help you in whatever way we can. Oh, this is too much for you to bear after . . . everything.'

'I seem to bring bad luck to women.' Terence's mouth twisted. 'Something wrong with me. But I don't mean any harm . . .'

'Let Patrick take you upstairs,' Maria said. She was weeping openly. 'Would you like anything to drink? We're having hot milk. Oh, brandy! Yes, that's it, pour him some brandy, Patrick.'

The nurse in Maevy spoke. 'I meant to ask Dr Wordie for a sedative.'

'He doesn't approve of them. He's homeopathic.'

Patrick had carried a full glass of brandy to Terence. 'Sit down and drink this, lad, then you'll come upstairs with me. The shock's been too great for you. You must rest . . .'

Terence took the glass. 'I'll take a sip or two and then I must go to Mother. She has to know.'

'There's no need tonight, Terence,' Maevy said. 'I'll go.'

He looked at her with dry eyes. 'You know I've got to go.'

'You take him, Maevy,' Patrick said. 'It would be better if I went back to Great Western Terrace to see if I can be of any help there.'

'And what about those poor children?' Maria asked.

'They're sleeping. Terence thinks they shouldn't be disturbed tonight. But there's tomorrow. Perhaps you could help then.'

'Yes, that's best.' Patrick and Maria were sensible, she thought, as Patrick went to get a cab. They would see to things at this end. And there was Mother. She could always be relied on.

She did not feel quite so alone as she got into the cab with Terence. A family was like a hap, supporting you in a crisis, but keeping their own counsel. There were some things, of course, which they could not be burdened with, like the letter. No one must know about that, except Mother. It was too great a burden to be borne alone.

12

Perhaps the brandy that he had drunk earlier restored in Terence's mind its ability to feel. Half-way to Sholton he started to weep, a harsh man's sobbing which the noise of the cab's wheels drowned, and Maevy held him in her arms as the silhouettes of the ugly ironworks jolted past, the winding wheels of the pits, the unnatural-looking bings of shale thrown up by the miners, and at last the quiet fields of home.

There was no need to say anything when Maeve opened the door to them at Braidholme. Their faces must have told her there was something sadly wrong. 'Come in,' she said right away, 'come in, both of you. I was sitting up late, reading.'

Is it late? Maevy thought wonderingly. She looked at the familiar wag-at-the-wa' clock as they passed through the hall. Nine-thirty. Maybe it was late in Sholton, but in the world of sickness there was little difference between night and day. And the last three hours seemed like an eternity.

'Catherine has died,' she said when they were in the sitting-room. She saw the start, the tightening of her mother's lips, the straightening of the back. She's preparing herself. Well, she'd always had a broad enough back to support most things.

'Sit down. I'm going to bring something to eat. You both look starved.' What a strange thing to say, Maevy thought, but already she was beginning to think everything was strange. She felt light-headed. She had to remind herself that it was not the middle of the night, that

121

this tragedy which had upset all their lives had taken place in a matter of a few hours.

The plentiful supply of hot tea and sandwiches which her mother brought quickly to the room took away the light-headedness. She had not eaten since lunch-time. She was surprised at how she enjoyed the rich pink beef between slices of Susan's homemade bread.

Terence was still distraught, ill with weeping his heart out. Her mother sat down beside him, her arm round his shoulders while Maevy told her briefly what had happened.

'It's a bad business.' She looked at her son's bowed head, anguish in her face, but her voice was calm, almost brisk. 'But there's the living to be considered. What you need now, Terence, is a good sleep and then you'll be ready to face your problems in the morning. You have your two boys to consider. Your life hasn't stopped because Catherine's has.'

How cruel that sounds, Maevy thought. I should have imagined she would have clasped him in her arms, let him weep on her breast. Terence had only moved his head in his hands as she spoke as if he was denying all possibility of life ever going on.

'Maevy,' her mother turned to her, 'I don't want to send Susan. You know what she's like. I saw Charlie McNab's light on when I had a walk down the garden. Would you go and ask him to come here? Tell him to bring his doctor's bag with him.' She nodded at Terence's bowed head meaningly.

'Yes.' She got up. All her weariness had gone. And Charlie, yes, of course, that was right. He was always brought into their family at times of crises. She remembered how good he had been during her father's illness and how he had made Mother smile at her saddest.

The cool air calmed her as she walked down the garden.

122

It was hardly dusk. The herbaceous border was at its best, a broad strip of variegated colour backed by bushes. The rosebeds were heavy with their sweet smell. The arbour of white ones she passed under drenched her in their sweetness.

Long ago, at Colliers' Row, they had had a red and white rose bush at the back door of their cottage which Father had planted. Mother had brought cuttings of them here, 'because they remind me of your father and me when we were young,' she had said. She stood for a second listening to the purling of the Sholtie down below, before she went through the wicket gate into the road.

She heard Charlie playing the piano as she waited in his porch for a second to pull herself together. Mother said that sometimes when she walked down the garden late she could hear him. 'It goes with the roses,' she had said. She lifted her hand to the knocker thinking he was lucky to have such a solace.

He opened the door himself in his shirt sleeves. Biddy must be in bed. 'Early to bed, early to rise, makes a man healthy, wealthy and wise.' 'The Sholton Jingle,' he had once said to her, laughing. 'Maevy!' His dark hair had fallen over his brow. It was usually under his white cap . . . why was her mind running on like this? She must be tired. 'What brings you here?' he said. He looked tired, too. 'Come in.'

'I'm sorry to disturb you, Charlie.' She stepped into the little hall. 'Mother sent me.' The comfort she had begun to feel at home was increased. Yes, Sholton was where her heart lay. Mother, Isobel, friends like Charlie. And there was John. Perhaps he could explain the sense in all this later. And whether she had been right . . . no, there was no need, of course she had been right to burn the letter.

He listened to her without speaking as they stood in his

sitting-room, and his keen mind sprang to the question she had feared from him. 'Didn't she leave a suicide note?'

'No,' she said, looking at the fire, 'there was no suicide note.' She turned to him, 'But you know what they were like with each other. Terence was eaten up by remorse about Bessie Haddow.'

He nodded. 'I've found there are two ways to deal with that state. Be eaten up or be spurred on.' His eyes remained on her, black, bright. 'So,' he said briskly, like her mother, 'how's Terence taking it?'

'He was shocked at first but now he's gone to pieces. Mother wondered if you'd be kind enough to see him, perhaps give him something.'

'Take the load off your feet while I get my bag.' He turned at the door. 'You're lucky to find me here. I sometimes stay overnight at the Infirmary.'

'Are things going well with you?' She tried to be calm, composed.

'Och aye.' He grinned at her. 'I'm getting the old codgers licked into shape.'

Walking through the garden with him, the red roses grey now but the white ones shining like lamps, she found her lips asking a question which surprised her at a time like this. 'How is Miss Wilcox?' He was behind her on a narrow stretch of the flagged path and his voice came to her, cool.

'Well, I believe. She's in America with her father where he's lecturing. We hope to be married next year.'

'I'm pleased to hear it.' Her weariness ran back through her like water.

Her mother was sitting close to Terence on the sofa. When she looked up Maevy saw she had been weeping. 'There, Terence,' she said, 'here's Charlie. Didn't I tell you we're surrounded by good friends?'

Terence nodded at Charlie. 'You shouldn't have bothered . . .' He tried to smile.

'And why shouldn't I bother and you one of my oldest friends?' Charlie went to him and put his hand on his shoulder, his face gentle. 'You're tired, lad. Come upstairs and take off your boots for a lie down.'

Terence stood up. He looked younger in his grief now. 'I'm sorry . . . I'm like this. It's . . . a bitter blow.'

'Aye, bitter. You've lost your wife, but tomorrow you'll be able to face it better. Come along with me.' Maevy opened the door for them and they went out together. Charlie had his black bag.

'Charlie has authority,' her mother said. 'You're never a good doctor without that.'

'Yes.' She sat down beside her. 'What's to be done?'

'What *has* to be done. He'll rally. He's down now but Terence is resilient. Patrick's the pessimist in the family. I'll go with him tomorrow to Great Western Terrace, perhaps bring the boys back here with Sadie. I've plenty of room.'

'Maria's willing to have them. We called and told her and Patrick.'

'We'll see, we'll see. My poor lad will have to get back to work as soon as possible. It's his saving grace, and with this strike brewing there are plenty of problems to solve.' She sighed, looking at Maevy. 'You're tired, lass. Can you take a few days off?'

'I won't go in tomorrow, and I know I can get a day or so off for the funeral. Will that be soon?'

'It depends on a lot of things. Has it been reported to the Fiscal?' Trust Mother to know the legal side of things.

'Yes, Dr Wordie went to see him right away. He said people would have to be questioned, the servants . . .'

'And you and Terence. You found her.'

'Yes, we found her.' The hammering of her heart made her feel faint again.

'As long as they don't find anything suspicious the Fiscal will tell the doctor to make out a death certificate. What suspicious circumstances could there be when the poor girl had slashed her own wrists? Terence told me the whole story.' She looked at Maevy. 'Did you see anything?'

'Anything?' Surely her heart had stopped?

'What she did it with?'

'No, I didn't. I think it would be a razor. It would drop into the bath.'

'That's what I thought. One of Terence's. But *why* would she do it?'

Again her heart froze. 'That's what the questioning will be about. Dr Wordie said she'd been attending him.'

'And then you went because Terence was worried about her, didn't you?'

'Yes.'

Her mother sighed. 'It's a sorry business. Anyhow I think that doctor they have over there will be able to rush things and get the funeral over. He ought to carry some weight. I know his fees are big enough. Poor Catherine. I can't understand her doing this all the same, can you?'

She shook her head, looking away. 'I know she was unhappy.'

'That was Catherine's natural state of mind. And she brooded. That's always a mistake. She cared too much about the appearance of things. But she had virtues, too, all that charity work she did. What a good thing her father's dead and gone. How could we ever have broken the news to him? He never thought Terence was good enough. But there are others to tell, an aunt on her mother's side, John and Isobel, and letters to America . . .'

'Yes.'

'I pity you that sight.'

'Yes . . .' There were no more terrors in the memory now. She was so tired.

'I'm surprised she didn't leave any kind of note.' Charlie had made it easier for her, had said, 'a suicide note'. She did not answer. 'Did she, Maevy?'

She looked at the fire. How did Mother manage to have such dancing, cheerful fires no matter when one called? She thought of the sullen red embers in Catherine's bathroom, and the feeble flame which had licked round the pieces of charred paper. 'Yes, she did,' she said.

'You read it?'

'And burned it.' She turned to her. 'It was evil. I knew it was the best thing to do. Mother, do you think I did the right thing?'

'Tell me what was in it?'

'That he'd got Flora pregnant, Maria and Patrick's maid . . .' She looked at her mother. She had gone deathly pale. 'Are you shocked?'

'In a way.' She was breathing deeply. 'Well, history repeats itself.'

'What do you mean?'

'My father did the same thing. He sent the girl to Dublin for an abortion.'

'Did he? I had a strange feeling . . . but this was different. Flora's married to a farmer now. It could even be *his* child. Still, the letter said Terence had been "carrying on with her".' She saw the letter before her eyes, its neatness, its clarity. 'It was done on a typing machine.'

'What!' She looked at her mother, surprised at the harshness of her voice.

'You know, very distinct, *printed*. I read it at a glance.' She saw her mother staring at her. Then she got up abruptly and walked to the fire. When she turned to

127

Maevy she was shaking. Her eyes frightened her, their blueness almost black. She spat out the words.

'I knew it. It was Ethel Mavor.'

'Ethel Mavor?' The name did not mean anything to her at first. 'Oh, you mean the girl who works for you in the office? It couldn't have been. She knows you, knows Terence . . .'

'She called here with a story that she'd seen Terence with a young girl in a tavern near the Gallowgate, that she thought I ought to know. I sent her away with a flea in her ear, but I knew it was true.'

'Did you say anything to him?'

'I told him I'd been hearing rumours, but he blustered, then admitted he'd only been having a bit of fun. That marriage was to blame for a lot.'

'Did you tell him who gave you the information?'

'No, I didn't. I thought I'd keep Ethel Mavor's name out of it. I didn't want to give her the satisfaction. I knew she'd always had a soft spot for Terence, but that's nothing new. What hurt me was to find out how much she disliked me. I gave her her books the next day. I can't abide clipes or mischief-makers.' She looked at Maevy, 'I was surprised she disliked me so much. I couldn't understand it.' She could. Ethel Mavor was plain.

'So you can't challenge her if she's gone?'

'Not unless I could find out where she is.'

'But you couldn't confront her with the note, nor even give it to the police since I've burned it. I've done a terrible thing.'

'You were thinking of Terence. He's always had people behind him . . .'

'It was the hurt to everyone, and nothing could bring her back . . .' She met her mother's eyes.

'I'd have done the same.'

* * *

Charlie came back into the room. 'He's sleeping, Mrs McGrath. I'll call in the morning and see if he wants to go back to his house.'

'They'll both have to go back for questioning. It's not over yet by a long chalk.'

'No.' He looked at Maevy. His eyes were apologetic. 'I hope you don't mind me asking. Had your sister-in-law any medical history?'

'I knew she hadn't been well recently, that's all.'

Her mother said, 'And Maevy was there tonight because Terence was worried about her. She was always . . . inward-looking.'

'Maybe the servants will bear you out about her general state of health?' He looked at Maevy.

'Kitty, one of the maids, told us Catherine had been in her bedroom all day without eating.'

He nodded. 'That ought to be enough for the Fiscal. You look dead beat. You're not going back to Glasgow tonight, are you?'

'No, she isn't,' her mother said, 'Maevy's had the heavy end of it.'

'She's a nurse, able to cope.' He said to her, 'Would you like anything to make you sleep?'

She craved complete oblivion to escape from the thought of what was ahead, but pride made her shake her head. 'No, thanks. I think I'll sleep all right.'

'Right. I'll call tomorrow, then. I'll be going to the Infirmary.'

'Maybe you'd have room for me, too,' her mother said. 'I want to be around when those two wee lads are told, and maybe bring them back with me.'

'Of course there's room.' He looked at the two of them. 'You're going to have a difficult time for the next few weeks. A lot of suffering. Maevy sees plenty of that.'

'It's different when it's your own family.' Her voice broke and she put her hand to her face.

'Get some rest,' he said. She saw his eyes flood with sympathy, a deeper depth than that . . .

'Don't show me any sympathy,' she tried to smile, 'or I'll greet.' She used the old word.

'"Wee chookie burdie, roared and grat . . ."' He smiled, encompassing her with a kind of comfort.

'I wish I was a child again,' she said, 'with Mother and Father and my brothers and sisters, I wish . . .' A longing rose in her for her youth and innocence and no suffering. She felt the tears running down her face, saw Charlie take a step towards her.

'Come away, my lovely.' Her mother put an arm round her. 'You're dead on your feet.'

13

There was a policeman on duty in the hall when the three of them arrived at Great Western Terrace, and the dreadful circumstances of Catherine's death filled Maevy's mind again. Driving into the city from Sholton with Charlie it had almost seemed that the tall elms, heavy with summer leaf, the foaming banks of cow parsley under the hedges, the freshness of the morning, denoted an ordinary fine June day. Colliers were hurrying along the Sholtie Brae from the night shift, their bate tins rattling, their clown mouths red against the black of their cheeks. She remembered as a child the hush in the house when Da was sleeping during the day.

'Remember,' Charlie had said as he let them out, 'I'll do anything I can to help.'

'We're lucky with Charlie,' her mother said. She was elegantly dressed as always, although in black, a question of meticulous attention to detail, Maevy thought, seeing the black kid gloves with the white veining. I seem only to be able to apply that to carbolic dressings . . . She was ushered into the drawing-room by the policeman while Terence and her mother went up to the nursery. Patrick and Maria got up to greet her when she went in.

'Did you sleep at all, my dear?' Maria asked.

'I thought I wouldn't and then it was morning. Mother and Terence have gone up to see the boys.'

'I'm here to take them back with me.'

'We'll see what Terence says. No one will be at the office today?' She spoke to Patrick.

He shook his head. 'No, I've closed it. Though things

131

are getting uglier every minute.' She supposed he meant the imminent strike.

'How was Terence?' Maria said.

'He seemed more composed this morning, but telling the children is another ordeal.'

'Mother will help him with that. How did she take it?'

'Like the rest of us, appalled. But she was calm. You know Mother.'

'I hope Terence will be as calm when he's questioned,' Patrick said. 'That will be a great ordeal for him. And for you, Maevy.' He walked over to the tall sash window, looked out. 'It's strange she didn't leave a note . . . maybe the poor soul was too deranged.'

Maevy sat silently, feeling the familiar bleakness flood over her. I'm not devious, she thought. I've never had any . . . tricks. She remembered strangely enough her mother's description of Emily Barthe, passed on from Kate, 'Full of tricks . . .'

'We've talked and talked about it,' Maria said. 'Hardly slept a wink. Catherine was never communicative with me. I wish I'd tried harder. Well, it's too late now.' Her eyes were full of tears as she looked at Maevy.

'Catherine was difficult. We hoped her lovely house and the children would compensate . . .' For what, she asked herself, for Terence's infidelity, or for her inability to really love him despite his faults? If she'd been able to love him, he might not have had any . . .

Terence and his mother came into the room. 'I'm glad you're here.' Maeve went to greet Maria and Patrick.

'We're here to do anything we can to help,' Maria said. 'I'll take the boys back with me, if you like, Terence. Are they . . . very distressed?'

He shook his head in an infinitely pathetic way. 'They're strange wee lads. I got the impression they were crying to please me, and then in no time they were playing with their toys quite happily.' There was a knock at the door and Jenny, the maid, came in with a laden tray.

'Did you manage to get my message to the Royal last night, Jenny?' Maevy asked her.

'Yes, Miss. I saw the Matron. She said to tell you to take as much time as you need.'

'Thank you. You were a great help.'

'That's a sensible girl,' Maeve said when the door closed. Maevy passed round the cups as her mother filled them. Terence shook his head.

'It will brace you,' her mother said. 'You took no breakfast.' She's a spartan, Maevy thought, a matriarch. 'They'll make it as easy as possible to spare you. Charlie told you that.'

'It won't be difficult to describe.' He looked at the rest of them. 'I can't get that picture out of my mind. I don't think I ever will. I can't bear being here, or going near that bedroom . . .' He turned away.

'I'm staying with you,' Maevy said. 'And there are plenty of other rooms in the house. Just leave it to me.'

'You could come to Braidholme with the children,' Maeve said.

'No, I want the boys' lives to go on as usual. They've had a big enough shock. Sadie's reliable.'

'And they can come to us as often as you like,' Maria said. 'We'll all support you through this, don't you worry.'

There was a knock at the door and the policeman who had been on duty in the hall came in, gingerly, as if he had been told that Catherine's fine Axminster was the best Templeton's of the Doges' Palace on Glasgow Green could supply. 'Will you follow me to the dining-room, Mr McGrath?' Terence got up.

'You can't believe it, can you?' Maeve looked at the others. 'I think that's what saves your sanity, the periods

133

when what has happened is unbelievable. Will there be anything in the papers, Patrick?'

'I'm hoping just a small paragraph tucked away somewhere out of the road. I should imagine Dr Wordie might have some influence there.'

'Once the funeral's over it won't be quite so bad. He'll only have his grief to contend with, poor lad. Is the office shut today?'

'Yes, but one or the other of us will have to go down there tomorrow and take up the reins again. The men are very restive.'

'That strike's coming.' She got up. 'Well, tomorrow's another day. I'll go down to the kitchen now and ask Mrs McLeary if she'll lay on a light lunch for us.'

'I'll have to go home to feed Mary, Aunt Maeve,' Maria said.

'Of course. How is the little lamb?'

'Getting on, I think. At least she's alive.' She looked at Patrick. 'We should count our blessings.'

Maevy was summoned to the dining-room while her mother was in the kitchen. Terence had come back looking white and shaken, but Patrick had taken him in hand. 'I think a good tot is indicated and not that peely-wally coffee.' She followed the broad back of the constable through the wide hall. Did prisoners feel like this when they were going to the gallows? You must be practical, like your mother, she told herself. You did it for the family. There's no going back now.

14

The sergeant was grey-haired with a thin Highland face, high cheek-boned, florid. His smile was kindly as he pointed to a chair. 'Sit down, Miss McGrath. This is bound to be hard for you. I'll try to be quick.'

'Thank you.' She clasped her hands together under the table.

'I'll tell you first that I'm acting on behalf of the Procurator Fiscal. It's my duty to find out the circumstances of the incident which happened in this house last night. The Fiscal is concerned to know if it was suicide,' he glanced at the paper before him as if to refresh his memory, 'in order to exclude the possibility of either accident or homicide.' He looked up. 'Suicide, if proven, is not a crime, but the other two are. Now, Miss McGrath, have I made that clear to you?'

'Yes, Sergeant,' she said.

'That's fine, then. You're a Sister at the Royal Infirmary, Glasgow, I believe?'

'Yes.'

'And sister-in-law of the deceased?'

'Yes. I came here with my brother . . .' He held up his hand.

'Now all you've to do is to corroborate or otherwise what he has already told me.' His eyes on her were pale blue. 'What time did you arrive here yesterday evening?'

'About six. Terence came to my brother's house in Claremont Terrace . . .'

'That's Mr Patrick McGrath?'

'Yes.'

135

'Did you expect to come here?'

'No, but Terence asked me. He said he was worried about his wife.'

'Can you remember what he said?'

She had to think before she spoke, conjure up that room in Claremont Terrace with that poor damaged child on her knee, Terence coming in, his usual jauntiness not quite concealing his anxiety. 'He said Catherine wasn't well. That she'd withdrawn from her charity work – she did a lot for the Temperance Movement – and just sat about the house all day. And that the doctor didn't know what to make of it.'

'That was all?'

'Yes, I think so. He thought that because I was a nurse I might be able to ask questions the doctor couldn't.'

He nodded understandingly. 'What happened when you reached his house?'

'We went into the drawing-room, both hoping, I think, that Catherine might be there, but she wasn't. Then Terence rang for the maid to ask her if she knew where her mistress was.'

'Which maid was that?'

'Kitty, she's called. She said Cook had been asking, too, as she generally went into the kitchen about that time to give orders for dinner.'

'Anything more, Miss McGrath? You're doing fine.' Was she? Did she appear honest, the type who would conceal nothing?

'Yes. I remember she told my brother that Catherine hadn't gone out, and that she knew she wasn't in the nursery, and then at the end that she might be resting because she hadn't been well all day and she'd turned away everything Cook had sent up.'

'Whatever didn't she say that for in the first place?' He said 'whateffer'.

Maevy smiled. 'I think that's what Terence thought as well. She's fairly new.'

The sergeant was looking at his notes. Now the pale blue eyes were on her again. 'You went upstairs with your brother and she wasn't in the bedroom. I've got it here.' He paused. 'What happened then?'

'I said she must be having a bath.'

'Where were you then?'

'Outside the door. I didn't want to . . . intrude.' His eyes prompted her. 'Then I heard him shaking the bathroom door – it leads off the bedroom – and he called me, so I went in.' She took a breath. 'And together we forced the door.'

'Was it locked?'

'No, Terence explained that they'd removed the lock some time ago . . .' He waved his hand to stop her.

'Now, even though you're a nurse, this is bound to be upsetting for you.' He read from his notes. 'Mrs Catherine McGrath was lying in the bath. There was blood in the water. One arm was hanging over the edge.' Pale eyes, veined. 'Right?' She nodded. 'What did you notice about that arm, Miss McGrath?'

The picture was in front of her. Catherine's breast, the staring eyes. 'The wrist I saw was gashed. Blood had been dripping from it but it had congealed on the floor.'

'Did you notice . . .?' Her heart stopped. She could not breathe. 'Did you notice any instrument lying there?'

'No.' She spoke quickly. 'It looked like a razor slash to me. I've seen the same thing in the Royal. Fights. You know what it's like on a Saturday night. And if it *was* a razor slash I thought it must have slipped into the water when she used it.'

'*When it was used.*' He emphasized the words. 'But you're quite right, Miss McGrath.' His face seemed to relax. 'We found a razor in the bottom of the bath when

137

it was emptied. Your brother identified it as his. He also said he saw nothing lying on the floor, no suicide note . . .' He looked at her.

She breathed naturally. It was an effort. 'There was no suicide note,' she said. Her heart seemed to be in her throat, choking her. She saw his face change.

'Would you like a glass of water, Miss McGrath?'

'No, thanks.'

'These enquiries have to be made. It can be an ordeal for the family. Do *you* think it was suicide?' A lawyer wouldn't have asked that.

'What else?' The bleakness was with her, making her calm.

'Why do you say that?'

'She wasn't well, hadn't been well for some time. She'd been to see her doctor about not sleeping. He told us that when he came, after . . .'

'Are there any others in the family who knew this?'

'I think my mother would, and Patrick's wife. And then there's what Kitty said . . .'

He consulted his notes, reading from them. ' "She hadn't been well all day and she'd turned away everything Cook had sent up." I've had a talk with the cook, Mrs McLeary, and she confirms this. She says she'd been worried about Mrs McGrath's health for some time.'

'I didn't see Catherine as often as I should . . .'

'Don't reproach yourself. Would you say your sister-in-law was a happy woman?' The question came quickly, almost casually.

'Never exactly happy. She was of a quiet, self-contained disposition. She'd been brought up by her widowed father, a minister.'

'Did she ever confide in you?'

'No, never.'

'She wasn't that type?'

138

'No, she wasn't that type.'

'Rarely gave way to her feelings?'

'Rarely, if at all. Not to me.'

His eyes were on her, searchingly, the pale blue so different from the deep blue of her mother's. Perhaps it was her guilt about the letter which made her imagine they were probing her. He was only a policeman, even although he had his sergeant's stripes. 'I don't want to prolong these questions more than necessary.' Yes, he was kindly, someone's father. 'Your brother tells me you asked him to help you lift the body out of the bath and together you placed it on a rug on the bathroom floor. You were quite sure she was dead?'

'Yes, I felt her pulse and put my head to her chest.'

'Then you asked him to go for the doctor. Why did you do that, Miss McGrath? Couldn't you have sent one of the servants?'

'I suppose I could, but I didn't think. Yes, I did think of that, but I had the feeling it should be kept quiet until the doctor came. And I thought it would be better if he had something to do . . .' He nodded.

'You'd covered the body with a towel. It must have been an ordeal for you, to be alone . . .?'

'I'm a nurse. And I suppose I was shocked, too . . .' She was getting tired.

He nodded again, gravely. 'Yes, I can believe that.' He looked at his notes again. 'I have the sequence of events here from the time the doctor came, followed by one of our men. Did your brother want to go as far as Sholton, considering the circumstances?'

'Yes, it was his suggestion. He and my mother have always been close.'

His look was understanding. 'And you came back here this morning with him. On your own?'

'No, Dr McNab, my mother's doctor drove us.'

'Well, then,' he seemed visibly to relax. 'This is not a court of law, Miss McGrath, though it might seem like that occasionally.' He gathered his papers together and placed his hands together on the table, big, knuckled farmer's hands. 'That's about it. I've to submit my findings to the Procurator Fiscal. A post mortem is taking place, and depending on the result of that and his reading of my notes, he'll make a decision as to whether or not the funeral is to go on.' He smiled at her. 'You've been very patient. I think you must have been a great support to your brother.'

'Oh, I don't know. I can go, then?'

'Yes. Thank you.' He got up. 'Good morning to you.' He had a dry Highland smile.

She went out and along the hall, trying to imagine she was walking through a ward in the Infirmary with her usual briskness. All she wanted to do was to curl up somewhere and cry her heart out. It was not easy to do something wrong for the right reasons.

They had a more or less silent lunch, and at the end of it her mother surprised Maevy by suggesting Terence might like to go to the stables with her. 'It will take your mind off things,' she said, 'and there's nothing you can do. Maevy will be here, and Patrick if he's needed.'

'Well . . .' Poor Terence, she thought. Being a man he's not supposed to shut himself up in his room and give way to his grief.

'You could have a talk with the men. They'll be hanging around the gates. There's something in the office I want.' Was it Ethel Mavor's address?

In the hall, while Terence was upstairs seeing the children again, her mother spoke to her. 'Are you going to be able to stay here for a few days?'

140

'Yes, I'm sure I can. I thought while you're out with Terence I'd go and see the Matron and explain to her.'

'You're a stout lass. You'll have a hard time with Terence. He's not out of the wood by a long way yet.'

'I'm used to it.' She thought of the many people she had comforted in the wards, the cups of tea, the ritual panacea in hospitals, giving as much comfort to the giver as the receiver.

'He was always your favourite.' Her mother's smile was tender.

'And yours.' How like each other they were, mother and son, dramatic, colourful, although Mother's practicality seemed to have become more noticeable since Father died.

'The prodigal son? Maybe so. It wasn't intended. You have all an equal share of my love.' She bit her lip. 'But don't you go carrying everybody's burdens. Get back to the Infirmary as soon as you can or you'll end up running this house for him. I know you.'

'I'd thought of that.'

'Don't. Terence has always been unpredictable. You never know with Terence.'

'I'll do whatever he wants.'

'Now are you going to make a carpet of yourself? Take it from me, a bit of constructive selfishness isn't a bad thing. You've always wanted to *donate* your life.' She went to the mirror to adjust her hat, and seeing her reflection wreathed by the gauzy veiling Maevy thought her extra paleness gave an added dimension to her beauty.

'Oh, I'm not holy, Mother.' She laughed. '"Where's your monkey Joe?"'

They laughed at each other in the mirror, then as quickly sobered. Her mother turned, head up, 'ready for the road'. 'Is that you, then, mavourneen, ready for the road?' Father used to say to her, love shining out of his eyes. 'You never had much time for the trappings of religion, like me. Maybe it was Catherine's father that put me off it. John's not so bad.'

The bleakness was there again. John would call today, offering his sympathy and help. Could she tell him? Oh, to lay her burden on him . . . her mother was still speaking. 'You wouldn't have made a good minister's wife.' She was always able to read one's thoughts. 'You've too good a sense of humour. Isobel's cut out for it. *She*'s holy enough.' 'You're bad, Maevy!' Isobel as a little girl with her rightness, her rectitude. 'They're well suited. I only hope Lizzie doesn't become like them. They're strict . . .'

'Mother . . .' The bleakness was like a great black wave laced with stones rasping against her, scoring her. 'I didn't tell the sergeant about the note . . .' Her mother was putting on her gloves, smoothing each finger, carefully. The blue eyes were on her.

'What good would it have done? And come to that, what good is there in my chasing Ethel Mavor?' Her fingers swivelled neatly on her wrists, buttoning the gloves. 'The deed's done. Let it be buried with Catherine.'

15

The funeral was over. There had been no difficulty with
the Procurator Fiscal. After reading the notes taken by
the sergeant his verdict had been suicide while the balance
of the mind was disturbed, and the death certificate had
been issued with respectful speed by Dr Wordie. He it
was also who saw to a discreet mention in the *Glasgow
Herald* which got lost amongst the graver problems of the
day, such as Home Rule for Ireland, not to mention the
hyperbolic article on General Grenfel winning the Battle
of Toski on the Nile 'with the minimum of loss which was
the sign of good generalship'. Widely reported also was
the new Eiffel Tower in Paris built especially for their
Great Exhibition. Maevy wondered if their visit to Emily
Barthe would ever take place.

She was still staying at Great Western Terrace although
slowly the family was returning to normal. She devoted
her time to Robert and Terence during the day, and to
Terence in the evening, sitting with him night after night
while he talked his grief out. And his guilt.

'Wives get to know,' he said to her once, 'but I don't
think that was the case with Catherine. I wasn't seeing
this . . . this lass very often, and by that time Catherine
didn't want anything to do with me. I'm sorry to speak
like this to you, Maevy, and you not married, but she
liked to keep up appearances in front of the servants. We
still occupied the same bedroom, although we weren't
close in any way. To tell you the truth, she never liked
that side of marriage, didn't see it the way I did. It should
be . . . fun.'

143

She listened patiently to this handsome brother of hers abasing himself, and tried to prevent him crossing to the decanter too often. And to smother her own guilt. If he was suffering just now from having betrayed his dead wife, how much more would he suffer if she told him about the letter?

John called to see her religiously – that was a good way of putting it. He took his duties as a counsellor seriously, and said a prayer with her each time before he left. 'The only way to survive a tragedy like this,' he said, 'is to put yourself in the hands of the good Lord. Catherine is at peace now, and you should gain strength from the fact that you were there when your brother needed help, that you did everything to support him in his hour of need.' She watched him praying through her fingers, and wondered once more why his expression, the sweet lines of his mouth, should stir a sense of familiarity in her.

'John,' she said, 'sometimes I feel I want to clear my mind of all doubts, to explain to someone what really . . .'

He was omnipotent. 'I know what's troubling you. It's the manner of Catherine's dying. It is not the way the Lord would have us choose, but we must be charitable. I am not amongst those who think that they should be buried in an unsanctified grave two thousand feet up on top of a hill.' But aren't you, she thought, noticing the look of distaste he could not quite conceal.

Charlie breezed in one day on his way back to Sholton. 'I'm charged by the great Mrs McGrath of Braidholme to see how you are keeping, and coping.'

She smiled at him. He seemed to fill the house with fresh air. 'I'm keeping and coping very well, tell the great panjandrum. I enjoy being with the children, but the days are long. I miss the Royal.'

'Terence leans on you, does he? Give him all you've got for the time being, but set a time limit. They miss *you* in the Royal. I was speaking to Matron the other day and she says you're one of her best nurses.'

'Maybe I make a better nurse than a housekeeper.'

'It depends who you're keeping house for . . . and whose children they are.' His eyes were bold and black.

'Maybe.' Sometimes when she took the boys to Kelvingrove Park she wondered if she would ever have any of her own. It was in the McGraths to love children. She and Terence could romp in the nursery with them, forgetting the gloom downstairs. Was she giving up too much for a career?

It was Terence who said she must go back to work. She had given him enough of her time. He had gone to bed disconsolate the previous evening and come downstairs calm and purposeful. Mother was right. He was resilient.

'I'm needed at the office and stables all day and every day. It's back to normal, and for you, too. Mrs McLeary's willing to act as housekeeper as well as cook, and she's got the girls well-trained. The boys couldn't have a better nursemaid than Sadie.' It was true enough. Even Kitty seemed to have got over her sense of drama and was being rapidly licked into shape by the doughty Mrs McLeary. 'I'll never cease to be grateful to you for how you stood by me and consoled me, but I've got to look forward, not back.'

'Are you sure you're up to it, Terence?'

'I woke up this morning feeling I was living again. I'll give it a try at least.'

'But you'll promise to call on me if you need me?'

'I promise, but you have your own life.' He was bright-eyed as he took up the morning paper.

Towards the middle of the month she had a letter from Maria saying she had arranged a day's sail for the family on the 21st July, and asking her to join them. 'Now that we're beginning to put Catherine's sad death behind us, I've taken Patrick's advice and rented a house on the Isle of Arran for the month of August. This is by way of a trial run.'

She wrote saying that she would be pleased to come, not adding that Maria might get more than fresh air sailing 'doon the watter'. Not for nothing was the Clyde known as the Sewage Canal. She hoped the wind would be blowing in the right direction.

But she did not accept her invitation of a holiday in Brodick. Perhaps she and her mother could still hold to their plan of going to Paris. She was surprised how much it had stayed in the back of her mind. She had even told Charlie she might be going, and he had been pleased, not surprised. 'Paris! Now that's what I call sensible. High time you enlarged your horizons.'

'What a nerve you have!!'

'Have I?' His quick smile illumined his face. 'Try and get time to see some of Whistler's work when you're there. He impresses me greatly.'

'How do you get time to know about things like that?'

'I make time. Everybody sleeps too much. And one thing leads to another. That's the delight of reading. Don't you remember Whistler was awarded a farthing damages against Ruskin? So I read Ruskin. And he painted a portrait of Carlyle so I read Carlyle. Then your carters' strike which is surely going to happen leads me to read William Morris and that leads me to Rossetti and Burne-Jones. And as a stern antidote I read Darwin which leads me to Huxley . . .'

'Stop!' she laughed. 'You're only trying to impress me.'

'I wish I could. And in between I play my piano.'

She thought of her own life, all work, mostly satisfying work, but not much more. 'You make me feel half alive.'

The light died from his face and in his quick abrupt way he said, 'Excuse me, I have to be back at the Infirmary.'

It was a sunny day when they set off from the Bridge Wharf of the Broomielaw. Everybody was making a determined effort to be in good spirits for the sake of the children. The McGraths had a great capacity for enjoyment, Maevy thought, looking around at their little gathering on the polished benches of the deck. She was seated beside Maria with Gaylord on her lap. He had listened eagerly to the loud clang of bells from the ship's telegraph, and given a little cheer when she had encouraged him. Now, the excitement of the early rising having proved too much for him, he was having a nap in his aunt's arms, snug in his white serge coat with its three tiered cape collar and white laced boots to match.

Little Mary, considered too much of a handful at four months, had been left behind in the care of Jeannie. Sarah, Robert and Lizzie were standing at the rail watching the thick foam being churned up by the paddle wheels, and little Terence was on his father's knee. Maevy looked at her brother's face and the little boy nestling into him. He craves physical contact, she thought. How long will it be before he finds someone to take Catherine's place?

'This was a good idea of yours, Maria,' she said, smiling at her, 'provided you hold your handkerchief to your nose for the first half-hour.'

Maria laughed. She looked pretty in her sprigged muslin, her hat tied on with white veiling which disguised the squareness of her chin. Her eyes were bright.

'Anyone like me who's used to mucking out stables back home doesn't bother about a few smells. I remembered the good times we had sailing on the Hudson with Kate and James and their family, and especially one

147

lovely day we had with Isobel and Aunt Maeve when they visited us.'

'Do you feel you've settled here yet?' The girl's face had been wistful.

'Well, where Patrick is I must be, want to be, but, yes, I still miss Wallace Point. It's the vastness, the freedom, freedom of spirit, too.'

'Are we narrow-minded here?'

'Engrained in your thinking perhaps. I don't find *you* narrow-minded, but some of the people we have to entertain . . .' she blew out her breath, 'sometimes I've a great desire to shock them! It's your old John Knox breathing down their necks all the time.'

She laughed. 'Douce bodies, we call them. How's Mary? Is she still improving?'

'I don't know.' She turned, her face serious. 'Already I can see how badly she compares with the other two at the same age. And yet I see how much she needs us.'

'Oh, she does. She'll only get on if she has loving parents wishing it.'

'I hope you're right. I sometimes wonder what Mother and Father would say if they saw her. Mother . . .' Her eyes filled and she bit her lip.

'They'll see beauty if they're prepared to love her.'

'They'll be prepared to love her, but I worry about upsetting Mother. Her twin brother did away with himself. It had a terrible effect on her.'

'But this is different.'

'You don't know my mother. She had a nervous breakdown after Uncle Gaylord's death. I nursed her before she had to . . . go away. And if her brother was flawed perhaps it runs in the family, and Patrick and I are cousins.' Her voice rose shrilly. It would have been better if she had broken down and wept.

She spoke quietly. 'You're letting this thing prey on

your mind, Maria. It's a long time ago. What age were you?'

'Seventeen. It was a bad time for Father and me.' She saw the girl's mouth tremble.

'You were vulnerable then. Don't think like that. You and Patrick have two healthy, normal children. Surely that proves something?'

'Not . . . when I look at Mary, see that strangeness . . .'

'What's wrong with her has nothing to do with your Uncle Gaylord, nor you and Patrick being cousins.' Was she sure about that? 'Will you promise me to put this out of your mind?'

'I'll try. Forgive me, Maevy. We all turn to you . . .'

'Rubbish.' She looked down at the sleeping child, Gaylord Grant, called after his dead uncle. How would *he* develop? Families were a mixed bag, so many skeletons in cupboards. Lift the lid and all manner of things came to view, like Pandora's box. Was she lucky *not* to be married? She turned to Maria, 'Once Mary's a year or two old you should think of going to America with her. Let your parents see her. They'll love her as you do. Everyone has dark patches in their lives.'

Maria smiled at her. 'You're right. Patrick has a great hankering to go back. I might think of accompanying him with the children. Oh, look at the size of that ship!' She was making a brave effort to be cheerful.

'That's one of the Irish boats!' She had caught sight of the red, white and black funnel. 'Mother . . .!' She looked along the deck and saw her walking with Patrick. She was restless, did not like to sit still for a long time. How elegant as always she looked with that straight back of hers. And that purple feather boa in a careless loop, and the way she held her parasol. 'She doesn't hear me. She and Father came from the west of Ireland. They always meant to go back but he died before they could.'

149

'Yes, Terence told me. Do you remember him singing those lovely Irish songs at that Christmas party of ours? Oh, that was a fine night! And Charlie McNab playing. Isn't he the grand pianist?'

'Yes, a grand pianist he is.' Maevy smiled at her sister-in-law. She knew what was coming.

'Do you ever see him?' Maria looked limpid.

'Yes, he called at Great Western Terrace once or twice after Catherine's death. He's been very kind and helpful.'

'But . . .'

'No buts. He's getting married to the daughter of one of the surgeons at the Royal.'

'Oh . . .' Maria subsided into silence, breaking it in a second or two with determined gaiety, 'Oh, those must be the liners! Don't they look immense! Floating palaces.'

'Yes, that's Queen's Dock we're passing.'

'Can you see the one which goes to America?'

'Not yet. Look at the Lascar seamen swarming all over that one. I expect it's bound for tropical seas. Yes,' she pointed, 'there's an Anchor liner. The *Columbia*. That will be the one that goes to New York. I shouldn't mind going on it.'

'Well, go, Maevy! And see Kate and James and my father and mother.'

'Some day I will. Mother used to tell me such tales of its beauties.'

'She appreciated my home.' She looked up. 'Oh, here's Terence!'

He was smiling down at them. The wind had whipped some colour into his cheeks and his curls were blowing across his brow. 'Little Terence wants to see the windjammers. Does Gee-Gee want to come?'

Maevy looked down at the sleeping face and then smilingly at Terence. 'Here's one passenger who's showing not the slightest interest in windjammers.' Her brother's face was open and happy. She watched him joining the other children at the rail, saw the eager faces raised to him, heard the laughter. He'd be all right. He'd always found it easy to communicate with others. Too easy, sometimes.

Soon they were round the great landmark of Dumbarton Rock, and sailing past the quay sheds and chimneys of Port Glasgow and Greenock. In the distance were the Highland peaks against the skyline, and then, as the steamer took a wide sweep, they were in the broad reaches of the Firth.

'It's as wide as the Hudson!' Maria exclaimed. 'Would you believe it?'

'Easily.'

'You are a tease! Shall we have to sail all this way when we go to Arran next month?'

'Goodness, no. You'll take the train to Wemyss Bay and cross from there. It's much quicker.'

John was now beside them with Isobel. She was holding on to her hat with one hand and John with the other. As usual she looked ethereally pretty. There was a little colour in the pale cheeks. Such fine skin. John must love it. 'Isn't this grand?' she was saying. 'What a good idea of yours, Maria.'

'Yes, indeed.' John smiled down on them with his comforting smile. 'I've come to say that the first sitting of dinner is being served. I'm rounding up the others.' Serenity and compassion. 'We owe ourselves this day after Terence's tragic bereavement, so shall we go down and do full justice to MacBrayne's fine cod with tartare sauce?'

Maevy got up, putting Gaylord on his feet. She bent towards him. 'Gee-Gee. Dinner. Nice fish.'

'I'll take him and you go and help John to round up the others,' Maria said.

Lizzie came running towards them, her curls bobbing under her straw brim. She was a replica of her grandmother, even to the purple boa dancing like her curls. Mother spoiled her with presents. 'Oh, Aunt Maevy! Uncle Terence is telling us grand tales about the windjammers and how the men clamber up the mast like monkeys!'

'He's a grand blether!' She laughed up at Terence who was beside them, and he tweaked the ribbons on her straw boater.

'A grand blether, is it? Well, I seem to remember you're pretty good at that yourself!' It was the old Terence restored, if only for this day at least.

In the dining-room John sat between her mother and herself and devoted his time equally between them, seeing that they had a plentiful supply of cod, that they helped themselves to the mountainous plates of bread and butter, and that their cups were kept well-filled. Her mother soon became engaged in conversation with Maria across the table comparing notes *vis-à-vis* the Hudson and the Clyde, and she and John were left sitting in a friendly silence. He was the first to break it.

'We can't participate in that discussion,' he said. 'Have *you* ever wanted to cross the Atlantic?'

'Yes, indeed. I'd love to meet Uncle Terence and Aunt Caroline, but most of all to see where Kate and James live. And I'd love to see how the boys have grown. You know Kate used to bring them to visit us at Sholton when she was nursemaid to them? That was before James's first wife died.'

'It was fortunate Kate was there to take her place.'

'Oh, it was more than that. She wasn't only useful to them. There's a deep love between her and James. And Emily and Victoria adore her.'

152

'It must be difficult being a second wife.' She wondered why he was pursuing the subject.

'I shouldn't think so. And they've got Kieran, their own child.' Did he disapprove of someone marrying again?

'Well, I can appreciate the pleasure that must be.' His smile was bathing her in its glow. 'Lizzie·is like our own daughter. She's literally saved Isobel's life, if not her sanity.'

'I've never seen her look better.'

'It was thanks to your mother. She's a fine woman, if a bit unorthodox.' Unorthodox? Mother? 'She appears to take nothing to do with the family, yet has a great influence on them.'

'That's Mother's cleverness.' No, that was the wrong word. 'I mean, nothing is deliberate. She has a natural talent for being helpful without interfering. And she's completely reliable. You could tell Mother a secret, knowing it would never be divulged.'

'That's certainly a great attribute.'

'Yes.' She wondered why she had to justify Mother to John. 'The thing is, she never passes judgement.'

'And that's a good thing, too?' His eyebrows were raised.

'Yes, only sometimes you'd like an opinion from her.'

'Or commendation? Only *you* know if you're comfortable with . . . happenings in your life.'

'But sometimes you *don't* know. Some things can be expedient, but not morally right . . .' She stopped abruptly. 'They say fish is good for the brain!' She laughed. 'It's obviously stimulated mine. May I have another piece of bread and butter?' She did not want it.

'Of course. I'm not counting.'

'It's included in the price.' She laughed again. 'Besides, it's Patrick's treat. I'm sure this outing was his idea although he lets Maria take the credit. That's Patrick.'

She felt full of love for him, for her family, and smiled round at them as she attacked the cod and sipped the strong yellow tea.

The band was playing on deck when they went upstairs again, and although they were too recently bereaved to join in the dancing, they watched the other people enjoying themselves to the tune of the piano and melodeon, and contributed generously when the velvet bag was shaken under their noses.

Then they were round Toward Point and sailing into Rothesay Bay where they had decided to spend a couple of hours instead of sailing all the way up Loch Striven. The children were getting restive, and Terence had told them of the delights of Ettrick Bay.

Maevy, her mother and Patrick walked on the wide sands while the children paddled, guarded by Maria and Isobel. There were excited squeals when they had to jump clear of the wavelets which ran towards them. 'Aren't you envious?' her mother asked.

'Of Maria and Isobel?'

'No, no, the children.' She might have known. 'If you and I weren't being so jecoe we'd be in there with them.'

'I'm surprised at you, Mother,' Patrick said, 'Maevy perhaps, but . . .'

She smiled at him, unabashed, 'You'll learn before long, son, that however old you appear to be to others, you remain a child at heart. I expect to feel the same at ninety.'

'Go on, Patrick!' Maevy laughed at him. 'Admit you'd like to paddle, too.'

He shook his head, genuinely puzzled, 'No, honestly. I think I must have been born old.'

'We'll have to tell Maria to get to work on him, won't we, Mother?'

'Yes, but not to influence him too much or before long

154

she'll be whisking him back to America for good. Her heart's still there.'

'I don't think there's much chance,' he said, but Maevy thought he said it without much conviction.

They were a happy party on the way back. There was another distraction for the children at Inellan, that of cheering the steamers as they raced up to the pier to debouch their cargo of travellers from Glasgow. 'Those are the summer folks,' Terence explained to them. 'The father goes up to Glasgow every day to his office and the mother sets up house in a rented cottage. Look, the passengers are nearly all men.' And to Maria, 'It's a quaint old Glasgow custom to go "doon the watter" for the summer.'

The children hugged the rail and cheered their chosen favourites as they steamed importantly past, the seagulls skimming furiously in their wakes, 'The yellow funnel's mine!' 'Red's winning!' 'Come on, *Jupiter!*' They expended so much energy that they were happy to sit for the rest of the journey, and it was a happy but fairly silent party which disembarked at the Bridge Wharf.

They dropped Maevy at the Infirmary, and as she stood waving to the overflowing carriage she felt the anticlimax like a weight on her. It had been a happy day, and yet with undercurrents, Maria with her secret worry about Mary. 'Dark blood.' The words came into her mind. What if the danger lay not with that poor wee lass but with the dead uncle's namesake, Gee-Gee? She had a longing to be with them all, caring for them, or was the longing for John Craigie? I'm tired, she decided, with all that sun and fresh air.

One of the nurses met her as she went in, thinking of bed and oblivion. 'Sister Connelly's been taken bad. You've to take her place on night duty.'

'Who says?'

'Who do you think? Matron.'

She stripped off her summer dress, put the straw boater in its box under the bed and got into her uniform. The cloth felt hard and unsympathetic against her warm skin.

16

Maevy lifted a paper one August evening in the Nurses'
Recreation Room and read that next morning two thousand men were expected to assemble at Townhead to be
addressed by Mr Robert Stevenson of the Horsemen's
Union. It was believed they would unanimously agree to
adhere to their original demands. The carters' strike had
begun.

She knew, of course, that it had been expected, and in
a certain sense she welcomed it. It had given Terence
something other than Catherine's suicide to think about.
Her mother had told her on her last visit home that he
turned up at the office most days now and was with the
men a large part of the time, talking and reasoning with
them.

'It'll happen any day,' she had told Maevy, 'and
although we gave them the advance they asked for, a lot
of our temporary carters will be swept up by the excitement and join in.'

'Can't Terence get it over to them?' she had asked.

'If he can't, no one can, but a lot of them don't want to
listen. He's told them we're willing to have discussions
about stable duty on Sundays, overtime on their rakes,
and so on.'

'But don't you already do that?' She had been
surprised.

'The overtime's under discussion, but as regards stable
duty, some like to come in. They're attached to their
horses. There's never been a hard and fast rule.'

'But, Mother, some of these men have to walk miles to

157

get to the stables! From one side of Glasgow to the other. And Sunday's their only day of rest.'

'Your father and brothers had to walk miles to the pit. And work nightshifts, don't forget.' Her eyes had pinpoints of fire in them.

'I know that. But carters have their own problems. They've to sit hours in the rain at docks and railway sidings, and groom their horses when they get back . . .'

'They know their horses are their livelihood. You're not accusing us of treating the men badly, are you?'

'No, I'm not.' She was exasperated, stopped herself from saying, 'It looks as if horses are more important to you than carters,' but she knew her mother's quick temper. 'I think McGraths are better than most, but I can see in general why the men are striking. It's not so long ago since carters were regarded as the scum of the earth, and yet when you think of it, where would we all be if they weren't there to move goods about? And I know Father and the boys worked hard, but in time people won't be willing to work like that unless they're better paid.'

'Our business is founded on fair treatment. You should get up on a soap-box on Glasgow Green.' Her mother's mouth had lost its curves, a sure sign that she was angry.

'Oh, Mother . . .' She had given her a hug, 'I know nothing about it and I know you're the fairest employers in the district, and that you've always been willing to meet the men, but it's the general principle . . .'

'You're trying to butter me up.'

She had laughed. 'Butter *you* up when you're on your high horse! What a hope!' They had parted on good terms. They had the same temperament in that neither ever bore a grudge for long.

She had wondered, nevertheless, despite McGrath's reputation for fairness, if her mother and the boys were shutting their eyes to what was happening around them. A new breed of men were coming into carting. The older ones had taken for granted the long hours, the soakings, the cold, the poor pay, but the new ones were beginning to demand their rights. Her family were caught up in the ramifications of business. They could not step out of line with the other contractors. I'm glad I'm in nursing, she thought, even although we get all the results of those poor working conditions, men who are worn out and tired of life at forty.

The morning after she had read the announcement in the *Glasgow Herald*, she could hear the sound of a band being played outside. She went to the window of the ward where she was on duty and saw that Infirmary Square was crowded with men milling around in every direction. There were waving banners held up above the cloth-capped heads, a lot of shouting which did not seem to be ill-humoured, even an occasional ragged cheer. She went back to dispensing medicines, kept busy answering patients' questions as she pushed the trolley round the beds.

'My folks are in the thick of this,' she told one of the men, 'they're haulage contractors.'

'They'll be skinned alive, then,' he said, 'they've marched from Brunswick Square this morning. Thousands of them. It tells you all about it in *The Crommonweal*, there. Aye, they'll be skinned alive, mark my words!'

'D'you think so?' She shook her thermometer. 'McGraths have a reputation for fair dealing. Ask anyone. And I happen to know they've paid the advance the men are striking for.'

His gaunt face was gleeful. 'It disnae matter. Once men get hetted up there's no stoapin' them, friend or foe alike. Take ma word for it, it's a struggle against capitalism.'

She looked down her nose at him, and replied with the only means in her power.

'Open wide, Mr MacPherson.' She stuck the thermometer in his mouth.

At their midday break she and another nurse decided to forego their meal and go out and see the fun, as Mag Petrie put it. The Square was still crowded, although there were some signs that the men were assembling under their respective banners. She overheard someone say that they were marching through the main Glasgow streets to the Green. There was a voice ringing round the Square.

'Let's listen,' she said to Mag, and to the man nearest them, 'Is that Mr Robert Stevenson speaking?'

'Aye, that's the high heid yin.'

'. . . and what I have to tell you, men,' Mr Stevenson's voice was loud and confident, 'is that I have a telegram – here it is – and this telegram which is from the Edinburgh and Leith Society says they'll support us to the tune of six thousand pounds, and that there's six thousand more if needed! What d'you think of that?'

There was a roar from the crowd. 'Bluidy guid,' the man beside Maevy said, then raised his cap above his head as another man took the speaker's place. 'Here's John Campbell to give us the rallying cry.'

'*There*'s an offer for you!' the new speaker shouted. 'Are we resolved to remain firm?'

'Aye, aye! Right y'are, Campbell!' There were cries on all sides.

'So it's on to Glasgow Green now! Form up behind your respective banners and keep it orderly. You'll be led by the Blind Asylum Band who've given their services free for our cause!' The crowd began to break up round the two girls.

'Are you game to follow them down?' Maevy asked Mag.

'Do you want to?' She looked doubtful.

'I'm in it in a kind of a way. I'd be able to give my family a first-hand account.'

'If the carters find out who you are they'll scalp you. All right, come one. Follow the band!'

High Street was crowded, but there were few women about. Probably they had more sense. Perhaps, Maevy thought, their nurses' uniform would give them official backing. Laden lorries pulled by two or sometimes more horses were being driven down the street to the imminent danger of the crowds walking in the middle of it. Instead of getting out of the way they stood their ground, jeering and booing, and Maevy saw one man, not content with this, jump at two Shires pulling a large load and try to loosen their harness. Others followed suit, and the drivers, not slow to retaliate, began to wield their whips ferociously to right and left of them, standing up in their seats. She saw one man retiring, blood pouring from a savage cut on his brow.

'It's beginning to look ugly,' Mag said, 'I think we'd better get back.'

'You go if you like.' It was her strike, in a way. 'I'm going to see what it's like on the Green.'

'On your own head be it.'

It was bedlam. There were several bands playing in competition with one another, it seemed. She recognized the Blind Asylum one, and the distinctive uniform of the Salvation Army, the Army of Peace, but always in the thick of things. The carters stood in groups, arguing amongst themselves, or listening to whichever speaker caught their fancy. The noise was deafening, roars of approval were drowned by jeering and loud clapping, and over and through it the bands played away for dear life.

In the middle of it all they found a stall where the Salvation Army were offering hot soup, and a young girl with bright eyes and curls under her bonnet held out two cups. They thanked her and stood drinking, pushed this way and that. 'I think we should go,' Mag said.

They began to make their way back to the Infirmary by the Broomielaw, and here the situation looked if anything uglier. There were some small attempts at organization by officials wearing arm bands, but the men were breaking ranks and fighting with anyone whose opinion they did not like. She saw fists pummelling, irate faces, and exasperated policemen rushing about with drawn batons.

Suddenly above the head of a large listening group Maevy saw and recognized the speaker, Arthur Cranston. His thin face was alight with proselytising zeal. 'Fair do's,' he was shouting, 'that's all we ask. We've been oppressed and underpaid far too long. Hit them where it hurts. They can't do without us.'

There was the loud rattle of wheels and the sound of horses' hooves thundering. The men gave way, forced to stand back as a Caledonian Railway carter drove his lorry through the crowd as if he was cutting a swathe through grass. Everyone seemed too surprised to try and stop him although there was the inevitable shouting and cursing. He was making straight for Arthur Cranston.

The next few minutes were pandemonium. Arthur jumped from the box he was standing on and was swallowed up by the crowd. He'll be trampled to death, Maevy thought, but the next moment he was there again, this time hanging on to the traces of one of the great carthorses which was plunging its head and raising its hairy hooves in fright. The driver laid his whip viciously along its back while it thundered on with Arthur hanging on to its collar, and then Maevy saw him being thrown off by its rearing and plunging, and disappear.

'That's someone I know.' She clutched Mag's arm. 'I must get to him.'

'Go into that crowd? Don't be daft! They'll murder you!'

'No, they won't.' She left Mag and pushed her way through the moving mass of cloth-capped men. Her nurse's uniform seemed to give her some kind of authority, for they made way for her. She heard someone say, 'He's under the bluidy wheels!' And the reply, 'He asked for it, daft bugger,' and then a third furious voice, 'Whit the hell ur ye talkin' aboot? It's Arthur Cranston!'

Faces were all around her, some pathetic, some angry, some frightened. They're like the miners in Sholton, she thought, long ago, over-worked, under-paid, desperate . . . *I'm on their side*.

Arthur Cranston lay on the ground with a little group of men round him. She saw his mangled leg and the red grazes on the side of his face where the dirty gravel had scraped it as he had been dragged along. He was conscious, but his lips were blue. She shook the arm of a man standing beside her. 'Get an ambulance! Quick! I saw one at the gates!'

'I'll no' get through.' He looked scared.

'Blow a whistle! Anything! Go on!' She knelt down and saw the sweat on Arthur's brow, heard the soft moaning coming from him. 'Arthur, it's Maevy McGrath. I happened to be passing. We'll soon get you all right.'

'Maevy . . .' His eyes flickered. 'It's my leg. The wheel went . . .'

'I can see that.' The right leg of his trousers was in tatters and soaked with blood.

She tore off her apron, pushed up the torn trouser-leg. There was a long, ugly gash on his calf, and she quickly bound it with a length of linen. The blood immediately seeped through it. And then she saw his knee, and the gap between the crushed bone, the purple bruising. Bad enough, a fractured patella, but thank God it was not compound. The dung on the ground from the frightened horses would have been sure to have caused infection.

'Oot o' the road!' It was two ambulance men making their way through the crowd, and then they were both kneeling beside her to look at Arthur. 'In the name o' Goad, nurse,' the elder of the two said, 'how did ye get here?'

'I came to see the fun.'

He threw up his eyes. 'C'mon, Jock,' he said, and then they were rolling Arthur gently on to a stretcher. 'We'll get him to the Royal right away.'

'That's where I work.'

'D'ye tell me that? Well, you'd better come as well.'

She could not see Mag as she followed them to the ambulance. She must have taken to her heels.

He was sent to her ward after he had been seen at Casualty. He was in a bad way, deathly pale, but after she had cleaned him up he seemed to revive a little. 'It's you again, Maevy. What's the damage?'

'You've been lucky. It's a simple fracture. You're concussed slightly from that knock on your head, and there's the gash in your leg. But I'll see that it heals.' She wished he had not lost so much blood.

She gave him meticulous attention. Each day she changed the dressings on his leg under a steam jet of carbolic. The knee was splinted. She made sure that he suffered from as little discomfort as possible, if she could help it. But despite all her care, after the first few days he began to slip back. His temperature went up and he slept badly, tossing and turning in evident distress. He never complained.

Bob Cranston, his father, came to see him, a grizzled

164

man now in his sixties, but still hale and hearty. Arthur's wife was tied with the children and found it difficult to come every day. 'What do you think of him?' he asked Maevy on one of his visits.

She was non-committal. 'Dr Maitchison said he'd like to see you or his wife, whoever came first.'

'Come on, Maevy. What do *you* think of him?'

'To tell you the truth, Mr Cranston,' she said, 'I'm not too happy about him. He's all nerves, your Arthur. He's had a bad experience, and it'll take him a week or two to get over it. But don't you worry, Dr Maitchison's giving him every care.'

'And you, I know.' He smiled at her. 'I never expected to see Kieran McGrath's wee lass nursing my son in the Royal Infirmary.'

'I'm glad I am. I remember you and Father sitting in the kitchen with a roaring fire between you when I came home from school. You were poring over your papers about the truck system.'

'Aye, we won that one, but only a year or two ago. Pity he didn't live to see that. He was a special man your father, gey special. Your mother must miss him sorely.'

'She still does, but she keeps herself busy with the stables and the family. You'll have heard about Catherine's death?'

He nodded. 'That was all round Sholton with embellishments, her being the late minister's daughter. That lad Terence hasny much luck.' She knew he was thinking of Bessie Haddow.

Terence came to see Arthur, a subdued and thinner Terence, but putting a brave face on it. The strike was over, the carters had had to step down in the end, but McGraths had been one of the first contractors to agree to pay them overtime. He had a word with Maevy before he went in.

'They may have been defeated,' he told her, 'but they've set the ball rolling. Did you read about the London dockers' strike?'

'Arthur told me. He feels he's been injured in a good cause.' She looked at Terence meaningly, 'He badly needs cheering up.'

'Is he not so good?'

'The doctor thinks he's not making the progress he should. Don't say anything to him.'

She listened to her brother talking to Arthur as she busied herself round his bed.

'Well, you old fraud, what are you doing lying there for instead of away down to London to join the dockers?'

'Oh, there'll be another strike here before long.' His mouth quirked. 'The Trades Council's going to rise up in support of the tramway servants. That's another bloody disgrace . . .' He stopped speaking, his face twisting in pain.

'Don't tire him with your talk, Terence,' she said.

'Me tire him? I haven't said a word.' They both looked at the thin face on the pillow, the sunken cheeks. He was barely forty. He could have been living in Crannoch helping on the farm, had a nice little cottage near it and a wife who was fat and rosy. His was like himself, thin, worried, not properly fed, and they lived up a back close near McGrath's stables in the Gallowgate. Women have the heavy end of it, Maevy thought, when their man has an obsession.

Arthur opened his eyes and smiled at Terence. His voice was weak. 'It's a long time since you and me larked about at Sholton, eh, Terence? Those were the days. Not a care in the world.'

'"We twa hae paidled in the burn . . ."'

'"And pu'ed the gowans fine . . ."' He finished the quotation. 'Life's funny, isn't it? I take the weight of the

166

world on my shoulders, deliberately, but a harum scarum like you doesn't escape either. I was right sorry to hear about Catherine . . .'

'Thanks.' Terence put his hand over Arthur's lying on the counterpane.

'And here's your sister tending me in bed. By Jove, she's a fine nurse. There's no one who's got more gentle hands than her. When that big lump . . . what's her name, Maevy?'

'We have no big lumps in my ward I'll have you know, Arthur Cranston,' she said.

'Well, whatever she's called . . .' He smiled at Terence. 'When she turns me over you'd think it was the winding gear at the pit doing it . . .' His eyes dropped shut again. There was a flush on the cheekbones of his gaunt face.

'You'd better go, Terence,' she said.

He nodded and got up. 'Buck up, lad.' He patted Arthur's hand. 'You'll soon be out and running the country again.'

Arthur smiled. His eyes remained closed. 'For a . . . bloated capitalist, I like . . . you fine . . .' His voice trailed away.

At the end of a fortnight he was no better. Dr Maitchison spoke to Maevy on his round. 'I think something will have to be done. The kneecap isn't uniting. I've told the Chief and he's coming to see him today. We don't want gangrene setting in.'

Mr McKendrick duly came and, to her surprise, was accompanied by Charlie. She remembered a remark he had once made about the surgeon. 'One of that stern breed of Scotsmen who think that to utter a few civilities is a sign of being soft in the heid.'

It seemed to be apt. Mr McKendrick grunted over Arthur as he felt his knee, barked instructions at her.

And yet his hands, although like a labourer's in size, were gentle and sure. 'Never get him out of bed like this.' He beckoned Charlie out of earshot . . . 'Can't be avoided.' They walked further away. If the Chief was a man of few words, Charlie appeared as voluble as ever, she thought, watching him. He'd always been able to talk the hind leg off a donkey.

Another week passed with no change in Arthur's condition. He said to her one night as she bathed his brow, 'Are you going to get me on my legs for the next strike, Maevy?' His eyes were bright with fever. 'Or should I say . . . leg?'

She redoubled her efforts. The 'big lump' as Arthur called her, a harmless girl called Nancy from the Highlands, was round-eyed. 'Oh, you're that careful, Sister! I've never seen anything like it, that spray, and everything soaked in carbolic! I can't get the smell of it out of my hair.'

'Success in nursing,' she looked up from dressing Arthur's leg, 'is a meticulous observation of a number of small details. You write that in your Nurse's Notebook.'

'I'll do that, Sister,' Nancy assured her.

Charlie did a round that evening. 'The Chief's going to operate on Arthur tomorrow,' he told her.

'No . . .?' She could not say it.

'No, no. He's going to wire the two parts of the patella together.'

'But that way we'll have an open wound and there's the risk of infection . . .'

'You know the alternative.' His voice was brisk. 'And if he's left any longer to moulder in bed without anything being done . . .'

'Gangrene?'

He nodded. She felt sure he was behind the idea of wiring the knee.

'Will you be assisting?' she asked.

'Yes. He'll leave the sterilization to me.' He smiled at her, his brief, flashing smile. 'And I'll leave it to you when he's back in bed.'

'It's dangerous, isn't it?'

'Only if the incision gets infected, and that's up to both of us. We're not like some of those old codgers who believe bacteria is produced by disease and not the other way round.'

'It's not for want of telling by you!' She had to smile. 'All the same, when it's someone you know, you feel doubly responsible.'

'Well, that's a good thing, isn't it?' He was gone.

He'd always had a habit of going away quickly, she thought, as she busied herself in the ward. Once when she'd laughed at this when he was visiting Father, he'd said that was one of the few things general practice had taught him, how to make a quick exit.

Mother had told her a bit about him. He had taken his surgeon's examinations at St Andrews but had seen no prospect of keeping himself alive as an assistant or dresser. You had to hang around unpaid for years in a hospital, he'd said, before you were able to build up a practice for yourself, and that called for a fine house in the West End where you could see private patients. His father had died and he'd had to earn money to support his younger brothers. He'd chosen general practice in Sholton to be near the Glasgow Royal. Maybe in time he would save enough money to buy that fine house and become a whole-time surgeon. Sholton will miss him if he does, Maevy thought.

The following night she was sitting at her desk in the ward, having volunteered to do night duty. She wanted to be with Arthur as much as possible. He had survived the operation well after the first distressing sickness from the

169

after-effects of the chloroform. You developed a sixth sense when you'd been nursing for a long time. She felt he was on the mend.

The ward was quiet. She had looked at Arthur and he was sleeping peacefully. Now, in the pool of light, she was busy writing up her notes. And yet she felt unaccountably tired. Not sleepy, but tired. She laid down her pen, felt someone behind her, turned. It was Charlie, soft-footed, smiling down at her.

'I didn't think you'd be on duty tonight.' The light threw black shadows across his face, highlighting his nose, the boldness of it, making deep shadows under his eyes.

'I stood in for someone else. I wanted to see how Arthur was doing.'

'How is he?'

'Peaceful. It was a grand operation, thanks to Mr McKendrick and you.'

'I was only the dogsbody, the mechanic. He sees eye to eye with me about asepsis, fortunately.'

'Arthur will walk, then?'

'Without a doubt. Maybe it won't be a hundred per cent success, but it's better than being short of a leg.'

'As long as he doesn't throw himself at another horse.'

'You'll never get Arthur to stop treading the path he's chosen.'

'A lot of us are like that.' She looked down at her desk. 'Mother talks about my stubborn bit.'

'I've experience of that.' She dared not look up. Well, he had got over it, hadn't he? His voice changed, 'Ah, well, the stubborn ones are the folks who get things done. I made up my mind when I couldn't work here full time, I'd at least carry Lister's ideas with me into general practice.'

She had the courage now. 'Maybe when you marry Miss Wilcox her father will arrange for you to get a full-time place here. Help to set you up.' She faltered at the look in his eyes.

'You sound as if you thought I'd sold myself.'

'I'm sorry if I did.'

'You'd never do that . . . compromise?' His eyes had steel in them. She was defiant because of her own anger and misery.

'No, at least I stick to my guns.'

'Guns or illusions?' His voice was bitter. 'You should take them out from time to time and dust them off, see if they're worth keeping.'

'Should I?' She thought of John Craigie and how she had believed her heart was broken when he married Isobel. Was it still broken? There had been that whiff of John Knox from him on the steamer, his sanctimonious attitude about Kate being James's second wife – or had she imagined it?

'You have wisps of golden hair on your brow, Maevy.' His voice was suddenly soft, tender.

'Have I?' She tucked in the offending wisps. 'Those curls! Terence hates his. He used to plaster them down with pomade when he was a boy.'

'I thought you might have left them out to tantalize Dr Maitchison.'

'He's married, you know that full well.' And to pay him back, 'Is your marriage date fixed yet?'

His eyelids dropped over his eyes. 'We've still to discuss it.' Then they were suddenly revealed again, black, brilliant, his voice was urgent, 'Maevy. It's not too late. I have to, I must ask you one last . . .'

'Nurse . . .' A wavery voice came from the end bed. It was the old man who was dying. He had a tumour.

She jumped up, aware of the self-righteous look on her face, hating it, 'Excuse me, I'm wanted . . .'

'Maevy . . .' Charlie put his hand on her arm. She felt

171

herself melting with tenderness, and then she remembered Miss Wilcox at the Exhibition, her proprietorial look, and the rumours in the Infirmary, 'He's Wilcox's pet . . .'

'I have to go.' When she went back to her desk he had gone.

17

Would you like to live here? Charlie asked himself as he walked along the select avenue to the Wilcox house. One side of it was bordered by the Botanic Gardens, and on this sunny September day the trees were still green, hardly a turned leaf amongst them. Ahead of him he could see the ornate glass and stone annexe of the Wilcox's conservatory, to sit in which always gave him the illusion of being in the country, but nowhere in the country would one find such exotic plants as grew there. He suspected the Wilcox's gardener got a few tips or even cuttings from the Botanic Gardens' staff across the road.

And the Wilcox house was not like, say Maeve McGrath's – his own was too unremarkable for comparison. Braidholme had been a farmhouse before Colonel Naismith had added two wings and built stables at the rear, but it still retained the character of a farmhouse with its low beamed-ceilinged rooms leading out of one another, its casement windows, its beautiful garden, a cottage garden with an abundance of flowers and no formal beds.

It bore the imprint of her personality; the Wilcox residence was the combined product of gardeners and maids. Only the cooking reflected Mrs Wilcox, her own *embonpoint* in its heaviness. He remembered his first dinner there and the plum duff which had stuck in his gullet. And most importantly, the Wilcox residence had never nurtured Maevy. It was at Braidholme that he had first seen her, a rounded girl of sixteen with her golden hair tied back in a bow. And where she had told him she wanted to be a nurse.

Now he was at the gate. I'm girding my loins, he thought, this is the only thing to do. Never mind if Maevy's mother says there are two ways one might choose, two persons one might be happy with. In the end you have to come down on one side or the other, and half a loaf was never better than no bread.

Effie opened the door to him, treating him like an old friend. 'Well, Dr McNab, it's yourself, and a long time since we saw you in these parts.' She had a pert, pretty face, with the shan gab sometimes found in Glasgow girls, a slight protrusion of the lower lip which would become more pronounced as she grew older . . . the Irish Mick face he had heard it called.

'Yes, indeed.' He gave her his hat. 'Is Miss Letitia at home?'

'Yes, and expecting you. She's in the conservatory . . . alone.' She nodded, meaningly.

'Thanks, Effie. I think I can find my way there myself.'

Letitia sprang up to greet him, lithely. She has a constant struggle to appear younger than she is, he thought, and then he was smiling at her, taking her hands, genuinely glad to see her. 'Back at last, Letitia.' They kissed, a cool kiss on her side, he noticed, as if they had lost ground by her absence.

'Back at last, Charlie!' She whirled around for his benefit. 'Do I look any different? I shouldn't be surprised if I'd put on pounds over there. The food! Oh, those pies and tarts!'

'You'll never put on weight. You're one of Pharaoh's lean kine.'

She pouted. 'That isn't very romantic. Come and sit beside me. I've much to tell you.' She patted a chintz cushion of the wicker sofa. 'Oh, thanks, Effie.' The maid had appeared with a laden tray. 'I thought you might like a cup of tea, Charlie. You doctors never seem to eat.'

'Is that all right, Miss?' Effie lingered, smiling on them like a kindly procuress.

'Yes, I think there's enough for a hungry man.' Both Letitia and Effie smiled on him with an indulgent air, very different from Biddy's purse mouth. Oh, I'm well in here, he thought, I'd be stupid to give it up . . . he stopped himself. Hadn't he lain awake night after night thinking of that last conversation with Maevy in the ward and the look of her, the *rightness* of her for him, those honest eyes? *She* would never think one thing and do the other.

'Go on, Letitia,' he said, having accepted the cup of tea and a generous slice of sultana cake, 'I know you're bursting to tell me all about America and your conquests.'

'It was Father who was fêted, silly boy. He was a great success there, indeed he was offered an appointment which he turned down.'

'Would *you* like to live there?'

'That depends.' She looked at him, head on one side. 'But it's a wonderful place, New York, and the hospitality is overwhelming. I was hardly in bed before midnight every night . . . but I told you all about it in my letters. I must say you're a poor correspondent. Is it that you're afraid to commit yourself on paper?'

'No, no!' He protested too vigorously. 'I'm a hopeless letter writer.'

'Or did you console yourself with some pretty girl like that one we met at the Exhibition? The one who was a nurse?'

'Maevy McGrath? No, she has no time for me. But speaking of her,' it was good to speak of her, even in this oblique way, 'a terrible thing happened to her brother. His wife committed suicide.'

'Oh, horrors!' She loved what she called 'scandal'. 'Do tell me about it. That's terrible. Was it near here?'.

'Yes, in Great Western Terrace. Maevy and her brother found her dead in the bath.'

'How awful. How terrible for your Maevy.' My Maevy . . .

'She's a nurse, more able to cope than most. She was a great help to her brother. He couldn't have got through it without her.'

'And you were a great help to her. I can see it all . . .' Her bright, knowledgeable eyes were on him.

'I live beside her mother. I've known the family for a long time. I've seen Maevy grow up . . .' He was being too fulsome, 'at least from when she was sixteen. You'd like their house, a real country home.'

'No, I prefer the city. The country bores me, so green, so dull. But tell me, because I'm interested, why did this sister-in-law commit suicide? Had she a shameful secret, or more likely, had she found out that her husband had a shameful secret?' He had forgotten her sharp mind.

'She was ill, deranged at the time.'

'Of course she was deranged at the time. How did she do it?'

'With her husband's razor.'

'Well, isn't that proof? But there must have been a trigger, like the discovery of her husband's infidelity when she was in a poor state of health.'

'How your mind jumps about, Letitia.'

She waved her hand. 'I should have been a lawyer if I hadn't been an only daughter and expected to marry. This sort of thing intrigues me. Didn't she leave a note?'

'No, she didn't leave a note.' Now that he came to think of it, it was unusual. The report in the paper had said nothing, and he had not liked to ask questions from the family. All the same, he had been curious.

'Take my word for it, there would be. Perhaps it was suppressed. I read of lots of cases like this. They have a morbid fascination for me. Perhaps she was being black-mailed systematically and there would be one that was the last straw, sent by some malignant person writing anony-mously. She wouldn't be able to bear it. She would read it in her bath, for the tenth time perhaps, drop it over the side in despair and slash whatever it was she slashed, having picked up her husband's razor first. There,' she smiled at him, 'I've solved your mystery for you. Don't say I'm not clever.'

'Clever?' He was vaguely alarmed. 'You're wasting your time sitting here with me. You should be a writer of novels, or a lady journalist, if there were such a thing . . .' Why did her words start up such a sense of uneasi-ness in him, in a way a confirmation of his own doubts? 'No wonder I thought of you often when you were away, a young lady with so many attributes.' Even to himself his words sounded false.

'But you said your days were full of work, and helping your nurse, Maevy, with her family problems.' How brittle her voice was, and how piercing her eyes.

'Nevertheless I thought often of your kindness, and that of your father, and how he encouraged me in my work. And how your mother welcomed me here. I'm deeply grateful to all of you.'

'You sound as if you were going away.' The tip of her tongue ran along her bottom lip. She watched him like a cat.

He swallowed. 'What I'm saying, Letitia, is that I can't take advantage of all this kindness which has been shown to me. I know our friendship has progressed to a certain stage, that there may have been an understanding . . .' She interrupted him.

'What you're saying is that after due consideration and

taking cognisance of the numerous advantages which would accrue to you, you still wouldn't want to marry me.'

'That's it.' It was out. 'I apologize if I've led you to understand otherwise.' Thank God I've got it off my chest, he thought, wanting badly to wipe his brow. The heady smell from some arum lilies in a pot behind him was in his nostrils, making him feel slightly sick.

'This is because you're in love with someone else?' She was smiling, a cat's smile. He was not out of the wood yet.

'Yes, that's the reason.'

'And you intend to marry her?'

He shook his head. 'She wouldn't have me in a gift.'

'How very unfortunate.' She laughed. The little white teeth showed. 'But fortunate in a way. If you'd been jilting me . . .' She jumped up and whirled about the conservatory in an agitated fashion, even her bustle seemed to quiver. When she turned to him she had her hand to her mouth. Was she still laughing? 'The whole thing's a dreadful mix-up. Oh, you're so solemn, and so . . . puritanical, Charlie! You wouldn't suit me at all, and I never took you seriously for one minute.' Her chin was lifted, her eyes cold. 'But I'm very much afraid Mother and Father did. They're getting desperate about me, an unmarried daughter at thirty-one! Left to myself, I wouldn't worry. I like to travel. I'm curious about the rest of the world. And I should want to settle down to please my parents, there's a doctor in America who's interested in me. I haven't told them because truth to tell I'm not interested in *him*. I believe I'm a perennial flirt who'll go on being so until my face is raddled and I become a joke. Besides, I don't think I'd at all like to be a surgeon's wife having seen how my mother is at the beck and call of my

178

father, and how she has to entertain the most *boring* people,' she looked down her nose at him. 'Glasgow's full of them, those douce men puffed up with their own importance who've never been further than Rothesay Bay!'

'You never loved me.' He made sad eyes.

'Oh, the vanity of men!' She made a small impatient gesture. 'Well, I'll confess I was attracted to you, your horizons did seem a little wider than most who come here . . . but *love* is another matter.'

'I think you should go and visit that doctor in America, Letitia. He sounds . . .' She interrupted him.

'Oh, no! I've no intention of throwing myself into someone's arms just to salve *your* conscience.' Her eyes had narrowed, her mouth become thin. She looked all and more of her thirty-one years. 'I think you should go now before I lose my good manners. I can bawl like a fish-wife. Ask the servants.'

He got up quickly. 'I hope I haven't been too abrupt. I have no niceties.'

'There you go again! You've always been a little presumptuous, Doctor McNab. What you've said hasn't affected me in the least. Don't stand there dithering and looking foolish. You're right . . .' She raised her chin, 'You have no niceties.'

He walked down the avenue in a mixture of relief and shame. What a conundrum of a woman all the same, he thought. He wished she *had* launched a full-blown tirade at him. He deserved it. Or burst into tears . . .

When he reached the corner he ran like a boy for the horse bus which was ahead of him.

18

Suddenly it was all fixed. They were going to Paris. Her mother expressed surprise that Maevy had ever doubted it.

'I thought that with Catherine's death, and Terence . . . and, oh, everything, you'd drop the whole idea.'

'Drop the whole idea! Kate will be there, and I wouldn't like to miss the chance of seeing her.'

'Neither should I, but Terence being alone . . .'

'Everybody has to face up to being alone at some time or other in their lives. Some thole it, some like it and those who don't like it do something about it. Take my word for it, Terence will be frequenting his favourite howffs before long. He craves company.'

They called at the manse to tell them of their plans, and found Isobel sitting in the dining-room with Lizzie who was doing her lessons. Lizzie was ecstatic. 'Thank goodness you've come, Grandma,' she said, 'I hate sums.'

'You want to be able to add up the money in your bank, don't you?' Maevy said. 'By the way, where is it?'

'I'll get it.' She dashed away, curls flying, checked skirt showing a swirl of white petticoat and black stockings.

'She certainly seems happy enough,' Maeve said.

'You've no idea the difference she's made to our lives,' Isobel said. 'Will you take a cup of tea?'

'No, thanks, Susan will have our dinner ready soon. We just walked over to tell you we're off to Paris next week.'

'Oh, you lucky things!' Isobel had on her 'I'm-a-poor-minister's-wife' face, Maevy thought, smiling to herself.

'Here it is.' Lizzie was back, waving her red pillar box bank. 'I'm saving for a white fur bonnet. I'm eleven now. I'm too old for dollies.'

'Are you, now?' Maeve 'posted' her shilling, followed by Maevy. 'When you were a very little girl you went in our phaeton at Christmas time, dressed in a white fur coat and bonnet. With grandpa and me.'

'Did I? Oh, I wish I'd been there!' She had her hand to her mouth, giggling, when John came in.

'Well, this is a surprise!' He greeted Maevy and her mother, then his face darkened as he looked at Lizzie. 'I hope you didn't *display* that bank. I've told you before, it's like begging.'

The girl hung her head. 'No, I didn't. Aunt Maevy asked me.'

'Yes, I asked her, John,' Maevy said. 'She wasn't even thinking of banks.'

Her mother supported her. 'She's been telling us about the white fur bonnet she's saving for.'

'For herself.' Isobel was now supporting John. 'How about the poor children in far-away countries?'

'The poor black children who have no clothes to wear at all, far less fripperies,' John said.

'It's too hot there.' Lizzie raised her chin. 'You've told me how the sun burns and burns all day long. They don't need clothes!'

'Certainly not a white fur bonnet!' Maeve laughed, and John and Isobel joined in, a little stiffly.

On the way back her mother said to Maevy, 'John's beginning to wear a halo, I think.'

They were walking through the village. The feeling of belonging was strong, the street with its familiar houses, the shop where they had bought liquorice straps with their Saturday penny, old Mrs Cochran's shop which sold

181

coloured hanks of wool, cards of safety-pins, inch-tapes – oh, the time she had taken to find anything – and there was Charlie's house with the surgery attached. Biddy was at the door chatting to a neighbour but when she saw them she scurried inside . . . I'm a homebird. I could come back and live here for the rest of my days. 'What did you say, Mother?'

'You heard me the first time. I only hope when he calls at Great Western Terrace on one of his errands of mercy he doesn't find Terence out enjoying himself.'

'Oh, Mother, you're the limit.'

'The limit, is it now? I saw your brows drawing together when John was reprimanding Lizzie, but you haven't the guts to speak out!'

'I see nothing wrong with John,' she said, opening the wicket gate into the garden. 'After you, Madam.' Her mother swept through.

They came back from Paris refreshed and rejuvenated. The principal reason for going had been to see Kate, but her step-daughter, Emily, had provided some unexpected excitement which had added a *je ne sais quoi* to the little trip.

Kate had arrived to greet them at their hotel in the *rue St Hyacinthe* looking ravishing in a Burgundy red velvet costume and a little toque of the same colour made of feathers. After the three of them had wept and laughed and chattered together they had been whisked away in the Barthe landau to meet Emily at Ledoyens in the *Champs-Élysées* for tea. The gentleman with her she introduced as Monsieur Paul Vincent.

It did not take Maevy's professional eye very long to decide that Emily's febrility was of the heart and not the constitution, and that Monsieur Vincent was the cause.

182

By her mother's bright eyes she knew she had not been slow on the uptake either.

Their suspicions were confirmed the following evening by the 'atmosphere', it was the only word for it, when they dined at the Barthes' sumptuous house near the Monceau Park, and the barbs, not so veiled, which husband and wife inflicted on each other across the table. Kate, she had told them yesterday, was there to try and 'sort things out'. Beside her tall elegance Emily was like a bright little humming-bird, brilliant and iridescent, her face just as brilliant with *maquillage*.

Next day, on an afternoon's shopping in the *rue St Honoré*, Kate told them that besides Emily having a lover, there was also the matter of Charles having a mistress . . . 'So French, so sensible,' Mother said to Maevy's astonishment, 'since Emily doesn't want to have any more children,' and Kate had concurred. 'Once you pierce her surface sophistication she's just an unsure young woman living in a strange country.' It was high time I came abroad, Maevy had thought.

She began to understand Emily's rebelliousness, even her extravagances of speech. '*Louis Quatorze*,' she remembered she had said when they had gone into the drawing-room, 'It all belongs to the Barthe family. Just look at that awful knee-hole table by Boule, so *demodée* now! And that candelabra with its ridiculous fountain of crystal drops! The pictures are all right, that little Boudin of the Normandy seashore is a dream – we spend our holidays there in our farmhouse – but that monstrous ormolu clock with its cupids, and those Sèvres vases . . .!'

But, oh, the gaiety of Paris, and driving in the *Bois de Boulogne* in the Barthe landau, and walking with Mother across the *Pont Royal* in search of Whistler's house in the *rue de Bac* (to tell Charlie). And seeing the beautiful houses in the *Faubourg St Germain* where the Barthe family had lived before the Revolution, with their carved stone foliage and shells, huge stone urns . . . no wonder the Barthes did not want their name besmirched because of a duel. Yes, a duel! It could only happen in Paris.

Charles Barthe had challenged Monsieur Vincent because Emily had been seen coming out of his *appartement*, and this was where Mother had been invited to step into the scene. She had been closeted with a tear-stained and overcome Emily for hours in her boudoir, because, as Kate explained to Maevy, she needed a 'mother figure'. She herself had always been more like a sister. 'She thinks Mother is very much *du monde*,' she had added.

At the last minute the duel had been called off. Mother had told Maevy later that she had persuaded Emily to plead with the doctor who was to be present, and he in turn had advised the seconds to shout 'Aim high!' to their gentlemen at the critical moment. Duellists always obeyed their seconds. 'Very much *du monde*,' Maevy had said, and her mother had said, 'Sometimes, Maevy, you can be quite dry.'

The trip had ended on a high note with a family expedition to the *Exposition* to see the new *Tour Eiffel*. Charles and Emily had been like cooing doves and had been very grateful to Mother who had said, smiling, '*De rien*.' Where had she learned French? And Maevy had ascended the wonderful *Tour* with Giselle and the twins, Marc and Olivier, and absorbed all their drolleries, such as, '*Je suis trois minutes plus âgé que Marc*,' so that she could tell Lizzie.

There was no doubt about it, being abroad did something for you, put things in their proper perspective, and people. Like John, for instance, who had seemed to dwindle, become more parochial, whereas Charlie had grown larger as if he was very much *du monde*, too.

19

Charlie had taken advantage of his first half-day off in that miserable winter of 1890 to gather some notes for his book. Winter was always busy in the practice with patients' ailments, mostly brought about by hard work in the mines and foundries. Colds and chills were liable to develop into pneumonia. Often death was the result.

Hadn't his father died from the same cause in the colliery at Fifeshire, and also that fine man, Kieran McGrath whose good health had been ruined by the long hours spent underground, for which he had been ill-suited? But he had lived long enough to see their firm become prosperous, and he had always had the support of a sterling wife. Anyone with parents like that was bound to be exceptional. But there was no point in thinking any more of Maevy . . .

His first call was at an unemployed carter's house in a miserable back street behind the McGrath stables. It was strange to think of a flowering business in the middle of such squalor. He wondered if it ever disturbed the two sons. One would never know what Patrick thought, but Terence was more open, at least up until that tragedy when his wife committed suicide.

His conversation with Letitia Wilcox suddenly came into his mind. She had let him off lightly, but maybe it wasn't over yet. Her father had been distinctly cool since then, and there had been no further invitations to visit at that opulent house near the Botanic Gardens. And no further mention of helping Charlie to set himself up in the same manner.

'Take my word for it, there would be.' Letitia's words came back to him. He had been telling her about Catherine's suicide, and she had asked if there had not been a note. 'Perhaps it was suppressed,' she had said. 'I read of lots of cases like it. She'd read it in her bath for the tenth time perhaps, drop it over the side in despair and slash whatever it was she slashed . . .' Suppressed? A peculiar word to use.

He had reached the close he was looking for, and when he entered it he was immediately choked by the smells that met him. In those cat- and rat-ridden tenements the close was a convenient place for the men staggering home from the ale houses to empty their bladders, or worse. No wonder the women did not 'take their turn', the rota of washing down the stone stairs and closes which was done by charwomen in the high-class tenements of Hyndland and Pollokshields.

The door he stopped at had a label on it, 'Three Adults'. The City Improvement Trust had tried hard to limit the tenants, but it had also created a breed of artful dodgers. He waited a long time at the black-painted door, scuffed white where many feet had kicked it, before it was opened by a frightened lad of about nine with a running nose and matter-filled eyes, his hair spiky with dirt.

'Is your Mammy in?' he asked.

'Aye.' He stood, holding the door.

'And your Da?'

'He's sleepin'.' He held tightly to the door.

'D'you think I could come in and see them for a minute?'

'Ur ye the Sanitary Inspector? Mammy says a've no' tae let ye in.'

'No, I'm a doctor.' He insinuated himself into the small space between the door and the wall, the boy had to

186

retreat, and he found himself in the usual tiny, dark lobby with, ahead, the door of the kitchen. It was a 'single end', with no sign of a lavatory. He remembered he had passed a door hanging on its hinges on the landing from which the stench was even worse than in the close. The boy ran into the kitchen and he followed him.

A woman was sitting, legs apart, at an ash-filled grate with a flicker of flame in the middle of the ashes. She turned, poker in hand, showing a thin, peevish face. 'Who the hell ur ye? A telt ye no' tae let anybody in, wee Boabie!' She shook the poker menacingly at the boy.

'I'm a doctor from the Royal Infirmary,' Charlie said. 'I'd like to ask you a few questions . . .'

'Whit aboot?'

'About your circumstances.'

She let out a hoot of laughter. 'Ma circumstances, is it? That's a guid yin, that is, ma circumstances! Well, that'll no' tak long to tell ye. *There*'s ma circumstances.' She pointed to the sleeping figure of a man under a dirty blanket in the bed let into the wall. 'A man who came in last night fair stottin' wi' drink and has lain in his dirty bed ever since. "There's nae work tae be had," he says to me, "A telt ye, a've been tae McGraths a hunner time and there's nae work." He's a bluidy liar! He never gets further than the Saracen's Head far less McGraths! And they weans half-starved. That's ma circumstances, an' that!' She pointed to a drawer half-open where Charlie could see only the head of a child, the rest of the body covered with a grey shawl. It was as if they all slept to escape the world they lived in. 'An' there's three mair oot playin' on the midden roofs wi' their bare feet and there's anither yin here,' she laid her hand on her swollen stomach, 'that would be better if it never saw the light o' day. Is that enough for you to be goin' on wi', dae ye think, *doactor*?'

187

Charlie had developed a tactic which seemed to work better than all the soft-voiced questions in the world. He anchored a pound note on the table with a packet each of tea and sugar and a bag of sweets, the latter being greeted with a whoop of delight from wee Boabie, 'Oh, Mammy, they're assoarted sweeties!'

'Haud yer wheesht!' she admonished him. 'A want tae hear whit the doactor's askin' me.' She pocketed the pound note and turned an attentive face.

She answered Charlie's questions after that, and the same sorry story emerged. No work, no money. Her husband was a drunkard, which was bad enough. It was even more of a heartbreak when he heard the same story from a respectable couple who did their best. Once caught in the treadmill of poverty, there was little escape.

He slipped a shilling into wee Boabie's hand as he showed him out. The hand was held out with a practised attitude. Maybe he was sent out on Friday nights, when the drinking was heaviest, to beg at alehouse doors.

He hurried along past the Tron steeple and up Castle Street towards the Infirmary. He would just be in time for the meeting. He had spent more time in that wretched house than he could spare. But what to do about such poverty in a city which had two extremes? He thought of the Wilcox house, and even his own. A book wasn't enough. You needed a solution.

There were one or two of the younger surgeons in the waiting room. He spoke to the one he knew, a man called Selkirk, one of the 'cold water and cleanliness school', and in his opinion, a bit of a bombast. 'Well, Selkirk,' he greeted him taking a seat, 'waiting to go in?'

'Oh, no, my ordeal's over. I've got another contract, as I expected. I'm waiting for Jamieson. He's in there now. We're going to celebrate, I hope.'

'There doesn't seem much to worry about,' Charlie

said. He would have liked to add, 'if they've appointed *you*.' He pointedly lifted a paper on the table and studied it, his mind still on the family he had seen. The boy was a clear case of malnutrition. He would not put it past the mother to keep him that way so that he would touch the hearts and pockets of the tipsy men at the alehouses. You're being unfair, he reproached himself. The woman's defeated.

Would they take his advice about the free Sunday breakfasts? Maybe, if they could get up early enough, and if they were prepared to send the children to Sunday School. And would she tear up the list of addresses of Charitable Societies he had given her, where she could apply for clothing? And would he have been better to save his breath to cool his porridge than expect that taciturn husband who had wakened bleary-eyed half-way through, to join the Temperance Movement? 'Me, doactor? A never touch a drap!' Nearly knocking you over with his breath at a distance of four feet. Even the promise of a good supper at the end of the meeting would never wean that one away from the bottle.

Jamieson came out and held up his thumb to his friend. 'I'm in! Where will we go?'

'Great! How about McArthur's? I fancy an ashet pie.' He turned to Charlie. 'Well, I hope they haven't run out of contracts when you go in, McNab.' He began to wrap his long scarf round his throat. Then smirking at Selkirk, he pulled the scarf up and over his mouth, 'À la McNab,' he said. He could hear their stupid giggling as they went out and down the stairs.

The clerk appeared at the communicating door. 'Dr McNab, will you come in, please?'

'Thanks.' Charlie walked into the room, outwardly confident. It was never difficult for him to assume confidence.

'Sit down, Dr McNab,' Mr McKendrick said.

Charlie smiled and sat down. He was at ease with McKendrick, especially since Arthur Cranston's operation. He had been encouraging since then in his quiet way.

'I won't beat about the bush, Dr McNab,' Mr McKendrick said, 'the voting is against your contract being renewed.' He looked down at his papers, as if he could not bear to meet Charlie's eyes. 'Five to four.' He looked up again, his face grim. 'I'd like to say personally that I'm sorry about this. I've always found you an excellent assistant, and I intend to put that on record.'

Charlie was stunned. They were not over-staffed. If he could have spared more time away from his practice he had been led to believe he could have even more sessions. He had considered going whole-time. Hadn't Mr Wilcox suggested it, made promises? He forced himself to his feet.

'Thank you, Mr McKendrick. I've enjoyed working here, especially with you, sir.' He looked round the faces at the table. One of them was Mr Wilcox's. The man turned away as their eyes met.

20

Paris had done something for Maevy because she came home determined to put the worry of the letter behind her. She qualified in midwifery that winter. The wretched homes she visited made her think of Charlie and his researches. Did he know that afterbirths had to be wrapped in newspaper for want of anything better? That often when a woman was in labour there were two or three other children in the 'hurley bed' she lay on, privy to their mother's wailing?

Often when the woman was settled with the new baby in her arms – it was strange how in spite of its poor future it was always welcomed – she would tidy the miserable kitchen, rake out and reset the fire, empty the pail of urine under the sink – nobody liked to venture on the cold stone stairs in the middle of the night to go to the communal lavatory – wash the faces of the other children and feed them with the meagre supplies in the kitchen cupboard.

A man was useless in such an emergency, she would think, taking pity on the poor shivering creature huddled in a chair. Maybe he felt guilty that he had added yet another one to his brood to be cared for because of a brief flare of lust, or love, she was not sure which. In any case, she had put all that behind her. She was Sister McGrath, in the running for Matron. She would give him a shilling or two and send him out for some hot pies as a treat, and hope he would not spend it at the corner alehouse to 'wet the wean's heid'.

She thought of herself as one of the New Women, who

fortunately did not have to defend herself against public opinion. Nursing was recognized as women's work. Her virtues were womanly virtues, her skills were womanly skills enhanced by her training. She even toyed with the idea of studying medicine. There was now the Queen Margaret College for Women and a female pathologist actually in her own Infirmary!

She played as hard that winter as she worked. Many people had acquired the new phonographs, and there were frequent parties where, instead of being pressed to sing or play, they danced to the music of this devilishly cosmopolitan machine with its waxed cylinders. She had two offers of marriage and was kissed more than once in someone's 'sitooterie'.

She hadn't as much time to go to Braidholme but she met her mother in Glasgow, either at Patrick or Terence's house. They both enjoyed putting Terence's boys to bed, now eight and three years of age.

'You spoil them,' she said to Maeve one evening. They had been promised a pony next time they came to Braidholme.

'Those ones need a bit of spoiling.'

'You're right, as always.' She smiled. 'How do you think Terence is managing?'

Her mother shook her head. 'I don't know. He's out a lot but he isn't settled. Terence has always needed a woman beside him. And I'm a wee bit worried about Sadie. She's got a young man. Robert's mostly off her hands now he's at school but Terence takes careful handling. He's . . . sensitive.'

She watched her brother later at dinner. He drank too much, but that had always been a failing of his. Catherine had complained to them often, and with justice. 'The children are the picture of health, Terence,' she said.

'Yes.' He nodded. He was thinner than usual, but if

192

anything more handsome. 'They're real fond of Mrs McLeary and I couldn't be better placed than with Sadie as long as she stays. Then there's Braidholme at weekends, and Maria's. It's not much different, from their point of view, than when their mother was here. You know how busy she was with the Temperance Movement until . . .' he lowered his head to his plate.

Maeve looked at Maevy, then at Terence. 'You could do with a holiday, son, when we get past the winter. You're losing weight.'

'I don't seem to have the same appetite for food, and that's a fact.' He had been toying with the meat and vegetables on his plate, and he laid down his knife and fork.

'There's nothing like a change of scene. Maevy and I found that out when we were in Paris. You get your skates on and think where you'd like to go. Maevy's got an invitation from Kate to visit them. How would you like that?'

'That's Patrick's territory. Anyhow, I'm not in the mood to make plans. There's plenty of trouble in the firm just now.' He lifted the decanter. 'Another glass of wine, Maevy?'

'No, thanks.' She pointed to her half-finished one.

'Mother?'

'No, thank you, son.'

He filled his own. 'No tellings off? Ah, well, we're both getting older. I'm not likely to make a fool of myself at this late date. The only exciting thing in life just now for me is McGraths. We're doing well with the Small Parcel business now, aren't we?'

She nodded. 'It's the railway companies who're grumbling. They've to put on more and more services and spend more and more paying people like us to collect.'

'You'll be working your poor old horses to death,'

Maevy said. She liked talk about the firm. She was a director, she reminded herself, appointed legally by Mother.

Her mother spoke to Terence. 'Patrick says the danger is that the railway companies will get fed up passing the profits on to us, and buy their own fleets.'

'Or try to buy us out.'

She was surprised. 'Would you let that happen, Mother?'

'I wouldn't like it, and certainly not as long as Patrick and Terence are in the business.'

'But you're not likely to draw out,' she appealed to Terence, 'are you?'

'It's my lifeline at the moment, but you never know. Sometimes I dream of being a country gentleman, a few horses to ride and train, a place in the country, not this eternal competition.'

'That's your grandfather Muldoon speaking,' his mother said.

'Blood will out.'

'Would Patrick ever give up?' Maevy asked.

'You'll never know till he does it,' her mother replied. 'America has always appealed to him, and he's more far-sighted than Terence and I are. He's never liked horses and has always looked forward to motor transport. He was saying the other day that he could see the beginning of the end with those express services springing up all over the place, specialist services for delivery of parcels and all that. You've got to set up receiving offices and shops, take the whole thing on, collect the parcels from the suppliers first, pack them in hampers, take them to the main railway station and on top of that arrange for their delivery at the other end. We would have to sink a lot of capital in a venture like that.'

'Mother's right.' Terence nodded. 'I'm angling just now

for Lipton's business, but they want our carts with their own name on them, *and* their own livery.'

'Sometimes I wonder if I'm getting too old for the whole thing,' Maeve said. 'I'm fifty-six now.'

Maevy looked at her mother. She was still a beautiful woman. Her colouring and her finely-set eyes would stay with her until she died. But her youth had gone from her. Perhaps now she hungered after a quieter life, time to visit her grandchildren, time to travel. 'I can't see you giving up the struggle, Mother,' she said.

'I can't myself.' She shook her head. 'But you never know.'

A week or two later, in early April, Maria sent out invitations to all the family, children included, to Mary's first birthday party. Maevy, walking along Claremont Terrace, and seeing the formal beds of daffodils following its curve, felt the spring tenderness of the air on her cheek. She had walked from the Infirmary along Sauchie-hall Street past Charing Cross, her step light.

And she had given in to Kate's entreaties and would soon be setting off for America. She thought of that talk she had had with her in Paris when they were driving in the Barthe landau through the *Bois de Boulogne* . . .

'You've a great capacity for love, Maevy. Don't look back.' And then, astonishing her, 'Believe me, John Craigie will never leave Isobel.' In her dismay at being so transparent she had mumbled something about having reached a bad patch in her life. The letter had been there in her mind again.

But Kate had been like Mother, practical, resilient, and beautiful, the little feathers of her hat stirring gently in the breeze to reveal the velvet underneath, with her rosy cheeks and her black glossy hair. 'Come and visit us!

James says we'll prove good wine *does* travel.' How lucky she was to have a sister like Kate.

Isobel, John and Lizzie had arrived before her, and she thought what a striking young woman Lizzie was becoming. At twelve she was tall, straight-backed, her luxuriant hair, although tied back escaping in curls on her brow, her eyes fine and deeply blue. She must resemble Mother at the same age, she thought, greeting her as she ran into her arms. 'Who's this beautiful young lady? I scarcely recognized wee Lizzie. We'll have to go back to calling you Elizabeth Maeve.'

'Oh, it's me all right! And I like Lizzie. Elizabeth Maeve sounds so stuck-up!'

'Don't turn her head,' John said, kissing Maevy on the cheek, 'you'll undo all our good work.'

'Oh, she won't spoil. Hello, Isobel.' Her sister was pale as usual, her delicate colouring like a shell, her hair still 'blind fair'. 'She'll never make old bones,' they used to say of her. If that happened, and if John were left alone . . . she was surprised at the swiftness of the thought entering her mind, as quickly banished it. And yet, talking to him there was that feeling that he resembled someone else in her life, the sweetness round the mouth. What I need, she thought, is a sudden flash of remembrance to dispel this . . . affinity, once and for all.

Maria was beside them, holding Mary, dressed in white with pink ribbons in her hair. Nothing could disguise the fact that she was a mongol. You could always tell, the small round head, the straight sparse hair, the squat, low-bridged nose, the lobeless ears. How bad Mary was, time alone would tell. It would kill Maria if she had to go into a home.

She took the child in her arms. 'And here's the birthday girl! What pretty ribbons you're wearing in your hair,

Mary!' The head rolled, the mouth widened. 'She's fairly coming on, Maria!' She felt hypocritical, saying that. 'Has she tried walking yet?'

'No, I've done my best to encourage her, but it's no good. She crawls about, and she sits on the floor like a little Buddha.'

Gaylord was holding on to his mother's skirts, a thin little boy of five, looking more normal, more handsome, because of his sister. 'She's funny, Aunt Maevy. She nurses her foot like a dolly!'

'Daddy said you weren't to laugh at her, Gee-Gee.' Sarah reprimanded her brother, severe with her burden of seven years.

'Can I hold her, please?' Lizzie had come running up. 'Oh, the wee soul!' Her eyes were bright with knowledge as she took the baby. 'She's a real wee cuddly thing, isn't she? Look at her laughing at me. When is she to open her presents, Aunt Maria?'

'Soon. We're waiting for Uncle Terence and the boys. And Grandma.' She said to Maevy, 'It's not like her to be late where family parties are concerned.'

Terence came into the room, the boys each holding a parcel. 'Well, Terence,' Maria greeted him affectionately, 'you must be proud of Terence and Robert. Such fine boys.' There was no envy in her face, but it seemed as if her youth had gone from her with the advent of Mary.

'Mrs McLeary's a treasure, and I'm more than lucky with Sadie, so far . . .' He, too, looked unhappy behind the surface charm. 'You're looking grand, Maria.' Patrick had joined them. 'I hope this taciturn brother of mine has showered you with compliments. It's like drawing water out of a stone to get anything from him.'

'He tells me all right.' She smiled at Patrick. 'But not in company.' Maevy saw the look which passed between them.

197

John, the practised talker, was dominating the conversation. 'I will say, the McGraths are grand folk for gathering together when they find an occasion to warrant it. And what better one than this, to celebrate a grand wee lassie's first birthday. I was dragged up in the slums . . .'

'Oh, John . . .' Isobel interrupted.

'I repeat, I was dragged up in the slums, and goodness knows where my relatives have got to, and so it was a grand day for me when the McGraths accepted me into their fold. There's only one person missing,' he looked around, 'the head of the family since her dead husband departed this life of care, the one who has set the pattern, I'm sure, for those convivial . . .'

'Yes, where is she?' Patrick spoke brusquely as if to stop the flow. 'It's not like Mother to miss anything.'

'Yes, where can the Queen of Ceremony be, I wonder?' John said playfully. 'Are the laws laid down that we must not eat or drink until she puts in an appearance?'

'Would you like a dram?' Patrick asked him.

'Now, that would be most acceptable, a libation, rather, if others feel inclined to join me . . .'

Terence spoke to Maevy when they were standing with their glasses in the window embrasure, 'Have you noticed John's getting a bit long-winded recently?'

'All ministers are the same. He's no worse nor no better than the rest of them.'

'No?' He sipped his drink, his eyes mischievous over the glass.

'What are you looking at me like that for?' She was suddenly angry, as much at herself as at Terence.

'I've sometimes thought that if it hadn't been for John you wouldn't have made such a damn fool of yourself.'

'The nerve of you! It's you and Mother again!'

He charmed her. 'Oh, I know it's a case of the pot

calling the kettle black. I've made a right muddle out of things.'

'You'd nothing to do with Catherine dying.' She was amazed at the turn of the conversation, how it had blown up like dry wood igniting. She looked around. The others were busily talking.

'I made her unhappy.' Her anger ran out of her. There was a letter, Terence . . . if only she could say it. 'We could never live in harmony, right from the first day. I was besotted with her as a lad, had to get her by marrying, although I knew she was the wrong woman for me.'

'It's no good turning up old stones.'

'Two women, dead because of me.'

'Catherine died because the balance of her mind was disturbed. Bessie died of puerperal fever and pneumonia.'

'Of having my child.' He took a gulp of whisky, looked around him, 'And now Lizzie's being looked after by a man who talks too much!'

'Stop punishing yourself.' She noticed Lizzie had placed Mary carefully on the rug and was running to the door, her dark red curls bobbing. 'Grandma! We're all waiting for you. Come and see Mary!'

They both stood at the doorway for a second and the similarity was striking. It was not only the looks, it was a certain inner awareness of living and liking living which showed in their eyes, in their confident stance. But there was a subtle difference today in her mother, Maevy noticed. Her back was as straight as ever, there were welcoming smiles for everybody, kisses for the children who ran to greet her.

She bent down to lay a little box tied with ribbons beside the baby, patted her head. It will be an expensive gold locket, Maevy thought, Sarah had been given one at the same age. She looked up at Maria. 'I'm sorry I'm late.

Charlie McNab called to see me just before I left. There's been a terrible accident at the Hall.'

'What's happened?' Everyone had stopped talking and drawn nearer.

'Lady Crawford was thrown at the hunt today. She's dead.'

'Oh, her poor husband!' Maria's sympathy was immediate.

'Poor bugger,' Terence said. 'Excuse me, John. Now he'll have to go through the whins, too. It comes to everybody.' He gulped his whisky. 'Aye, it comes to everybody.' There was a sombre satisfaction in his voice.

They talked about the accident during the buffet Maria had provided with its usual American delicacies from the Italian Warehouse in Howard Street.

'Left with one boy, Nigel, isn't it?'

'What age is he?'

'Ages with Lizzie.'

'Is he at a boarding school?'

'They all go.'

'But he'll be home for the funeral?'

'Aye, I expect so.'

'It will be a lonely house for Lord Crawford when he goes back, that big place.'

'Do you remember him when he was the Honourable Alastair . . . you knew him then, didn't you, Mother . . .'

'Yes, long ago that was . . . long ago.'

21

When, on her next day off, Maevy went to Braidholme, she found Lizzie sitting companionably with her mother on the sofa in front of the fire. It was one of those unpredictable days in spring when the season went tumbling backwards. There was a snell wind blowing off the Sholtie, and the garden looked uninviting in its windswept greyness. Even the daffodils had their colour drained out of them.

But her mother was one of those people who created her own environment and the room was cosy with a clear bright fire burning in the old brick fireplace. What a comfortable room it was, she thought, with its hunting prints of Father's, its chintzes, its great bunches of daffodils lighting up the dark corners.

'Look what the wind's blown in!' Maevy said, hugging Lizzie when she came running towards her. 'What are *you* doing here?'

'Aunt Maevy, you'll never guess! Grandma's sending me with you if you'll take me.'

'Sending you where?'

'To America! Isn't it the best news you've ever had? *Is* it the best news? I'll be as good as gold. I'll do whatever you tell me.'

'Is she making this up, Mother?' Maevy asked her.

'Devil a fear of it. Would you take this spalpeen with you?' She laughed at herself. 'Lizzie, run to the kitchen and tell Susan to let us know when the carriage arrives. And have a look at the new kitten she has. It's in a nice wee bed at the grate.'

'What's all this?' Maevy asked when Lizzie had gone out. 'Carriages at the door, and Lizzie coming with me to America?'

'Sit down and warm yourself. I was wondering if you'd come on such a day. Well, first we're going to a birthday tea at the Hall. I met Lord Crawford at the kirk last Sunday and he said it was his son's birthday today. And he suggested that maybe I could bring Lizzie, someone of his own age.'

'I thought he would have been back at school by this time.'

'He would have been, but he's been in bed with a chill, it seems.'

'But Lord Crawford won't want me.'

'Yes, you're invited. I said you would be here today.'

'That's very kind of him. Do you think he's getting over the death of his wife?'

'As well as he can, I imagine. There's no alternative. You do it for the children's sake if nothing else.'

'I'd have dressed better if I'd known.'

'You look fine, my lovely. That navy sets off your fairness. Before Lizzie comes back, tell me honestly, would you mind taking her with you?'

'To tell you the truth I was a bit fearful of going on my own. She'll be great company. But what will Isobel and John say?'

'Oh, they're pleased. At least I had to talk them round, but one thing, they think well of you as guardian. I thought it was high time she saw a bit of the world and got away from them for a while. If they're not careful they'll be making a Holy Willie out of her. Besides, I want her to get to know her American cousins.'

'Have you told Kate?'

'I'll write to her today. She'll be pleased. She has a big heart and James is the same.'

'You should have come, too.'

'No, it was Lizzie or me. Besides, I'm needed in the business just now. Terence is setting up a new office in Dalmuir to try and catch some of the shipping trade, and another one out at Shettleston for the ironworks. It's a case of having as many irons in the fire as possible in case our contract with the railways finishes.'

'What would you do?'

'Think of something else. If, as Patrick always says, we go into motor transport in time, there are always removals to fall back on. The first money your father ever made was shifting a widow's things to her daughter's house in Sholton. She gave him that desk in the window. Her daughter hadn't any room for it. Five shillings, he charged, but you can't put a price on that desk, not for me.'

'I can believe it. So, we've constantly to be one step ahead?'

'It's the same in everything, and we're living in exciting times. Patrick says we'll soon have electric trams and telephones . . . well, you know our firm was one of the first to be on the Douglas Exchange. He'd like one in their house now so that he could 'phone the office. And maybe in time you could telephone me from the Infirmary instead of coming all this way to say you're not coming!' She laughed. 'There, that's Irish for you!'

'Those poor horses – no longer needed after all their faithful service.' Lizzie came running in.

'The carriage is here from the Hall, Grandma. Susan says to tell you.'

'Well, we're ready. Are your hands clean?'

'Yes, I've washed them again. Susan made me at the sink after holding wee Ginger. Oh, he's lovely!'

'I hope he isn't a rampager like his father or we'll be polluted with Gingers.'

203

Maevy got up to put on her coat again. 'This is too much excitement in one day for me, a visit to the Hall, and Grandma telling me I've to take you to America.'

'Are you going to take me?' Lizzie's eyes were anxiously on her.

'On one condition.'

'What's that?'

'You've to coorie doon in my hamper the whole way, and I'll feed you on bread and water . . .'

'Oh, Aunt Maevy! You're going to take me. That's great.' She threw herself into Maevy's arms.

'Here, don't knock me over, you big lump.'

But she was on her best behaviour when they reached the Hall, quiet, copying her grandmother's dignity, shaking hands shyly with Lord Crawford and then his son, Nigel. Maeve had given her a present to take to him. 'Happy birthday, Nigel,' she said, as she had been told.

He was a tall, dark-haired boy, not yet as elegant as his father, but with the same sloping shoulders and amber eyes. He had none of his mother in him at all, Maevy thought, remembering the woman at Maria's Christmas party four or five years ago now. She had been haughty, 'distant', as they called it at home, only seeming to come alive when the talk turned to horses.

'Oh, thanks a lot,' the boy said. 'What is it?'

'Open it and see,' Lizzie said, forgetting her dignity.

'That's a sensible suggestion.' His father smiled. 'How are you, Mrs McGrath, and Miss McGrath?' He shook hands with both of them. 'I'm glad you were able to come.'

'It's good of you to ask me,' Maevy said. 'I was sorry to hear of your bereavement, Lord Crawford.'

'Thank you.' His amber eyes rested on her. She remembered him in the kirk when he had been the Honourable

204

Alastair and the dash of him as he had walked up the aisle after his father and mother. The dash had gone, but not the looks nor the elegance. He looked more of a lord than his father had done.

Mrs Robertson, his housekeeper, was standing in the background, and she led Maevy, her mother and Lizzie upstairs to leave their coats. 'It's nice you've brought Lizzie with you,' she offered. 'He's a lonely young lad, Nigel. Best when he goes back to school. He's had a troublesome cough and cold and Dr McNab advised keeping him off for another week.'

'That was wise.' Maeve smoothed her hair. How this place suited her, Maevy thought, patting her own hair at the mirror, with her dignity, the lift of her chin. You had to feel proud of her.

When they went downstairs Charlie was there chatting with Lord Crawford. He shook hands with them.

'I haven't seen you in the Infirmary for some time,' Maevy said, taken aback.

'Maybe not.' He was short. 'How are you, Mrs McGrath? I've got to ask her that, your lordship,' he said, turning to him, 'she never graces my surgery.'

'She's impervious to minor ailments, I should think.' Maevy saw how their eyes met. 'You'll join us for tea, doctor, I hope. We're just sitting down to it, a full-sized birthday tea, I'm told by the kitchen. Nigel's twelve today.'

'Well, many happy returns.' Charlie shook hands with the boy. 'It's kind of you, sir. I just looked in to see that he was all right to go back to school. If I could just sound him before . . . ?'

'Take the doctor up to your room, Nigel,' his father said, and when they had both gone, turned to Maevy. 'You'll be a good judge of doctors, Miss McGrath. What do you think of Dr McNab?'

She was surprised at the question. 'He's highly thought of in the Royal, but Mother's a better person to answer that than I am.'

'I've little doubt what *her* answer would be.' Again the smiling look, but of course they had both lived in Sholton a long time . . .

'He's seen me through a lot, and he's blessed with a sense of humour. I can't tell you how he helped me through Kieran's illness . . . and death.'

'Ah, yes.' He sighed. 'Well, let's hope he can see me through my loss. It's how it affects the young that I worry most about. An only child . . .'

'They have to know death sooner or later. And there's Maevy. She sees it every day of her life.'

'You never get used to it,' she said. She looked at Lizzie who was sitting, on her best behaviour, feet together, hands clasped on her lap.

What went on in children's minds while their elders talked around them? She remembered lying in bed with Isobel long ago at Colliers' Row on that night when Patrick and Terence had come home drunk. And how puzzled she had been. One moment she had heard the boys getting a telling-off, and the next moment, it seemed, she could hear her mother and father's smothered laughter from their bed in the kitchen. She had felt shut off from a world, a parents' world, which she would only know when she became a parent herself.

Charlie and Nigel came back, Charlie with his arm round the boy's shoulders. 'Well, there's nothing to worry about with this lad, Lord Crawford. His chest is as sound as a bell. He can go back to school as soon as he likes.'

'That's good news, Nigel, isn't it?'

'Jolly good news, sir.' Maevy saw Lizzie's head rise. She would be treated to an impersonation of the Honourable Nigel later.

A young footman came in. 'Tea is ready, my lord.'

'Thank you. And will you tell Mrs Robertson to set an extra place? Dr McNab will be joining us.'

It was an enjoyable meal, thanks to Lizzie and Charlie, Maevy thought. She herself felt subdued. The visit had been sprung on her, and then Charlie's presence had been a surprise. She studied him while he was teasing Lizzie about eating too much, getting Nigel to smile, too. She noticed Lord Crawford and her mother were deep in conversation on their own.

Charlie was thinner, but then she always thought that when she saw him after a lapse. He was getting older, like her. He must be in his middle thirties now. Mr Wilcox had been back since September, and presumably his daughter, so why had their wedding not been announced? It's none of your business, she told herself, watching him applauding with Nigel and Lizzie when the young footman came in bearing the birthday cake. They had never had birthday cakes at Colliers' Row. A clootie dumpling was all they could afford, but how good they had been with their shiny beige-coloured skins holding such a richness of fruit.

Nigel's present from Lizzie had been a set of dominoes, and after tea they played with them at a small table. She saw his father look approvingly at them when they laughed together.

The day had brightened, and from the tall windows they could see the park and the curving drive with the spring sun shining weakly on the red blaes. Charlie had not sat down. 'It's getting near the time for my evening surgery,' he said, 'I'm afraid I'll have to be going. Don't worry, I'll show myself out.'

'I quite understand,' Lord Crawford said. 'By the way, MacFarlane has a few cuttings for you in the greenhouse.

You must have made the mistake of admiring one of his pride and joys.'

Charlie laughed. 'It was a barberry, I think. He said it was early flowering. I'll stop on the way and collect them.'

'And there's also one of my special orchids for Braidholme there,' he smiled at Maeve, 'a *Bella cymbidium*.'

'That's kind of you. I've never had the patience to grow them.'

'Would you like me to bring it back to you?' Charlie asked her.

'No, you're in a hurry. You go with him, Maevy. The fresh air will do you good after being shut up in that Infirmary.'

They walked down the curving drive together. At Braidholme the flagged paths were so narrow in places that you had to walk in single file. 'Mother's convinced the Royal is like a leper colony,' she said, 'but I seem to survive. I haven't seen you there recently.'

'Have you missed me?' She felt him looking at her.

'No, I just thought it was strange. We used to meet.'

'I haven't had my contract renewed.'

'Oh, Charlie!' She turned to him. 'What a disappointment for you!' She felt the hurt as if it were her own. 'Someone must have stopped it. There were no complaints about you . . .'

'I'm no longer visiting the Wilcox household.'

She was astonished at the delight which surged through her. Was he implying there was a connection? It was well-known in the Royal that if a young surgeon attracted the attention of one of his elders, he was as good as made. 'I'm sorry . . .'

'I thought of writing to you but dismissed it. You've let me know pretty definitely what you think of me.'

'I've always had . . . a high opinion of you . . . something's been in the way, but, now, oh, I can't explain . . .'

It's this new, incredible lightness of heart, she wanted to say, gave up. 'Are you going to apply to another hospital?'

He looked at her, puzzled. No wonder, she thought, with this babbling. 'No, I'll finish my book, my panacea. Besides, my heart's in general practice, always has been, though I'll miss surgery. Maybe they won't miss me. I was a thorn in the flesh of quite a few.' They reached the greenhouses. 'There's Mr MacFarlane inside.' The old man looked up, saw them, and beckoned. They went in, the damp green smell in their nostrils.

'Well, doctor. And young Maevy McGrath isn't it?'

'Not so young now, Mr MacFarlane.'

'Just as bonny anyhow. I've got a fine orchid here for your mither. Nothing but the best, his lordship said.'

'And have you got my humble cuttings as well?' Charlie asked.

'Aye, doctor, waiting for you. You'll have fine flowers on them in another month. And tell your mother to keep the orchid in a warm place, Maevy. They're delicate things.'

'She's a dab hand with plants but I'll tell her.'

'A capable woman, your mother.'

'It's a big place to run,' Maevy said when they were walking back to the house. 'Lord Crawford will miss his wife.'

'If he does he won't show it.'

'I suppose not.' *I'll finish my book, my panacea* . . . Of course he had lost interest in her long ago, and no wonder . . .

'Do you ever feel,' she said, 'that the whole system is wrong? Look how he's looked up to in Sholton, how they speak of the Hall with bated breath. Look at the sense of privilege that boy, Nigel, is going to be burdened with.'

'Maybe he won't regard it as a burden, more of a responsibility.'

209

'There's a lack of freedom anyhow.'

'Freedom is of the spirit. They're in an enviable position, providing jobs, for instance. I counted three men in those greenhouses, and there are the stables. Lady Crawford never spared men there. And look what the pits and the foundries have done in giving jobs to the folks around.'

'There was enough work for the real Sholton people. It's incomers who're getting the advantage. And when the pits and the foundries peter out, what state will Sholton be in then?' Why doesn't he stop me? she thought, change the subject, ask me what I meant when I was stuttering and stammering . . .

'You're in a thrawn mood, Maevy.' He shook his head at her. 'I thought you were all for advance.'

'I am and I'm not, and that's contrary, if you like. It might be because my father and mother had different upbringings and I see both sides.'

'Mine didn't, but I'm like you in many ways. I want to see advances in medicine, but I've got a picture of myself as the country doctor driving with my pony and trap to my cottage.'

'And roses round the door?'

'Yes, there's only one thing missing.'

A warmth enveloped her. It would come all right. Give it time . . . she did not want to go away from him now, to America. They had reached the main door with its broad flight of steps. She turned to him. Her voice sounded shy in her ears. 'Have you your horse or are you walking?'

'Walking.' His eyes were brilliant, and yet moist. Like blae-berries. What a thing to think! 'It's no distance. So you'll be off to America soon?'

'Yes, I'm taking Lizzie with me.' *I don't want to go* . . .

'She'll keep you busy. Maevy . . . damn it,' he pulled out his watch, 'I'm always in a rush. They go mad if I keep them waiting, and so does Biddy . . . when my contract wasn't renewed I wanted to come and tell you, but I stopped myself. You'd made it so plain you weren't interested.'

'Folks change. You could have tried me.'

'All those years I've tried. You gave me no encouragement. But the fact of the matter is, Maevy McGrath, I can't get over you.'

The happiness expanding in her made her pull her mouth straight. 'And you're not desolated because Miss Wilcox broke it off?'

'Desolated?' He laughed. 'Me desolated?' He leaned forward and planted a good sound kiss on her mouth. '*That*'s how desolated I am. God, I must go. These patients . . . Will you think of me, of us, when you cross the mighty ocean? "I had a mighty notion to cross the mighty ocean . . ." What's that song? I'm babbling. I'm as light as air. I've got to go . . .' She called after him.

'I'll think of me, us . . .!'

'I'm counting on it!' He turned and waved.

22

The Blue Riband liner which Maevy and Lizzie sailed on was if anything grander than that which her mother and Patrick had described to her. The gracious staterooms, the deck areas where they played quoits, the wonderful orchestras and the luxurious food, lived up to the Anchor Line's reputation for floating palaces.

And yet in the midst of all the excitement of their two-berth cabin and the steward who waited on them hand and foot, and careering about the ship after Lizzie – 'You're as good as a poodle,' she told her, 'everybody speaks to me because of you' – she thought a lot about that last meeting with Charlie at the Hall.

Was it that which made her glow like an oil-lamp inside, dance in the evenings with feet as light as a feather's, feel herself at times as young as Lizzie? 'Oh, Aunt Maevy, it's great fun to be with you. The dullness of the manse, you've no idea. Daddy used to be fun, but he's got *that* serious, and he babys Mother. When I grow up and get married I wouldn't let a man baby me, we'll be equals. Why have you not got married? Oh, I'm sorry, Mother told me not to ask that.'

'Maybe I haven't met anyone who's taken my fancy.'

'I saw Dr McNab looking at you that day we went to the Hall. Nigel says he's "awfully jolly, don't you know".' It was a perfect rendition of Nigel's English way of speech.

'It's rude to make fun of people.'

'I did it when we were playing dominoes and he said I was "quite a card". And I said, "It's *dominoes* we're playing!" That made him laugh. I was doing my best to cheer him up.'

'And I think Grandma was doing her best to cheer his father up.'

'Did Dr McNab need cheering up?'

'No, he's "awfully jolly, don't you know".'

'Oh, don't make me laugh!' The girl's face was a pleasure to look at, the liveliness of it. 'Aunt Maevy, I was thinking of that tea later in bed, and do you know what struck me? We were three *couples*, me and Nigel, Grandma and Lord Crawford, and you and Dr McNab . . . as if we were meant to be that way.'

And she felt as young as Lizzie, dizzy with excitement when the great ship was berthing at New York and they got their first sight of the jumble of buildings lining the water-front. 'I can't understand how there's room for them all on that little island. Do any ever fall into the water?'

And Lizzie's presence helped her with her shyness when she saw the figure of James, Kate's husband, Mr Murray-Hyslop, waiting for them after they had docked and been cleared. His clothes had an American dash, a grey waisted frock-coat with a black velvet collar, a grey top hat banded in black, a silver-topped cane, a New York city gentleman.

'Welcome to America,' he said, sweeping off his hat, 'I knew you at once! You still look like that little girl whom I last saw on the Broomielaw.' He had changed little, perhaps a little more girth, but the wry charm was the same as she remembered, and the humorous lift to his mouth.

'And this is Lizzie,' she said, when he had embraced her. There was a smell of pomade from him, a man's smell, new to her after the smells of the wards; Kate's man, she thought, enjoying the masculinity of it.

213

'You don't have to tell me that.' He kissed Lizzie, too. 'She's your mother all over again.'

The journey to Wanapeake was swift and, as she said to James, she knew every inch of the way. Both her mother and Patrick had given her vivid descriptions, Patrick calling it Vanderbilt's triumph and extolling the engineering of such a difficult track, the cuts and tunnels, her mother the beauty of a railway which followed so closely the course of the river. The Hudson was all Maria had said, lapping up to the very rails, broad like the Firth of Clyde, and as busy.

And her first sight of Wolf House as the carriage drew up was no surprise, because a clear picture of it hung in her mind from her mother's description. The setting sun was flushing its red brick, warming its many white painted windows with their white shutters open like welcoming arms. There was the 'French style' roof and the four rooms set in it – that one on the right might have been Emily's which she shared with her sister, Victoria, before she married, before men fought duels over her! And there was the wide porch which she had always peopled with Mr and Mrs Murray-Hyslop as it had been at the beginning, the children, small as she had known them when they came to Sholton, and Kate dressed in her navy-blue high-necked dress with its small band of white, her uniform as the children's nurse.

And the trees. 'So many tall trees,' Kate had said in that first letter home, 'that you can imagine Chief Sachem himself creeping through them with his bow and arrow and his row of scalps on his belt.' But beyond them, she knew, was the shining river which had become already like a friend.

But nothing could have prepared her for the welcome in the large drawing-room when James ushered them in with the words, 'And here's the Scottish contingent.' She was in Kate's arms, both weeping with happiness, then she had to meet Kieran, their son, seven months younger than Lizzie but as tall, and so like the pictures of his grandfather that her eyes overflowed again.

Then there was Victoria, a toned-down replica of Emily, older by two years and already matronly-looking, and with a stout young man tightly buttoned into his frock-coat, who was introduced as 'Jason, my husband,' with a smug air. And her brother, George, who looked, unlike his father, as if he had the cares of the business on his shoulders. Ernest, who was finishing at Yale, would be home on Sunday when they would have a family party. Kate had mother's liking for family gatherings.

And last, but certainly not least, there was a straight-backed man wearing a floral waistcoat, with deeply blue eyes and the manners of an Irish gentleman which he was, as her mother had often said: Uncle Terence, very much in the flesh. 'Maevy McGrath! The last of the bunch. Well, they say you should keep good things to the end.' A warm embrace. 'And Lizzie!' Another hearty embrace. Lizzie's feet left the ground. 'The Muldoon blood's there all right. Did anyone ever tell you how like your grand-mother you are?'

'Yes, *she* did,' Lizzie said. 'She's always telling me to sit straight in the saddle, like the Muldoons.' Terence roared with laughter. 'What do you think of that, Caroline? The same all over again, wouldn't you say?'

'She certainly reminds me of dear Maeve.' The petite woman with the golden curls and the lined face kissed them in turn. 'And dear Maevy. Not so like, but it's there all the same.' She was fussily dressed, 'all buttons and bows', Mother had said. 'When you get your breath back you must tell me all about my darling daughter.' Her hand trembled as she touched her hair. Maevy remembered what Maria had told her about the nervous breakdown.

215

Kate took them upstairs to 'freshen up' after their journey. American expressions were creeping into her speech, and she had almost lost her Scottish accent. Lizzie will be storing it all away, she thought. 'We'll just have a light supper tonight and let you get to bed early, but tomorrow Ernest will be home for the family party. It's a double celebration. He's just got his degree, then he goes to New York to work in an accountant's office.'

'I thought he'd be going in with his father and George?'

'No, James says he prefers them to sow their wild oats first without him looking over their shoulder.'

'It'll be lovely to see everyone gathered together. And Victoria has children, hasn't she?'

'Yes, two at the moment, but I doubt if she's finished. Her interest lies in the home. Not like Emily.' She sighed, but her eyes were full of laughter. 'That farcical duel! She worships Mother as a result.'

'Very much *du monde*.' They laughed together. 'Maybe we'll get to the bottom of that some time. It was all so exotic to me. Life is real and earnest in the Royal. And now, coming here and seeing your lovely home . . .'

'Yes, I'm blessed, but it doesn't count compared with James. There I'm truly blessed.' She looked at Lizzie who was standing at the window. 'Grown-up talk, Lizzie. But we have a special surprise for you.'

'What is it?' Lizzie turned, her eyes bright.

'Can you ride a bicycle?'

Lizzie shook her head. 'I think I could if I had one, but I haven't. I've been saving up for a long time, but they cost a terrible lot, Mother says.'

'Well, there's one for you to ride in the stables, and you, too, Maevy. They're the greatest fun.'

'I've never tried it. What a boon it would have been for me when I was doing my midwifery.'

'Well, tomorrow you'll try, and you, too, Lizzie. And

then when you're proficient in the grounds we'll set off for a picnic ride. Ernest is very keen, Jason might join in although the prospect of falling off is not so appealing to him, James and I ride tolerably, but Kieran is the best performer. We tell him he ought to go into a circus!'

'Oh, I'm glad Grandma had the idea of sending me here,' Lizzie said, clapping her hands, 'I'm going to have a grand time!'

It took Maevy and Lizzie a few days to get the hang of bicycling, and in between Kate took them shopping and bought them riding costumes, navy-blue bloomers, white blouses with ties, and boaters which were worn with elastic under the chin to keep them on in the wind. In the privacy of their bedroom Maevy and Lizzie tried on their costumes, and the sight of themselves in the mirror was so inexpressibly funny to them that it had them rolling on their beds.

'Oh, oh!' Maevy wailed, 'I've a stitch in my side . . .' It was true. For a second she was doubled up with the swift pain which shot through her like a red-hot poker, and then it was gone.

'What's wrong?' Lizzie said, sitting up.

'Nothing. I mustn't laugh so much.' Her legs felt like jelly.

Another day they took the ferry to Wallace Point and Springhill, Uncle Terence's fine house overlooking the Hudson. Again there was the sense of familiarity from Isobel's and Mother's description. There was the columned portico, much grander than the Wolf House porch, however pleasant that was to sit on during the fine evenings, and inside the wide central staircase dividing at the top, a staircase for sweeping down in a ball dress.

Aunt Caroline showed them the bedroom Isobel and Maria had shared, but best of all was the beautiful view from its window of the wide lawns, the even wider

Hudson, the broad shining expanse of it, and on the other side, the tall square roof of Wolf House could be seen through the trees.

'Now, my dear,' she said to Maevy, 'you must sit down here and tell me every little thing about Maria.' Maevy did her best, minimizing her description of Mary.

'Sarah and Gaylord adore their little sister,' she said. 'With all that love round her she could grow – the way a flower does.'

'Oh, do you think so?' The woman touched her hair with a nervous hand. 'Such a tragedy. We've had enough tragedies . . .' she looked away, biting her lip.

'Maria doesn't think of it that way, Aunt Caroline, she feels she's lucky compared with Terence because of Catherine's . . .' She stopped herself in time, but perhaps not. Her aunt had got up, smoothing her dress, touching the curls behind her ears which seemed to tremble with agitation.

'Perhaps we should go down now. Tea will be served.'

'Certainly.' How tactless of me, she thought, and again, no wonder Maria has those fears about Mary with such a nervous mother. Sometimes the dead, she was thinking of Maria's Uncle Gaylord, can cast a shadow on the living. There was a small blot on the pleasant afternoon, no bigger than the sail of the yacht tacking out on the river while they sat at the window. And with the slight lowering of her spirits came the thought of the letter . . .

After tea her uncle walked with her in the grounds while Caroline took Lizzie to see the stables. Before they left she was to have a short ride under his direction. 'We don't want you to land on your head and then they'd be blaming me back home!'

'Is it all you pictured, Maevy?' he asked her.

'Yes, all of it. It's like a picture book come to life. Mother still talks of her visit.'

218

'She must come back. But has she never returned to Ireland at all?'

'No. She's sorry she didn't go with my father. She once said to me, "That was the only wish of his I didn't honour." He had a great love for the old country. Perhaps Mother not so much.'

'Ah yes, I'm sure the love was there, but truth to tell, we didn't have a very happy time at Woodlea. It seemed my father was irascible and my mother always whining, you know the harsh judgements of the young. So I got out as soon as I could. Maeve did the same. Kieran was the means.'

'But he loved her.'

'Yes, he was steadfast. And a sweet-tempered lad. Kieran McGrath was liked by everyone although no one ever thought of him as a suitable match for my sister. She'll go back to Ireland, mark my words. There will be a right time.'

'Terence has a notion to go. Mother says there's a bit of his grandfather Muldoon in him.'

'Well, I hope it's the right bit, because there was a lot I couldn't admire in my father when I was young. But there it is, Maevy, you reach the years of discretion and your opinions change. Now I see him as an unhappily married man at odds with himself. Take it from me, the people who say they never change their minds are the ones to be feared. We grow all the time, in my case outwards.' He laughed and patted his round stomach.

She thought of her long obsession with John Craigie, and how, slowly, that was diminishing, as if his image had been cracked, how in fact *his* mind was not growing but becoming more rooted in his prejudices. And how Charlie, with his volatile searching mind, was a man of quicksilver in comparison.

Now when she thought of Charlie it was with a feeling

of delicious anticipation. John no longer claimed her thoughts. Miss Wilcox had dropped out of the picture. And, in addition, there were those piercing thrills which she was experiencing as she lay in bed, strange, disturbing. Had she done that incredible thing, at last fallen in love?

'What have I said to make your eyes shine so, Maevy?' Her uncle was speaking to her. 'Was it that high-falutin' philosophy of mine?'

'Maybe.' She laughed, feeling vibrant, even her fingertips were tingling. 'And I'm just suddenly happy, Uncle Terence.'

'That's good to hear. And do you think my daughter is happy in Scotland?'

'I'm sure she is. She and Patrick are ideally suited.'

'Your aunt worries a lot about the baby.'

'I know. Is it because they're cousins?' She could be franker with him than his wife.

He nodded. 'A feeling, I think, that weaknesses come out when the parents are too closely related.'

'But lots of cousins marry and have healthy babies. No blame can be attached to anyone.' She smiled at him. 'And there's the McGrath and Muldoon blood as well to be taken into account. It's all just luck.'

'But poor little Mary . . . she's definitely not normal?'

'She's a mongol. Maybe Maria feels she would find some miracle cure here if she came back. It isn't likely.'

'No, it isn't likely. I tell Caroline that.' He sighed. 'Patrick writes to me. He's taken by America.'

'He sees changes coming back home. The carters aren't as ignorant as they were. They're beginning to demand their rights.'

'And why not? The class system in Britain is the curse of their industry. Only when the owners stop regarding

220

themselves as superior beings will they get their relations right with their workers.'

'Oh, I agree! I don't think I'd succeed in business at all. I'd be on the wrong side.'

'Maybe it's people like you they need in it. But you're happy in what you're doing?'

'It has its own rewards.'

'Well, you stick to what you want to do and pay no attention to what the women-folk tell you. They've got, even the best of them, the "Come in, the water's fine" mentality, but they don't tell you that you can drown in it as well.'

'I'll remember what you say,' she said, laughing.

23

They chose the following Saturday for their picnic ride as Ernest would be home from Yale, and the week after that Lizzie and Maevy would be going home. The day dawned warm and sunny, and after breakfast they all trooped out to the stables to collect their steeds, as Ernest put it. He was a carefree young man, very smart, very conscious of his new degree and determined to show the world how things were done by a Yale man.

Lizzie had confided to Maevy in their bedroom that she thought he was very 'posh'. 'He speaks to me as if I were grown up, too,' she said. 'He asked me where I was being *finished*. He nearly laughed his head off when I said I hoped I wouldn't be finished until I died. What does it mean, Maevy?'

'A finishing school is what Emily and Victoria went to in Paris. It's to improve your manners and deportment and your foreign languages, and so on.'

'I think I wouldn't mind being finished here with my American cousins. What are the French ones like?'

'Very formal, "*bien élèvé*". That's a phrase I learned from Emily.'

Lizzie was thoughtful. 'It's strange. Before I came here I thought Sholton was the world. Now it's suddenly grown much bigger, America and France, and it's not only the size, it's discovering that people think differently. I thought there was only one way to think . . .'

'What was that?'

Lizzie looked at her. 'I don't know the word for it. The manse way?'

'I know what you mean. You're finding out that travel broadens the mind.'

Ernest had brought his own bicycle, the very latest model, but James had provided solid-tyred drop frame 'safeties' for the ladies while he and George rode 'ordinaries'. Perched on the top of their fifty-six inch wheels, they were monarchs of all they surveyed, but as Lizzie said, 'Thank goodness Uncle James doesn't expect us to mount these. It would have been most unladylike.'

'That's the reason for the bloomers,' Maevy said.

When they assembled in front of the house she could see Lizzie's eyes on Ernest who was resplendent in his Club costume, sage-green knee breeches, a tight-fitting tunic with silver buttons and liberally befrogged, a Yale badge on his pork pie cap and pedalling shoes of white, laced with green.

'What a sight you look!' Kieran said to his step-brother.

'Better than your hairy Norfolk! You'll be sweating like a pig long before we reach Wanapeake Point.'

'Language in front of the ladies,' James said. 'You aren't in a Yale pot-house.'

Uncle Terence and Aunt Caroline arrived in the carriage which had been sent to meet them at the ferry, the hampers were stowed in beside them, and with Terence assuring everyone that in fact he was a champion cyclist but that he had only agreed to ride in the carriage so that it would be available as an ambulance, they were off, Maevy shakily in the rear with Kate, Lizzie ahead between Kieran and Ernest, and George and James leading the cavalcade.

'This is the grandest fun,' Maevy said when she could safely look sideways at Kate. 'Wait till I tell Mother all about it.'

'She likes riding a horse better, but we had a lovely sail one day up the river. I hope you've time for that, too.'

She gained confidence as they pedalled through the village, and by the time they had crossed the bridge and were on the road which ran round the Point, she was riding with such *élan* that she was able to look round and admire the scenery. 'I can get an "old" feeling here,' she said to Kate, 'a sense of mystery. That long ago there were a different kind of people . . .'

'It's where the Indians once lived. Ernest and George found an arrow-head of theirs about here. I get that "inhabited" feeling, too. Once it came to me very strongly indeed. I was walking with the boys and someone had lit a fire on the beach. It was very quiet, a *still* quietness, and there was the smell of driftwood in the air. I thought that I might find Indians sitting round the fire . . .'

'It makes you believe in spirits.'

'Especially when you crunch oyster shells under your feet. This was their last outpost and they defended their control of the Hudson fisheries with terrible battles. Listen!' She put her hand to her ear.

'What?'

'Can't you hear their war-cries?'

'You are a tease, Kate!' But wasn't that a faint rhythmic shouting coming from beyond the swampy land beside the shore?

'Am I scaring you?' Kate laughed. 'It's all long ago. The Peace Treaty was signed with Henry Hudson at the beginning of the seventeenth century.'

'Was the Hudson named after him?'

'Yes, he discovered it. He was with the Dutch East Indies Company. James knows more about it than I do. Oh, here he is.' James had cycled back to see how they were getting on. 'Just the man we're looking for. Can you hear me up there?'

224

'Yes, my darling, but don't ask me to gaze into your eyes when you're speaking, much as I love you.'

'Some love!' she laughed. 'We're talking about the Indians.'

'A much maligned race. Did you know that it was the Dutch who taught them the gentle art of scalping? It's a shame to blame the Indians, poor souls. They're being slowly decimated everywhere. Over a million in the fifteenth century and now just a fraction of that.'

'Kate's been trying to scare me. I could even hear the soft pad of their moccasins in those bushes. Perhaps they're looking at us at this very moment.'

'You've got the right type of mind, imaginative. I say,' his eyes were looking ahead, 'look at that young niece of yours! She's racing with Ernest. She's very like her grandmother, isn't she? Full of spirit.'

'She's having the time of her life.'

Kate nodded. 'I get the feeling she's held down somewhat at the manse. Is she?'

'Well, it *is* a manse. They have to set an example for Sholton. Maybe because she isn't their daughter, they're being extra careful.'

'They've never told her of her real parentage?'

'No.'

'That's a great mistake. The shock will be all the greater if she finds out.'

'Mother and I think that.'

'They'll have difficulty with her when she's older. James believes in a more liberal attitude.'

'*Do* you?' Maevy asked him.

'Yes, although I try to instil the essential values. But we've found, haven't we Kate, that environment isn't everything. Look at Emily, wilful from the first day, and look at George there.' He had wandered away from them.

225

Maevy could see him standing gazing out across the Wanapeake.

'Quiet, sober and industrious, but do I detect a certain dreaminess?' She smiled at Kate.

'He's mooning about a girl, Mr Van Dam's young daughter, a near neighbour. One of the old Dutch families around here. She's away at school just now.'

'He's in love.' She felt she could understand. 'Why aren't Jason and Victoria here today?'

'She sent a note this morning. She was feeling a little sick. I thought as much.' She smiled. 'And Jason is very husbandly. He wouldn't leave her.'

There was the roll of carriage wheels and Terence and Caroline came into view round the bend. The coachman brought the horses to a halt. Terence, with a wave, jumped out, then helped Caroline. 'How are the speedsters? Don't tell me you're resting already?'

'We're waiting for Kieran and Lizzie,' James said. 'They're being poled across the creek by the boatman.'

'Ah, yes. Ben,' he turned to the coachman, 'lift down the champagne, if you please. I think it's time for refreshments.'

'Champagne!' Maevy said, watching the white napkin being wrapped round the bottle. 'I've only had it at weddings.'

'Here we do things in an altogether grander fashion.' He winked at her and opened the bottle with a flourish. 'Ben, glasses, please.' They were being handed around on a silver tray when Kieran, Lizzie and Ernest joined them.

'You're doing us proud, Uncle,' Ernest said.

'Well, knowing how you young fellows at Yale have it every morning for breakfast . . . here you are, my dear.' He handed a glass to Lizzie. 'This will refresh you after your trip.'

'Oh, isn't it fizzy! Thanks. What is it?'

'D'you mean to say you don't know?' Kieran said. 'It's champagne, of course.'

'You've never had any,' Ernest said. 'You were too young at the sisters' weddings. So don't show off.'

'Well, I think he's old enough now.' Terence raised his glass. 'To our travellers. And may they return to our shores before long.'

'To our travellers!' they all echoed. Lizzie looked shy as she sipped, unusual for her.

'Thank you,' Maevy said, and as if inspired by the bubbles rising up in the glass under her nose, 'Lizzie and I are having a wonderful time. We'll never forget America, will we, Lizzie? And now that we know you, it will be like . . . hands across the sea.'

'Hands across the sea!' Ernest cried, raising his glass, 'I'll drink to that!'

George strolled back. 'What's going on here? I heard shouting.'

'It's our champagne stop, George,' Terence laughed. 'Sorry to disturb you. Here you are.' He poured him a glass.

'What are you smirking at, Ernest?' George was blushing. 'Thanks, Uncle.'

'Knock it back, old fellow, you look as if you need it.' Everyone laughed, at George, at Ernest, his pork pie cap pushed to the side of his head. His thin face, Maevy thought, had all the volatility of Charlie's.

How is he getting on, she wondered, in far-off Sholton? And why did she have total recall of every word they had exchanged that day, and of his face, especially the dark, searching eyes. And then he had kissed her, like a seal. Long ago he had done more than kiss her in the Sholtie Woods. She had resented his eagerness, the feel of his body against hers, now she wished ardently (she was

227

surprised at the word which sprang into her mind), to be in his arms, to be swept away by passion.

Everyone knew of this strange passion except her, wanted it, even quiet George was disturbed by the dark blood surging in him for a girl still at school. James and Kate knew of it. It was in every gesture they made, every look they exchanged. Terence adored Caroline, a tender, mature love for someone weaker than himself, but there must have been passion at first. Ernest had surely known it briefly in his escapades at Yale, Lizzie was made for passion. There would be no half measures with Lizzie when she fell in love. And hadn't she herself been born of passion? She felt her body melt . . .

James was at her side, smiling. 'You aren't feeling homesick, are you? You had a faraway look.'

'No, not at all, but yes, I'll admit it, I was thinking of home.'

'There's nothing quite like getting away from well-known places, or people, to make you appreciate them.'

The champagne released her tongue. 'I was thinking how happily married you and Kate are, almost envying you.'

'It's no cause for envy. "Enough for today . . ." I remind myself of that all the time. But the married state doesn't appeal to you, Maevy?'

'It didn't, at first. All my life I'd dreamt of being a nurse. In any case . . .' No, she would not say, 'The man I loved married someone else.' It was not important now. 'I told myself my career came first.'

'Your mother has a career, and I don't think there was a better wife.'

'It was a love marriage all right. "Cooin' doos" we called them. You won't know what that means?'

'You forget I'm a Scotsman, first and foremost. No, marriage is a fulfilment in every way. She'd be able to give more to the firm because of it.'

228

'I never thought of it like that.' She glowed inside. It was not only the champagne.

They had left the scattered houses behind them, the little school-house, the large white clapboard house – George, who had attached himself to her, said it was occupied by a recluse who studied birds, the vineyards on the south shore. The track narrowed, the wind blew freely round them, and Maevy had to cycle harder to make any progress against it.

Now there was a feeling of even greater freedom. They were on the tip of the land surrounded on three sides by the confluence of the Wanapeake and the Hudson. Here there was a strong sense of the past. She could imagine the men of the Militia George was telling her about, the British man-of-war, full-sailed, rocking under their fire, being steadily driven downstream.

'You're like your father,' she said, 'you make me see it. And hear it. The noise . . . Oh!' She felt herself go white with the sudden fierce pain which shot through her. She doubled up, vomit rushed to her mouth, and hardly seeing where she was going, she managed to stagger a few yards away from him. With her back turned she was violently sick on the tussocky grass. She sank to her knees, holding her side because of the pain, her head swimming.

'What is it, Maevy?' He was beside her, his face frightened.

'I don't know. A terrible pain. It's gone, I think. Oh, I'm sorry, George!' She wanted to hide her face. What a spectacle she had made of herself. She was mortified at the sight of the vomit on the grass, its stench rising up to them. She put her face in her hands. If only he would go away . . .

'I'll run back to Uncle Terence and tell him to bring the carriage. He thought it was too narrow . . .'

'No, no,' she put her hand on his arm, 'it's gone, the pain's gone, truly.' She forced herself to speak calmly. 'Look, George, let this be a secret between us. It's nothing. I know. I'm a nurse. Maybe it was the champagne, or something I ate.'

'Let me tell Kate, then. She always knows what to do.'

'Not even Kate. Why should we spoil the picnic?' She got up slowly, stretched her body experimentally, carefully, yes, the pain had gone, as quickly as it had come. But the intensity of it! Her knees were still trembling. Had it been a touch of colic? Certainly she and Lizzie had been indulging themselves in American food, especially crab and lobster which were new to them and a great treat. She had been unwise, that was all.

'I honestly think I should tell Kate.' George looked miserable.

'No,' she said, making herself smile, 'I forbid you to spoil the day. Besides we'll soon be going back. I promise you if there's the least recurrence, which there won't be, I'll let you ask Uncle Terence to drive me home.'

'As long as you promise.' He smiled boyishly at her. She had given him the fright of his life. 'We have a very good doctor, Doctor Studebaker. He attended us all when we were small. Kate swears by him.'

'Well, that's comforting to know. Let's join the others now.' I know a very good one, too, she thought, as she cycled, for George's benefit, with a panache she did not feel. Her legs were still trembling. But he's too far away . . .

George was a young man of his word. He went to New York with his father on Monday to their export business, and it was obvious he had not told Kate, who would have been full of commiseration and insistence that Maevy should see a doctor immediately, and which she was convinced would put a blot on this wonderful holiday.

Besides, there were only a few days to go and they looked like flying past. At the beginning of that week also, Ernest left for his new job with the women fussing around him, a state which he seemed greatly to enjoy.

'Goodbye, fair cousin,' he said to Lizzie, and she threw her arms round his neck and hugged him. Kieran looked disgusted.

'Steady on, there,' Ernest said, laughingly disengaging himself, but Maevy thought he looked pleased.

Kate was full of instructions about eating – he was to share a bachelor apartment with a friend from Yale – but it was touching how he embraced her warmly before he went. 'Thank goodness *you* haven't flown the nest yet,' she said to Kieran, her arm round him as they waved goodbye from the front steps. Her eyes were wet.

But there was no sitting down to mope. There were friends to visit in order to show off the Scottish relatives, and more visits across the ferry to Springhill where Lizzie seemed to forget her 'pash' for Ernest, as Kieran called it, in riding Starlight, Maria's old horse. The only drawback was the heat which tired Maevy unaccountably. When she mentioned it to Lizzie she said, 'You must be imagining it. It's much cooler now.'

The night before they left she touched Kate's arm with fondness. 'It's been a wonderful holiday. When it comes to goodbyes tomorrow, I know it won't be said in the rush, but you've opened out my life, you and James. I'll carry back such good memories. Do you remember in Paris you said, "Come and visit us. I've got a cure"?'

'Yes?'

'Well,' she was shy, 'the cure has worked, I think. I'd struck a bad patch, then. Distance lends enchantment, they say, but it's not that. I think it makes you see clearer. I see . . . how blind I've been for such a long time.'

Kate turned to her. 'Do you mean you're thinking differently about Charlie McNab?' She had Mother's frankness.

'Yes, at least beginning to get things in perspective. It may be too late.'

'It's never too late. Once you know what you want it's never too late.'

Her dear big sister did not know of the obstacles, the permanent cloud of that letter, and now the pain, lying there like a beast ready to strike. Never too late? She was afraid.

The first day of the voyage she and Lizzie felt miserable. 'Now I'm homesick for America,' Maevy laughed, trying to banish her low spirits. 'Did you ever know anyone as thrawn as me? When I was in America I was homesick for Scotland!'

'I wasn't,' Lizzie said, 'at least, not much. It's never as exciting in Sholton. Oh, the times we've had bicycling and riding and sailing and visiting! Did you ever know anyone so good and kind to us as Aunt Kate and Uncle James, and then Uncle Terence? He was the grandest man, wasn't he, and little Aunt Caroline with her curls who couldn't do enough for us. And the boys! Who did you like best?'

'Now, that's difficult to say.' Maevy kept her face straight. 'I found George very sympathetic and a tower of strength; Ernest was playful and he'll be a great flirt with the ladies, I'm sure, but Kieran, yes, I think Kieran was my special favourite.'

'Why was that?'

'I think because he's so like my father. Do you remember your Grandpa?'

'Yes, like a dream somehow, or maybe it's because

232

Grandma told me. Sitting between them in a wee carriage, and feeling the softness and whiteness of the fur coat I was wearing. And singing. It's the happiness that comes back to me.' She pursed her lips. 'I can't decide between Ernest and Kieran.'

'I don't think it's necessary yet.'

'You're laughing at me. It's just that I like to get things clear in my mind.' How like Mother she is, Maevy thought.

They were sailing up the Clyde, and she and Lizzie were standing on the deck when the beast rose again. That was how she thought of it, a beast stirring in its lair. The familiar outline of the shipyard gantries wavered in her sight with the intensity of the pain, and she had to clutch the rail. This time she was not sick, as if her body was accommodating to the pain now, had recognized it as a familiar. But her knuckles were white, and her body trembled. She was surprised Lizzie did not notice. She looked at her. Her face was alive, she was almost dancing with excitement.

'There are a lot of people standing on the platform, oh, bother, the dock, I mean. Who are they, Maevy, do you think?' Fortunately she did not turn her head. 'I can't see. Oh, yes, I can. It's Father and Mother. I recognize Father's black coat, and Grandma. Yes, it's Grandma, look, it's that lovely green costume with the mauve velvet toque, oh, doesn't she look grand, like a queen, and there's someone else, it might be Terence, or Patrick . . .'

She made herself speak as naturally as she could. Mind over matter, she told herself. She saw people being braver every day in the Royal, dying . . . she was not dying, was she? 'When Grandma and Isobel went to America I was on the dock waiting with your father. And Isobel, your mother, my sister, went straight into his arms. That was when I knew she was the one he loved . . .' When I thought my heart was broken. But Lizzie was not listening.

'They're waving! They've seen us. Oh, and do you see who it is? It's Dr McNab!'

They docked. She could not understand how she was able to walk, to get on the gangway with Lizzie, to say, 'Yes, I see them. You're right. It's Charlie . . .' The rail was a help. And the crowd pushing her along. She leant backwards and was propelled slowly the length of the gangway by the people behind her, praying silently, 'Don't let me faint, don't let me faint . . .'

They were amongst the first off, and the pain cleared a little enabling her to see their faces. They were smiling, Isobel, John, Mother and Charlie, and then as she went towards them, she saw their expressions alter, as if something was worrying them. They were no longer smiling. She saw Isobel speak to her mother, her mother turn to Charlie. What was all the fuss about?

He was striding towards her, now half-running, seeming to clear people out of his path. His face suddenly loomed large in front of her and then she was in his arms. The same again, she thought, feeling his strength, Isobel and John, now Charlie and me. That was how it happened on docks. It was right, a pattern. 'In the name of God, Maevy,' she heard his voice in her ear, 'What's wrong with you?'

She tried to smile, to lift her head to her mother whose gloved hand was on her arm, but a new shaft of pain tearing at her insides twisted her mouth, bringing saliva into it. 'It's lucky,' she said, 'that . . . we're fine . . .' her tongue was heavy. 'It's lucky . . .' she tried again, 'that we're fine and near . . . the Royal.'

'Help me, John.' How curt Charlie's voice sounded. They were hovering round her, Isobel, Mother, Lizzie.

She wanted to reassure Lizzie, her faithful companion on their great jaunt.

'Some homecoming, Lizzie,' she said, hoping she was smiling.

She had no recollection of the short drive through the familiar streets. There was some kind of commotion at the end of it, of being wheeled somewhere and hearing her mother speaking to her, her voice more Irish than usual. Wasn't it a strange thing how that often happened when she was upset? 'Not long to go now, my lovely. Sure and it's only a hop, skip and a jump to a nice soft bed where they'll be after seeing to your comfort.'

There was a hand in hers, not her mother's gloved one. Charlie's, broad-knuckled, capable, capable in an operating room or sitting at his piano, working in his garden, driving his pony and trap.

'Charlie,' she said, she was ashamed, 'this is terrible . . . in my own Infirmary, too.' Then nothing.

24

She was in the surgical ward, she realized, when she opened her eyes. She had worked there for quite a long time. Would it still be Nurse Allan, fat, jolly Nurse Allan who had a boyfriend in Pathology? Maybe they were married.

But all speculation about Nurse Allan was gone in a new onslaught of pain. She was being undressed by two pairs of chattering hands, put into a calico nightgown, the tapes were being tied at the back of her neck (the biter bit, she thought), and then she heard Charlie's voice. He was speaking to someone.

'Who's on duty doctor?'

'It's Mr Wilcox today.' The voice belonged to yet other hands which turned back the bedclothes, probing, searching for her pain. She cowered, moaned when they found it, heard the voice again. 'You're quite right, Dr McNab. Right ileac region. Tender enough for an abscess. I'd say Perityphlitis, right? He'll drain it.'

Charlie's voice was a soft hiss. 'But that might go on for months! They're *operating* on them now! There was one done a week ago in this very city.'

'One swallow doesn't make a summer. Anyhow, I'm only his assistant. I'll send a message to Mr Wilcox right away if he isn't on his round already.'

Now Charlie's voice was very close to her ear. 'Maevy,' so softly, 'Maevy, my love, is the pain bad?'

The tenderness made her want to weep. 'I can thole it. But I'm very hot.' She moved her head on the pillow. 'I was stupid in America . . . Lizzie said I was imagining the heat. I must have had a temperature . . .'

'We'll get a nurse to sponge you down. Mr Wilcox will be here to see you soon.'

'That's . . . ?' She could not say it.

'Yes.' Letitia's father. 'He's good. Very sound.'

'Is it my appendix?'

'Yes. Don't talk.'

It was he who was not going to talk. But then he was not Mr Wilcox's assistant any more. Difficult. Ironical. 'Is Mother still here?'

'Yes, she's in the waiting-room. Would you like to see her?'

'Yes, please.' It gave her a little respite, to stop tholing the pain, to let the beast have its way with her body, rampaging . . .

Her mother was there, bending over her, and her perfume. Was it anything like the white roses in her garden? It had a fresh, dewy sweetness. 'Maevy, my lovely, you're all right now. They'll see you all right. Not much longer.' She felt the pain, too. You could tell by her voice.

'So they should, considering what I've done for *them*.' She tried to laugh, knew it died in her throat. 'Mother, go home. Get Charlie to take you.'

'Wild horses wouldn't get Charlie to go home. You know that. He's waiting to hear what the surgeon says.'

'Well, take the train yourself, or a cab, splash out on a . . .' She could not be bothered speaking any more.

'John and Isobel have taken Lizzie back to Sholton. I thought that would be best.'

'Yes . . .' I do not want a gathering of the clan. It was easier to think words than to say them. It took too great an effort.

Her mother was stroking her hand softly, murmuring.

237

'Try to sleep, maybe the pain will go away, try to sleep . . .' 'Wee Willie Winkie runs roon the toon . . .' Just as this pain ran round her body. Nothing would make it go away. She turned her head on the pillow and some kind of sound escaped her lips. She hoped it was not a moan. There were always moaners in a hospital. She did not want to be one of them.

She heard the nurse's voice again. 'You'll have to wait outside, Mrs McGrath. The surgeon's here.'

'Certainly, Nurse.' The Irish lady. A swish of skirt. A swish of perfume.

There were eyes round her bed, and nearer to her the eyes of a grizzled-looking man with bushy eyebrows. What if she said, 'Are you Miss Letitia Wilcox's father?' The consternation in the retinue, the surprise in the eyes. Or would they just think she was delirious, which she was. Her bed was like the solid bed of a winter fire. It must be scorching her night-gown, not hers, the hospital's. A solid red bed of burning coals, not like that surly little fire in Catherine's bedroom which had licked eagerly at the letter . . .

'When did the pain first occur, Sister?' She heard the Kelvinside voice. Lizzie would make short work of that.

'It occurred . . .' How difficult it was to remember, and then to put her thoughts into words, 'when I was . . . laughing with Lizzie . . . nothing, a stab.'

'When was that?'

'When was that?' Concentrate. 'About two weeks ago when I was in America. Then some days later. Much worse.' She saw George's concerned face, felt the deep shame again at the pool of vomit he could not avoid seeing. 'Much worse. And I was hot all the time. I should have known I had a temperature, me a nurse . . . oh, my God!' Mr Wilcox had put his finger on the pain, cornered

238

it. The beast snarled once, then retreated, grumbling around her inside.

'That's it. I'm sorry.' He sounded pleased. 'I didn't mean to hurt you.' He covered her up and then she heard the scuff of feet going away from her bed, heard again the familiar noises of a ward, the clink of someone's glass as they poured water, two patients talking, the quick rubber slap of a nurse's feet going down the middle, a running cistern from the sluices, smelled it, the Lister smell.

The pain was still growling around, petulantly, but growing less fierce as the circles spread out from its centre, bigger and bigger circles. Charlie was there again. She saw him through half-closed, pain-filled eyes.

'You're going into theatre in an hour, Maevy. Nurse will get you ready.'

'Oh!' Her first thought was the ignominy of having her pubic hair shaved. How often she had done it to other people and never given a thought to their feelings. 'That's quick.'

'It's the only thing. You can't go on suffering like this. I hope he . . . you know it's the only thing.'

'Yes, I know.' She must act like a Sister although she was flat on her back.

'I'm going to wait till it's done. So is your mother. I can't get her to go away.'

'It's her stubborn bit.' Everything was topsy-turvy here.

The nurse who prepared her was thin, or was it that her eyes were so blurred with pain that she could not see properly.

'You're not Nurse Allan?'

The girl laughed, wielding the cut-throat razor with what Maevy thought was unnecessary relish. 'Nurse Allan? No, I hope I'm not as fat as her! She's off duty.'

'She's a good nurse.'

239

'Yes, she is.' Scrape, scrape, a small nick. 'Sorry. There you are, dear. Now we're going to give you a bed bath.'

'Not an enema?' She might as well have the whole works.

'Oh, no! Mr Wilcox said no enemas.'

'It's an abscess, then, inflammation of the appendix?'

'They don't tell me anything, Sister.' The young nurse was brisk. 'No enemas, no hot fomentations, that's all I know. Now, you just lie there quietly till they come for you.'

'That's not the way I did it,' she thought. 'I reassured the patient. I prepared her with words of kindness as well as with a razor and a face flannel.' There was one thing about having a temperature. Everything was at one remove now although the whole ward was a burning hot womb for her body, the noises were dull, she could lie like this, hands crossed on her chest and wait till she was wheeled into theatre to those rows of staring young eyes. Once a patient had said to her, 'When I saw all those young fellows standing round the table I said to myself, "Thank God for chloroform!"'

But it was afterwards. She had nursed patients in bed for months with draining abscesses, changed the filthy dressings day after day, not minding, like some nurses, because wasn't it easier to be in her shoes rather than those of the poor man or woman with a tube sticking out of them and that constant sickly smell in their nostrils? 'All the perfumes of Arabia . . .' Maybe some of Mother's white perfume – white roses.

Why didn't Charlie come? Had he been debarred by that young efficient nurse because he was no longer on the staff? But he was her mother's doctor, and hers when she was in Sholton. She wanted Charlie. She needed him beside her. If only he could come into the theatre with her, make sure everything was being done all right, according to Charlie and Lister, maybe they should suggest they should take the thing out. Was it because he was too forward-looking that his contract hadn't been renewed, or was it that Mr Wilcox was annoyed at him because of his daughter?

He was there. She could feel his hand on her brow, professionally, or was it the hand of a lover? I'd like to tell him what I found out in America, she thought, that a career isn't enough . . . about those thrills, up and down, delicious . . . she began but was too tired. Later would do if there was a later.

'You'll be fine, Maevy.'

'I know. I was just thinking . . . I wish you would come in with me.'

He did not answer. Medical etiquette. She understood that. Then, 'I'll be close by. So will your mother. We'll both be thinking of you. You're in good hands.' He was loyal to Mr Wilcox.

'You're telling the truth?'

His hand was grasping her hand now, making her feel strong. 'Yes. You've got to be all right. We have to be together.'

But the strength went, and the grasp of his hand was lost and his face with its black eyes was lost in a welter of pain and a small flurry when she was lifted from the hot bed of coals and wheeled away.

25

The Manse, Sholton, Lanarkshire, Scotland.
3rd May, 1890.

Dear Kieran,

I'm sitting in our dining-room and we've had our supper – we had it early because Mother and Father go to a prayer meeting tonight – and I've been given permission to write to you if I do an hour's piano practice.

I think all that business of playing duets or getting up and singing at parties is beginning to go. Even in Sholton I know someone who has a phonograph, Nigel Crawford. They're very rich but his father isn't as good to the kirk as the old Lord Crawford was. At least, so *my* father says. I told Grandma that, and she said the old one was trying to buy a ticket to heaven! We had a good laugh at that.

There's not much laughing with us just now all the same. I know my mother has written to yours to tell her all about poor Aunt Maevy. We're all very worried about her and we say special prayers for her at each meal as well as in the kirk.

The trouble is she isn't getting better because there is a lot of poison in her system and it has to be drained away. It makes her delirious, and Grandma says she's lost a lot of weight. She tries to make me laugh, and she says Aunt Maevy would be quite glad to know she's lost two stones because she always wanted to be slim like my mother, who's like a Dresden doll. 'A puff of wind would blow her away,' I heard one of the old ladies at the kirk saying.

Between you and me, Kieran, if Aunt Maevy died I don't know what I'd do. We had such good talks in our cabin about life and everything, and I told her a lot of my secret thoughts. She said she felt the same way about many things when she was my age, very sure and confident, but it was only now that she was beginning to realize that some of her opinions had been wrong. She called them 'illusions', and said they could be a spur, and she wouldn't have been a nurse if she hadn't had hers. But you had to be ready to change when the time came. I asked her how I'd know when it was the right time, but she said I'd know.

'Now you feel kept down at the manse, Lizzie,' she said, 'and you're dying to do all kinds of things, but the one thing you can do is take advantage of the good education Isobel and John are giving you.'

I don't have to be told to pray every night for Aunt Maevy.

Anyhow I mustn't make you feel sad, too . . . I expect you're swotting away at your boarding school and having great times with your chums, sailing and playing games and maybe working at your books as well. And the tracking you told me about. I'll never forget that grand bicycle trip we had to Wanapeake Point and the feeling all the time that those Indians who used to live there might *just* be lurking behind a bush and they'd come rushing out with their tomahawks raised and dance a war dance round us. I dream a dream like this, and strangely enough, the Indian chief has a face like Ernest.

How is he? Is he liking New York and living in a house of their own with his friend? I expect they 'paint the town red' every night. If you see him tell him Lizzie sends her love and best wishes. I expect he'll make millions of dollars in New York and marry a rich heiress called Vanderbilt!

Uncle Patrick and Aunt Maria came to see us last Sunday with the family. He's kind, but very quiet, and he always asks me sensible questions about school and he gives me lovely presents at birthday and Christmas, the last thing was a swivelling pencil box and a leather satchel.

Aunt Maria's gone much quieter than she used to be, and I'm sure she worries about little Mary. She's getting no better. She drools on her bib and her head wobbles and she must be terrible to look after. I offered to go and push her in her pram in Kelvingrove Park, and tell her the names of the birds and flowers. But Father said I wasn't allowed to travel in the train alone so that was that.

I hate to see people sad, and indeed everybody's sad nowadays because of Aunt Maevy. And now I've made myself sad, too, with all those problems, so I'd better stop. Write to me if you can spare the time and tell me all about America and my American cousins. You seem to have such fun there. I think in Scotland life is greyer somehow. Maybe it's the climate.

Your loving cousin, Lizzie

243

26

All day as Charlie did his rounds he was preoccupied by
thoughts of Maevy. It was impossible to get to Glasgow
to see her. Jim Geddes was having his half day, and he
had been very good at shouldering more than his load to
allow Charlie time to visit at the Royal. He was a quiet
man who did not ask questions. Charlie had told him the
bare facts about Maevy's condition. He knew and
respected the McGrath family. That was enough for him.
If he was reading between the lines he did not say so.
Biddy was fussing in the hall when Charlie thankfully
stabled his horse, pushed the trap in beside it and went
indoors.

'Oh, there you are, doctor. The dinner's near spoiling.'

'I've never eaten a spoiled dinner of yours yet, Biddy.'
He hung his hat over a pair of antlers he had bought in a
Crannoch junk shop. 'That will be the day.' He hoped to
God she had not cooked too much for it. He had told her
some fairytale yesterday about having an upset stomach.
His appetite had left him, and he had wished in the last
few days that he had had a dog under the table. That was
one of the things he had promised himself in the married
life that was to be his some day, a dog, a laughing kind of
dog that would come bounding up to him, children . . .

Biddy brought in a large ashet of toad-in-the-hole,
golden brown and crisp on the top, her solution to his
request for 'light' food. Her ideal of a 'normal' dinner was
a good bowl of vegetable broth to stick to your insides,
roast beef, potatoes and two vegetables, followed by a
hearty wedge of apple pie with cream.

'Thank you, Biddy,' he said, 'I didn't know we were entertaining the elders of the kirk as well.'

'You ken fine we're not, doctor!' He had forgotten she had no sense of humour. 'I've done something light as you said.'

'It looks very nice.'

His mind was already back with Maevy before Biddy had gone. Mr Wilcox should have taken the damned thing out. *He* should in his place. What was the point in leaving a vestigial piece of anatomy in Maevy's body which was useless and had been the seat of the trouble anyhow? He had seen it all before, the endless suppuration, the lowering of the body's resistance, the constant pyrexia, and in the end septicaemia and . . . no, he could not even think the word. She would get better. She was bound to. She had a good healthy constitution like her mother, not at all like Isobel, who always looked as if she had such a frail hold on life. Sometimes they were the ones who lived the longest.

Should he go and see Mr Wilcox, ask him what he thought of Maevy, what were her chances? How would he receive him? Would he still be holding a grudge against him for leading his daughter up the garden path, and even worse, for turning down his offer of professional help?

It seemed fairly evident that he was. A word from Mr Wilcox would have made sure that the contract was renewed. He was the senior surgeon. I was in the wrong, too, he told himself. I should have gone to him after I saw Letitia, explained my feelings, or lack of them. I was brash, thoughtless . . .

But it was immaterial now. It was Maevy he was concerned with, and it would be a mistake to see Mr Wilcox and perhaps end up by saying more than he should. Any surgeon was bound to resent being told how he should deal with his patients, even from someone who

245

had once worked with him. If only it were five years on, he agonized, when very likely there would be no difference of opinion, when appendices would be taken out routinely. Already it had been done successfully in one or two cases. In a few years it would have been proved too often that they could be a source of trouble.

But my poor Maevy, what about her, here and now? He was in such anguish that he pushed away his meal half-eaten and got up. He met Biddy in the hall now bearing a smaller ashet, semolina, he guessed, seeing the brown top, like a scab. 'Biddy, I'm sorry, I've just remembered. I've forgotten to call and see Mrs McGrath on the way home.'

She rubbed her hand over her pug nose, flattening it, a favourite gesture of hers when she was annoyed. 'But surely it'll wait, doctor!'

'No, it was important. She'll be anxious . . .'

'But the pudding . . . specially for stomachs . . .' she almost wailed, 'A pit twa fresh eggs in it . . .'

'Put it in the larder. If there's anything I like it's a cold semolina pudding. Like a poultice. Now you wash up and get away to your bed. I know I've kept you up.'

She glanced at the wag-at-the-wa', slightly mollified. She scampered to her early bed every night as to a lover. 'Aye, it was gey late when you cam in.'

'It always is on Dr Geddes' half day. Off you go, now. The toad-in-a-hole was grand. I'm only sorry I couldn't do full justice to it.'

He went into Maeve McGrath's garden through the wicket gate and walked up the flagged path towards the house. There was a clarity, a last glow of light before darkness came, falling on the beds of flowers, and the air was full of the scent of them. She graced everything she touched, gardens, her own person, she created beauty . . . I'm tired to be thinking like that.

Her curtains were not drawn, and he could see her at her desk, the flame of her piled hair against the light dress. She looked up as he passed the window, and waved. She was at the back door to greet him. 'Charlie, come away in. I was just writing a few letters.'

'Am I disturbing you? It's late.'

'No, no, you know I'm not an early bedder. I wouldn't go to sleep if I did.' He followed her into the room. There were bowls of flowers everywhere. She had brought the garden inside. 'Would you like a drink? Sit there.'

'No, thanks. I've just finished my supper. I'd get maudlin if I had one. Were you at the Infirmary today?'

'Yes, I left the office early. Terence drove me up and waited. They wouldn't let him in.'

'Is there any change?'

'Not except for the worse.' She bit her lip. 'I'm writing to Kate to give her the news. I'm glad you came. I was only relieving my own anxiety. I'll tear it up.'

'Was she lucid?'

'Only fitfully. Her eyes are fever bright and she dozed a lot. She was muttering most of the time. I couldn't make head nor tail of it. Once she grasped my hand and said, "Don't you worry, Mother."'

He looked at her. 'Apart from her condition, is there anything she thought you *would* be worrying about?'

'Nothing in particular except the usual family things. She was very involved in us all, Patrick and Maria's baby – I don't see much change there for the better either – the business. She was always interested in the business. She worked in the office, remember. She knew more about Trade Unions than any of the rest of us. I tried to tell her about the Horsemen's Union, even took in the paper thinking she would be pleased about that, but she turned her head away. Then she always worries about Terence.'

247

'Even yet?' There was something in her way of speaking. He could not place it.

'Well, she discovered Catherine's body with him.' She spoke with her head turned away from him. 'He's probably confided in her more than the rest of us.' There was one thing he had noticed about Maeve McGrath since he had first known her. She always looked you in the face. Perhaps that was why you remembered her eyes more than most people's. 'She's the most tender-hearted of them all, my Maevy.' Her voice was tender, too. 'You'd think it would be Kate, but she's got a lot of common sense mixed in with her thought for others. With Maevy it's all or nothing. No half measures.'

He sighed. 'I didn't get in today. I couldn't rest till I knew how you found her. I'll go tomorrow. I can manage it between the afternoon and evening surgeries if I put a spurt on.'

'You'll wear yourself out.'

'Not me. I'm tough. I'm half-thinking of trying to see the surgeon, ask him what his opinion is.'

'Would that do any good?'

'I can't bear to be in the dark. I'm not a doctor when I go there, remember, just a visitor. If I'd still been assisting Mr Wilcox I would have known all about it.'

'I never understood why they didn't keep you on there, a good worker like you.'

'Quite simple. My contract had expired. Anyhow, it's not important. What's important to me is Maevy. I'm out of my mind with worry about her.' He had not meant to say that.

'You love her?' Her eyes had lost their colour in the dusk. She had not lit the lamps.

'I've always loved her.'

'Try reminding her.'

'She knows. I was beginning to hope . . .'

248

'She went into your arms when she came off the liner.'

'I was the nearest doctor.' He laughed. 'Still . . .' He thought again of that quayside and her white face rigid with pain, how he had caught her just as she was about to fall, thought of the joy of having her in his arms, half-fainting as she was, the indescribable joy that she had come to him. 'All I want is to be given the chance to care for her. If I lose her . . .' The thought drove him to his feet. 'I'm being selfish, not thinking of your anxiety. I'll get away back now. I'll have to be up betimes tomorrow morning and get through my list.'

She rose, too. 'Will you come in on your way home and tell me how you found her?'

'I'll do that.'

'Have dinner with me.'

He shook his head. 'Your Susan would give me black looks like Biddy for not doing justice to her cooking.'

'I know. Why does that poor lamb have to suffer so much, Charlie?'

'Don't ask me. I'm only the doctor. Your son-in-law, John, could give you a better answer.'

'Does he know? I sometimes wonder. He goes often enough to see her. It upsets Isobel to visit and you know how careful he is about her health. Lizzie's pleaded with him to take her but he'll have none of it.' She smiled. 'She and Maevy had a grand time in America. Maevy can get down to her level. She has a child-like quality at times.'

'I think it's the goodness in her.' His throat filled, and his eyes. 'I'll say good-night.' He turned on his heel and went out, blessing the unlit room.

Walking back through the garden he let tears run down his face for the relief of it. Nobody would see him. There was comfort in being woman-like, feeling the wetness on his cheeks in the soft night air. He breathed deeply, a

249

sighing breath, and caught the strong perfume of a lavender bush nearby. Sheer indulgence, he said to himself, a grown man of thirty-five greetin' . . . 'Wee chookie birdie, roared and grat . . .' He had said that to her once. When was it? When her sister-in-law died?

He let himself quietly into his house and went to bed in the dark.

27

Thank goodness it isn't a hundred years ago, Charlie thought, hurrying up High Street. Ahead of him was the plain bulk of the cathedral – they might have made it more imposing when they were at it – and beyond it the more satisfying lines of the Royal Infirmary. The Adams brothers at least knew what they were about.

What would the state of hospitals have been like then, with no surgery to speak of except amputations, and no antisepsis? Someone had once shown him an old etching of the valley of the Molendinar, where he was now walking. 'The sacred river' they had called it, where St Mungo had baptized many of his converts. Such rusticity, but no one would dare bathe in it now, an open sewer at some places, and not so long ago the *trottoirs* (strange how many French words remained in the old Scots tongue), the pavements, under his feet smelling to high heaven with discarded filth. Things were better now, even if Maevy was still lingering weeks after the operation while her body fought the poison running through it like the Molendinar.

He knew the nurse who was on duty, Nurse Allan, a jolly soul and not too much of a stickler for discipline. She would not hurry him away like the thin one. 'How is she today?' he asked her.

She shook her head. 'That poor lassie. She doesn't know whether she's coming or going. Maybe you'll be able to do her some good, Dr McNab.'

She led him to the bed and they stood looking down at Maevy. Her eyes were closed, her hair loose about her face. You couldn't call it fair any longer. It had lost its shine, its bright liveliness. Sometimes in the sun or lit by a lamp it was like pure gold. He remembered that time he had come upon her on night duty, and how the tendrils lying on her brow and white nape had turned his heart over.

Nurse Allan bent over her. 'Here's a visitor to see you, Maevy.' She looked back at him. 'I call her Maevy though she'd half kill me if she was up and about.'

'I hear you, Nurse,' Maevy said distinctly, not opening her eyes. 'That's another thing I've told you. Don't discuss the patient in front of her.'

Nurse Allan laughed. 'You caught me out there, Sister.' She looked pleased. 'It's Dr McNab.' She brought forward a chair. 'Take the weight off your legs, doctor.'

'Thanks.' He sat down, took Maevy's hand. How thin she was. Her beauty, which was a combination of her psychological and physical healthiness, was gone, this gaunt-faced girl with black circled eyes and lank hair was scarcely recognizable as the Maevy he knew. 'It's Charlie. Can you not be bothered to look at me?'

Her eyes opened suddenly, and he saw their brightness, the fever in them. He shifted his fingers to her pulse, racing, erratic, and the hand itself was hot and dry. 'I knew it was you. Is John a man of God?'

'John?' He was taken aback. 'Your brother-in-law?' He saw her nod. 'Well, the whole of Sholton believes he is. They would be right dumbfoonered if they found out to the contrary.'

'He says it would be morally wrong . . . I asked him. I . . . put it to him.' Her voice stopped, the eyelids, like a china doll's dropped over the bright eyes. A china doll would have had rosy cheeks.

'You put what to him?' She did not reply. The eyelids quivered. Her other hand plucked at the sheet. He

252

watched her face, saw the hectic flush on the cheekbones, how the whole shape of her face was altered by the gauntness. A slight smile lifted one side of her mouth.

'Trust *you*, Charlie. I knew you had . . .' there was a long pause. She seemed to forget she had been talking. '. . . a . . . searching mind. Searching . . . eyes. Pity you can't see into someone's head. That would be good. Better even than seeing into . . . bodies. That's what . . . you were always after. Progress . . . is that it?'

'What did you tell him, Maevy?'

'"Morally wrong," he said, "sin . . . to withhold . . . information . . ." It was bad enough before,' her voice came in a sudden spurt of energy, 'always remembering when I wanted to forget, now he's put me . . . into . . . a black hole . . . a black . . . hole . . . of despair.' She made no sound, but tears escaped from between her lids and trickled slowly down her face. He took his clean handkerchief and wiped them away. He could have wept himself.

'You're doing yourself no good at all.' He spoke severely to her. 'Breaking your mother's heart, breaking mine, not trying to get better. Tell me what's bothering you, my darling . . .' Her mother's words came back to him, 'Then she always worries about Terence . . .' He wiped her eyes again, gently, putting love into it. A terrible thing had happened to Terence. But his mother would never speak if she was protecting her daughter in any way. She was a strong woman who had been fired to strength by life.

'What did you say, Charlie?' Her voice was soft.

'Tell me what's bothering you. Let me help . . .'

'No, the other thing. You called me something. Say it again.' She was cajoling, shy.

'My darling.'

'*Am* I your darling?'

'You've always been.'

'What about Miss Wilcox?'

'I told you, she doesn't count. Never did. I was stupid, because I thought you'd never want me . . . I thought it would at least help my career . . . something daft like that.'

'I like it. "My darling."' She said the words with tenderness. 'But I can't be your darling . . . not now. You wouldn't want me.' Her voice was infinitely pathetic, breaking his heart.

'Well, I'll just have to be yours, like in the song, "Charlie is my darling, my darling, my darling . . ."' He sang the words softly to her.

'". . . the young chevalier."' Her voice broke on the words. 'Can you remember any more of it?'

'Let me see . . .' He spoke the words now, half-whispered them, '"He set his Jenny on his knee, All in his Highland dress . . ."' He laughed, 'They'll put me out for disturbing the patients. How does the rest go? Ah, yes, "For brawlie weel he kend the way, To please a bonnie lass . . ."' She was weeping again and he stopped. 'You are my bonny lass, my darling. What is it that's worrying you? Tell me. I'll bear it for you.'

'Oh, Charlie . . . I'd rather have the pain than this . . . all this horrible stuff . . . draining out of me. Jenny Allan tells me lies. Says the dressings are getting cleaner. I know they're not. I can smell them. Don't come near, it's horrible! It's all the badness draining out of me, but there's no end to it . . . no end. I can't get the smell out of my nose. I can't eat because of it . . .'

'Maevy, listen to me.' He bent and kissed her cheek, kept his head down as he spoke. 'You smell fine to me. I'd put my head under the bedclothes up against your wound if it would help. You're getting better. It takes a

long time to drain. You know that. You're getting better.'
Her eyes were closed. 'Maevy, do you hear me?'

'I want to die.' He could scarcely hear the words, but
he was suddenly angry because of his fear.

'What's this nonsense you're talking? Want to die when
I'm waiting for you, weary of waiting for you. I never
heard such nonsense'

'I've done a terrible thing. It was morally wrong. He
said so. John . . . there was another . . . John. Long ago.
Long . . . I was to blame . . .' She suddenly screamed,
'Mammy's coming, John!' It was Maeve McGrath's voice.
His teeth gritted together with shock. 'Hold on to wee
Maeve and catch that branch . . .' Her eyes flew open,
bright, terrified, her fingers clutched his. 'I was to blame.
She couldn't . . . He floated away. She told us to look
when they . . . got him. Bessie Haddow's mother said it
wasn't nice . . . But you know Mother,' she laughed
shrilly, grown-up, 'she always called a spade a spade. *She*
never blamed me.' She suddenly screamed again, 'Oh,
I'm sorry, Isobel, I know I was bad, I didn't mean it, I
didn't mean it . . . Oh!' Her voice rose even higher and
Charlie could hear murmurs from other beds, 'I didn't
mean it . . .!' Nurse Allan was there, her plump face
concerned.

'What's happened?'

'She's delirious. Could you sponge her down, do something . . .?'

'I think you'd better go, Dr McNab.' She bent over
Maevy, put her arm under her shoulders and lifted her
against her bosom like a child. 'There, there, my lamb.
I'm here. You're just a bit hot. I'm going to get you a
fresh nightgown and give you a wee sponge down. Jenny'll
look after you.' She looked up at Charlie. Her mouth
shaped the word, 'Go.'

'Will I tell the other nurse to get the doctor on duty?'

'Yes, please.' She nodded. 'There, there now.' She looked down. Maevy's eyes were closed. She was muttering unintelligibly. He thought he heard the word, 'letter'.

He met Mr Wilcox on his way downstairs from the ward, as if he had conjured him up from his thoughts. After a preliminary start of recognition Mr Wilcox's West End manners did not desert him. Charlie was to a certain extent preventing him from ascending, and he accepted the inevitable, offering his hand with a show of pleasure. 'Well, well, Dr McNab. This is a surprise. Visiting the old alma mater?'

'I've been visiting a patient of yours and a friend of mine.'

'Indeed? Who is that?'

'Maevy McGrath, a Sister here.'

'Ah, yes.' He put on his consultant's face. 'A long business, drainage. But she seems to be pulling through. So Dr Maitchison tells me.'

'Does he? She's been here for three weeks and she's still running a high temperature.'

'You know as well as I do that is to be expected. When the abscess is cleared, the temperature will go down. It's as simple as that.' He looked down his nose. The senior surgeon.

'But during that time the patient's constitution is being weakened by continuous pyrexia, by lack of nourishment, by dehydration!' He cursed himself but could not stop. 'Is she getting saline injections?'

He saw the man's face change. He had annoyed him, forgotten his resolution not to question him if they should meet. 'I think I have to remind you, Dr McNab,' his voice was icy, 'that you are no longer employed in this Infirmary. In your capacity as a visitor to Sister McGrath it's not within your province to question her treatment, nor her surgeon. Not at all.'

'I'm sorry. I forgot myself. But . . .'

'I know very well your attitude of mind. You don't have to explain it. At first I was deceived, thinking I had found someone who was willing to sit at the foot of experience, but, oh, no, not for you. You know better. There's no spirit of modesty in you! You would have every inflamed appendix removed routinely . . .'

'I apologize, Mr Wilcox. In my anxiety for Miss McGrath's condition . . .'

Mr Wilcox's eyeballs seemed to enlarge, his face followed suit, became purple, tight-looking. 'I could wish your thoughtfulness could have extended to my daughter in your summary taking leave of her after having taken up so much of her time, after having been entertained in our home!'

It was the irrelevancy of bringing Letitia into it which struck him at first. It was Maevy they were concerned with for God's sake! 'But that was a mutual arrangement as it happened, Mr Wilcox. We parted on good terms.'

'It's good terms, is it, when she shuts herself into her room for days, won't speak to anyone? And you walk off without as much as an apology to her mother, or to me for that matter!' There was spittle at the side of his mouth. He shouldn't do this to himself, Charlie thought professionally, he's getting on.

'I thought it was a matter between Letitia and myself. I see now I was mistaken. Besides, she told me she had a suitor in America.'

'She may have told you she had a suitor in America! But why then should she worry her mother to death refusing to attend soirées she arranges for her, balls . . .' Mr Wilcox stopped short, pulled himself upright. 'I don't know how my daughter came into this discussion, except as an example of your ungentlemanly behaviour. But we'll say no more about that.' He had command of himself now. 'As for Sister McGrath, she is getting the best treatment this Infirmary can offer, and if you aren't pleased with it, you must write to the Board of Governors. I believe you're quite capable of that, too.'

'There's no point in that.' Charlie drew a deep breath. 'I feel I owe you an apology on several counts. Perhaps when Letitia and I ceased our relationship I should have come to you. It is, as you say, a further example of my uncouth behaviour. I know you had been prepared to help me in my career, and I see now I should have been franker with you. You're probably well rid of me. I've decided to remain in general practice, maybe use the experience I gained here for the benefit of my patients.'

'That's your affair.' Mr Wilcox was lofty, trying to erase his outburst of a moment ago. He took his watch from his waistcoat pocket, looked at it. 'Of course, some are more suited to the higher echelons than others.' He put it back, as if the small act had restored his confidence. 'I have a consultation at six. You must excuse me.'

'Don't let me detain you.' Charlie bowed.

This time Mr Wilcox did not offer his hand. 'Too frequent visits to a patient in Sister McGrath's condition are a mistake, if you will allow me to say so.' His voice was cold.

'Do you think she's going to get better?' Charlie put his hand on the man's arm but he shook it away.

'Your guess is as good as mine. I bid you good-day.'

28

When Charlie called at Braidholme after he had finished his evening surgery he found Lord Crawford's carriage at the door. If he had not recognized the eagle crest on its side he would have known it by its coachman. 'A fine evening, doctor.' He touched his tall hat with his whip.

'Indeed it is, Tom. How's the new bairn?'

'Doing grand, sir. The wife called him after you.'

'But he's healthy in spite of that?' The man laughed and shook his head delightedly at the drollery.

Charlie rang the bell and was ushered in by Susan, looking important, but with a frown between her eyes. He had seen the same frown on Biddy's face when her meal times were disturbed. Their souls lay in their kitchens.

Maeve welcomed him warmly, and he shook hands with Lord Crawford. A widower calling on a widow at seven o'clock in the evening! If it had been anyone else than Susan who did not 'hobnob' as she put it, it would have been all round the village by tomorrow. 'A nice evening, your lordship.'

'Yes. We can do with some more of these for the farmers.'

'They'll grumble all the same whatever the weather.' He remembered as he accepted a chair and sat down how pleased his mother had been when, in the first flurry of pride at having won a scholarship, he had announced his intention of becoming a doctor. 'A doctor! You'll be able to mix with anybody!'

Lord Crawford seemed to be explaining his presence. 'I

259

looked in to hear if Mrs McGrath had any news of her daughter, and she persuaded me to wait as she said you were visiting the Infirmary today.'

'How was she, Charlie?' Maeve asked. He thought she looked particularly beautiful tonight with her red hair dressed in a softer manner perhaps, although still piled up on top of her head, such luxurious hair, and a white muslin dress with a faint mauve stripe through it. There was a velvet ribbon of the same colour round her neck. What a white skin she had, like all true redheads. This evening it seemed particularly luminous.

'She talked a lot but she's still fevered, I'm sorry to say. I'd like to see her making quicker progress.' He had intended to go over Maevy's remarks with her to see if she could throw any light on them. It was a pity Lord Crawford was there.

'That's the way with fevers, I imagine,' his lordship said. There was sympathy in his voice. 'They hold back recovery. My mother was the same in her last illness. It was strange. It seemed to stir up old memories for her.' His eyes sought Maevy's mother. 'Perhaps you remember?'

'Yes, you're right. You know, Charlie,' she turned to him, 'Lady Crawford used to take a short cut through our garden at Colliers' Row. Once we sat on the bench at the back door and talked. She admired the roses Kieran had planted for me there. "The white ones have the sweeter scent," she said, "but they fade sooner . . ." Or maybe I said that . . .' She paused. The room was very still for a moment.

'The fever does the same thing with Maevy,' Charlie said. 'But I'm afraid it's not only the happy memories that are stirred up . . . However,' he spoke briskly, 'there's often a dramatic recovery as the fever wears off. Perhaps tomorrow she'll be much better.'

'I worry about her. My youngest, and maybe my dearest. How her character stands out when I think of her – her steadfastness and devotion to duty.' She smiled. 'And her thrawnness. We joke now between us about what I call her "stubborn bit".' Her eyes were deeply blue, and moist. He had never been more struck by her beauty. 'Ah,' she said, 'sure and I'm brimming over with self-pity. I tell you what, you two must stay for dinner and cheer me up.'

'It's too much trouble,' Lord Crawford said.

Charlie muttered, 'Biddy . . .'

'Now, Charlie,' she was playful, 'don't let any woman put the fear of God in you like that. It's high time you showed her who's master. What do you say, Lord Crawford?'

'About Biddy putting the fear of God into Dr McNab? Well, it's hard to imagine, and I'm no judge there being a mere man, but to your kind invitation I have a mind to show Mrs Robertson where she stands once and for all if the doctor will support me.' He looked at Charlie with great good humour, and he thought what a distinctive looking man he was, far more so than his old father, who had always been hanging round the Reverend Murdoch with promises of money for the kirk, at the same time as that scoundrel who ran the truck shop at the pit was flogging bibles and whisky in equal proportion.

'How are we to let the two ladies in question know?' Charlie said smiling at him. He'd like fine to stay here for dinner. He would only torture himself with thoughts of Maevy at his own lonely table.

'Simple. I'll send Thomas back with my apologies and on the way he could stop at your house.'

'That has all the virtues of simplicity,' Charlie said, laughing. 'I agree.'

'I'll ring for Susan, then.' Maeve laughed with them. 'Don't forget, I have a dragon in the kitchen, too.'

'Yes, Mrs McGrath?' Susan was there with alacrity, arms akimbo. She had never gone in for those high falutin' ideas of calling her employer 'Madam'. If they were not equal on this earth they certainly would be in the next where they were all headed, God willing.

'Lord Crawford and Dr McNab will be staying for dinner, Susan. Set two extra places, please.'

'It's only a *scart* of beef, Mrs McGrath!'

'I know your scarts, Susan,' Maeve said calmly, 'they'd feed a rampaging tribe of Zulus and the rest for their dogs . . . if they have dogs.'

Susan drew herself up, sniffed, then looked sourly at the two men who had broad smiles on their faces. 'The vegetables will be a bit scarce. I was only doing some of the fresh peas and new tatties frae the gairden.'

'You couldn't do better. And as long as you have some Dunlop and an apple or two that'll do. Neither of the gentlemen have a sweet tooth.'

Susan bridled. 'Ma aipricot tairt's just oot o' the oven, Mrs McGrath! It'll no' be up to much the morrow!'

Maeve looked queenly. 'Well, perhaps they'll have a taste, to please you. On you go, Susan.'

When the door shut behind her they looked at each other, hiding their laughter. 'That last stroke was masterly,' Lord Crawford said.

'The aipricot tairt? Oh, dear!' She wiped her eyes. 'Now, Alastair,' Charlie noticed the name came naturally, 'don't tell me you've never heard of "Mary, Mary, quite contrary". Surely you know by this time that if you want a woman to do anything you must insist on her doing the opposite?'

He laughed, his eyes on her. 'I've a lot to learn.' Is her name trembling on *his* lips? Charlie wondered.

It was a delightfully pleasant dinner. Most women, Charlie thought, are in any case happy if they are the only representative of their sex amongst men, and Maeve McGrath was no exception. The talk was wide-ranging, covering every topic, but they were wholly at ease with one another. Only rarely did he feel superfluous, and then it was merely by a look which he imagined did not include him. He told them of his meeting with Mr Wilcox.

'Do you find all surgeons tend to be autocratic?' Lord Crawford asked him.

'In a way, but I mustn't attack them since I used to be one myself. These are difficult times. Since Lister and asepsis, the way has been opened to perform operations of a more difficult kind. They have to be pioneers, launch themselves into the unknown. Some surgeons fight shy.'

'They're not all pioneers?'

'It's a question of temperament. Take this matter of removal of the appendix, better medical men than they have come out strongly against it being removed, Dupuytren, for example.'

'Is that the Frenchman?'

'Yes. He's of the opinion that no structure so insignificant as the appendix could possibly have such widespreading effects as others claim.'

'You might as well say a diseased limb shouldn't be amputated,' Maeve said.

'True.' Lord Crawford looked at her, then turned to Charlie again. 'So what's your opinion about the removal of this "insignificant structure"?'

'Well, it seems immodest to take up the sword against such a renowned authority, but I hold the opposite view. This very year, for instance, it's been done successfully. A diagnosed appendix abscess.'

'Will it get to the stage where they will operate before

263

the abscess has formed, I mean at the first onslaught of pain?'

'It's possible.'

'Does Mr Wilcox share your view, Charlie?' Maeve's voice was quiet.

'He's cautious, and rightly so. No two patients are the same. Some present with recurrent pain over a long period, some get very little warning. Maybe it's better to be safe than sorry.'

'So there are the "take-it-out" and the "better-safe-than-sorry" schools?' Lord Crawford put in.

'Inevitably. If you live in the middle of a transitional period it's difficult to see the wood for the trees, and doubly difficult for the surgeon with the knife in his hand.'

'It's certainly a transitional age all round. You'll see the difference in Sholton?' He looked at Maeve.

'Yes. The workers aren't worked to death, there isn't the evil of truck . . . do you remember how Kieran and I worked so hard on that after he was injured in the pit explosion?'

'We had no truck with truck, may I remind you.' Charlie saw their eyes meet. I'm out of my depth here, he thought. 'But, yes, I agree, those were the bad old days. An invidious system to mortgage a man's wage.'

'If Kieran were alive today he'd still be working for the men. That's one thing we've always done in McGraths, tried to look after the carters' welfare.' She looked proud. 'Some of the less reputable employers only pay them twenty-one shillings a week for a twelve hour day!'

'I'm no business man,' the excellent port helped Charlie to intervene, 'but it strikes me that the men are beginning to look after their own interests, aided and abetted by men of Arthur Cranston's character. It may be the transition age, but it's also the rise of the Trade Unions, don't you agree, Lord Crawford?'

'Yes, I do. There's no reason why management and labour shouldn't work well together for their mutual benefit. I'm a radical,' his eyes sought Maeve's again, 'unlike my father.'

Charlie told them of his book, of the squalor and poverty he had found in the black spots of the city. 'Chiefly around the cathedral. Ironical, isn't it? Maevy knows all about it. She's told me of going into a house where a dead child has been lying on the table for three days because the whole family lived in a single room and it had to lie there until they buried it. She's on their side . . .'

The effects of the port seemed to run out of him. He was back with her, saw again that gaunt face on the pillow, heard that voice, so unlike her own bright one. 'I want to die.' His spirits plummeted. If this smooth-talking personable man had not been here he could have asked her mother if she had any idea what was worrying her. Together they could have gone over what she had said, tried to unravel it. He looked at Maeve, at her beautiful face as she listened, chin on hand, to Alastair Crawford. That was how she thought of him, he was sure.

But she would only tell what she wanted to. There was steel under her beauty. She would protect her family to the last.

'If you'll excuse me, Mrs McGrath,' he said, 'I'd better be on my way home. I'm expecting a late call from Colliers' Row. Maybe two.'

Lord Crawford rose, too. Proprieties must be observed. 'A doctor's work is never done. Thomas will be outside. He'll take us both home.'

They made their adieus and thanks, and left.

29

A week later Maeve went back with Terence to his house for dinner. He had accompanied her to the Infirmary, but although he was not allowed in, he had insisted on waiting for her. Driving afterwards in the cab along Sauchiehall Street to Great Western Terrace, he put his hand on hers. 'Don't worry, Mother. She'll get better in the end. You know what a stubborn wee thing she is.'

'Her stubbornness has left her, Terence. For the first time since she fell ill, I was afraid today. She looked terrible, like a skeleton, my bonnie lass. Her life is draining out of her. This is the middle of June, the fourth week since she went in there, and far from an improvement she's getting worse by the hour.'

'You see her at the end of the day. Patients are always lower in their spirits by that time.'

'What surprises me is that she has so little fight in her. You know how she always went straight for anything she wanted, becoming a nurse, for instance. It's as if she had nothing left to live for.' You're not telling the strict truth, Maeve McGrath. You know something crossed your mind when you looked down on that poor girl, her constantly-moving lips, those spots of colour on those paper white cheeks . . .

'She's not still pining for John Craigie, is she?'

She looked at him. 'You knew about that?'

'Yes, we once had a talk.'

'No, I've a feeling that's over, although he's the only one that's allowed in to see her, except Charlie and me. Maybe it's because he's a minister.'

'Maybe he doesn't do her any good with his holy talk, gathering her into the Eternal Arms before she's ready. She'd have been better with me. I could have cheered her up.'

'Aye, you used to be the one, Terence. Her favourite brother. She'd do anything for you, save you from anything within her power.' She did. Would it do any good to tell him now about the letter Maevy had destroyed? She couldn't see any sense in it. He'd had enough to bear.

Her mind was on Maevy as the cab made its brisk way along Sauchiehall Street. She could remember when she was a young woman the north side here was all gardens. Look at it now. And here was Albany Place, not so elegant as Claremont Terrace, but handy for the Grand Hotel. She remembered Catherine and Terence going to functions there for the Temperance Movement . . . I mustn't have a gloomy face for the boys, she thought.

Sadie asked if she could have a word with her when she was in the nursery later. It sounded ominous.

'It's about my intended, George Rintoul, Mrs McGrath. You know he's gone to Canada to seek his fortune?'

'Yes. Is he doing well?'

'Yes, fine. He's a good worker, learned his trade in Denny's in Dumbarton. He says once he gets settled and has a house, he'll be sending for me. It's the boys, you see . . . and Mr Terence.'

'Will you soon be going to Canada, Sadie?' Robert asked anxiously.

'No, no, not for a while.'

'Where's Canada?' Terence's lower lip stuck out.

Robert looked down his nose at his young brother. 'Mr Rintoul told you all about it, the grizzly bears, and the snow, and the Great Lakes!'

'The Great Lakes?' Terence echoed tearfully, 'Are they bigger than the one at the park?'

'That's just a wee one for the fountain!'

'Don't you worry about a thing,' Maeve told them, 'and you've lots of good times to look forward to at Braidholme. That pony, Benjamin, is just dying for your summer holidays to come.'

She did not mention anything about Sadie to Terence when she went downstairs to the dining-room. Mrs McLeary waited on them herself and there was no chance of any private conversation. She expected, although on the whole a sensible body, a reasonable modicum of praise from Maeve for her running of Terence's household, and Maeve was not slow to give it.

'A lovely piece of brisket, Mrs McLeary. And the gravy!' She was quietly ecstatic. 'You can always tell a good cook by her gravies and sauces.'

'There's only one way to make gravy and that's with the good juices of the beef and a wee tait o' flour to thicken it. That's the secret.'

'You're right. I think you could give my Susan a few tips.' She kept her face straight.

In the drawing-room she looked around surreptitiously. Mrs McLeary's creativity with gravy did not extend to arranging flowers, indeed to flowers *per se*. She had seen some nice moss roses in the garden as they had come in that would have looked grand in that wee white Doulton bowl . . .

'You're thinking this is a cheerless kind of place, aren't you, Mother?' Terence said. He had filled himself out a large whisky. 'I can read you like a book.'

'You haven't been able to read me that well or you would have offered me a whisky when you poured your own.'

'But you never take it!' Terence hurried to the side table, poured her a generous amount.

'Never say never. Thanks, Terence. The great mistake is never to change. Tonight I feel like a whisky. Yes, I admit I'm feeling a bit depressed. I'm worried sick about Maevy. And while I know you could be a lot worse, you could be a lot better. This room looks like you, sufficient, that's all. A place for going from rather than coming to.'

'I don't spend much time indoors, that's true. I need the company. When the boys are older . . .'

'I'm not criticizing. There's no one I've more admiration for than you, how you've shouldered your burden. It's just that every mother wants to see her family happy, although she knows in her heart of hearts that isn't possible. But here, son,' she looked around again, 'you strike me as just existing.'

'Aren't most people doing that? There's not much real happiness about. Even Patrick's and Maria's is tempered by that child of theirs. That must break their hearts.'

'They can share their grief with each other.'

'Yes.' He sipped his whisky, his face sad. What a difference between the Terence of Colliers' Row and this defeated man, she thought.

'I knew about Flora,' she said. The words were out before she could stop them.

He looked up, startled, and for a second she saw the boy, Terence, that look when he had been caught out – Terence's pout – even imagined the tumbled curls falling over his brow. 'That's a long time ago,' he said.

'Not so long.'

'Who told you?'

'Never mind. I knew. But that turned out all right. She married, didn't she, and the baby has a father, maybe its own.' He did not answer. His head was bowed over his glass, and she reproached herself bitterly, except that the air had to be cleared. Then, maybe she would tell him about the letter . . .

'My life's been a series of mistakes with women,' his voice was low, 'Bessie, Catherine and Flora. Bessie was the only one I really loved. Flora came out of it better than the other two. She's alive. But it tortures me to think that maybe Catherine knew of her, and maybe that was why . . .'

'We all make mistakes. The strange thing is that when you get to my age they sometimes turn out for the best.' She thought of Alastair Crawford, how she had blamed herself at the time for betraying Kieran, how now he had come back into her life. If you lived long enough you began to see a pattern. 'And,' she said, 'I've begun to think you should keep your promises to yourself.'

'What do you mean?'

'It was your father's dearest wish to go back to Ireland. He talked about it often, said he would like to "feel its softness on his cheek". Your father was a poet but there was never enough time for poetry or for going back to Ireland.'

'Ah, don't grieve.' He had his father's quick sympathy.

'Patrick could take care of things for a while . . .'

'What are you saying, Mother?'

She raised her head. 'I've been full of fear since I saw Maevy tonight. Fear of death, her death. I'd die a thousand times if I could take her place in this suffering. And just now the thought's come to me, why the devil am I thinking dark thoughts like that? I've got to concentrate on her getting better! And then when I see her out of bed and being looked after by that man who's nearly dying himself out of love and worry for her . . .'

'Charlie McNab . . .'

'Yes. Then you and I will be off to Ireland. You never know how long Sadie will be with you.'

270

'I know about Georgie Rintoul. I'm prepared for it.'

'That's best. And who better to accompany me since I can't have your father with me?'

'Second best, is it?'

'No, next in line. Maybe he'll see us sallying forth from wherever he is and be giving us a wave. But only when Maevy's better. Not *if*, you notice, *when*. Would you like to come along?'

'I'd like it fine.' It was his old smile, the one that charmed the girls, always would.

'I've never said it before, but my heart aches for Woodlea . . .'

'Your old home? You hardly ever speak about it.'

'That's why. But, oh, those early mornings and the hooves of the horses ringing on the hard frosty ground and the strip of silver that was Lough Arrow across the fields.'

'Woodlea . . .' She saw the name had a magic in it for him. 'Do you think there will be anyone living there now?'

'I don't know, son. It's a long time ago. But we could find out, couldn't we?'

'Yes, we could find out . . .'

30

Charlie was at the piano as she walked up the garden path to his house. That must be how he wound down at the end of the day, lucky man, she thought, a man of many parts, the right man for Maevy. She admired his garden as she rang the bell, nothing niggardly about that huge clump of variegated delphiniums, that dense bed of stocks, and he had an eye for blending colour.

She heard him shouting, 'I'll get it, Biddy!' and then he was at the door, his smile taking away the gauntness from his face, a gauntness akin to Maevy's. 'Come away in,' he said, and then, almost immediately, 'Did you go today?'

'Yes. It couldn't wait till tomorrow. I'd like a word with you.'

He led the way into his sitting-room. 'Here, this is a comfortable chair.' His room was like his garden, to be used, and again showing an eye for placing the few pieces of furniture, as unlike Terence's mausoleum as night from day. 'Was she any better?' He could not hide his tenseness.

'Not that I could see. I had a word with Mr Wilcox. He said everything had been done that was possible. I thought that sounded ominous. What do you think?'

He considered. 'It's a typical surgeon's remark. Once you've wielded the knife you have to hold by your decision.'

'Right or wrong?'

'Something had to be done. We must give him the benefit of the doubt. The abscess is being drained.'

'But it depends how far it's spread?'

'There's that.' He looked at her. 'What I can't understand is . . . she was such a healthy girl, good constitution, the right candidate for an operation, I'd have said. Oh, you would expect pus, filth, plenty of it, the site of the trouble has to be cleared, but it's as if there's an invader in her mind as well as her body that she can't or isn't prepared to fight.'

'Do you think,' she spoke hesitantly, 'that in such a cut-and-dried thing as surgery the mind can influence the body in some way? That's what's worrying me. She's getting good attention, that Nurse Allan is an angel. Maybe Mr Wilcox didn't go far enough, but it should have come right by this time, shouldn't it?'

'Most of the time it does.'

'Do *you* think there's something on her mind?'

He got up and paced about the small room, stopped to look out of the window at the darkening garden. She could smell its scent coming through the open window. This was the best time for the sweetness . . . He turned to face her.

'Maevy is as honest as the day, straight with everybody, straight with herself. Maybe hard on herself. And if her standards slip, if she lets herself down in any way, she'd suffer. How much more would she suffer when she's lying in bed, ill for the first time in her life, when she's been given time to think . . .'

'And if she couldn't find peace with herself, couldn't come to terms with what was troubling her . . . that would make her worse?'

'There's no saying. One thing I'm sure about, you can't separate the mind from the body. The more I read the more convinced I become of that. And I'm beginning to think as well that our early memories have more importance than we know. I don't mean so much "memories", as a particular instance in the past that stands out like a

273

peak in our consciousness, and in a way explains what we are today. You'll likely have something similar yourself.'

She smiled. 'Funnily enough, I was telling Ṭerence earlier of a memory which always crops up with me. It's of riding early in the morning at my home in Ireland with Kieran. The sensation of that will never leave me.'

'I doubt if that's far enough back. To me that just shows he was your true love, the only one you could share joy with. And youth.'

'I think you're right.'

'Mine is of getting lost when I was five. We were shopping in some big town, probably Dundee, and I ran from my mother to look at something and when I turned she wasn't there. My memory is of searching, searching, and eventually finding her, or of her finding me. Maybe that's why I go on searching, hoping . . .'

'Charlie, there was a letter.'

'What's that?' His eyes pierced her.

'There was a letter. She destroyed it, burned it.'

He came swiftly and sat down opposite her, leaned forward. His eyes were brilliant. She had always thought they were black. Now she saw they were the deepest indigo, there were even golden flecks in the iris. 'Tell me everything.' His voice was harsh. 'Don't leave out a single thing.'

She told him of Ethel Mavor, and how she had admired Terence, followed him with her eyes. 'He never gave her a thought. Terence's girls had to be pretty, but you know his charm. He never passed her desk without speaking to her. He likes to be liked. Maybe she thought he was showing interest in her. Well, she saw him with a girl in some howff or other and started writing anonymous letters to Catherine.'

'Were they true?'

'Oh, yes. The girl, a servant girl with Patrick,' she was

pleased his eyes did not flicker at that, 'had a child. Whether or not it was Terence's, I don't know.' She looked at him. 'I'm sure it was possible. Anyway, she got married to a farmer, Maria told me. I wouldn't be surprised if she used Terence to make sure of the other man.'

'So this woman, Mavor, wrote to Catherine and told her about the child?'

'Yes, you have to understand Catherine, always snobbish about her background, her standing in society. I don't say this vindictively, Charlie, she was a born old maid who got married because she was flattered, and probably infatuated a little. She didn't like the marriage bed. Don't ask me how I know it, but I'm one who did and I can tell. She knew she couldn't hold Terence in that way, knew in any case that his only love had been Bessie Haddow.'

'Why in God's name didn't he marry her and not Catherine Murdoch?'

'That's a man's question.' She smiled at him. Why had he wasted his time with Miss Wilcox when he loved Maevy? 'Terence became obsessed with Catherine when he was a lad. Maybe he was taken by her being a minister's daughter – he's always been susceptible to "class", maybe by her air of inaccessibility which he thought he could break down. He never did because there was nothing to warm. I think that his regrets about Bessie, too late, led him to seek love with other women.'

'Lizzie should have gone to live with them. He would have at least found Bessie through her.'

'You know about Lizzie?'

'It's a village and I'm the doctor.' He smiled at her.

'It was impossible. Catherine would never have stood a constant reminder of Bessie in her own house.'

'And the letter?' His eyes were fixed on her.

'A series of them, I'm sure, until the final one telling her about the child. That was the end of her world. You've just talked about the influence the mind has on the body. Then when Maevy found her dead, she hid the note to save Terence any more distress and later burned it.'

'Ah, my poor love.' The words seemed to burst from him. He got up again as if he could not bear his thoughts, walked to the mantelpiece, fingered a small *cloisonné* box lying there, came back again. 'It wasn't a suicide note.'

'No. She was asked by the policeman if there had been one. She didn't have to lie. But it had a bearing on Catherine's suicide. I have to tell you, Charlie, that when she told me what she'd done I said I'd have done the same. I don't know if I would or not, but that poor girl's face was there before me, and besides, I was burning with hate against Ethel Mavor.'

'Is she still working with you?'

'No, she's disappeared. I've never heard a word from her. I was going to wreak vengeance on her,' she smiled wanly, 'but then there seemed no point.'

'She was a blackmailer all the same. She'd committed a felony. I'll go and see Maevy tomorrow.'

'What will you do?'

'I don't know. Try and get her to talk, try and help her, maybe let her know that I know about the letter. Have I your permission to do that?'

'Surely. You don't blame me?'

'Blame you? I'd as much think of blaming you as Maevy. There was love in both your hearts.'

'Now I'm tired. I'll get home.' She got up.

'I'll go with you.'

'All right.' She was too tired to desist. For the first time, she thought, I'm feeling my years.

'You use yourself up in the service of others,' he said, as they went out.

276

'Oh, I'm not like that, I'm selfish, pleasure-loving, but Maevy . . . she's a special lass. I couldn't bear it if . . . anything happened to her.' It was in Charlie's hands now. He would know what to do for the best.

'Nor could I.' He repeated more softly, 'Nor could I.'

They did not speak going through the quiet gardens, but when he left her at her own door, he kissed her.

31

She had deteriorated in the two days since he had seen her. His professional eye told him that, the dryness of the skin, the cracked lips, brown, not pink, the scored circles under the eyes, the dull hair. These were physical signs. Above and beyond that, even although her eyes were closed, there was a look of exhaustion, of bone-weariness, of an inability to fight any more in the way her head lay low on the pillow, the hands limp at her sides. Her body under the counterpane scarcely raised it, as if it had been drained flat, like an empty skin.

'She's weary,' Nurse Allan had said before she led him to the bed, 'the only thing that keeps her going, strangely enough, is the fever.'

'That's still with her?'

'Aye, it'll be the last to go.' She must have seen his face, 'Oh, I didny mean that, doctor, it's just . . . it breaks my heart to see that lassie going down the hill like this. She's like . . . a lamp on the glimmer.'

He had signalled towards the bed. He could not trust himself to speak. When she had finished fussing with nursely touches and had gone he took Maevy's hand.

'How's my bonny lass?' He spoke softly. Her eyelids quivered.

'Is that you, Charlie?'

'Yes. You've disappointed me. I thought I'd find you sitting at the side of the bed today.'

'Ah, if I could.' She sighed.

'Nurse Allan tells me your dressings are almost clean

now. If you were nursing someone, you'd be pleased, wouldn't you?'

'If I . . . ?' She did not seem to understand.

'Sister McGrath,' he said, 'that's you.' He raised her hand and kissed it, holding it to his lips. He saw the ghost of a smile.

'Am I still your darling?'

'You're still my darling, always will be.' He bent his head to her, put his face against hers, 'Maevy, when you're up, will you marry me?'

There was not enough blood in her, but it seemed to him that the fever spots on her cheeks deepened. He watched the tears seep through her eyelids and trickle slowly down her face. She did a childlike thing. She put out her tongue to lick them.

Didn't someone in the McGrath family once tell him that she'd been called 'Wee Maeve'? In severe illness, he had noticed, grown-up behaviour often disappeared. He remembered the old woman who had sung 'Wee Willie Winkie' when she was on the point of death. All Scottish children knew the rhyme, Maevy did, he was sure. Miller, the man who wrote it, was buried up there in the Necropolis. And that other man, Motherwell, whose poem to Jeannie Morrison he had come across on one of his sleepless nights recently.

> Oh lay your cheek to mine Willie,
> Your hand on my breast-bane . . .
> Oh say you'll think on me Willie,
> When I am deid an' gane . . .

He looked down on Maevy's face and knew terror. 'You didn't accept my proposal.' She lay like death, but the tears were still trickling down her cheeks. 'Maevy,' he said gently, 'why don't you answer?'

She turned her head against the pillow, again like a child. 'I'm not . . . worthy. A sin, a moral . . .'

'Is it the letter you're thinking of?'

Her eyes flew open and he could see her soul cowering in them. He hated himself for his crudeness, his coarseness, in speaking like that. 'The . . . letter?'

'The one Ethel Mavor wrote to Catherine. Yes, it was Ethel Mavor in McGraths' office. You didn't know that. She was jealous of Terence's wife . . .'

'Ethel . . . Mavor?' she said, wonderingly. 'Oh, she would have been far too plain for Terence . . .' He laughed at that woman-like remark, and then the terror returned. She was shaking. He even heard her teeth rattling, saw how her hand went up to her mouth. 'What do you know about the letter?'

'Everything. What was in it. That you found it and burned it for Terence's sake.'

'That was bad, wasn't it?' She was shivering like a dog that had been kicked. 'I knew all the time it was bad, and then John said it, too. Morally wrong.'

Wee Maeve. Bad. Long ago Isobel had told her she was 'bad', that she had caused her brother's death . . . 'It wasn't bad. But there's only one person who could decide. You know that, don't you?'

'You mean . . . God?'

'No,' he laughed, 'the Fiscal. Maybe he thinks of himself as God, but I'm sure he's a kind man. Dr Wordie, Terence's doctor, knows him well, doesn't he?' He saw the slight nod. 'Maevy,' he took her hand again, 'will you let me go and see him? Tell him what you did?' He felt the feeble jerk of her hand, held it firmly. 'And then when you're better, we'll call and see him together. I'm sure that will be the end of the matter. He knows nothing will bring Catherine back. He's concerned with the living, not the dead.'

'It's cowardly,' her voice seemed to have gathered a little strength, 'to let you go in my place.'

'No, no. Of course, if you'd been well you would have gone yourself, but I would only be acting as your envoy until such times as I could take you.'

'I'm frightened.'

'You wouldn't be frightened with me beside you. And you know you'll only be frightened all your life if you *don't* go, plagued by the feeling that it was morally wrong.'

'Do *you* think it was, Charlie?' Her voice was pitiful.

'I'm no lawyer. It would take Aristotle himself to argue the rights and wrongs of the case. My belief is that if you do something legally wrong for the right reasons, the law will be lenient.'

She did not answer. The heightened colour drained from her cheeks, the tears dried. Nurse Allan came back, pounding quietly on her rubber soles.

'I've strict instructions not to let anyone stay longer than five minutes, Dr McNab. She has to guard her strength.'

'She's still got strength,' Charlie said, and bending close he kissed Maevy's cheek. 'Haven't you? To marry me?' He felt the corner of her mouth move under his lips.

'Do you hear him, Nurse Allan?' She was making an effort to joke and that was even more pitiful, 'Trying to play . . . the Gay Lothario . . . for your benefit.'

'And isn't he the picture of it?' the girl said enthusiastically. 'By Jove, if I was in your shoes . . . or bed-socks,' she let out a tirl of laughter, 'I'd be louping out of that bed and away doon the watter with him for a sail!'

'I've done louping.'

'Who's this old woman I have lying here? Do you hear her, doctor?' She nodded meaningly at him, eyes slanting to the door and pounded away, full of tact.

He said softly, 'What is it to be, Maevy? Do you want me to be your envoy?'

'Aye,' she sighed, a long sigh, 'you be my envoy.'

He sat for a few moments, his fingers on her pulse. It was flickering, but he fancied it was slightly stronger. Maybe the last bit of pus would drain away now. He bent and kissed her forehead before he left.

He had looked at his watch when he came out of the Infirmary and found he had just time. His surgery was an hour later than Dr Wordie's, the difference between a town practice where the white collar workers were free at five, and his own practice where they had to wash the grime off their bodies before they could present themselves at 'the doactor's'. He summoned a cab.

He hoped Dr Wordie would be at this moment doing justice to a good tea to put him in a receptive mood. The tea, if it were anything like Biddy's, would be 'set'. Only the gentry had it on wee tables in their drawing-rooms, even those with West End practices were scarcely gentry despite his mother's fond hopes. The table, again if it were anything like Biddy's, would be groaning with home baking, every variety of scone, bannock, teabread, pan bread and fruit bread, and at least three varieties of jam, strawberry, raspberry and 'aipricot', to spread on top of the thickly-laid fresh butter. And oh, what sonsy vehicles those treacle scones, cookies and pancakes made!

He was shown into Dr Wordie's consulting room, vast, panelled, with a circle of straight-backed chairs round a table laden with magazines mostly depicting some aspect of the hunting field. Why did every Glasgow man of substance like to pretend his roots were in the country?

He watched the people going in one by one, silent, respectful, carrying their complaint or illness like a secret. No swapping of symptoms here as in his own surgery, where often he was greeted by a cheery, 'Mrs MacPherson back there says aw a need, doactor, is to pit ma feet in a mustard bath and wrap a gravat roon ma' neck.'

I'm better off where I am, he thought, and surprisingly enough, for it seemed like the first time the thought had come to him, better off in general practice than an operating theatre. Much better to live amongst people who can answer back, give them the benefit of my hospital experience, to have time at the end of the day to read a little, or play a little. Pray God Maevy will be with me . . . He was surprised when the man beside him nudged him in the ribs and said, 'The doctor's bell's ringing. You're next.'

He came to himself and got up, knocked on Dr Wordie's door and went in. 'Good evening,' he said, 'I'm Dr McNab from Sholton.'

Dr Wordie hid his surprise well. 'Ah, good evening to you, Dr McNab. Sit down, if you will. I thought you looked too healthy for a patient. But you should have presented yourself at my house. I would have seen you there.'

'I didn't want to intrude. I'll be brief, Dr Wordie, as I have an evening surgery myself. You'll remember the case of the sad death of Mr Terence McGrath's wife?'

'Indeed I do.' This time he did not hide his surprise.

'I'm a close friend of Miss Maevy McGrath, his sister.'

He nodded. 'I remember her well. A sensible young lady. Her brother would have been lost without her.'

'She's ill just now, in the Royal – she's a Sister there, as you may remember – and she's asked me if I'd clear up a small matter with the Procurator Fiscal on her behalf.' He hurried on, seeing the curiosity in the doctor's eyes, 'Could you give me his address, if it isn't too much trouble? I knew you'd be the best person to approach.'

'Well, yes, I can give you that. I don't know if he'll

. . .' he looked at Charlie who looked back blankly, 'but, yes, I know how people are when they're ill, small matters become large. Is it serious?'

'She's had an operation to drain an abscess – her appendix.'

'Ah, yes, well, she'll be in good hands in the Royal. My friend, the Fiscal, lives just a few doors away from here, number 27. Would you like me to write to him . . . about the matter?' His upward glance was masterly, tact struggling with curiosity.

'That's kind of you, doctor, but it isn't necessary. I've been entrusted with this mission, if you understand. The lady in question and I intend to marry when she's fully recovered in health.'

'Ah, well, that's different. A sad case that, Mrs McGrath's, er . . . death. Between one medical man and another, although the last thing I expected was *that* outcome, she hadn't been in robust health for some time. Physically she was all right, but she confided in me quite a lot . . . about other matters. Of course Mr and Mrs McGrath are vastly different in temperament, I mean, *were* . . . he's the soul of conviviality, likes a communal life, while she was of a quiet almost brooding, religious disposition, didn't you find?'

'I didn't know them very well.' He was an old woman.

'I suppose like me you see many sides of marriage. I've found the most lamentable ones are where the public have the opposite impression. It's especially important for a medical man to choose a good wife, one who doesn't mind being left alone, who can create a good impression when she has to receive, as I, er, have, let us say, *important* patients. But there, I'm sure Miss McGrath will meet your requirements to perfection . . .' He'd go on for ever, Charlie thought, rising. At Sholton, if you took this amount of time with a patient, you would hear the shouts of impatience from the other side of the door, even the drumming of tackety boots. Yes, he liked it better there.

'Is that you, Charlie?' Her eyes flickered open. They were washed clean of the fever. He saw that at a glance.

'Yes, it's Charlie. Your envoy.'

'My envoy.' She repeated the words. 'You're a funny lad.' Her hand moved on the counterpane towards him and he took it firmly.

'I'm your darling.'

'So you said.' She smiled but her eyes closed again. She was still weak, but the last two days had made a difference. Her skin was moist, her hair had life in it. The tendrils on her brow were golden.

'Maevy, I fixed it with the Fiscal. He'll see you when you're well enough. He was understanding. You'll like him. You have nothing to fear.'

Her eyes were wide open now. 'You'll be with me?'

'Of course I'll be with you.' He lifted her hand and kissed it. 'I'm your intended. Had you forgotten? Just as soon as you feel up to it we'll be married. You can't back out of it now.'

'I wouldn't want to.' The colour was back in her eyes as well. She was beautiful to him. 'I've had plenty of time to think, lying here. And to feel. Aye, no matter how ill you are, you get the feel of people coming to you.' She smiled at him. 'If you'll have me, I'm yours.' Straight as a die. His eyes filled and he turned away.

'What is it, Charlie?'

He cleared his throat. 'If you knew the length of time I've waited for you to say that . . .'

'It's my stubborn bit.' The blue eyes were tender, not stubborn. 'But I know when it's time to give in.'

He bent and kissed her. Her skin was blue-white round the eyes, he must be gentle with her. 'Oh, we'll get on fine, you and me,' he said.

BOOK TWO

Going Back
1890–1900

1

Maria sat at the dressing-table of the rented house in Brodick on the Isle of Arran, brushing her hair for the night. The bracken smell and the smell of brack, which was a different thing, Patrick had explained to her, came to her from the open window, tangy, essentially Scottish, the smell of the sea. 'You haven't lived,' he had told her once, 'until you've popped bladderwort or swung long ribbons of it above your head, or looked for wee crabs in the pools with a jam jar. *That*'s doon the watter!'

'Leave it loose,' he said now from the bed. She smiled and met his eyes in the mirror. He was sitting up on the pillows watching her, his eyes ardent. My secret, she thought. Despite Terence's reputation as a lady-killer, Patrick is probably more passionate than he is. Only one other person knew that, and she, poor girl, was dead. It was the philandering Terence liked, the chase rather than the conquest, with the exception of Bessie Haddow. She could see her in Lizzie, whom Patrick said resembled her 'except where she resembled my mother'. Catherine had not left the same sweetness. Maybe that was the true immortality.

'It ripples under your brush,' he said. 'Lovely hair, like a raven's wing. Tie it back while we're here, my love. Don't dress it. You're still a girl.'

'Am I?' She took a satin ribbon from a box on the dressing-table and passed it under her hair at the nape of her neck, tied it in a bow at the front. Yes, it made her look younger. 'What a day it's been.' She wanted to delay the delicious moment. 'I never thought we'd all get here without mishap. But Mary liked the sail from Wemyss

Bay, didn't she? She laughed at the seagulls. Her eyes followed them.'

'I thought Gaylord would fall over the rail. But trust our Sarah. She kept an eye on him.'

'She helped me to pack the trunks this time, folded things so neatly.'

'I've never understood why it's necessary to have three trunks as well as all those suitcases. A feminine mystery. Thank goodness at least the firm took the lot to the station for us. The poor horses were buckling at the knees.'

She laughed at him, powdering her face and arms with a swansdown puff. 'Men never understand because they refuse to concern themselves with domestic affairs. We've Jeannie and the other girl here with us, there are the three children, and you and I, and maybe guests. Do you want them to sleep on bare mattresses like in Sing Sing, and wipe their faces on their petticoats and shirts instead of towels? Do you realize I have to calculate what we'll use for the month since the shops here aren't as good as Glasgow? The great wooden box you complained of is an order from Mr Lipton.' She was ticking off the items on her fingers. 'Then there are the children's toys and books. And your books, all before I start packing the suitcases with clothes for us all.'

'Sure and you're a wonderful organizer. Do you think you could organize yourself into bed before I die of love for you?'

She laughed, stood up, took off her negligée and crossed the room, slipped into bed beside him. Immediately his arms were round her, he was pressing her body close to him. 'The Brodick air's gone to your head already,' she said.

'It's not the air, it's you.' He was on top of her, lying still for a second, his head on her breast. 'Your heart's racing. You want me, too, don't you?'

'I've never not wanted you.'

Their love-making had been a pleasure from the first day of their marriage, at first too quickly over. Now they had learned to temper it, to savour its sweetness, the slowly mounting passion, the inevitable pounding urgency of it.

His voice was rough against her ear now. 'I'm mad for you. It's like the first year. Maybe it *is* the Brodick air, Maria . . . my love . . . let me stay inside . . . let me . . .'

The heart-breaking sweetness of it. She wanted him to be in her, to feel his life moving inside her, more than anything that was what she wanted, and then came the brake, remembering not to move too suddenly . . . Mary. Another child. Perhaps another tragedy. She needed all her strength to cope with her. 'You promised, Patrick . . .'

'Ach, yes, I promised . . .' He handled himself out of her and lay palpitating at her side. 'It's like . . .' he was breathing heavily, 'never knowing . . . the end of a book.'

'You knew it before, when Sarah and Gee-Gee were coming. It's only since Mary . . .' She knew his hurt because she felt the same, but she knew also how to console him, to love him tenderly, to talk to him. 'We're lucky, my darling, to have our love, even with its restrictions. I'll get over my fear. Mary will grow older and less of a worry. You know how I love you. You've made my life for me. You're the man I waited for all those years at Springhill.' His head lay between her breasts, and she stroked his hair. 'Remember that sad lad who came to visit us, full of grief, and how you wouldn't talk at first? And then I told you about my Uncle Gaylord, and the tragedy of his death, and it took your mind away from your own tragedy. When you first smiled at me, really at me, I wept in bed with happiness. There will be other times, many times. We'll relax here, take the children to

the sands, walk on the hills, make love at night . . .'
There was a high wailing from the bedroom where the
children were sleeping. Mary, she thought, the heaviness
returning to her heart. It went on and on, high-pitched,
plaintive, rising in volume.

'It's because of the new house,' Patrick said. 'Jeannie's
not managing to quieten her.'

'She'll waken the other children.' She lay for a moment
or two. 'Like a seagull's cry . . . I'll go and get her.'

'Yes.' He took his weight off her.

'My poor darling.' She did not know whether she meant
Patrick or Mary. She went quietly along the corridor and
found Jeannie already in the bedroom, a long plait
hanging down her back, the wailing child in her arms. She
could see the head rolling, the clutching hands. She did
not cry like the others, it was hoarse, rough . . .

'Oh, has she wakened you, Madam?' Jeannie looked
up. 'I tried my best.'

'I'm sure you did. Give her to me, Jeannie, and you get
back to bed. Are the other two all right?'

'They stirred a bit in their sleep, that's all.'

'Go to sleep yourself. You've had a long day.'

She went back to their room, and got into bed, putting
the child between them. Her sad wailing stopped, as if the
warmth soothed her. The gurgling noises began, her sign
of pleasure. Patrick's voice was gentle.

'What are you doing in our bed, Mary, you wee rascal?'
She won't understand, Maria thought, only the warmth.
She stroked the child's head, murmuring endearments.

'She can't tire herself out like the others, that's what it
is. Nearly a year and a half and still showing no signs of
walking. Do you think her bad chest weakens her?'

'Don't fret. Girls are always longer, Mother says.'

'Yes, I know.' She tried not to sigh. 'She's a big girl,
isn't she? Can you feel the length of her? She ought to be

292

walking. Shh, shh,' she said, stroking Mary softly, 'go to sleep, my precious, you're safe now. It's nice, Patrick, isn't it, her between us? She's at peace. She's happy now.'

'Aye, she's happy now, but we won't have to make a habit out of it.'

She smiled in the darkness. 'Oh, she'll settle down. Maevy once said that routine means more to children . . . like her.' She had never been able to say the word. 'But we'll soon instil a nice routine into her life. She can play on the sands every day and build castles and who knows she might even walk while she's here. Maevy says her legs are quite strong now and I've been massaging them.'

'Did she tell you to do that?'

'Yes. Isn't it good she's out of that infirmary now?' She spoke softly. Their hands met across the child's body.

'Yes, I feared at one time. We all feared. Mother said Charlie McNab was like a ghost. It's touching how he cares for her. I never saw a happier man.'

'What a wedding that will be! When do you think they'll have it?'

'My guess is they'll leave it till next year. She needs a lot of fattening up. What a wraith she was when she first came home! But she and Mother will have a fine time shopping for the wedding when she's well enough. Have you ever seen my mother in a shop?' He laughed softly. 'How she queens it! And yet she's gracious and friendly at the same time. The assistants just dance attendance on her. It's a performance, a true Irish lady's performance.'

'Do you think she'll give Braidholme to them?'

'I doubt it. Charlie has quite a decent house and it's always been known as the doctor's. They'll start off there.'

'James and Kate will be delighted about Maevy. Not to mention Father. He wrote to me saying how much she'd

293

impressed him. "Something special about that girl," he said.'

'Yes, he's a lucky man, Charlie, but I think it cuts both ways.'

'Ah, she's asleep now, the lamb.' Mary had given a quivering sigh. 'I still get homesick, Patrick. Mostly for Springhill, the beauty of it, and the river. Always the river. Its vastness.'

'You'll fall in love with the Firth of Clyde, too, mark my words. Give it time.'

'Yes, but I'd still like to go back.'

'We will. Once Terence and Mother's visit to Ireland is over, and the wedding's over. When I can be spared.'

'Next spring?'

'Yes, maybe next spring, or the summer. There are going to be great changes in transport. I've been saying that for years, but it's coming now. We're working up to the end of the century. If only things would move faster here. By God, they know how to do things in America! Their railways are being built at a terrific rate. They're pushing everywhere. Think of the cartage of railway freight in a place the size of that! Here the railways are trying to grab at them themselves. I admit we've made a few good deals with them, but there isn't the same scope. You always talk about the vastness of America and that's what's beginning to haunt me, its vastness, its scope. It's beginning to seem like an . . . Eldorado.'

'It's mine, too.' Her voice was loaded with sleep. 'Some day we'll go back . . .'

2

'I told you,' Maeve said to Terence, 'it's the softness on your cheek.'

They had travelled fairly comfortably from Glasgow to Portpatrick for the short crossing to Larne, the latter 'a bit short on luxury' Terence had said as they had stood on the deck buffeted by the wind. After that it had been a weary trip by train to Dublin and from there a horse-drawn bus, and lastly an Irish jaunting car for the final few miles to Boyle.

They had put up at the Freeman's Inn there, with the Boyle flowing swiftly under its windows. 'Bianconi's stage-coach used to leave from here when I was a girl,' she said excitedly. 'Four horses. From Boyle to Sligo. Did you see the size of the stables at the back? Father met the local horse dealers here on market days. Oh, the place would be alive with people, sure enough.'

After they had unpacked and refreshed themselves, nothing would do for her than that they should take a stroll before their evening meal, up steep Bridge Street to the Crescent to show Terence the tower erected by the tenants of the local estate, back again and across the Boyle, then along the main street to see the Abbey, its old stones silver-grey against the limpid light.

'You're right, the softness, no bite in it like back home. But it's more than that,' he looked around, 'it's the light.'

'Yes, it's the light, my clever boyo.' She was like a child in her enthusiasm. 'Look at it on that white-washed wall, and even the warm colour of that thatched roof. And wait till you see it in the countryside round Woodlea.

Especially when it's dying on the Curlew Mountains. The sad beauty of it. Sometimes I slipped round to the stables between tea and dinner (I was forbidden to go there latterly), and there was a kind of pale washed pinkness on the white walls. And a stillness. The noise of your father, or maybe Peters, he was the head groom, hammering nails into a hoof, was loud . . . supernaturally loud. It would echo round and round the yard. Even voices took on a different quality. You spoke softly in case you would . . . shatter the silence. The stable clock would strike and even that was like a tuning fork . . .'

Terence looked at her, smiling. 'I don't know how you stayed away for so long.'

'Now that I'm back I don't know how I ever did! The truth of it is, I put it out of my mind. A chapter closed. I've never been one for regrets, as you know. What's done is done. Your father was more . . . tender. He kept this place alive in his heart, often yearned for it, sang songs about it.'

'Patrick and I used to listen to him when we were in bed. It was like a lullaby for us. I'd sing softly along with him under the bedclothes till Patrick gave me a nudge with his sharp elbow.'

'It was like a lullaby to me, lying in his arms . . .' She laughed embarrassed. 'This place is putting its magic on me already. My tongue's running away with me.'

'It suits you. I even think your hair's turning redder by the minute!'

'Just wait till I start talking to the folks round Woodlea, if they remember me. My brogue will get thicker every word I speak. Will anyone remember me? Shall I have the courage to call, in any event? Have I the courage to walk up that drive to Woodlea after all those years?' She shook her head. 'The memories are flooding my brain, my tongue wants to tell them. But, honestly, son, don't you feel your heart lighter already?' She took his arm as they walked, turning eagerly to him.

'Yes, it's getting at me, too.' He smiled at her. 'No, I'm trying to please you. It hasn't got to me yet. I need a good dinner and some of your Irish poteen. But I've weathered the worst of the storm, nearly a year since Catherine . . . killed herself.' Only recently had he been able to say it straight out. 'The guilt takes longer. I wasn't a good husband to her. I failed her. I wasn't ever what she wanted.'

'Leave over grieving now. You've got the boys and you're still young. Let this be your first forward step, coming here.'

'Forward step!' He laughed. 'You'd make a great general. Is there by any chance an Irish marching song?'

'I can't think of one and that's a fact despite their bloody history. All their songs are softer, or sadder, like the air, like the Wild Geese . . . give me a minute, Terence, and I'll tell you who the Wild Geese were.'

'I didn't say a word.'

'Your eyebrows were up amongst your hair. It was after the surrender of Limerick when the Irish officers and soldiers left and gave their swords to France. They kept Ireland alive in their hearts with their songs, like the wild birds with their wailing cry . . . sure and I've got a touch of the blarney now all right.' She smiled at him and sang softly, ' "I hear you . . . calling . . . me." ' Her voice was true and sweet.

'You'll have the tears running down my cheeks.' He laughed at her. 'Aye, Scotland's the one for the warring songs, a different breed, "Scots wha' hae, wi' Wallace bred . . ." ' he mimicked the song, his voice rough, his elbows going at his sides. 'I never realized it until I came back here. The rain must soften the folks up.'

'You're right. Did you notice the easy-osy way of the

little servant-girl in the hotel back there? "The dinner's ready whenever you have a mind to eat it"? Well, maybe you were looking rather than listening. It would suit you here, Terence.'

'Maybe, but it wouldn't suit Patrick. All that wasted time in getting here in the first place. No timetables. No push.'

'It would irk him to distraction. If he thinks we're backward in Scotland, God alone knows what he'd say about it here!' She squeezed his arm as they walked. 'No, it's not for Patrick. We'll keep it for ourselves.'

Over dinner in the cosy dining-room they talked incessantly. Maeve's tongue was loosened by the excitement of being 'in her own place' as she said, and by the excellent wine poured by the 'easy-osy' maid who could not keep her eyes off Terence. And he himself seemed to throw off the trials of the last years and revert to the young careless boy he had been when they lived at Colliers' Row.

It was the rarest of bonds, Maeve felt, that of mother and son, different from the relationship between husband and wife, but as sweet. He's ready to go forward now, she thought, laughing with him, sometimes singing snatches of songs which came to her . . .

'Then up comes Ted without any legs
And in their place he has two wooden pegs.
She kissed him a dozen times or two
Saying: "Holy Moses 'tisn't you." '

His burst of laughter made the other diners look across at them.

'Oh, haven't you a terrible mother, Terence, sure enough. Tomorrow,' she said, 'we'll visit my home.' He nodded, smiling, his eyes on the little maid.

* * *

298

When the cab they had hired dropped them at the gates of Woodlea, Terence asked the man if he would wait. Maeve had had a sudden onslaught of nervousness when they were coming near the house.

'No, I couldn't drive up, Terence. I'm there whether I want to or not that way. Too . . . precipitate. I can always take to my heels and run, if we walk up the drive.'

The man was accommodating, if surprised. 'Whatever way you want it, to be sure. I tell you what. The village is only half a mile further on. I've a few cronies there right enough. When you're ready you stroll back and you'll see me horse standing thereabouts. We'll work in fine with each other that way.'

Things had changed without a doubt, the scale mostly. She thought the long walk up the drive would give her plenty of time to think, to decide, to turn back if she wished and no harm done, but it was shorter than she remembered.

Certainly it was autumn, the trees had not the luxurious foliage of full summer, but it seemed lighter, sparser, and she could not decide, although she looked carefully, where the spot was where she had met Kieran all those years ago. Forty, was it not? Then they had had to force their way through a thick tangle of laurel, now you could see through the border of shrubs to the stone wall behind, overgrown with moss and ivy.

Already she could catch glimpses of the house, and her heart began to beat rapidly. She was breathing quickly, and Terence must have heard her because he put a hand under her elbow in a reassuring way.

'Are you all right, Mother? Sure you want to go on?'

'Right as rain,' she said falsely.

This was the last bend before the house would come into full view, her last chance to turn back, but her feet were leading her onwards, albeit more slowly. Fifty-seven you are, she thought, and still accepting challenges. She felt her jaw muscles tighten. When they had rounded the bend she stopped. 'A minute, son.'

It was smaller than she remembered. That was the first thing, but still typically Georgian with its wide sweep of gravel in front of it and its flat windows. There had never been enough money, thank God, to add any of the Gothic excrescences of some of their wealthier neighbours. The stone was lighter than she remembered, or it had been bleached whiter by the sun. More likely washed whiter by the rain.

There were the drawing-room windows above the columned front door with the decorative stone detail above them. And the Corinthian pillars on either side of the heavy door through which she had slipped that night long ago, blessing Mick because he kept the hinges well-oiled. And the stone gryphons on either side of the flight of steps.

Her nervousness had disappeared. She realized she was looking at the house objectively for the first time. She had been conscious of it as a girl, it had been part of her, but she had never appreciated it aesthetically. Now she could admire the fine windows, their satisfying proportions to the rest of the house, the key-patterned stonework where the roof met the walls.

And there was a young lad raking the gravel, looking like Kevin. The name of old Mick's assistant came back to her. She laughed at herself. Kevin would be her age now, and Mick probably dead a long time ago. He had been shaky when she was a girl . . .

'So that's Woodlea?' She heard Terence's voice and turned to him. His eyes were bright, alert, she had not seen that expression in them for a long time. 'Your family home.'

'Is it like what you imagined?'

300

'Well, you never gave us much food for thought, but Patrick and I used to talk about it and wonder. Knowing about it, even if vaguely, made us feel . . . different from the other lads in Sholton.' He looked again. 'It's . . . gracious.'

'Yes, it is. I can see that now. And it's been looked after. Look at the windows, they're sparkling. And the steps haven't moss on them. They tended to gather moss . . .'

'It's a bit bare altogether.'

'Bare?' She was indignant. 'Well, you don't want to smother the fine lines of a house like that with climbing stuff! Beauty needs no adornment.' She met his mocking eyes and laughed. 'Well, it's true. Look at that fine door. Heavy. It . . . *swung* open. Inside the hall is black and white tiled, and there's a grandfather clock. Old Mick had the job of keeping all the clocks going in the house. He was especially proud of the grandfather one. Father always checked his watch by it before the meet.' She was suddenly nervous again. 'I don't know whether I should! There are people living there, that's obvious. I can't just walk up and knock at the door and say, "I'm Maeve McGrath and I used to live here a long time ago . . ."'

A girl came round from the back of the house, a dog at her heels. It immediately left her and came running towards Terence and Maeve where they stood. Not another Murphy, Maeve prayed. She had been through that once, cowering in the shrubbery, the terrier throwing itself at Kieran, snarling, biting . . .

It was a harmless enough dog, a spaniel. Her father would not have had one like that. He said their snivelling ways annoyed him, and sure enough, the stupid beast was now rolling at their feet. Terence stooped down, patted its stomach, then straightened. He waved in a friendly, reassuring fashion to the girl, put his hand under Maeve's elbow, and together they walked forward. She was standing looking at them, not smiling, that was the first thing Maeve noticed.

'Can I help you?' she said, polite, cold.

'You must excuse . . .' she started, but Terence took over.

'We shouldn't have barged in on you like this. We ought to have written first . . . my mother used to live here. She was Maeve Muldoon before she was married.'

She gained a little courage from him. 'We took a drive past the house and asked the man to drop us . . .'

'Did you say Maeve Muldoon?' The girl looked from Terence to her, astonishment in her eyes.

Maeve smiled at her. 'Yes. My father was Major Muldoon. I left here a long time ago, eighteen-fifty-one, to be exact. We went to Scotland, my husband and I, Kieran McGrath.' The girl's face had been changing as she spoke, from haughtiness to doubt and then to pleasure. It seemed to Maeve to open like a flower, and her smile became friendly, lighting her face.

'I can hardly believe what you're telling me. But it must be true. You're Maeve Muldoon, and your mother was a . . .'

'Daly.'

'And she had a sister, Maud, in Dublin?' Maeve nodded, smiling. 'But why am I keeping you standing here and questioning you?' her hands waved, 'like . . .' she looked at Terence, including him in her smile, 'like someone come for a job!' She laughed, 'Come away in! But why didn't you drive up?'

'Mother suddenly took fright.' Terence laughed, too. 'We told the man from Boyle who brought us to go on to the village and we'd pick him up there.'

'If it was Seamus Byrne you'll have to root him out. He's a great man for getting his feet under the table. You

302

shouldn't have been afraid to come,' she spoke to Maeve as if she were a child 'you belong here.' She was ushering them towards the steps as she spoke. 'You're my relations, for goodness sake!' She flashed Terence a smile over her shoulder, 'Maybe I'm your long-lost cousin.' She was excited, she looked like someone who welcomed excitement.

They went up the steps into the hall, the dog following, and immediately three little girls like a pack of puppies launched themselves on her. 'Mama, Mama! Where have you been?' They clustered round her, pulling at her tweed skirt.

'This is my brood,' she said, laughing, 'Mind, girls, you'll knock me over. Moira's the eldest, Dymphna's next and then Clare. Say how do you do, girls.' To Maeve's amazement they curtseyed, the youngest one, auburn-haired, teetering on her heels.

'How do you do,' she and Terence said, smiling, and Maeve added, 'What lovely curtseys! They must have been practising.'

'It's Moira's idea. She read in a book about being presented to the Queen. They're always play-acting. Come away into the snug.' She led them into a room off the hall, the little girls falling back shyly in spite of Maeve holding out a hand to them.

'This used to be my father's study,' she said, looking round.

'It's mine now. Oh, I didn't mean it that way!' Her cheeks flared, 'I meant I *use* it as my study. I've been trying to write . . . sit down, please. That's not a bad chair. And you, too . . .' she bit her lip, still embarrassed at her gaffe, looking at Terence.

'I'm Terence,' he said, 'the eldest son, the bad boyo of the family. Isn't that right, Mother?'

'Away with you. So you'll be?' She looked at the girl.

303

'Honor Daly.' She laughed at the astonishment in Maeve's face. 'My husband was a Daly. We'll get a paper and pencil and work it all out, but first you must have some tea. Moira, run and tell Edna we're ready.' She turned to Maeve again, said almost shyly, 'Do you know what decided me you were genuine? That's the wrong way of putting it, but I've got to be careful, living alone here. You'll understand that. Your lovely red hair. It's the real Muldoon hair, I've been told.'

'Aye, it persists. What ages have the little girls?'

'Moira, the eldest, is six, Clare's three and Dymphna's in between, so you see I had no time to get into mischief.' Her voice was cold for an instant, and then she was smiling at Terence, 'And you've got that famous hair, too, Mr McGrath.'

'Terence,' he said. 'You said I might be your long-lost cousin, and you wouldn't call *him* mister, now, would you?' Maeve looked at him. This was the tonic he needed. A change of air, a fresh person in his life with no connections with Catherine or Glasgow.

The autumn sun streamed in on them as they had tea, 'lashings of good strong Irish tea,' as Maeve said, sipping appreciatively. 'What do you think's the secret?'

'Sure and it's the *watter*,' the girl said, emphasizing the brogue. She spluttered into her cup with laughter, and the three little girls did the same. She's nervous, Maeve thought, and she hasn't laughed for a long time.

'Are you . . . alone all the time here?' she asked. She was young for a widow.

'Yes.' The laughter died out of her face. 'My husband passed on a few months ago. It was very sudden. Fortunately he'd made a will when we were first married leaving this place to me. Otherwise . . .' she stopped, frowning, as if she regretted saying what she had, 'I needed a place for the girls.' Her glance went to them and they looked

304

back at her, round-eyed, solemn, from the three stools they were sitting on. Maeve had watched them as they followed the conversation, laughing when they laughed, munching solidly.

Terence nodded. 'I can understand that.' He put down his plate on the low table. 'To the devil with pencil and paper. My mother's Aunt Maud in Dublin was a Daly . . .'

'I was being sent off to her when Kieran and I decided . . .' Maeve said. 'Oh, I wonder what happened to my mauve crinoline and bonnet to match that I had to leave behind . . .' Kieran's young face flashed before her, total recall. 'He might be descended from the Kings of Ireland for all you know,' she had told old Mairi once, through her tears. 'He should have been here with me, my Kieran.'

'Is he dead?' Honor Daly's face became sorrowful. She was very vulnerable, but then she was recently bereaved. And young. And yet with three children, she must be closer to thirty than twenty.

'Yes, eleven years ago. He loved Ireland, loved Woodlea. Ah, well, it's ancient history now. But I interrupted you, Honor. I can't call you Miss Daly, knowing we're related.'

'You've probably guessed the rest, and oh, I do wish I knew what happened to your trunk with the violet crinoline! We've a fine assortment of them in the attics. Your mother left this house to her sister, Maud, and as she was a spinster when she died it went to her brother, Daniel Daly. My husband was his grandson.'

'So we're cousins after all,' Terence said.

'Only by marriage.' She turned to the three little girls. 'You've got new relations. Isn't that exciting?'

'What's relations?' the one called Dymphna asked. Her

305

hair was a tone lighter than her mother's, but she had the same broad, pale brow.

'Family connections, Dymphna, on your father's side.'

'You can call me great aunt,' Maeve said, smiling.

'I'd like an aunty,' the small auburn haired one said, 'we haven't got an aunty.'

'But we have uncles!' The other two turned on her.

'Still, they're *men*,' Dymphna said. She frowned like her mother, 'I don't like men. I didn't like Daddy!'

'Hush,' her mother said, 'she isn't asking for your opinion about men.'

'*I* didn't like Daddy!' Clare said, her round face indignant, 'he made you cry! And then we all cried and he said . . .'

'Hush,' her mother said again. She studiously avoided looking at Terence and Maeve. 'Would you like another piece of cake?'

'Yes, please.' She took the slice, eyeing it appreciatively. 'He gave us sweeties,' she said to Maeve, 'sometimes.'

'I used to buy jujubes in Boyle when I was your age. What are *your* favourites?' She met her mother's eyes briefly as they listened to the child's prattling. There had been suffering . . .

After tea they walked round to the stables. The shadows were lengthening in the yard, and Maeve stopped, overcome by memories. Honor and Terence were talking easily together as she led him to the loose-boxes. Their voices seemed to be at one remove from her, like the cries of the children who were swinging on the white gate . . .

'*A bad hunt, then, was it, Miss Maeve?*' Old Mick shutting up his greenhouses against the January frost, bent head raised, respectful.

'*Yes, bad, Mick, bad.*'

Stumbling as the soaked skirt swung heavily between her legs. '*Pray God he's there.*' Righting herself, '*Pray God he's there . . . Kieran . . .*' His name choking in her throat as she saw him, Blackthorn's hoof on his knee, and then his raised face, the love in his eyes, '*Kieran . . .*'

Such enduring love, lasting from then until eleven years ago, faithful, loving, tender . . . She looked away to the back of the house, her hand across her mouth. Stupid. She shouldn't have come here. Memories. And hadn't she boasted often of not looking back?

'Mother!' It was Terence's voice with life in it. 'Will you come and look at this old horse of Honor's? I'm telling her it's ready for the knackers, but she won't hear a word of it.'

She went towards them, saw the girl's flushed smiling face. 'Now, he's the greatest tease that ever was, Honor! That's his way. This horse, is it?' She stroked the mare's nose. 'Well, I would say this old horse as he calls it has a good ten years in her anyway. And look at those docile eyes. No malice in them at all. She'll make a grand mount for those girls of yours, steady, reliable, better than a pony. They can be fickle.'

'See,' the girl said, 'your mother knows more about horses than you.'

'Now, that's a moot point,' Terence was smiling at her in the old way, 'maybe Irish horses, but when it comes to Clydesdales, I'm your man.'

'Why Clydesdales?'

'Because we're hauliers in Scotland, and we've a fleet of a few hundred. It's not the first time I've acted as a trace boy on our steep Glasgow streets.'

'My goodness!' Her brown eyes were alive, interested. 'Oh, there's so much to know about you! How long are you staying here?'

'About a week, I should think,' Maeve said. 'The travelling takes about another week on top of it.'

'Come and stay here! I'd love the company. You know there's heaps of room.'

Maeve saw Terence's eager eyes. 'No, thank you, Honor. We're nicely fixed up at the Freeman's Inn. I always feel that's the best thing when you visit friends. Then everybody's happy.'

'But we aren't just friends. We're relations.'

'Nevertheless, I'll have a few friends to visit and a few jaunts to take. It works better that way. I did the same when I visited my daughter's step-daughter in Paris with my daughter, Maevy.'

'Stop! Your daughter's step-daughter and your other daughter! I can't take it all in. Paris! Well, you must promise to come here as often as you can. We have so much to talk about. Now, there,' she said, smiling, 'and I thought this was going to be a sad autumn.'

'I liked autumn best here,' Maeve said. 'So did Kieran. The brisk mornings, and yet the melancholy, lovely feel of it. I think that suits the Irish, the undertones.'

'It was melancholy till you came.'

'Come to the hotel tomorrow evening,' Terence said, 'and we'll have dinner together. And talk and talk.'

She laughed. 'Come for lunch and then I'll let you know for sure. You, too?' She looked at Maeve. 'Unless you have other plans?'

'I might have. I'd like to get that Seamus Byrne to drive me about my favourite places, maybe visit some old friends. But you go, Terence.' She saw the quick look pass between them, and to make them think she did not, 'Do you know anything about the old staff? Old Mick's dead, I expect, but there was Kevin and Sean, no, he said he would go when Kieran went, and Mairi, the cook . . .

308

I'm afraid she'll be gone, too. And the two maids, Deirdre and Jenny . . .'

'They weren't here when we came. The place had run down. My husband said it was best. New brooms had to sweep clean.' Her face was set in a sternness, then it had gone and she was full of enthusiasm, 'Well you must do all those things, of course, for it's a homecoming, and if you won't come tomorrow, maybe the following day we could have a picnic lunch. The girls adore that. We have a favourite place not far from the house, Crow Wood . . .'

. . . Lying in Kieran's arms in the old shack, safe, they thought, but not knowing Peters was prowling around, a creature of the night, spying, not knowing because all she knew during those times with Kieran was passion and ecstasy and Kieran's body heavy on hers and the beating of their hearts . . .

'Yes,' she said, calmly, 'I know it. I remember Crow Wood.'

And many other places, although not so sharply. The next day, with the talkative Seamus Byrne as her driver, she visited the market up at the Crescent – the same old man was skirling on his pipes, or his grandson – and Lough Key with its Castle Island, and then off along the road to Ballinafad with Seamus talking nineteen to the dozen and pointing out the Curlew Mountains to her and Lough Arrow and everything she knew already.

'And those will be the Ox Mountains to the west,' she said, surprising him. She knew by the way he pushed back his tall hat to scratch his forehead.

'Aye, sure we're rich in mountains about here, and you've got Knocknarea and Benbulben ahead of you, indeed overpowered with mountains hereabouts we are, it's no wonder the rain breaks on them night and day without a stop.'

'Is that what makes it so green?' she asked with innocent relish.

She asked him to wait while she called at Kieran's old house, long, low, whitewashed, half the thatch replaced by corrugated iron, old wheels and carts lying about, a midden with some drookit hens pecking on top of it, an unloved place, she thought. She found her sister-in-law, after the first surprise, too preoccupied with her own affairs to be at all interested in hers. The family had never liked Kieran associating with her in any case, taking their cue from his father, who resented the Muldoons and thought of them as usurpers. Maybe he was right.

She listened politely to Kieran's sister. Her grandchildren were all angels and clever with it, her husband's arthritis was worse than anyone else's in the district, her son the most caring son that ever lived and just desperate to have them beside him in Dublin. Maybe long-lost relations and memories were better left alone.

3

Honor was up early feeding her horse, Moonlight. Twilight as a name would have suited him better, she thought, seeing his sad eyes, his spavined hocks, the sagging back. She had sold Dermot's mount because she knew it would fetch a better price, and it had. It had paid for a year's fodder, Rory's wages, and the roof to be fixed. It was such a relief to dispense with the basins and bowls in the attics. And there had been enough left over to buy a bolt of muslin from the packman from which she had made dresses for the girls and herself.

She had wanted them to have something light and summerlike to wear instead of the dreary black. They did not fully understand death in any case, just that Papa had 'gone away', that he had 'made Mama cry', and that the sweets he had tried to win their favour with were a thing of the past.

He had been awkward with children, not like this new-found cousin who seemed to have a natural gift. He had admired their dresses at lunch-time, making them simper, and also her own skirt with the ruffled hem, maybe even her red stockings. She had seen his eyes on them.

Later, when they had set off on their own she had told him of her writing and how she had been afraid to start with fiction, not that she had too little to say, but too much. History was more severe in its discipline and Irish history more severe still because of its mythological underlay. But he appeared to take more delight in driving the jaunting-car than in listening to her telling him of megaliths and forts and Maeve's cairn on top of Knocknarea. For the first time she had thought it was like a woman's breast. What's coming over you, Honor Daly? she wondered.

'I'm happy behind a horse,' he told her, 'like my father was. Patrick's the one who wants the march of progress to march even quicker and land us into the mechanical age.'

'Tell me about Patrick,' she said, 'and his wife, who's American, and your sisters, tell me about everybody. And Lizzie who lives with your sister and her husband but isn't their child. Whose is she?'

'Mine,' he said. 'She was mine in the real sense but I was already married so my brother married her mother when she was pregnant. She died after Lizzie was born. It broke my heart at the time . . .' He looked at her. 'I'm sorry. I shouldn't be speaking like that. You've just lost your husband.'

'It wasn't the same for me,' she said. 'We were married when I was barely twenty and then the babies came thick and fast. I had a miscarriage and a still birth to begin with, "a bad breeder" he said I was, and then he died . . .' She was appalled at the way her tongue ran on. 'Do you see that tower over there, Terence? This country-side's bristling with them . . .'

'So much unhappiness in the world,' he had not looked, 'my wife committed suicide.'

After that they had not talked much, driving back in the pale washed pinkness of the setting sun. He told her, smiling sideways at her as he drove, that it made her face rosy.

The girls had been annoyed at the 'relation' keeping her so long, but he had got round them with his charm and said they would all go for a picnic tomorrow to the sea, provided it did not rain, and he would buy lots of good things in Boyle for it.

312

Clare had said she had been to the sea lots of times and Dymphna had said she was a bloody liar. She picked that up from Rory. 'I'm ashamed of you girls,' Honor had said, and to Terence, 'It never rains in Ireland.' 'Who's the bloody liar now?' he had laughed, and by the way the girls had joined in she knew he had won their hearts.

Moira was the first to be ready, being capable of brushing her long dark hair herself. 'Shall we bathe, do you think?' she asked. She was trying on the pink ribbon her mother had given her, her head to one side.

'If you want to. We'll take the swimming costumes and rubber shoes anyhow. You can always paddle.'

'Can the relation swim, Mama?' Clare asked in her sprigged muslin.

'I don't know. Call him Uncle, darling. People don't go around saying "relation" like that.'

'But you said it.'

'That was different.'

'What for the lady?'

'She told you. Great aunt.'

If there had not been this childish chatter, how would I have got through the first month, she thought, quickly brushing her own hair. Five months now, long enough for the scars to fade, the guilt that maybe it had been partly her fault. How could she have known at barely twenty that a man could have two faces?

Mrs McGrath looked fresh and lovely and so well turned out that Honor shuddered inwardly at her own badly-made dress. 'I wish I could wear muslin like you, Honor,' Maeve said. 'I've decided to be patriotic and wear Irish linen instead.' That helped.

Of course she must be over fifty, but what a glorious figure she still had, and her eyes . . . you could not pin down her beauty, really. 'Linen's always cool,' she said, 'and I do like your hat. I hardly ever wear one.'

'Why should you at your age? Terence is outside with your little daughters packing the hampers.' They were in the black and white tiled hall. 'Could I ask you a favour?'

'Why, yes.'

'I'd like very much to see my old room. It's so long ago.'

'Of course. Which one was it?'

'The one beside the servants' staircase. Deirdre used to come running down in the mornings, give me a knock. But I forget, you haven't a Deirdre now.'

'Only an Edna.' She smiled. 'I've made that room my sewing room, I'm sorry. The girls have the two next to it, and then there's the master bedroom next to that. We . . . my husband and I were there, but I've moved into a smaller room now. Come along. Oh, I forgot, I don't need to show you the way.'

It was strange walking beside this woman in her violet linen gown with its pleated bodice, the cream folded parasol matching the cream straw of her hat, the elegant feet in cream buckskin taking the steps so surely. What must be going through her mind?

Maeve stopped when they reached the landing and looked through the window to the wide gravelled driveway. Her son was there with the girls. Honor could see him laughing with them as they put the food into the hampers Rory had carried out. Clare was looking very important as she bustled about, doing what her 'relation' told her. A flood of love went through her for her children.

Terence was wearing knickerbockers and polished brogues, like his mother his clothes were of fine quality, and he had taken off his jacket, rolled up the sleeves of his white shirt. He was very handsome, the same grace as her in the way he held his body . . . 'That view, the same,' she heard Mrs McGrath's voice, low, as if she was speaking to herself, 'and, yes, there's the turn in the drive . . .' Her voice changed, she said briskly, 'Terence lives for the moment, thank goodness. That's what has saved him.' They passed on, up to the head of the staircase, down the long corridor and into the sewing-room.

'I'm sorry,' Honor apologized. 'Such a mess. I'm always in the middle of something and it's so convenient to be able to leave it . . .' Mrs McGrath was not listening. She walked to the window and stood, looking out. 'It's a good view,' Honor said, 'being at the front.'

'Yes . . .' She did not turn. She was perfectly still, her head slightly bent. Even from the back, there was a sadness about her. Honor stood inside the door, wondering if she should speak, or if she should offer her a chair, but she saw that the only one without heaped-up material on it was the one with the broken webbing.

'Uncle . . . !' The high childish voice floated up to them. Dymphna. She tended to scream. She had told her about it. She did want them to grow up to be graceful and contained. It was quite a responsibility, being their only parent. The laughter from the driveway drifted up to the quiet room, seeming to slide into its corners, to drift out again.

Mrs McGrath turned. The brim of the straw hat shaded her eyes, but Honor got the impression that they were deeper in colour, almost black, or perhaps it was that her cheeks were if anything paler. 'I left all this behind me. I didn't know where I was going. It's strange to come back.' Her voice seemed different, not so clear.

'It must be . . .' She had been going to say 'heart-breaking' but that was such an exaggerated kind of word. 'Be careful of hyperbole' she was always saying to herself when she was writing, '. . . moving for you. I should have

315

asked you earlier. Would you like to see the rest of the house?'

They walked out of the room and were at the top of the staircase. The cream shoes were emerging from the violet linen skirt, left, right, surely but slowly, almost reluctantly. Mrs McGrath stopped once more at the landing window, stood for a second or two, then moved down again. She still had not answered. Honor, slightly behind her, thought that her back had lost some of its straightness. 'Yes,' she said, 'I would, thank you, but not today. One room at a time is . . . enough.' The petticoat which showed under the lilac linen as she took the steps was cream-coloured lace, like the scarf round the hat. It was detail which counted.

Terence was in the hall with the girls, now fully accepted by them and being treated as a new and unexpected plaything. He was in high spirits. He praised her for having chosen such a fine day, rainless so far, for providing such capacious hampers for the picnic.

'You must have raided Docherty's,' she laughed when she had inspected the cold meats and fruit and the cheeses, the napkined bottles of hock. The game pie, she suggested, must have cost the earth, not to mention the rich cake, the bon-bons and the sugared pineapple rings.

She found Mrs McGrath more interested in the history of the place than Terence had been. 'You know much more about it than I do, Honor,' she said. 'When you're born and brought up here you don't appreciate it. It's the incomers like yourself who know the whys and the wherefores of it.'

She was flattered. 'Oh, I'm sure you can tell me lots I don't know. You have the feel of it, not like me, coming from Dublin. Do you know what first started me off with history? Even before I went to school in England which is a great place for history, sure enough.'

'Tell us, what first started you off?' Terence laughed over his shoulder. He looked as happy as a sandboy with the reins in his hands and two fine horses to control.

'I read somewhere that the Pale was an area around Dublin which stayed in English hands despite all the anarchy which followed. And then I realized where the phrase, "beyond the pale" came from. It was so *neat*. History's neat because it's all been sorted out before you get to it. Not like life. Of course I had to give it up when I got married and the children came, but I've taken it up again. The day I discovered it was there waiting for me to go back to was the day I started living again. Sure enough.' She looked down at her hands. She was talking too much.

'Something outside yourself,' Mrs McGrath said. 'You've discovered the secret, too.' She smiled across at Honor. 'It's the only way to live.'

The place they had chosen was Strandhill on the Sligo Bay, a long strand practically deserted now that the holiday-makers were gone and the children back at school. They found a smooth place on the sand, which was grainy with pebbles and boulders strewn about. She directed Terence gaily as he spread a rug for the picnic and unfolded some wooden garden chairs she had put into the wagon at the last minute. He was full of life.

'Lovely sea-smell,' he said, 'kelp, isn't it? Don't you make a pudding of it? That's what makes your hair curl. Reminds me a bit of Brodick in Arran. Patrick and Maria take a house there every year.'

'You've an Isle of Aran, too?'

'Different spelling.'

'I like how the breakers roll in along the strand. Lazy, they are, as if they had all day.'

'I'm tempted to have a swim. I bought a costume in

317

Boyle, just in case.' He pointed to a long tongue of land on their right, 'What's that?'

'Rosses Point. And in the channel there's the Metal Man.'

'What queer-like names you have. Is it a landmark?'

'I remember going to Deadman's Point out there, long ago,' Maeve said. She had taken off her hat. Her hair lifted from her forehead in the gentle wind.

'I might go in, too.' Honor laughed up at Terence. 'I learned by default at Minehead, in Somerset. That's where I went to school.'

'Don't do anything rash! Meantime, while you're cogitating, we'll go down and see if it's cold. Come on, girls!' He was followed by his now faithful band, laughing and shouting with joy.

'Thank goodness Clare's stopped calling him "relation",' Honor said to Maeve as they watched them capering on the edge. 'She has such a literal mind.'

'Terence will soon win her over. He's happy with children.'

'Does he take it from his father?'

'I'm sure he does. We had five, six until John was drowned. He was beautiful.' She turned to Honor. 'I say that with no false modesty. Beautiful in spirit as well. It was a blight on our lives for many years, Maevy particularly, but we were the better for knowing him.'

'If you can say that about someone who's died, that's something.' She had lain down on the rug beside Maeve's chair. She reached for one of the cushions and tucked it under her head so that she could watch Terence and the girls. But the autumn somnolence of the sun seduced her with its golden, mellow quality. She closed her eyes . . .

Someone was touching her arm. She looked up and saw deep blue eyes looking into hers. Mrs McGrath had bent down to her. 'Won't you burn?'

'No, I haven't that kind of skin.' She sat up, fully awake now.

'My daughter, Isobel, wouldn't dare expose herself. She's fair, delicate, like a pink pearl.' She laughed at herself. 'That's going a bit far!'

'Not if it's true. She sounds lovely. Tell me about your other ones.'

'There's Kate, in America, dark like a red rose – there I go again – and as sweet. I wouldn't say that to her face, of course. But the principle thing is she's happy, and makes everybody else happy who claps eyes on her.'

'Ah, but she'll have a happy marriage.'

'Yes, but some wouldn't have thought so. She's a second wife. There are grown-up daughters and sons. Anyone else would have made a task of it, but Kate went about it the right way. She won their hearts.'

'Yes, that's not luck. And have you any more daughters?'

'Maevy. She's a nurse, but she's been very ill recently. This holiday with Terence is a thank you for her getting well again . . .' I did not think she was religious, Honor thought, and then heard her say, 'a paen of praise to the good in everything.' She laughed. 'That's as far as I dare look. Oh, I must be the despair of my son-in-law, Isobel's husband! He's a minister. He thinks I stray from the flock.'

'I've never had much time for them. They're either trying to herd you in, or pretending they're as sinful as you to make you feel at ease. And they pry.' She remembered the questions her own minister had asked her when he had called. It had been evident he had heard rumours . . . she did not want to think of Dermot today. This was too pleasant. 'Isn't Maevy married?' she asked.

'She's going to be quite soon, to our doctor. Maybe when I get back they'll have fixed the date. That will be the wedding to end all weddings.' Honor heard the excitement in her voice, the happiness. 'Sholton will rise to the occasion. There's no one who won't wish Charlie and Maevy well.'

She said, knowing it was a miserable kind of thing to say, 'If they knew what was ahead of them some girls wouldn't go into marriage at all.'

'Ach, that's so, but a happy marriage is the finest thing in the world.'

'Mine wasn't.' She sat up abruptly, shading her eyes. 'I think I'll go for a swim. It's the last chance this summer.' The thought of the bleakness of winter overcame her for a second. Can you not be happy for half an hour? She scolded herself. She stood up, waving her arm. 'Terence!' He was paddling with the children, his knickerbockers pushed up above his knees, 'I'm going for a swim.'

'Right!' he shouted. She saw him hand the red bucket he was carrying to Dymphna. They would be gathering shells.

She took her swimming costume, went behind a nearby dune and undressed quickly. The salty air playing on her skin was delicious. She remembered the shivering anticipation of many swims, the plunge, the acceptance. There was nothing like it.

'Tell Terence there's a fine big towel there.' She stopped for a second at the rug. Mrs McGrath smiled up at her. Some tendrils of her hair had became loose, making a halo round her face. Her paleness had a luminous quality. She could be painted like that, she thought. She ran past Terence who was half-way up the beach.

'Is it cold?' She felt shy standing there in the serge costume, her bare arms and legs.

'Ask my big toe.' He smiled at her with the same charm as his mother.

She ran on. How fortunate she was that the McGraths

320

had come into her life, however briefly. She must stop having a chip on her shoulder, really stop this day. But it was more than a chip . . . ah, shut your gob, will you? Life was too good to spoil. What was it Mrs McGrath had said? 'Something outside yourself.' Yes, that was the secret, to stop this concentration on one's past unhappiness, to change it. There were the children, and her writing, and those new friends . . .

She was swimming strongly when Terence joined her. 'Here, who do you think you are? Captain Webb's daughter.' He had made up on her easily. 'I didn't think you'd be so good.'

'I didn't think *you* would. Glasgow isn't on the coast.'

'No, but we have a river beside us, the Sholtie. I learned to swim there. It's almost part of the family. Oh, yes, the Sholtie Burn is quite a character.' He dived suddenly, like a duck. She saw the white soles of his feet, narrow feet. She was suddenly happy, a pure, brief kind of happiness.

Mrs McGrath was there when they came out, holding towels for them. 'I thought you were going to swim across to America.' There was a hint of motherly anxiety in her eyes although she was smiling.

'That would save the fare,' Terence said, laughing. Honor watched him as he dried his hair, thinking what a taut, fine body he had, and liking the way his head was set on his shoulders. Men's bodies were a snare and a delusion . . . She raised her eyes and found him looking at her. His were appreciative, masculine, reminding her of Dermot without that glittering excitement which had always warned her.

'We'd better get dressed,' she said, 'or we'll catch cold.'

She came to Boyle with the children to see them off. 'We'll miss you,' she said, 'you've made this last week for us. I'm going to weep when you go.' They were standing on the station platform. She thought her remark sounded soft and she said, smiling, 'Although I'd better not start now. The train's always half an hour late.'

'That's Ireland for you,' his mother said. She was standing with the children, and by their smug expressions she had been doling out money. She saw each of their right hands tightly clenched round a coin and could hardly restrain a smile.

'You shouldn't spoil them,' Honor said.

'It's you who've spoiled us,' Mrs McGrath said.

'You must come back. Bring all my cousins.'

'The business will swallow us up for a time,' she shook her head, 'but why didn't I think of it before? You come to Maevy's wedding and meet them all! We'll fill up Braidholme with relations.' She smiled down at Clare. 'You love relations, don't you?'

'Mama,' Clare was single-minded, 'could we go to Leary's to spend my silver penny?'

'Hush. Oh, I'd love to, Mrs McGrath, but what about the children?'

'The more the merrier. Bring them, too.'

'I'll see. I haven't been in Scotland since I was in England, if you catch the Irish drift.' She laughed. Something to look forward to now. This new family, nothing to do with men ever again, despite Terence's charm, but a loving family . . .

'Here's the train!' the girls shouted. There was instant confusion because it had done an unmentionable thing, arrived only fifteen minutes late instead of half an hour. People darted here and there, lifting their luggage, bumping into one another, shouting goodbyes.

Mrs McGrath kissed her, Terence enveloped her in a hug. His eyes were laughing when he released her. 'Don't forget you're my long-lost cousin, now found.' Then he was helping his mother up the step into the compartment. She had a fine trim ankle.

They waved and waved until the train disappeared round the bend. 'Come on, then, girls.' She stepped lightly to the jaunting-car. You had to act like that when children were around. She was all they had.

4

Maevy looked out of the window of the cab as they sped along Great Western Road. There was Cooper's Stores where possibly Catherine had shopped . . . Catherine. No, do not think ahead, think instead of those many fine stores in Glasgow, Cooper's and Lipton's, Sir Thomas Lipton, that dapper little man with the big yacht. Hadn't Catherine once entertained him because he gave so much to charity? Catherine again. Glasgow liked rags-to-riches stories, there was very little envy of anyone who 'got on'. It was a feather in the collective cap of Glasgow's pride.

· When she had been staying at Braidholme after she had come home from the Infirmary, and before that, she had never found any envy of her mother in Sholton. The Colliers' Row days, where she had had her enemies, were long since forgotten. She was respected, admired, just a bit different, maybe, but that was the Irish in her. And now that her youngest daughter was engaged to the doctor . . .

But what would they think if they knew what she had done? What if the Procurator Fiscal said when he heard her story, 'I'm afraid I can't condone your act. Withholding evidence is a felony. There's nothing for it but to let the law take its course'?

Prison. Incarcerated in a cell, bars on the window, not able to see out, day after day with nothing to do but think, cold, hungry, anguished. What would Sholton think of her then? They would not like their doctor to marry a jailbird, would they? 'Oh . . .' She put her hand to her mouth to stifle the moan. Charlie's arm went around her.

'You aren't losing heart now?' His voice was tender.

'No . . . it's just my imagination was running away with me. I was locked up in Barlinnie . . . chains round my ankles.' She tried to laugh. Hadn't she promised him last night, in his arms, that she would remain cheerful? Everything had been all right then.

'The Procurator Fiscal seemed an understanding man,' he said. 'I told you. He didn't say much, but that's the way of them. They never commit themselves. But the fact that he was willing to see you . . . I told him how ill you'd been, and that you were a Sister in the Royal. I'm sure he'll be lenient.'

He had told her all that before. He was so patient. 'I wish we were there. I wish it was all over, that I knew what he was going to do with me.'

'He'll do nothing with you,' he squeezed her shoulders, 'except listen attentively. You've been over it with me many times. Keep a clear head, my darling. Let him see that your only concern was to save your brother any further distress. Your motives were good.'

'That's what a surgeon says when he chops off some-body's leg.'

'Oh, Maevy!' He laughed at her, and she had to laugh as well.

'Yes, I'll hold on to that.' 'My motives were good,' she repeated to herself without much conviction. And to show him that she was holding on to herself, 'It's a fine road, this. It has a sense of opulence and solidity, a look-at-me kind of road. No wonder Catherine chose it.' She could say her name more easily now. 'It exemplified everything she cared for.'

'Would you like to live here? If I'd become a surgeon full-time . . .'

'No, I prefer Sholton, and you're a fine doctor, as important in your own way as any surgeon in Glasgow. The country suits me. I have to have green round me, to rest my eyes on it.'

'Maybe when we've finished with this we'll stop off at Sauchiehall Street and look at those new furnishings for our house.' He called it 'our house' now.

'No.' That would be tempting fate. How could they marry if she were in prison? 'We'll wait till we set the date.'

'I thought the spring.' She saw through him, that he was trying to calm her, and she played along with him, feeling tenderly maternal.

'Mother thinks the American relations might come. Aunt Caroline has always been afraid of sailing. If she were buffeted in winter on rough seas, that would finish her.'

'The spring, then. I want you properly better. You'll get a new lease of life when the primroses come.'

'I'd like that, not to feel this tiredness any more.'

'You'll be fine, then. I've waited a long time. I can wait longer.' He looked out. The cab was slowing down. 'That's Dr Wordie's house. It's quite near the Fiscal's. Yes, he's stopping.' He turned and looked at her. 'I've never seen you more beautiful. One look at you and he won't be able to listen to a word you're saying.'

'I'm too thin. Aren't you for ever telling me to eat up?' She felt like a dressed-up skeleton, with a skeleton's grinning face.

'You're elegant and lovely and the pride of my heart. Come on, now, think of it as paying a visit to the doctor who's going to make you better.'

'Or chop off my leg.' She got up, trembling.

The Procurator Fiscal was not as she had imagined him. She had thought of someone tall, handsome, silver-haired, silver-tongued, with a thin nose and pince-nez, thin hands which he put together at his desk while he listened. This one was more like the man who used to come to kill their pig, Roly Poly, every winter, a different pig each time, of course, but to a child's vision, the same. He would jump off his cart at Colliers' Row, apron over fat belly, with the smell of blood on him and large hands.

But the eyes of this man were different. Rab Haw's, the butcher – he had been called after Rab Haw, the Glesca Glutton because of his fat stomach – had been like those of the pigs he killed for a living; small, just two twinkling dots almost lost in his face, whereas Mr Corstorphine's were large and of a piercing quality when he looked at you. They seemed to take in her thinness in one direct glance, her new hat of golden brown velvet (the velvet, she had thought, would soften the angularity of her face), her too thin waist, her nervous hands which played with her gloves.

'How are you, Miss McGrath?' he said. 'I understand from Dr McNab you've been ill for a long time.'

'I'm almost recovered, sir, thank you,' she said.

'Hospitals aren't the kind of place we want to spend much time in, but perhaps I shouldn't say that to you. I understand you're a nurse.'

'Yes, I was.' Charlie would not hear of her going back.

'It was good of you to see us,' Charlie said.

'A moment.' He busied himself with papers in a green cloth-covered folder, reading a little here and there, turning over the pages.

The silence lengthened in the long room with its two flat windows on to the front. Across the road she could see the trees in the Botanic Gardens, their leaves the colour of her hat. An autumn hat, she thought. I didn't realize that when I bought it in Mr Wilson's Millinery Department. She was distressed how her mind flitted about. It was something new to her, this nervousness, a hidden terror which had been with her since her illness. This was the day of judgement. This man fiddling with papers across from her held her fate and her future happiness in his hands.

She could not marry Charlie, of course, if she had to go to prison. It would spoil his standing in Sholton . . . she looked across at him, taking in every detail of his face as if it were her last chance. He had been gazing down at his hands, but as if he felt her eyes on him, he raised his, and the brilliant blackness of them seemed to put new life into her. She heard the man's voice.

'Tell me, please, Miss McGrath, what happened in the bathroom in Great Western Terrace when you found your sister-in-law.' He barely glanced at her, his hand still turning the pages.

She glanced at Charlie, but this time he looked away as if he did not want to be seen prompting her.

'My brother and I forced our way into the bathroom, his wife had wedged a chair under the handle. She was lying in the bath, one arm hanging over the edge. There was a deep gash in her wrist. There was a piece of paper lying in the congealed blood which had dripped to the floor. I put the piece of paper into my pocket.' It was like a well-learned lesson. 'Don't tell him how you felt,' Charlie had said, 'just what you did. Let him ask the questions.'

'Why did you do that, Miss McGrath?'

'I didn't know at the time why. It was . . . automatic. I thought, one thing at a time for Terence.'

'You wanted to spare him?'

'Yes, I wanted to spare him. He couldn't bear to look at her. He turned his head to the wall. It was easier for me, being a nurse.'

'What happened then?'

'I said, "Help me to get her out, Terence," and he did what he was told. He was in shock. I could see that. I listened to her heart, felt her pulse. I knew she was dead.'

'What then?'

'I led him to the bedroom and sent him for a doctor. He went . . . like an obedient child.' She was surprised how lucid she was being. It was as if the whole picture was in front of her eyes and all she had to do was to describe it. It was easier because there was no longer the feeling of intense shock, nor the need to tell herself to hold on to herself.

'What did you do when he'd gone?'

'I took the letter out of my pocket and read it. I can remember the words.' She looked at him.

'But you can't show it to me?'

'No, I burned it in the fire in the bathroom. Catherine like a fire . . . in the bathroom.'

'And you can remember the contents?'

'Yes.' She could not say, 'they're burned into my brain.' 'They were, "I told you he was carrying on with his brother's maid, didn't I? Now that she's pregnant, will you believe me?"' Her self-composure left her. She put a hand up to her eyes. Charlie touched her arm.

'Are you all right, Maevy?'

'Yes,' she nodded, ashamed, 'I'm all right.'

'You were wise to bring your medical attendant, Miss McGrath.' Charlie laughed, and she realized the man's remark was meant to be humorous. His voice was kindly. 'Do you feel well enough to go on?'

'Yes, I'm quite well. I'm sorry.'

'This isn't a court of law, you understand. But if it's too difficult . . .'

'It isn't too difficult.'

'We'll continue, then. Did you regret what you'd done, knowing it was wrong to withhold evidence of any kind?'

'Not right away. I thought it wouldn't have made any difference in any case. It wasn't a suicide note. The damage was done, Catherine was dead, and nothing could bring her back.'

'So you were quite happy with your action?'

She looked at her hands, then at the Procurator Fiscal. His eyes were certainly not like Rab Haw's, they were used to looking down on miscreants from high places, to getting a reply. 'Not for long. At first I told myself it was for the good of the family, then the doubts started. I was never free of them. They were always there at the back of my mind. Even knowing who had written the letter didn't help . . .'

'Who told you that?' The lofty gaze was like an eagle's. She was caught out. Truth stands all investigation. Where had she read that?

'Dr McNab.' She dared not look at him. 'He was told by my . . . mother. She had been approached . . .'

'By whom?'

'Someone in the office who . . . liked Terence, was jealous . . .'

'She had *presumed* this person was the author of the letter?'

'Yes.' Caught in a trap. Now she had brought her mother into it. Why had she and Charlie never thought about that? But, then, had she ever told Charlie she had confided in her mother? Or had *she* told *him*? Truth stands all investigation. Why did that old saying keep coming back to her?

'And your mother condoned what you'd done, compounded the felony?'

Legal words now. 'No, it wasn't like that. I'd done what I'd done. My mother is practical . . .'

'She didn't advise you to tell the authorities?'

'No. She'd never do that. She treats us as capable of dealing with our own problems. That's how she is.'

'I see . . . I see . . .' His eyes were hooded now, as if he saw fully her perfidy.

'Did you believe the accusations in the letter to be true?'

'I knew they were. But I also knew from my other sister-in-law that the maid mentioned was happily married to a man who was prepared to father the child, which might have been his in any case . . .'

Mr Corstorphine wrote busily for a few moments, then threw down his pen. He stood up, pulled his frock-coat straight behind his back, and walked to the window. He seemed to be examining something interesting outside. He even peered. She heard him say musingly, '"Oh what a tangled web we weave, when first we practise to deceive . . ."'

She could not see his face. She looked at Charlie, biting her lip, and he moved his head, whether in impatience that she had made a hash of it or nodding encouragement she could not tell. Charlie had been wrong. She should never have come, and yet, what a relief it was to have emptied her mind, even to bringing Mother into it, which she had not meant to do.

Mr Corstorphine turned slowly round to face her, his black bulk enormous against the glass, like an avenging angel. 'Dear, oh dear, oh dear, Miss McGrath,' he shook his head at her, 'I'll have to give you a good telling off, I'm afraid . . .'

'You're not going to . . . ?'

'Clap you in irons? No, not this time. What do you say, Dr McNab, should we let her off since it's a first offence?'

Charlie's face was straight. 'Maybe since we're going to be married . . .' Now they were both torturing her.

'But,' he shook his finger at her, 'I would be failing in

my duty if I didn't deliver myself of a homily as befits the occasion. Do you agree, Miss McGrath?'

'Oh, yes, I agree!' She began to see a glimmer of light.

'First of all, you made an assumption which you weren't in a position to make, namely that your sister-in-law had killed herself. Fortunately, this was proved to be the case. Then you withheld evidence. That was naughty, do you agree?'

'Yes.'

'Would it surprise you to know,' Mr Corstorphine was speaking slowly, as if she might not be able to understand him, 'that what you've told me comes as no surprise?'

She was stunned. She stammered, 'Because you saw Charlie? I mean, because Dr McNab called when I was in hospital?'

He shook his head, his lips pursed. 'It was still no surprise.'

She heard the slight noise of Charlie moving in his chair. 'Yes, it surprises me,' she said. She could not look up. Those eyes would easily read her thoughts. So they had been watching her all those months, the way a cat watches a mouse, wondering when they should pounce.

She felt anger burning in her. They should have told her long ago, at least saved her those endless sleepless nights, those terrible dreams in hospital when she could think of nothing else, when she felt she was going to die with the secret. 'You might have told me!' The words burst from her. She heard Charlie move again in his chair. He would be annoyed at her for speaking like that. She had said she would be cool and calm . . .

Mr Corstorphine crossed the room and sat down again at his desk. 'The case was closed as far as I was concerned, Miss McGrath. It was you who opened it. You see, I had a letter from a Miss Mavor confessing to be the author of several letters on the subject you spoke of.'

'You'd had . . . !' The words choked in her throat. All that agony for nothing . . .

'She has since died. The sister with whom she was staying informed me. Had she been alive, naturally I should have instituted further questioning.'

The blood was pounding in her brain. She sat, gripping the edge of the desk. Breathe deeply . . . Ethel Mavor dead. Dead! Had she gone to her sister because she was ill? Had she spent sleepless nights – I know all about sleepless nights – and in the end been driven to confess to the Fiscal for her own peace of mind? What had she died of? A wasting illness? How lucky *she* had been in comparison. 'I'm sorry,' she said, 'to hear of Miss Mavor's death.'

'A sad life, and a sad end. Cancer, I was told.' Mr Corstorphine closed the green cloth-covered folder, and got up. Charlie rose, too. 'I should take Miss McGrath away now, Dr McNab, and give her a good strong cup of tea. My wife speaks highly of the new tea-rooms which are beginning to blossom in Sauchiehall Street.'

'Yes, I'll do that. Are you coming, Maevy?' He put his arm round her as he bent. She still sat. 'Maevy?'

'Yes.' He helped her up. 'It's finished, then?' She looked at Mr Corstorphine. 'You don't want me?'

'No, the case is closed as far as I'm concerned.' He shook a playful finger at her, 'Off you go, but don't do it again.' And then, 'I trust your brother is recovered by this time from his wife's death?'

'Yes, thank you. He manages very well.'

'And that you'll soon be completely recovered, too.'

'I'm better already.' She smiled at him, relief flooding through her.

'We're to be married in the spring,' Charlie said. 'She'll be able to concentrate more on the idea now.' He held out his hand. 'Thank you, Mr Corstorphine, for sparing us the time.'

'Not all all. Permit me to offer my congratulations.' He came round his desk and held out his hand to Maevy. 'And to wish you every happiness.'

'Thank you, oh, thank you.'

He ushered them out, saying formally, 'I bid you good day.' He had a dry smile.

In the cab Charlie put his arm round her. 'You're like a little shivering bird.'

'I'm not little and you know it.'

'We'll obey the Fiscal's orders and have that nice cup of tea.'

'Yes . . .' The opulence of Great Western Road became commercialized with its rows of shops, and then they were in busy Sauchiehall Street with the cab driver going slow so that he could find a place to stop at one of the new tea-rooms. Two people dead, she thought, Catherine and Ethel Mavor. She had got used to Catherine's death, but that of Ethel Mavor's touched her deeply. Perhaps hers had been even a sadder life.

5

It was the biggest wedding there had ever been in Sholton, and, although the Sholton people were unlikely to use such a word, the most cosmopolitan. The *Crannoch Adviser* had used it with much aplomb the week before, in their column headed 'Coming Events'.

It has been announced that Dr Charles McNab of Sholton, a well-known figure there, is to marry Miss Maevy McGrath, youngest daughter of Mrs McGrath of Braidholme, Sholton, well-known in the district as founder, along with her husband, the late Kieran McGrath, of the McGrath Carting Company of the Gallowgate, Glasgow.

Guests are expected from far and near. There will be two contingents from America, Mr and Mrs Terence Muldoon, Mrs McGrath's brother and his wife, and Mr and Mrs Murray-Hyslop, Mrs McGrath's daughter with her husband, accompanied by their son, Kieran James. Mrs Dermot O'Rourke Daly will be arriving from Ireland, and Monsieur and Madame Charles Barthe from Paris, both these parties being related through marriage. A truly cosmopolitan occasion.

The Reverend Mr John Craigie, minister of Sholton Parish Church will officiate, the bride's two sisters, Mrs John Craigie and Mrs Murray-Hyslop, will be matrons of honour, the bridesmaid will be Miss Elizabeth Maeve Craigie, and the bride will be given away by her uncle, Mr Terence McGrath of America.

Among those local people who have accepted invitations are Mr Robert Cranston and his family, the well-known Crannoch farmer, and Lord Crawford and his son, the Honourable Nigel Crawford of the Hall, Sholton.

The whole district extends felicitations to the happy couple. The bride-to-be was a Sister in the Royal Infirmary, Glasgow, and such is her standing there that a guard of honour of nurses from that august establishment will attend . . .

335

'It puts the fear of death in me,' Maevy said, reading it out to Charlie. She had called to discuss the disposition of the various guests between the three houses, the manse, Larkhill (it had always been known simply as 'the doctor's house'), and Braidholme.

'Not me.' He kissed her. They were sitting on the sofa in front of the fire. 'I like a *splary*, I want everyone to know, everyone to be there to share it. The only thing that worries me is if I drop the ring when it's handed to me.'

'I'm glad to know you've some worries.' If he had, he kept them from her, only intent on her getting well. She looked round contentedly. She loved this room already. During the long winter months she had spent a lot of time here, probably shocking Biddy, except that whatever the 'doacter' did was all right, which included anything to do with Maevy.

She had browsed through his books, and become accustomed to the long waiting times when he was busy on his rounds, seen how after his fond greeting he liked to sit at the piano, 'unwinding' as he called it. They had discussed Carlyle and Ruskin, Kier Hardy and Frazer's 'Golden Bough'. The reading of those books and those discussion sessions were all part of the treatment, Charlie said. She had to learn to relax.

At first he made gentle love to her when she was still frail, but later, as her strength grew, she had no doubt of his feelings, and of her own.

'For two pins,' he had once said, his voice shaking, 'if it weren't for Biddy barging in . . .'

She was trembling herself. 'Ah, but then I couldn't wear that white gown that Mother and I have spent so much time over! Unless we do as she did and elope?'

'No, Sholton would never forgive us.' He had released

her. 'We'll not spoil their show. But, oh, Maevy,' he turned to her, his eyes full, 'that first night . . .'

'Don't make me feel as if I'm being fattened up for the slaughter.' She leant against him. Nothing could go wrong now.

'There will be no slaughter, I assure you.' He stroked her hair. 'I don't intend to have another wife. You're mine, always will be. Nothing can go wrong . . .'

Honor Daly was to stay at Braidholme. Terence had had a word with Maevy and his mother. 'You'll remember how unsure she was at times, Mother. Of course she hadn't been a widow for long, but it wasn't only that.'

'I think it was an unhappy marriage.'

He nodded. 'We've written back and forth, but she hasn't told me anything. She's been hurt. You can tell by what she *doesn't* say. She wanted to come to the wedding, as if she needed friends.'

'Are you beginning to think about her, son?' Maeve asked. Trust Mother, Maevy thought, to come right out with it.

'Well, she's an Irish beauty, isn't she? That colouring . . .'

'There speaks the connoisseur,' Maevy teased him.

He grinned at her. 'There's something more I warm to. She's . . . lonely in her soul.' He sobered. 'I understand that.' He looked at Maevy, shook his head. 'That terrible time, and the days and months afterwards . . . but I don't think she warms to me, much. Men . . . she says she's had enough of men.'

'She'll tell you in her own time what's bothering her,' Maeve said. 'It's early days.'

'There's another attraction,' he said, 'I don't know how to explain it. Honor is Ireland, and Ireland is Honor. They're one and the same thing. I think of that house and the beauty of it, and that Irish landscape, and there's something there that draws me. Sure and I don't know which it is at times, her or the place.'

'It's the Irish in you,' his mother said. 'You're looking back to your roots.'

'Aye, maybe so.' He's smitten, Maevy thought.

They also invited Kate and James and young Kieran to Braidholme. They had decided that Kate was the best one to put Honor at her ease. Isobel had begged to have her uncle and aunt, since she had stayed with them at Springfield, and Terence and the boys were staying the night before the wedding with Charlie to 'bolster him up' as Terence put it. Charlie did not look as if he needed any bolstering, but he was quite amicable to the arrangement.

And the 'French contingent', Emily and her husband, Charles, would be put up at Claremont Terrace with Maria and Patrick, and would drive to Sholton in the morning. Charles wanted to get a glimpse of another city than his own.

Indeed, Maevy thought, when 'the dark beauty', Honor, arrived, she certainly needed some putting at ease. She was nervous, talked too much at first, apologized for being early, for not bringing her three little girls although they had been included in the invitation. There were difficulties in the way, she said, looking vague. Maevy wondered if it was a question of money for the outfitting, because Honor's clothes were far from being *haute couture*. 'The lass makes them all herself,' her mother had informed her.

'I hope it's all right my coming, but, oh, I wanted to meet you all!' Honor said. 'I can't tell you how happy I was that day your mother and Terence came along. I was going through a bad time. To know I had relatives here, took away from that feeling of being quite alone . . .'

Kate was the one to handle this. 'Now, don't I know that feeling, Honor. It's like a bulwark. James laughs at

338

me and my ideas, because the Murray-Hyslops don't hold together at all, but then he's very happy to be one of us. As you are now, and very welcome. Isn't that so, Mother? It'll make a difference to you, you'll feel you're never really alone any more, that however far away, there is this link with those who love and care for you . . .'

'Is my wife making herself clear?' James said. His side-whiskers were grey now, but he was still the handsomest man Maevy had ever known, leaving out Charlie and Terence.

'If I hadn't had my relations,' young Kieran said, 'I shouldn't have had this trip to Scotland. I can tell you, the boys at my school in Albany are going to be fiercely jealous!'

'That's the stuff to give the troops,' James said. 'Are you convinced now, Honor?'

'Oh, I know it, Mr Murray-Hyslop. Am I not feeling it in my bones!' That rare rose colour of hers had flooded her pale cheeks, her brown eyes were moist. There was a wonderful quality about the girl, Maevy thought, a great capacity for feeling, perhaps too much.

But then, after a quiet dinner, she herself was being bundled off to bed by her mother with a hot milk drink with nutmeg and honey in it, and white gloves on her glycerined hands. 'You want them to look nice, don't you, when Charlie puts on the ring?' and she was in bed, soothed and happy, but not able to sleep for a long time. Tomorrow . . . that first night . . . would Charlie be surprised to know she longed for it as ardently as he?

'That white gown that Mother and I have spent so much time over.' The words came back to her as she stood in front of the mirror while Kate spread out the lace train at the back 'to see the full effect'. Indeed the gown was all lace, Irish lace. It had been Mother's idea when they had seen it at Walter Wilson's Bridal Department in Jamaica Street.

'Nothing could be more fitting,' she had said. 'And you could wear a satin petticoat to warm it up a bit.' She had been right, unerring in her taste as usual; the magnolia satin gleamed through the crusty lace and seemed to catch the lights in Maevy's newly-washed hair . . . the best hairdresser in Crannoch had come early to put it up.

'No pinks with it,' Mother had said, 'something deeper, warmer, but in the same tone,' and so her bouquet was composed of golden spring flowers with a sprig of white bride's blossom tucked in here and there. Kate, standing behind her now, was in primrose panne velvet, Isobel and Lizzie were to wear the same colour, but Lizzie, being a young girl, was to have a chaplet of primroses.

'A spring ensemble,' Mother now said, standing, satisfied, in her striped satin gown of silver-grey and beige which had been intended, as she put it, as 'a foil, but played-down, it's your day', but which only enhanced the flame of her hair, her erect carriage. Maevy straightened her own back in an effort to live up to her.

After that it was a confused impression of Uncle Terence arriving for her in full fig, silver waistcoat, silver cravat, 'piece of shamrock tucked in the lining of me lum hat', and driving through the village, of seeing people she knew at their doorways, of waving and being surprised at the beaming faces, at some children who waved and even ran behind the carriage for a time shouting, 'Good luck!' There would be more of them when she and Charlie drove away, scrambling for the pennies he would throw.

The church to her was like a giant nosegay with the floral decorations and the varying colours of the women's gowns. Emily, she noticed, had ignored the spring theme and was in a brilliant gown of peacock blue, Aunt Caroline had played safe and worn her inevitable sugar pink, but best of all in her eyes were the Sholton people themselves in their variegated gingham gowns who had come to see, as well as her, their 'doactor gettin' hitched'.

Someone assembled them in the vestibule, Lizzie's chaplet of primroses was straightened by Kate, and then she was off, on Uncle Terence's arm, veiled like a sacrifice, 'there will be no slaughter, I assure you,' Charlie had said, down the aisle to the altar.

She was in her own world behind the veil. She remembered a story she had once read at school about a girl who had been afraid to cross the ice to reach her brother, who had gone through it. It had been well written. She had entered into the girl's terror, had been so gripped by it, that when she read, 'And then she found she could touch her brother's hand,' she had been overwhelmed with the same shock of happiness as the girl. The frozen pond had been crossed.

And here was the same experience! One minute she was at the far end on Uncle Terence's arm, the next she was standing beside Charlie, without having any memory of having walked down the aisle. He looked at her and said, 'Hello,' in such a natural voice that it was better than a reward.

After that it was easy. John was in his element, 'He's good at weddings and funerals,' Isobel had said. He had a fine delivery, and he used it to full effect.

'Dearly beloved, we are gathered together here in the sight of God . . .' and so on and so on. Well, she did not know of any impediment. The Fiscal had seen to that. And no one had jumped up in the church to denounce Charlie.

'Wilt thou have this woman to thy wedded wife, to live together after God's ordinance in the holy estate of Matrimony? Wilt thou love her, comfort her, honour and

341

keep her in sickness and in health . . . ?' Charlie's strong, confident reply gave her courage when her time came.

There was no bother about the ring. Mr Robert Dick, his young surgeon friend from the Royal, was as neat in handing it over as he was with a scalpel. It was safely on her finger, she was that incredible thing, a married woman.

She stood with Charlie while the benediction was pronounced, able now to look John fully in the face. There was the sweet mouth that she had once longed for, or had she? The kind eyes which had seemed to understand all, but had they? Not about the letter. He had looked at her gravely and shaken his head. 'A sin,' he had said, 'a moral sin.' What other kind was there?

But now he was smiling at her, his arms raised, God's personal envoy, and this time the teasing sense of familiarity was gone. She knew. She wanted to cry out, to interrupt him, 'Blessed are all they that fear . . .' It was the *other* John he had been reminding her of all those years, her poor drowned brother. The same sweet mouth, the eyes which had always been older than his age. Mother had always said he would be a minister . . . she felt herself tremble against Charlie's side, and then she conquered it, straightened her back, and turned with him to walk back up the aisle.

It was a *fait accompli*, the end of the old and the beginning of a new life, married to the man she loved, but also leaving behind her that old obsession about John which had plagued her senses since she was sixteen. It had been like a gift from John's God, a little extra thrown in to make it perfect.

She smiled brilliantly, confidently, as they walked, at one side and then the other, glad to see the familiar Sholton faces, village faces under unfamiliar hats, the guests from further afield, Emily Barthe a brilliant little parakeet amongst the sober gowns, Charles, so French amongst the Scottish faces, skin parchment-like against their ruddiness, Lord Crawford smiling in his private pew with the crest on its door, his tall son, Nigel, now at Eton, beside him. She smiled right and left with relief and happiness and felt like Persephone whom she had once read about emerging from a long winter. The world seemed to open to her.

'You look as if you were enjoying yourself,' Charlie said to her later at Braidholme where the reception was being held. 'I thought you would have been nervous.'

'Me! Nervous!' she said. 'I was in full command. I made an important discovery during the Benediction . . .' but he had not heard her. He had turned to shake hands with a well-wisher.

She did not neglect her duties, Mother herself could not have shown more aplomb. She circled the room on her own, stopping to talk to Emily and Charles. Emily's gestures seemed more foreign than in Paris, she spoke French sometimes by mistake, or design. 'You look *ravissante*, Maevy. Such assurance! No one could take their eyes off you, isn't that right, Charles?' He agreed. He looked like a strange black and white bird which had come down in the wrong country. 'And that little brides-maid, Leezie! So like your mother. What age is she?'

'Thirteen. Yes, she's looking lovely.'

'Well, you must promise to send her to a finishing school I know in Versailles. Giselle will go there when she's old enough. But it gives them an air of . . . *je ne sais quoi*, am I not right, Charles?'

'Certainly Paris did a lot for me,' Maevy said.

'You should have spent your honeymoon there.' Charles looked pensive. 'It is a place for lovairs.' His pensive look made her wonder if there had been a little love nest on the Left Bank he had been forced to forsake.

343

Charlie was speaking to Arthur Cranston and his wife and she joined them. What about wives of husbands with causes? she thought, seeing Arthur's zealot eye, his wife's look of discontent. When he is responsible for yet another Act being passed, will they recognize in 'Commonweal' her support? Would *she* have to fill the same rôle with Charlie, the one to come home to, who never got a chance to venture forth on her own? She was surprised that in the midst of her happiness she should feel a slight regret for her nursing days.

The nurses who had stood in a double row as she went into the church made no bones about which they would have preferred. 'No more bedpans, Maevy!' Nurse Allan laughed. 'We thought of making an arch of them for you!' They did not disguise their good-natured envy. Every girl's aim in life was to be married. Of course, nursing was a vocation, but so was marriage, a woman's true vocation, that and to procreate.

Charlie had thought she was strong enough now. He, too, thought it was her vocation.

She spoke to Lord Crawford who was with her mother. 'This is a proud day for your mother,' he said, shaking hands, 'leaving her alone, but happy in your happiness.' He sounded hopeful. A little pleased that the way was being made clear for him? 'Allow me to add my good wishes to hers.' He had already done so in the shape of a handsome crystal decanter despatched from Mappin and Webb, by Royal Appointment to the Queen.

'Thank you,' she said. 'I'm very glad you were able to bring your son.'

'I want him to enter into Sholton life whenever possible, and your mother said children were welcome.'

'The more the merrier.' She looked round to identify for him some of the children who were present. 'That's

Robert and Terence, my brother Terence's boys, with my uncle and aunt from America.'

'You must meet my brother and his wife, Alastair,' Maeve put in.

'And at the other table,' Maevy pointed, 'are Sarah and Gaylord, my other brother's children. They've another little girl, Mary. She's too . . . young to come.'

'I told you about her, if you remember?' Her mother looked at him.

'Ah, yes, very unfortunate. We don't realize how blessed we are.' His eyes went to his son, Nigel, who was standing talking to Lizzie and Kieran in the centre of the room. Nigel was adjusting Lizzie's chaplet which was once again askew, tall, dark-haired like his father, the elegance there although there was still an engaging awkwardness. Lizzie was laughing, animated, looking from one boy to the other.

'Lizzie's enjoying herself,' Maevy said.

'She seems to be a young lady of spirit.' He turned to her mother. 'She resembles you, Maeve.' He's taken his cue from her, Maevy thought. 'If you're interested in girls' schools, by the way, my late wife knew of quite a few.'

'Emily was saying, Mother,' she looked at him, 'that's my sister Kate's step-daughter, Lord Crawford, that she knows of a finishing school near Versailles.'

'Ah, yes.' He looked impressed. She and her mother exchanged glances, kept their faces straight.

And when they had done their rounds and met up once more, Charlie said, 'Ready?' and she said, 'Yes.' They were travelling to Dundee for a short honeymoon to look for, not very seriously, he admitted, any relations of his who might like to know they were married.

But he longed to go back to the East Coast, he said,

'just to feel that drier, keener air again. Here it's like a damp cloth sometimes. I'll take you to Broughty Ferry,' he said, 'to give you the smell of the East Coast, the smell of fish.' And she had agreed, because it did not much matter to her where they went as long as they were together.

'I'll find the best hotel in town with a four-poster bed,' he promised, 'and every night we'll draw the curtains and tumble about in it to our heart's content.' And she had agreed to that, too.

This was what they did. During the day they hired a cab and got the man to drive around Charlie's old haunts – 'you have to go back to your roots occasionally,' he said – and searched, not very seriously, for long-lost relations. And in the evening, when they had had dinner and wine, they went upstairs and undressed in front of the glowing fire. 'I told you East Coast coal was good,' he said, and he did not draw the curtains on the bed so that they could watch the flames in between tumbling about. Even the first night had been easy.

'I'm not going to jump on you like a fox on a poor wee hen,' he said, 'I'm going to take you in my arms like this, see, it's nice and friendly, the warmth of two bodies together is a singular thing, and we're going to lie quietly savouring it until one or the other makes a move.'

He was right. It was a singular thing, complete in itself, in the pleasure it gave, and yet only a foretaste of a greater pleasure. She moved in his arms and he said, 'It would be even nicer if we hadn't any clothes on to spoil it. Let me help you.'

His hands were gentle on her. She raised her arms and the silky material passed her ears and went over her head in a soft rush. The result of their skin touching each other was even more pleasurable.

She was aware of her own body for the first time, the

346

hills of her breasts, the slope of her belly to the smaller hill, the thin thighs, the bony shins. It was a pity she had not put on much weight yet since her illness.

For the first time she was aware that those shapes of her body, those hills and valleys, had a purpose, in that they matched his, and with the realization came more than a warmth, a tingling excitement, a wish to mould and meld them against Charlie's body.

'I'm ashamed,' she said, 'to be twenty-eight and still a virgin.'

He laughed. 'I'm thirty-five and not, so that balances things.'

'That's smug. You speak as if men were different.'

'I didn't mean that. But aren't men's passions supposed to be stronger, more imperative?'

'Supposing I told you that some nights I was tormented out of my wits, that I . . . used a pillow?'

He laughed and hugged her. 'That tore your heart out to say. As bad as going to the Fiscal, my honest darling.'

'It did. But I don't want to be one of those clinging vines, lying here as if for a sacrifice.'

'I said there would be no slaughter.' He was finding her secret places, agitating her senses.

Her voice trembled. 'I've had more time than most to think about it. I want to play a part, an active part . . .'

'Oh, you will, you will. You're what I want, have always wanted. Waiting has made it sweeter, but, oh, the joy of not having to wait any longer . . .'

They were matched, at least, in the strength of their love. What had been a warmth, then a tingling excitement, became a smooth flowing river carrying her onwards with the force of the current in the Sholtie, not to the Falls which would have plummeted her downwards, but to some kind of whirlpool of desire and striving, and striving and desire, sucking her into the depths to raise her to the surface again, time after time until, together, they were thrown on to the shore.

'Better than a pillow?' he said. His voice was rough with love. It came from far away.

'Better.' She turned to him, winding herself into him, feeling the incredible texture of the skin which had taken part in their loving.

6

A year later, in April 1892, little Elspeth was born. It had been Charlie's mother's name, and Maevy was glad to use it, but said their son, when he came, would be called after his father. She was surprised how easy the birth had been remembering the agony she had seen in some of the women she had attended when doing her midwifery cases in Glasgow.

At least it was short-lived. When Charlie came bounding up the stairs after Jim Geddes had left her, she assured him she was all right. His usual medical detachment had temporarily left him. He was trembling. He had not taken time to shave.

'Maevy, dearest heart,' he knelt down beside her, 'are you sure you're all right?'

'Of course I am.' She looked down at her new daughter in her arms.

'And the baby?' He gently pulled back the shawl from the child's face.

'Didn't you hear her lusty crying? You could have heard her in the middle of Sholton.'

'I was nearly up those stairs long before that. Why didn't they tell me what fathers have to go through?' he joked, bending forward to kiss her brow.

'You're old-fashioned, Charlie. Mother once told me that my father delivered Terence before the midwife came.'

'It will come to that, or at least they'll let fathers in. Much more sensible.'

'That'll be the day! Jim Geddes would have been horrified.'

'It doesn't take much to horrify Jim.'

Little Ellie, as they soon called her, was a joy and a delight to them. They did not go away that summer because of her, although Maria and Patrick invited them to Brodick, but in the fine evenings, when Charlie had finished work, or the rare Sunday afternoons, they sat in the garden at Larkhill, perfectly content.

She said once to him, 'I've never known such happiness. It's funny how biblical phrases come into your mind when you want to express how you feel. "My cup's full and running over . . ." That's how it is with me. I'll remember this summer in the years to come.'

Her life broadened out with Charlie as they talked, about politics, art and music. She had never had the time nor the leisure, nor such a companion. They followed the Home Rule question, were pleased when Gladstone took control again that year at eighty-three years of age.

'He's worked hard enough for us,' Charlie said, 'but the country's too undecided to go along with him. The golden years are beginning to go. There's unrest about and a smell of change.' She agreed. 'And the trouble in South Africa goes rumbling on. I think we're going to be tested there in time. As usual we'll be totally unprepared. And then when we're on the point of losing, we'll gather ourselves together in the nick of time. It's always the same.'

'I used to admire Florence Nightingale,' she told him. 'She was one of my reasons for going into nursing. I almost hoped for a war so that I could go out to the front as she did. What would you do, Charlie, if war came?' It was a hypothetical question. They were safe here in their daily life, wrapped in a cocoon of happiness. Besides, if it came, it would only be a little war . . .

350

'I don't know. If there was a call to surgeons, for instance, if men were dying because of lack of them, I'd be tempted. I joined the HLI in 1881, at twenty-six. Full of patriotism, then.' He laughed. 'Like you, I've seen myself on the battlefield, saving lives, but having you and Ellie makes dreams like that frightening.'

'I couldn't bear to lose you.'

'There's no chance of that. Here, why the solemn face? The politicians will sort things out.'

They went to the choral and orchestral concerts in the St Andrew's Hall on Saturday nights if Charlie's surgery was finished in time, saw an occasional touring company at the Royal Theatre, they read, discussed every subject under the sun from Oscar Wilde to whether their son would follow in his father's footsteps, from Ibsen to the Sholton Sunday School Picnic, they entertained their family and friends.

And if the days were happy, so were the nights. Her sexuality which had been kept in tight rein for so long had full play. She loved with a mature woman's love, giving everything, so that in the morning some of the ecstasy would still be with her, and Biddy would say, hearing her go singing about her tasks, 'My, somebody's happy this morning!'

Terence with his two sons went to Ireland during the Fair Fortnight to visit Honor when the office in the Gallowgate was closed down, but Maeve stayed at home.

'I'm a bit unsettled,' she said when she came one day to have tea with Maevy. They were sitting in the garden. 'I think it's because the boys are unsettled. I sense it. Terence's mind is in Ireland, and goodness knows where Patrick's is. I think Maria still hankers after America, and that makes him the same.'

'Leave them to settle down again,' Maevy said. 'Everybody gets like that at times.'

'You don't anyhow.' Her mother looked at Ellie sleeping in the perambulator beside them – it had been bought by her for Lizzie – 'I've never seen such a happy face.'

'It's what I am. I must look like that Cheshire cat.'

'It's peaceful here.' Maeve looked around her. 'I love your garden and mine, and the Sholtie purling down below. I wouldn't be wanted over there in Boyle.'

'Do you really think he's in love with her?'

'That's a state Terence has no difficulty falling into. But whether she's in love with him is a different matter. There's something holding her back. There's sadness behind that girl's eyes.'

'I've yet to meet the one who can resist Terence's charms. Have you heard from Maria and Patrick yet?'

'Yes, they've had a bad time with Mary since they got there. She got a midge bite the first day, and her leg's swollen so badly that she's had to be pushed everywhere in her go-cart. Just when she was beginning to be steady on her feet. Sometimes I wonder if they'll ever rear that wee one.'

'I don't know what they'd do if they lost her. Still, it's not like you to refuse a trip to Brodick, Mother.' She said the words idly as she added more hot water to the teapot. 'You, the great traveller. Or you could have done what you did last year at Boyle and stayed in a hotel.'

'That might have been embarrassing if Terence was at Woodlea. Besides, I've got other things on my mind.' The tone of her voice made Maevy look up. She surprised a look of what seemed to be embarrassment on her mother's face.

'What other things?'

'Lord Crawford has asked me to marry him.'

'No!' She set down the teapot in her surprise.

'Is it so outlandish?' It was not often she used that sharp tone.

'No, of course it isn't. You've been friends for ages, you live alone, so does he. It seems . . . eminently suitable. Are you thinking of accepting?'

'That's the trouble, I don't know.' She looked at Maevy. 'Well, you're a married woman now. I can tell you the whole story. Are you shockable?'

Maevy laughed. 'Charlie's got rid of that in me, thank goodness.'

'Charlie's a man of the world. He keeps an open mind, not like some doctors, Jim Geddes, for instance. Though they tell me that eldest daughter of theirs, Belle, is a handful. No, Jim's got what I call a "Sholton" mind.'

'Poor Jim. There's room for everybody. Go on, try and shock me.'

'Alastair and I had a kind of affair when we were young. Oh, it didn't get to . . . what you might call the final thing, but pretty close all the same. Your eyes haven't blinked once. You're coming on.' She smiled. 'I'd become discontented with the hard life I led with your father, working from morning to night, bringing up bairns. And *I* hadn't been brought up to it. Alastair's mother offered me the use of her horse. We were sisters under the skin . . . Annabel, she was called, a shy creature. Without having to be told she knew what I'd left behind me in Ireland.'

'I remember her at the Sunday School Picnics.'

'Yes. She sent for me before she died . . . Well, Alastair used to join me on those rides. I looked forward to them, and then I realized it was Alastair I was looking forward to. He made me a proposal. An . . . arrangement.'

'You turned it down, of course?' It was she who was sharp now. Terence had hinted long ago, but she had not imagined . . . this.

'I thought you said you couldn't be shocked?' Her

mother's eyes slanted towards her. 'Charlie's got more work to do on you.'

Only mothers can make you feel like this, she thought, take away your married status with a word. She murmured something unintelligible.

'No, I didn't turn it down. I . . . played with the idea. It would have meant a better job for your father, that was the sop, but I also liked the danger in it. There's something in me that likes danger, a challenge. You're different, Maevy.' Thank you very much, she thought. 'And then I was brought to my senses when your father was trapped down the pit.'

'Oh, that awful day! I well remember it. And keeping the fire stoked up with the black kettle boiling away all the time. We boiled it dry once or twice, Isobel and me. And you rushing in and out. Your face, like death . . .'

'Well, by the grace of God he was saved, as you know, and my mind was made up for me.'

'But now, Mother, with all that behind you, there's no reason why you shouldn't . . .'

'No reason. That's the trouble. If I had a good reason for or against it would be easier. I'm fifty-eight now. Maybe I'd look too ridiculous?' Her glance was shy.

'*You* look ridiculous? If anyone could be Lady Crawford it's you. You'd be a credit to him in every way.'

'Oh, I don't doubt that. That's not sprowsing. Anything I put my hand to I do well. It's . . . other things.'

'What?'

'The boys. I told you they were worrying me. They're not single-minded about the business just now. I'm the one who's holding it together. Alastair wouldn't want a business woman for a wife, would he?'

'I don't know. They talk about the New Woman, don't they? Things are changing. Charlie and I were talking about that only the other day.'

354

'Not fast enough. Then there's Braidholme. I love that house like a person. It was ours, Kieran's and mine. I'd feel I was deserting him. I have a lot of myself invested in that house, happiness and joy, fear, disappointment, sadness, everything that makes up life. It's sheltered me for such a long time, comforted me, been a place for my children and grandchildren to come to. I tell you, Maevy, it would be easier to leave a person than leave Braidholme.'

'I can understand that. The thing, surely, would be not to *tear* yourself away, like wrenching a plant out by the roots. Think about it, visit the Hall from time to time, see if you can imagine yourself there . . .'

'It's all right Alastair visiting me at Braidholme. He's the laird, and if it was a little oftener than usual it wouldn't matter. Folks in Sholton think I'm an eccentric – oh, don't laugh, they do – and Susan wouldn't carry tales for a hundred pounds, even when she spends a weekend with Tibby Simpson, her crony. But if the news went round that I was visiting the Hall, we'd *have* to get married.'

'You're not far wrong.' Maevy laughed. 'Well, you'll just have to take Ellie and me for chaperons, won't she, precious?' She bent over the child's perambulator to kiss her cheek, to let the small fingers curl round hers.

'It's nothing to laugh about. I was perfectly content with things as they stood until he had this idea of marrying me . . .'

'Well, why don't you offer *him* an . . . arrangement? That's what he did long ago, isn't it?'

Her mother looked at her, astonishment in her face. 'My goodness,' she said, 'Charlie *has* done a thorough job on you.'

'I think Mother may take a lover,' she said to Charlie in bed that night.

'What did you say?' He got up on one elbow to look at her.

'You know perfectly well what I said.' She gave him a limpid look, tapped his nose with her finger. 'Dinna fash yersel.'

'Who?' he said.

'Lord Crawford. He's asked her to marry him but she isn't sure. Patrick and Terence are giving her some concern in the business.'

'She still feels very involved in the firm. She wouldn't want to leave it in the lurch.' He lay down. 'Come closer. I like this bit as well as the bit that went before. Titled ladies aren't as yet moving in business circles . . . but, on the other hand, taking a lover has always been in fashion with them.' He laughed. 'Your mother's cut out for it. She's as much an aristocrat as any of them.'

'I suggested it,' she said smugly, 'but only till she makes up her mind. Lord Crawford offered *her* an arrangement long ago. I thought, tit for tat.'

'In the name of God,' Charlie said, 'what kind of family have I married into? You'll give me fair warning, will you, when you intend to do the same?'

'I will,' she said. But there was no possibility. She was one of the faithful kind. Charlie was her man, always would be till the day she died . . . or he died. She drew close to him in one of those moments of fear which inflict even the happiest of people.

7

The Manse, Sholton, Lanarkshire, Scotland
1st August, 1894

Dear Kieran,

It was nice to get your last letter. I've kept them all. Of course, if you're feeling smug, let me tell you that I keep others, Nigel Crawford's, for instance. You'll remember meeting him at Aunt Maevy's wedding, Lord Crawford's son.

Well, I have a wonderful piece of news for you. It's all fixed for me to go to a finishing school in Paris when I'm eighteen. I'm so thrilled. 'You'd think you were glad to leave your parents,' Father said. 'I myself would have thought that one of our fine academies for girls in Glasgow would have been sufficient for your later years, but I've been overridden in the matter. Your grandmother is paying your fees and your mother has accepted, so I have no further voice in the matter.'

My cousin, Sarah, thinks that *everything* her parents say is right, but I must say Father can take the gilt off the gingerbread, but I suppose it's all for my own good. The school I'm going to was recommended by your sister, Emily, at Aunt Maevy's wedding, and I'm looking forward to visiting her in Paris, also her children, Olivier, Marc and Giselle.

I was sent to Grandmother's to thank her, and Lord Crawford was there. He told me a lot of interesting things about Paris, the flea markets, Montmartre where the artists are, the sewers, the cafés, not the usual things like the Louvre. Grandma looks very happy these days. Aunt Maevy says she's having her Indian summer whatever that may mean, but I noticed she and Uncle Charlie looked at each other and laughed.

I'm glad you enjoyed yourself at George's wedding. 'Abigail Van Dam.' What a grand name, really American. You'll be able to visit them when they set up house in New York, and Ernest. How is he getting on there? If you can find the time would you please send me some postcards from there? I collect them. Nigel

Crawford travels a lot in the 'hols' as he calls them, with his father, and he's sent me some wonderful ones from Spain, and Italy and France.

I'm supposed to be looking out my clothes for going to Brodick, so I'd better stop. I send my love to everyone, to George and his new wife, Abigail, to Victoria and Jason, and Deborah, Judith, Thomas, and now Priscilla. Goodness me, the children in this family! I suppose George and Abigail will be next. And special love to your mother and father, and great uncle and aunt at Springhill. Will you ever forget that wonderful bicycle ride we all had round Wanapeake Point?

I won't send you my love as you'd say it was 'soft', so I'll just send a big hug to Ernest!

Your cousin, Lizzie.

8

They were back at Strandhill, a special treat because it was the last day before Terence and the boys went home. The children were playing in the shallows, running in and out of the water to fill their buckets. Robert and Terence were making a moat, the girls were helping, taking directions meekly from their cousins.

'Look at the boys bossing the girls about,' Honor said. She was sitting on the sand beside Terence who was sprawled on one elbow. They were surrounded by a medley of picnic baskets, cushions and rugs.

'Still, they get on well together.' Terence was watching Robert wading in up to his knees to fill a bucket for Clare. She was shrieking with delight at his bravery. 'Will you be sad when we go?'

'I'm always sad.'

'Four years now.' He felt hesitant, knew he was speaking slowly. Once Honor had said to him that he spoke like a tap being turned on and off. She was very perceptive. Perhaps it was something to do with her writing, a capacity to observe . . . 'Do you feel at ease with me now? At first I was never sure if you really wanted me to come.'

'I'm at ease with you, Terence.' He looked up and thought there was a new sweet expression on her face. Usually she looked slightly tense.

'Well, that's something.' He laughed. 'Next step to being in love with me. I'll be honest with you. Although I've loved you for a long time it didn't happen right away.

I thought you were lovely, sad, but there was an invisible barrier there. It damped my ardour.'

'You weren't used to that with women?'

'Right first go.' He laughed. 'So, coming to visit you here for the first year or two was just something pleasant to look forward to, a cousin-by-marriage relationship.'

'A "relation". Do you remember Clare that first time?' They laughed together.

'It was Ireland that drew me as much as you. I feel an affinity with it, my whole body feels it. Even my skin relaxes, it's moist and supple, there isn't the constant tautness I feel in Glasgow, a determination to get through each day, no pleasure in it.'

'It's the Irish in you. Your mother noticed it. You take after your father.'

'Oh, I know that. Well, that's how it was, but now you're inextricably mixed up with it.' He laughed. 'I copied that big word from you. It's a strange kind of situation for me especially. I didn't even want to carry our relationship any further. And let me tell you, that's a different Terence McGrath speaking. But now it's changed. When we were having that special dinner last night and I saw you looking across the table at me, the candlelight in your eyes, I thought . . . I've come home.' His voice dropped on the last words.

'What are you saying, Terence?' Her voice was level.

'That I love you, will always love you. You're the right woman for me at last.' He sat up and put his arm round her shoulders in a companionable way. 'See how circumspect I am. I've never touched your body once in all that time.'

'The barrier must have been very powerful.'

'Yes. I knew it was because of your husband. I guessed long ago that he'd ill-treated you.'

'What an understated way of putting it!' Her voice was

360

suddenly shaking. 'He treated me like a possession, like a slave, like a tart! God . . . !' She turned to look at him. 'Why after all that time has it still the power to hurt me?'

'Because you haven't let it out.'

'I know, I know . . . don't run away with the idea that I was a prim little miss. I wasn't. Untutored, yes, but never prim. I was . . . ready. But not for being physically ill-treated, kicked, whipped.' Her voice was calm and now it was he who could not control his voice.

'What are you saying?'

'You haven't a clue, Terence. Maybe you've built up some kind of reputation for womanizing, you're handsome enough for that, but you simply don't know the . . . degradation that can be inflicted on women by men. You, with all your charm, have never assaulted a woman. Isn't that right?' He shook his head, unable to speak. He had slapped Catherine once. Puny . . . 'I've been whipped like a hound by Dermot.' Her voice was low and rapid, she could paint a picture in words, well, of course she could, he saw the fair-haired man in his riding coat, the livid face, the upraised arm . . .

'Why did you take so long to tell me?' He took her in his arms, ashamed of his sex.

'Guilt. Deep humiliation. He assaulted my spirit as well as my body. The first time I really began to feel I was a woman again was at your sister's wedding. So many kind people treating me well, that lovely sister of yours with the happiness shining out of her eyes.'

He said jokingly since it was the only way to say it, 'Since you didn't do him in, how did he die?'

'That's where the guilt comes in. Sitting across the table from me just a week later. I'd told him I was leaving the next day. Cerebral haemorrhage. Bloody foam at his mouth, his eyes bulging. His head crashed down on the table. That was a blow sure enough in spite of everything. You see . . . he won.'

He pulled her back against him, could feel her shivering. 'We've both known it, violent death and the constant sense of being to blame. Like a hump on your back you can't shake off.'

'Sure enough, sure enough . . .' She held herself away from him. 'You have to work through it on your own till you emerge into some kind of sanity.'

'You've done that?'

'Yes, I knew it last night. Suddenly. You've helped by coming year after year, by your patience. Unlike you, I felt *your* attraction right away. I knew you weren't in the habit of waiting, even to have a flirtation. That touched me, your consideration. Each year it got better for me, even your boys helped. My chief lifeline was my writing, and that was a struggle. Now it's easy, well, it's never easy, but it flows. Life has become wonderful for me again.'

'Does that mean you love me now?'

She turned and faced him. 'I've loved you since you came here with your mother.'

'Could we get married, then? I'm not spiritual at all, Honor, very much flesh and blood.'

'That's easy, too. The hard bit would be leaving Woodlea, and my writing. I'm not ready to give them up. Marrying you would mean living in Glasgow.'

'My work's there.'

'I know that. Is it an impasse, do you think? Woodlea and my writing have been my support. I don't know if I'm able to stand without them yet.'

'Lie down,' he said. 'We've got so far. Lie down.'

'The children will see us.'

'No, they're too far away. Lie down.'

* * *

362

Usually his love-making had been confident. There had been an acquired knowledge through experiment and experience, that secretly women liked a man to be masterful (except Catherine who had not liked men), that he could browbeat them, oh, just a little, sexually, make them whimper with delight, not to be cruel, of course, but to be, well, dominant, a king.

He kissed Honor, his hands at his sides, and they lay close, joined by their mouths only. She moved at last and said, 'I'd forgotten the closeness, the dark pleasure, I want more.'

He was tremulous. I'm like a woman, he thought. I begin to understand how she must have felt when her husband broke into her body, the loathing, but worse, the loss of self-respect. He liked this feeling of submission, the newness of it as if he had been given an extra dimension, or even another sex.

But as she moved in his arms and became eager, he pulled the rug over them, and there was singing in his ears. This love would be different. It would be the last time, the best time. It would be her wishes which came first, not his. They would talk out their future calmly, happily, safe in the knowledge of their love. It had been worth waiting for.

A long time later he opened his eyes to a circle of eyes.

'And what are you staring at?' He heard Honor's laughing voice.

'You and Uncle Terence,' Clare said. 'You'd gone to sleep. You're both funny to go to sleep in the middle of the day. Under the rug. See what Robert has found for me.' She swung her red bucket under Terence's nose and he looked down on a crab struggling in the water in it.

'Take it away! Take it away! I'm frightened!' He cowered against Honor in pretended horror.

'Never mind.' Honor put her arms round him, laughing. 'Isn't he a big cry-baby?' Her cheek against his was warm. He could imagine its rosiness.

9

'I like visiting on Sundays,' Maevy said. They were driving to Glasgow in Charlie's high-stepping pony and trap, bought so that she could sometimes accompany him with Ellie on his rounds.

She looked at the little girl sitting between them in her sapphire blue velvet coat and bonnet, her fair curls spilling over the cape collar edged with fur. 'Is it fun, Ellie?'

'Look, look!' she pointed, her eyes bright with excitement.

A bevy of cyclists passed them identically dressed in bright red and white with visored caps pulled down over their brows.

'Cyclists,' Maevy said distinctly, and to Charlie, 'The Sholton Ramblers. Lizzie and I cycled at Wanapeake before they'd even started here. Patrick's right. They're always ahead of us in America.'

'I'll buy you one, if you like, then we could go out together on Sundays.' He smiled round at her. 'Would that . . . help?' She knew what he meant.

'I was wondering, maybe, if I could act as part-time midwife in the village till they got somebody permanent. I wouldn't mind using my skills again. Work takes your mind off things,' she tried to sound light-hearted, 'far better than pleasure.'

'You're no hedonist. I don't mind. It may set the village by the ears, but you might as well be in the vanguard. I saw in the paper the other day the first woman surgeon has just qualified.'

'Do you miss it, Charlie?' She thought he had sounded wistful.

'No, I made a deliberate choice, but like you, I wouldn't mind using my skills sometimes. There are great strides being made in that field, especially now we've got the Roentgen rays. I've dreamed about that for years. With this war coming nearer and nearer, that's where it's going to be needed. War always advances surgery, about the only good it does.'

'You still think it's coming?'

'I think it's here. The Jameson Raid was the beginning of it. What, my pet?' He bent down to Ellie.

'Will you make wee Mary better, Daddy?' She looked up into his face.

'"Wee Mary"!' Maevy laughed. 'She's three years older than this one.'

'I'll try.' He looked enquiringly over Ellie's head.

'I was telling her that Mary had been ill for a long time and to be gentle with her, poor wee soul. Look, Ellie, there's the Tron steeple. Oh, you're lucky. The clock's just beginning to strike. Listen . . .' They drove briskly along the Trongate with the sound from the huge bell resounding in their ears.

She spoke again when Ellie was occupied in watching the unfamiliar traffic. 'Maria asked me to bring Lizzie as well since she knew this was John and Isobel's busy day, but they wouldn't allow her to come.'

'They're too rigid with her but we can't interfere. We won't do that with Ellie. We'll keep her on a loose rein.'

'But a boy needs more discipline.' She was sorry she had said that. She looked around pretending interest in the plate-glass windows of the emporiums in their Sunday calm.

'I don't think so. We shouldn't make such a difference

between the sexes. They should be treated according to their temperament.'

'Do you think we'll *ever* have a son, Charlie? Oh,' she shook her head, 'I'm out of patience with myself, and on such a fine day. And me the happiest person alive.'

'You'll have him, don't worry.' He turned and his smile made her feel ashamed. 'We were lucky the first time, but maybe Mr Wilcox guddled about too much in your insides. There's no accounting for the vagaries of the feminine constitution.' He laughed, but his voice was tender. 'Don't grieve. If you do that, it will affect you physically as well.'

'I'll try not to. It's just, I'm in a hurry . . .'

They had passed through Charing Cross, and Charlie was going more slowly now, ready to turn into Claremont Terrace. As always, when they entered it, Maevy admired the satisfying sweep of the building, the fine stonework, but counted her blessings when she remembered that sickly child behind the elegant façade.

Charlie dropped them at the door while he drove his pony and trap round the back – nothing less than a carriage could grace that imposing front entrance – and Maria received her warmly. Ellie was whisked upstairs to the nursery by Jeannie. 'What a nice day you had for your drive.' Maria looked pale and strained. 'And here are your two brothers ready to greet you,' she said, as they went into the drawing-room.

'Hello, Patrick. You're looking well.' She thought he had the same look of strain as his wife, 'but not so well as this lad, he's fair bursting with health.' She kissed Terence fondly. He was more the man he had been, his resilience had returned, and yet there was a new maturity about him. His heart was in Ireland without a doubt.

'Will you excuse me?' Maria said. 'I want to take

367

Charlie up to see Mary when he comes in. I value his opinion.'

'How is she, Maria?'

She shook her head. 'So weak . . .' She went quickly out of the room. Maevy saw Patrick looking after her.

'Where are your two?' she asked Terence.

'Mother has them at Braidholme for the weekend. She teaches them riding. The last time they were there they had a lesson from Lord Crawford as well.'

'Is that a fact?' She met his eyes and they both laughed. 'Don't say a word and I won't,' she said.

'Not me. And look at Patrick, pretending he doesn't understand a word. No, happiness is rare enough. You should take it when you get it. But I can't think why she doesn't marry him.'

'She'll have her own reasons,' Patrick said.

'Quite.' Terence sobered. 'I wanted to have a talk with you and Patrick.' He got up from the sofa where he had been sitting with Maevy. 'I've something on my mind. Thanks.' His brother was handing him a glass of sherry. 'And I apologize for bringing up my affairs when you've got your own worries. That wee lass . . .'

'Go ahead. Maria and Charlie will be upstairs for a bit. She's still looking for reassurance . . . or a miracle.'

'Is she worse?' Maevy asked.

'She's that frail.' He shook his head. 'The doctor says to keep her in bed which only makes her the more frail. It was that midge bite that started it all. I'm convinced of it.'

I'm not the only one with obsessions, Maevy thought. 'Don't think that, Patrick,' she said, 'the poison's cleared out of her system long ago.'

'But now he says her lungs are damaged. That she's not to make any effort. Winter's the worst for her. We're over the worst of it but it's taken a fearful toll of her

health, this damp, cold air all the time. By God, sometimes I long to get away from it all . . .' he passed his
hand over his brow. 'Excuse me. It's good to get your
wind out with your own. What was it you wanted to say
to us?' He looked at his brother who had taken up his
stance before the fireplace.

'I hardly like to mention it now, and you with this
worry on your shoulders.'

'Fire away.'

Terence emptied his glass, put it down on the mantelpiece behind him. 'I'm thinking of drawing out of the
business.' There was a pause.

'You're what!' Patrick seemed to pull himself together.

'I thought I'd tell you first, see if you had any idea how
Mother would take it.'

'It's Honor, isn't it?' Maevy said.

He turned to her as if looking for support. 'She's been
through a bad time, a hell of a bad time if you knew the
whole of it, but she's willing to marry me now. She
doesn't want to leave Woodlea, and, well, it's no good
putting it all on to her. I'd like to live there. The life
appeals to me, and she'd welcome the boys. Sadie's
leaving me soon to get married, and that would leave me
in a fix. Besides, I'm fed up with Glasgow. Every time
I'm in Ireland I feel worse about coming back. I'd like to
breed horses, to live with her there. It isn't a sudden
decision. I've been thinking about it for a long time . . .'
He looked at Patrick. His brother turned away from him
abruptly, walked to the window, stood there with his back
to them.

'You can't blame Terence for seeking happiness,'
Maevy said. 'You'll have to think about it at least,
Patrick.'

'I am.' He turned. They had been close for so long,
Maevy thought, as boys together at Colliers' Row, in their

369

escapades at Tweedie's Farm. Their terrible enmity over Bessie Haddow had been a kind of closeness, too, and the seal on it had been when they had striven together at the stable fire which had resulted in their father's death. Such closeness. She could have wept, looking at them. 'I'll miss you, Terence,' he said.

'I'll miss you. I've thought of that. There's never been a brother like you. Through thick and thin. But you wouldn't stand in my way?'

'No.' He shook his head. 'You deserve some after Catherine. Happiness is a rare enough . . .' The door opened and Maria and Charlie came into the room.

'How did you find her?' Maevy met Charlie's eyes.

'Poorly.' He never minced words. 'Very poorly.'

'You think the doctor's doing all he should?' Patrick asked. 'You don't think she should be got up occasionally, just to keep her legs supple?'

'You must do what he tells you. Her heart's far from strong, and any effort might be too much for her. Don't distress yourself. You've done everything you could for her.' He knows she's going to die, Maevy thought.

'I think we should go in for lunch,' Maria said. She was very pale. Had Charlie tried to warn her? 'You must be hungry, driving all that way.' She was a changed woman from the bright girl Patrick had brought back from America, thin, her once glossy black hair without its former lustre. Maevy put her arm round her waist as they walked to the dining-room.

'Don't fret too much, Maria,' she said. 'She may get better when summer comes.'

'I know she won't.' Her face was calm when she turned to Maevy. 'A mother always knows. It's Patrick I'm afraid for. He can't accept it.'

At lunch gloom hung over the table although Charlie did his best to banish it. Terence was abstracted, Patrick monosyllabic, which was not unusual, and Maria, although scrupulously polite, looked as if the strain of sitting there at all was too much for her.

'We'll have to leave fairly soon,' Maevy said, thinking this was the kindest thing to do. 'I'll just have a look at Sarah and Gaylord when I go up for Ellie.'

'She's enjoying herself with her cousins. I heard her laughing when I was upstairs. What a bright little girl she is, so healthy . . .'

'She's a wee rascal.'

'We used to call *you* that,' Terence said. 'Remember, Patrick?' It was as if he held out his hand to his brother in sympathy.

He nodded. 'Another slice of beef? There's plenty here.'

'No, thanks. Honor was saying when I was last in Ireland that I have to watch my pot, as she puts it.'

'They're getting married soon,' Maevy said to Charlie. She was desperate to give them something to talk about. 'You don't mind me telling, Terence?'

'No. We were talking when you were upstairs. I'm happy enough to tell the world.'

'I'm so pleased for you, Terence,' Maria said, 'she's a beautiful girl.'

'And he's thinking of clearing out of Scotland as well.' Patrick's voice was louder than usual. 'By God, Terence, I've been green with envy often enough before when we were boys, but never as bad as this!' He looked at Maria. 'He wants to live with Honor at Woodlea, become a country gentleman, and I don't blame him! This country,' he looked at the others, putting down his knife and fork, 'has never suited Mary right from the start. That creeping, miserable dampness! Maybe, Charlie, you with your medical knowledge are saying that's not the right way of it at all, but I know better. Sarah and Gaylord are as right

371

as rain, aren't they, although we're cousins?' The words
fell from him, surprising in someone who never used two
words when one would do, 'Oh . . . !' It was like a groan,
'I look back on the time I spent in America with Maria's
parents, and that beautiful weather, the sun on the river,
warming your very bones. The winters are crisp and dry,
Maria tells me. None of this continuous dampness that
congeals your very marrow! Do you know what they say,
Maria, that Glasgow's only good for rheumatism and
roses . . . ? or used to be before they made a cess pit out
of it with their works and their foundries and their smoke
and dirt . . .'

'There are quite a few cities as bad in America, I'm
hearing,' Charlie said, lightly, smiling. 'Isn't that so,
Maria?'

'Patrick's thinking of Springhill and the Hudson. I do,
too, often.' She looked wistful. 'But you're right. It's not
all like that.'

'But trust Terence!' Patrick brushed this aside. '*He's*
found his Eldorado, isn't that the way of it?' He looked
at his brother. 'I'm pipped at the post as usual.' His mouth
widened. Not a smile. A grimace.

'Oh, go on, Patrick!' Maevy smiled at him, trying to
coax him out of his black mood. 'Nobody's trying to pip
you at the post. He was only . . .' He looked through her.

'For two pins I'd chuck everything as well and take my
wife and family back to America! I've thought about it
for a long time, kept putting it off. I knew it would be
better there for Mary. And for myself. Things move at
the pace I like there. There's room to stretch your legs
. . .' There was a loud, hurried tap at the door, a kind of
scuffling, a voice. Maria got up, startled.

'It can't be the next course already . . . Jeannie!' The
girl was in the room, twisting her apron in her hands,
weeping. 'What is it?' Her voice was harsh.

'Oh, Mrs McGrath . . .' Sobs choked her. She put her hand to her eyes.

'Stop that at once! Is it . . . Mary?' Maria's voice dropped to a whisper.

'I'd propped her up in a chair when I was changing the sheets, oh, and I don't know how to . . .' She moved her head back and forward.

'Take it easy, Jeannie.' Charlie was round the table in an instant and beside them.

'She slumped forward, doctor . . . I laid her down . . . Oh, Oh, Mr McGrath said it was good . . .'

'Stop drivelling!' Patrick was half-way to the door.

Maevy met Charlie's eyes as she jumped to her feet. 'Look after your wife, Patrick.' She spoke sternly. Maria's face was bone-white. Strange how the 'Royal' voice comes back, she thought, as she and Charlie ran upstairs together. Jeannie was at their heels, still weeping. 'I got such a shock, Mrs McNab. Maybe I shouldn't have lifted her. Oh, I don't know . . .'

'You go to the children,' she said without turning, 'and keep them in the nursery.' They had reached the landing.

'Yes, Mrs McNab,' the girl nodded, wiping her eyes with the end of her apron, 'but you'll let me know?'

'Yes, on you go.' She patted the girl's shoulder.

'I didn't think it would be as quick as this,' Charlie said. His hand was on the doorknob. He turned it . . .

She's dead, she wanted to say, we both know, she's dead, but then she braced herself. How often had she done the same thing, standing outside the interview room before she opened the door to break the news to relatives? They went in. Before he shut the door behind them she could hear the children playing in the nursery, Ellie's excited squeals. She would have tantrums tonight. What a funny thing to think now . . .

There was no doubt about it. Mary lay, her head on

one side, the pale-lashed eyes open, as pathetic in death as she had been in life. But, no, that wasn't true at all. There was a look of gentle surprise on her face, and her mouth had a slight lift in it.

Charlie drew his hand over the child's eyes and turned to look at her. He shook his head. Unnecessarily, she thought. Doctors liked to go through the motions. He bent down and put his ear to the child's chest for a second, straightened. 'You go down and tell Patrick and Maria. I'll stay here.'

'All right.' She looked down on the dead child. A great wave of pity overwhelmed her, and she bent down and stroked the side of her face. It was cold. Had it been worth it? she wanted to say to this poor dead creature. Where was the point?

'And I should bring them up, Maevy. Better to see her like this. Their grieving will start here, then.' But their grieving had started long ago.

She went slowly downstairs, the children's laughter ringing in her ears.

10

'Sand and driftwood and fishing boats,' Maria said. 'I suppose a child who grows up near this always feels a little different.' She was thinking of her dead Uncle Gaylord.

Patrick nodded. 'It's the smell chiefly, salty, fishy, and the limitlessness of it.' He waved as if to take in the whole of the Atlantic Ocean. 'You're brought up short by a hill if you're country-bred or a building if you live in the city.'

'Mother will be glad we've seen it. We'd better get back.' The cab driver was waiting for them while they had a short walk on the shore.

Yes, he knew the Grant place, he assured them as they drove along. 'Loblolly House it's called locally on account of the trees round it. Loblolly pines.' There was a Miss Grant, an elderly spinster, still living there.

They filled their lungs with sea air as he drove at a spanking pace along the sea front. After a time he turned down a narrow road, immediately darker because of the dense forest trees on either side.

'Even the trees are different,' Patrick said, 'thicker, taller,' and to the man, 'Could you tell me the names of some of them?'

'There's every kind, I reckon,' he said, taking off his hat to scratch his head, 'let's see, sycamore, live oak, maple, then there's magnolia, crape myrtle, fig, and pines, of course. They stand up to the winds we get here, and the heat. Sometimes it's like a swamp in summer.' He pointed, 'See them houses?' They nodded. 'Summer folk. Once the Marshall Parks got here they all come.'

'Are they the summer folk, too?' Patrick asked.

'Lord, sir, no!' He laughed. 'That was the name of the Norfolk Virginia Beach Railroad. The engine was named after the man who thought it up. Decided this would be a good place for folks coming from Norfolk and round-abouts. There's some terrible slums there. Reckon the rich folks would be glad to get away from it all for a breath of good sea air.'

'We visited at a fine old house there,' Patrick said, 'friends of my wife's mother. Seventeen hundred and ninety-two they said it was.'

'Aye, Norfolk was a great port then.' He was ready for a chat. 'Some merchant gentlemen came from New York and settled there. Worshipped at St Paul's Church, they tell me. You can still see the British cannonball stuck in the wall. High-handed, them Britishers were. Burned down the town.'

'Are you going to tell us to dismount?' Patrick said laughing.

'Lord no, sir. Don't I know which side my bread is buttered on? Whoa, there!' He reined in his horses. 'Well, then, there's your Loblolly House, the Grants' place.'

Maria had always thought of it as buried in a vast estate like, say, Lord Crawford's at Sholton, but the house facing them across the creek was virtually on an island, with certainly plenty of trees at the back, but the front was lawn only, possibly to allow an uninterrupted view of the water. They both sat and looked at it.

'Different from either Springhill or Wolf House,' Patrick said. 'They're all of a piece, but this one sprawls all over the place.'

'Mother's friend at Ghent said the summer houses were quite big. It has a seaside air, hasn't it, maybe because it's all white. And don't you like the high central bit and the two lower wings on either side? And all those mansards? Oh, Mother will be so pleased we've seen her old home! Look, there are the drawing-room windows above the front entrance with their wrought-iron balconies. It's southern-looking, and higgledy-piggledy, somehow.'

'I've counted twenty-five windows already,' Patrick said, 'most of them at the front so that everybody can have a view of the water,' and to the cab driver, 'Do we have to take a boat to reach it?'

'Not on your life, sir, it's on its own piece of land jutting out. We follow the road and come in at the back. Ready to go, are you?'

The woman who opened the door was older than her mother, possibly in her seventies, but she had a look of her cousin in her features, the same short nose, the high apple cheeks, but her hair was white and pulled back severely from her face and her gown had none of the ornamentation of her mother's. 'It's Caroline's daughter!' The woman's voice rose in a shriek. 'I've been waiting ever since I got her letter. Come in, do, both of you, and don't stand at the door.'

'The cab . . .' Patrick said.

'Well, pay him and send him off, young man. You aren't turning back as soon as you arrive, I hope.' She led Maria into a large hall full of heavy furniture and cases of stuffed birds, and towards the stairs. She went up them with a surprising agility, beckoning Maria to follow her. 'Such a naughty girl. She doesn't come nearly often enough. Of course I know why . . .' She pursed her lips as she turned, 'You're not at all like her. Dark where she's fair. So was Gaylord.' She put herself to the stairs again. 'Skin like a girl's if he hadn't burned it nearly black in the sun every summer. That boat . . .' She talked nonstop, not at all breathless, until they reached the upper landing. 'Nice young gentleman she married, though, and

377

yours looks nice enough to eat. Not so boisterous as Mr Muldoon, maybe?'

'No. Patrick's quiet. Shouldn't we have waited for him?'

'No, old Jonah's hovering about. Missed your knock. Deaf as a post. But not me. I've got all my faculties.' She ushered Maria into a large drawing-room. 'Don't you worry, Jonah will see to him.' She nudged her with her elbow, said slyly, 'I knew you'd come today.'

'Did you?' Maria smiled at her. 'How?' The sunlight, a greenish sunlight reflected from the water, was in her eyes.

'I just knew. The older you get the more you know without being told. One of the few advantages of old age. Now sit there at the window and admire the creek while I admire you. You must tell me all about yourself, and your husband and your family, and where you live, and how your dear mother's health is . . . ah, here's your husband.' Patrick was being shown in by a man about the same age as his employer. He wore a navy-blue skipped cap on the back of his head and huge horned toes showed through his old sandals. 'Tea, Jonah.' Miss Grant shouted, 'Tell them in the kitchen.' He saluted rakishly, and she beckoned to Patrick, 'Come along, young man, and sit beside us. I've so many things to ask you, and since I live alone, you must excuse me if I talk too much.'

They were captive, for the rest of the day, except for a brief sortie to see their room and 'freshen up'. 'Wouldn't hear of you putting up in one of those new-fangled places along the beach.' It was only after dinner, in the drawing-room with the green-skirted lamps giving it a mysterious under-water quality, that she spoke of 'cousin Gaylord'.

'Always quiet, he was, nice manners, wouldn't have thought looking at him he could handle a boat as good as the watermen around here. But he could outsail them, big brawny men that they were. Sometimes went all night fishing. Scarcely tired the next day. Like silk thread, he was, fine, strong, hard to break. Only thing, he would never go to visit his sister up in that place.'

'Was he ever ill, or delicate?' Patrick asked. He's thinking of Mary, Maria thought.

'Not till that summer, let me see, eighteen hundred and seventy it was. He'd always been quiet, but he wouldn't speak, nor eat, his mother told me, stayed in his room all day. Now folks do get like that, out of sorts with themselves, I've been that way myself, but this went on too long.

'His mother told me she spoke to Dr Seaborg about him, but he behaved real queer-like, looked away from her and muttered something about Gaylord having his problems . . . Old Seaborg thought unless you were married and had a brood of children dancing around you, you had problems. *I* don't have problems, except that sometimes I get to thinking what's going to happen to me here on my own and not getting any younger . . .'

'You look as fit as a fiddle,' Maria said.

'The strings can go slack in a fiddle . . . where was I? Gaylord, and being sick . . . Well, this morning he comes down as bright as a lark and says he's going fishing. His mother didn't try to put him off because he knew all the creeks and crannies like the back of his hand, how to avoid the marshlands, you could get sucked in there. It was a bit blustery, but he knew Broad Bay better than most. She said he gobbled up a plate of pancakes with maple syrup, laughing and joking with her all the time.

'"A waterman who's scairt, Ma," he said, "better look out for some other line of business." He liked to imitate the Bay fishermen's way of talking. "If the fish are too smart for me I'll buy you some number one Jimmies off somebody for supper."' She took a breath.

'What are those?' Maria looked from Miss Grant to Patrick, puzzled, smiling.

'Crabs, they are. Sooks are the females, number one Jimmies the males. You've missed a treat if you haven't eaten a Bay crab. Well, he set off, and he never came back. That was the end of it. His mother could never fathom it, how could a good-looking man of forty do that to himself? But I could. I could see it . . .' Her old voice ran on. She made *them* see it . . .

The lightness of the boat was like the lightness of his heart. All the heartache over now, the misery of those last years. Now he knew how to get rid of the pain, the memory of that face like a flower, mouth the pink of dogwood beneath the wedding bonnet, the golden ringlets piled high out of sight because she was a married woman. Coming to a decision would get rid of that pain. And the other one that had grown slowly over the years. 'Your problem', old Seaborg called it.

The creek was dancing and flittering in the sunlight, and he looked at the house as he rounded the curve, a friendly house of bits and pieces assembled over the years, always full of sea light, a sea house. It would be better off without him. His folks would be able to live their own lives now, not be forever worrying about him, would he stay in his room when the Websters came, or the Amers, or the Tandoms, bringing their daughters with them, Poppy and Marian and, what did it matter what their names were?

He was in Broad Bay now, and the wind caught him. He enjoyed the tussle, of pulling at the sheets, the spray drenching him, the bugeye joining in the fun and the fight. 'Hold on tight, Caroline!' he shouted into the wind, not turning, pretending she was there.

How often they had set off in the bugeye, tacked along

the creek, waving to the neighbours. 'There go the Grant twins, always together,' and into Broad Bay. He knew it as he had never known a woman, every current, every eddy, the short steep seas of winter, the limpid ones of summer, every bird, the snowies, the sedge hens, the ibis . . . 'My brother knows everything that swims or flies. He even knows where the deep channels of the old Susquehanna lie.' He heard her light, pretty voice in his ears.

He knew about crabs and how they mated. She had laughed out loud when he had shown her a mating couple for the first time. Doublers, the female cradled beneath the male, and how it protected her until her hard shell dropped off and she was soft and vulnerable . . . 'We're doublers, Gaylord,' she had said. 'You'll always take care of me.' But she had gone off with that Irishman.

He steered the bugeye into a small creek out of the wind, put down his anchor and put out the line. It tugged almost immediately, and he hauled in a sea bass, glistening and blue-scaled, let it lie panting in the foot of the boat because he could never bear to kill them. That had been Caroline's job. She could 'bring herself to it', just as she had 'brought herself' to marry the Irishman and go off with him to some unearthly place in the north called Wanapeake. He sat motionless, staring across the Bay into nothingness.

Three flounders now, floundering . . . He laughed. Why am I so happy? A dog choker, a perch, and then his luck changed and there was only trash which he flung back saying as the watermen had taught him, 'See you tomorrow', for good luck. That was enough now. For proof . . .

He looked widely and for a long time, behind him the fine sand of the Bay and behind that again the loblolly pines and the live oak. He stretched his eyes as if to take it all into himself. To his left marshlands where the waterfowl lived, and ahead of him the choppy, frisky blue sea, agitated now because of the wind blowing up again.

It would be easy now, since Dr Seaborg had no pills for it. And if the boat were found there would be the catch in it to show he had been fishing when it happened. It would be easy for his folks. He headed into the Bay and when he was running fast he turned the bugeye broadside on and took down the sail. He could have got the smart of it. He was a good sailor, knew the Bay's changing moods. The sailor in him felt a slight regret, but it passed quickly. He no longer cared. Let it get the smart of him . . .

The first wave which came bounding into the boat like a lively puppy made the rock fish jump about belly up and the sight of it sickened him. Better to go cleanly. He went over the side saying her name as he sank. But he was too good a swimmer not to come up to the surface again. And too fit not to have to swim for a long time into the nothingness before he tired and sank for the last time . . .

The voice like a cracked bell had stopped.

'Sad,' Maria said. 'Sad . . .' she looked at Patrick.

'There was a fisherman mending his nets and wondering what was going on out there. Their minds don't work awful fast. When he got to the bugeye it was too late . . .' Miss Grant looked tired.

11

'I'm glad we took Maevy's advice,' Maria said when they were driving away from Loblolly House the following morning. 'She said finding out about Uncle Gaylord would help us with our grief about Mary. I think it has. There's a poignancy, but no bitterness now, washed clean . . . poor Uncle Gaylord. It wasn't necessary . . .'

'She's wise, my sister. She thinks with her heart. And we're indebted to her for other things as well.' She looked at him, saw the tenderness in his face. Was he thinking of last night in that white bed, the smell of damp sheets, and the sea-smell from the open windows? They had laid a ghost together. 'Come into me, Patrick,' she had said, and then, 'Stay . . .' A special night, that dark river flowing unabated for the first time for so long.

'I can talk now,' he had said, when they were lying exhausted. 'About so many things. Terence. My jealousy about his special relationship with Mother. He charmed her, the way he charmed every girl he met, including Catherine who should never have married him at all. I envied him that charm, that lightness. I felt dull and heavy beside him.'

'You grew up under his shadow, the younger brother.'

'But I don't hate him. I . . . love him. It was love which made me rage at the table that day when Mary was dying upstairs, not hate. I thought, I'm going to lose you, my brother and that . . . tore at my heart.'

'He'll know that. All those rows you had with each other are forgotten, forgiven. Look how happy he and Honor are with that brood of children around them.'

'Yes, the country squire, with his horses and the children. And him so proud of her writing, and her first book published.'

Now with the morning sun shining on them in the open carriage she put her arms round him and kissed him. 'It's helped so many things.' He drew back but she laughed and would not let him go. 'Nobody's watching.'

'Kissing in a cab!' he said, smiling at her, doubtful, but quite liking the idea.

The sun was shining on the Hudson river when they arrived back at Springhill, laden with presents.

'We've had a grand time, Mother,' she said, kissing Caroline. 'We had a lovely welcome from Miss Grant. She sent you her love. We talked and talked. I loved the sea, but . . . I'd rather have this all the same.'

'I've come to think that, too.' She had wrinkles round her eyes and mouth now, her curls were faded, and it was a pity, Patrick thought, greeting her, that she still wore such fussy clothes. Or was it, he asked himself, a new, more tolerant self. They were part of her.

'How are you, son?' Terence was as jovial as ever, but he seemed to have shrunk a little, and his gait was stiffer than Patrick remembered. 'Now we're going to drink tea on the terrace and admire the sunset and listen to all the details of your visit south, and what that train journey was like through Williamsburg and Washington, and if the people all have the same southern drawl as my dear wife.'

They talked the sun down, and when the ladies had retired to Caroline's boudoir upstairs, the two men sat smoking on the terrace.

'So you laid Gaylord's ghost?' Terence said.

'No ghost. Just an unhappy young man who was over-attached to his sister. There are different kinds of love,

384

each one as good as the other. I think old Miss Grant understands that. People say families are a source of contentment, but sometimes it seems to me there's more unhappiness in them than outside.'

'It's life. Everyone belongs to a family. You had the sorrow of Mary, and you know how her twin brother's death affected your aunt. But that's all past history. Did you talk over matters with Maria about settling here?'

'Yes, we're set on it. I'll go ahead with the arrangements when I get back. It'll take some time. I'll have to increase the Glasgow staff, upgrade others. Tom Johnson's son wants to join us. If you can help us to get a branch going here, as you said, I'll be grateful.'

'Anything I can do I will. I've got more time now since I'm drawing out gradually from my own firm.'

'What's Ernest Murray-Hyslop doing these days?' He had had an idea.

'Buckling down very well in New York as an accountant. A different type from George, more of a flair.' He looked at Patrick. 'It occurs to me, how would you like Ernest to stand in for you here while you're busy back in Scotland?'

'I'd had the same idea. We need someone on the spot.'

'I know he'd welcome the chance of working in Glasgow later as well. He's keen to see the world.'

'Is there any chance of seeing him before we leave?'

'Indeed there is. He's coming over with his parents this weekend when they come to say goodbye to you tomorrow.'

'This time it won't be goodbye.'

'No. You'll have no regrets?'

'Many. Leaving my family, especially my mother. I always think of her as ageless, but I know that isn't so.'

'None of us is ageless. I expect that's occurred to Maria but we've never put pressure on her, believe me.'

'I do. I console myself by thinking Mother has Lord Crawford, Maevy, Charlie, Isobel and John . . . Lizzie.'

'That's still a sadness?'

'Yes. She's called Craigie by deed poll. Some day I'd like her to know she's a McGrath.'

'Isobel and John are still against it?' He nodded, turning away his head. He had seen the sympathy in his uncle's eyes. 'Leaving families aside, you're sure yourself?'

'Sure. And the firm agree with me, Tom Johnson and Bob Carter and Mother. She's still good at not letting sentiment clog the issue. She says my father would be proud at the thought of an overseas branch, although she's never been quite sure how he'd know! I think she's the despair of John Craigie.'

Terence laughed. 'Maybe he'll be mollified that he's related to a Lady.'

'He wouldn't be if he'd heard what she said to Maevy and me, that she couldn't go on being a blot on the Crawford escutcheon!'

'You mean . . . ? What a girl my young sister is!' Patrick, looking at his bright eyes, made an important discovery. Age did not matter. To his uncle, his mother was still that young girl who had run about Woodlea long ago, her red plaits flying. It was good to think that Terence was there now . . . 'What made her make up her mind to marry?'

'Lord Crawford's health. He's older than her and he's getting very lame. It's all that port, she says.' Patrick laughed.

'She'll grace his house as she did her own, as she does any place. Will she be drawing out of the firm?'

'She's officially retiring on her sixty-fifth birthday, but she still goes to the Gallowgate office once or twice a week. It's surprising how much we need her yet, even with all those new departmental managers we've got. I don't know what we'll do when she leaves for good.'

If Patrick had any doubts about not settling in America, they were dissipated the following day when the Murray-Hyslops arrived, 'in full force', as James said. They came across the wide lawn in a phalanx, Kate and James, George and his Abigail, a flaxen-haired girl, broad in the beam, Patrick thought, Victoria and Jason, prim and proper they looked, vastly different from Emily whom he had met at Maevy's wedding, and her Frenchman, and a young man, Ernest, of course, with Victoria's children, he could never remember their names, romping around him. And that must be another one of theirs whom Kate was carrying. It was difficult to keep track of them all. This is the American branch, he thought, my new life, and his heart quailed, but only for a moment. They were all smiling, Kieran was pretending to blow a trumpet, a lad with the look of Terence in Ireland, the same charm . . .

'Kieran said we should hire a band.' James was smiling, doffing his hat, going to kiss Caroline and Maria. They were ushering Kate to a chair, petting the baby she carried, Kate who alone was a good reason for coming here, so complete in her happiness, spreading it around everywhere she went.

'Mother said she would sew a banner with the words, "The Murray-Hyslop Contingent",' Kieran laughed, handsome in his summer flannels and boater with the colours of his school on the band. 'She's let us down.' Later, when everyone had been found chairs, the children been given cooling drinks and the grown-ups offered sarsaparilla or something stronger, he came and lay on the grass beside Patrick. 'How's Lizzie?' he said squinting up at him.

'You know she's at a finishing school in Paris?' He listened to himself saying the words, Patrick McGrath who had worked with puddlers at Crawford's Ironworks, washed the grime off his back in his mother's scullery. He looked at the sparkling river, an *American* river, wanted to shake his head . . . 'I hear she likes it. Isobel . . . her mother, says she's been visiting your sister in Paris and has had a fine time.'

'Lucky her. I'd like to get a chance to go to Paris. She hasn't written to me. I expect she's too busy.' Kieran tipped his boater over his eyes to shade them from the sun. 'She writes an amusing letter.' Patrick listened and wanted to shake his head again as the boy talked on about Lizzie, his school, about how he hoped to visit Paris before he went to Yale.

He was in a kind of limbo, mentally transferring himself from one continent to another. He was half-fearful, half-excited, but in the back of his mind, confident. It was what he had always wanted, to be in the vanguard of progress. Scotland was slow in the uptake, dour. He had a rare flash of insight, recognizing himself as essentially Scottish, essentially dour, but he would bring with him the Scots' pioneering spirit, their capacity for hard work.

And these strange people were family, too. Not all strange. He looked across at Kate, still beautiful, talking with Maria about domestic arrangements possibly, she would be a rare help to her, James greyer than ever but at ease with the world, strolling about the lawn with Uncle Terence and George, deep in business talk, no doubt. Victoria was with Aunt Caroline at the tea-table, her husband, Jason, playing with his brood with a ball, a bit spineless to look at, but good at fathering. Abigail was nowhere to be seen.

The voices of the children came to him as he sat, their American intonation, and he thought, why is it that children's voices everywhere have a melancholy sound? Is it their happiness, their spontaneity reminding us that nothing lasts? 'Gone, alas, like our youth too soon . . .' Father. You still had moments of grieving after all this time, for his gentleness, for the example he had set.

'Hello, Patrick.' He looked up to see Ernest standing in front of him, not so handsome as Kieran, nor at twenty-six as tall as his step-brother at seventeen, but with all his father's urbanity in his lean, smiling face. His straight sandy hair was lifting from his brow in the soft wind. 'Uncle Terence said you wanted to have a chat with me.'

'Yes, indeed, Ernest.' He got up.

'Don't listen to a word that chap says, Uncle Patrick.' Kieran spoke from behind his boater. 'He's a clown of the first degree.'

'Shut up, little man,' Ernest said, giving Kieran a gentle kick with the side of his foot. 'Let's get out of hearing of this . . . schoolboy.' He put his hand on Patrick's arm. 'He's got ears like a lynx.'

'Better than your little rosebuds. No wonder you cover them with all that hair.' It was long, but maybe that was the American cut.

He had thought at first that Ernest would be too 'light' for him, his own word for anyone whom he thought was his opposite in temperament, but he soon found that the young man was astute. And he was enthusiastic when Patrick told him of his plans to open a McGrath branch in New York.

'I think it's a splendid idea.' He had lively brown eyes, his best feature. 'I might be able to help you. I'm in touch with a lot of business firms there. I visit them to do their books.'

'I'm convinced we're going to move into a new era with transport and I think you'll be in the lead here. I want to be ready for it.'

'But New York's the place to be. They'll take a chance there, Uncle Terence found that out when he came. By Jove, it sounds an interesting prospect.'

'Would you be interested in getting the branch going while I tie up my affairs back home?' He stopped on the lawn where they were pacing and faced Ernest.

'Interested?' There was no doubt about his enthusiasm. 'I'd jump at the chance! I don't think there's room for George and me in Father's firm. Do you mean a permanent position?'

'Certainly. I would be managing director, of course, but you'd be second in command. I'd depend on you at the beginning when I've got a foot in two camps.'

'Oh, keeping in touch gets easier every day. There's the telegraph already, and there will be the telephone, and soon we'll be taking to the air, and all driving about in motor cars as well. Yes, New York is the place to be. You should see Wall Street just now because of the rush to the Klondike. People are going mad with excitement.'

'You've convinced me,' Patrick laughed at his enthusiasm, 'although I scarcely needed convincing.' He held out his hand, 'We'll be glad to have you in the firm. When I get back I'll have the office make out a definite agreement and let you have it right away.'

'Fine. And if there's any chance of me getting to Scotland in the future, I'd jump at it.'

'And here am I planning to get out of it. Yes, I'm sure that could be arranged.'

'Thank you for giving me the chance to work with you.'

'We'll get on well.' We recognize the qualities in each other, Patrick thought, so different and yet complementary.

They gathered together in the drawing-room to drink Maria and Patrick's health. The Murray-Hyslops could not wait for dinner because of the children, and Abigail's condition, now discreetly admitted by George.

'Good health! Safe crossing! Come back soon!' Patrick stood with Maria, sipping the unaccustomed champagne, feeling released, and relaxed. Terence had the same feeling about Ireland. Why had they both to seek it so far from home? Later he knew he would say to Maria, this is the first time I've felt we can let Mary rest in peace.

Kate was holding up her glass. 'And be sure, my dears, there will be a welcome here for you . . .'

'"If your name . . . is . . . Timothy or Pat . . ."' Uncle Terence burst into song, waving his glass.

Family gatherings. The best times. Sentimentality lapped him or was it sentiment, gatherings in the summer-house at Braidholme, Mother and Father, lovers till the end. What did it matter now, that ridiculous fight he had had with Terence when they had both ended up in the Sholtie? What mattered was the loving kindness which surrounded you, either here or at home.

What would happen to Braidholme now, he wondered, if his mother went to live at the Hall? That took a bit of swallowing. Lady Crawford . . .

12

Maeve lay in her stately bedroom in the Hall after the wedding party. They had kept it small and intimate – after all they had both been married before, and they were not, to put it mildly, in their first youth.

Sixty-two, she thought, feeling the soft satin on her limbs, running her hand over her still thick plait of hair lying on her shoulder. What am I thinking about? In a marriage bed instead of sitting knitting at my own fireplace for my grandchildren. That man has the gift of tongues . . .

He had looked just as handsome, though, as he had seemed that first time when she had talked to him at the Sunday School Picnic, the laird's son, tall, narrow-headed, sloping shoulders, and those strange-coloured eyes. She remembered them bent on her when her horse had thrown her . . . so long ago. They had been galloping together on their way back from the ruined monastery across those fields out there . . .

'Your hair has come loose. Beautiful,' he had said, 'you need love . . .'

Her hand began slowly to unplait her hair. Maybe tonight she should have tied it back with a piece of ribbon which could be pulled . . . sixty-two, she cautioned herself, you're sixty-two, that kind of thing is past for you.

But was it ever past if you wanted it? She and Kieran had been lovers until he died, and it was only by throwing herself into working for the firm that she had been able to still that need, long after the first terrible grief had gone

. . . Her hair fell about her shoulders, the plait finally undone.

A ribbon now. There was a box of them in the dressing table drawer of this stately home. Would she get used to it after the cosiness of the Braidholme one with its view onto the dark garden and the sound of the Sholtie rippling below?

It had not occurred to her that of course she would not share a bedroom with Alastair. You had to think of the servants. The gentry were different. Well, she should have known that. Her mother and father had never slept together at Woodlea.

She got up and rummaged in the drawer, found a piece of blue velvet and tied back her hair. There, that was better. In the dim light her face swam in the mirror as she looked, not that of an old woman but a young girl, the Maeve that had been, the dark eyes . . . 'To the devil with it,' she said, 'if he won't come to me, I'll go to him!' She took the satin negligée which matched the satin nightgown from the back of a chair and shrugged herself into it, lifted her hair with both hands so that it fell over the lacy collar, and opened the door.

A dim light was burning in the upper hall. The great house was silent, the servants tucked away in the attics, Cook and the kitchen maids in their quarters off the kitchen ready to start the breakfast, just as it had been at Woodlea. How grand it was to think of Terence there with Honor and their children, happy as he had never been happy, except in his first careless years, a fulfilled man at last. 'This is it, Mother,' he had said to her the last time she had visited there . . .

How unfamiliar this place was to her, that great Chinese vase on its carved ebony stand, that armoire with the copper *jardinière*, the portrait of old Lord Crawford frowning above it. Would he have thought of her as an interloper?

She had reached Alastair's door. It was uncompromisingly shut. She stood looking at it, drawing her negligée closer around her, feeling her bare feet cold on the polished wood. What had made her forget her slippers? And what had happened to *him*, for God's sake? Had the man gone to sleep on his wedding night and forgotten all about her? She lifted her arm, the satin slipping down it, and knocked decisively, three smart taps. And almost fell into the room because of the speed with which the door was opened. Alastair stood there in his floor-length robe, his lean face surprised.

'Maeve! I was . . . Come in.' He looked sheepish.

'I thought . . .' She walked in, feeling the same. 'Were you on your . . . way?'

'Yes, I was. Here, sit on the bed, my darling.' He put his arm around her and steered her towards it. She walked slowly because of his bad leg.

'I began to think . . . I wondered . . .'

He sat down beside her, took her hands, smiling. 'We're both as awkward as children, aren't we, and us of a mature age.' She looked into his eyes. They were full, moist. 'I had a sudden attack of nerves, would you believe it? I wondered if you would want me tonight. So different from Braidholme, suddenly formal, and the two bedrooms . . . ridiculous. I should have told the servants.' He kissed her lightly. 'I was unsure . . .'

'I know, I know.' She touched his cheek. 'But we're old friends as well as old lovers.' She took him in her arms and they lay back on the pillows, his head cradled on her breast. She heard him sigh. 'I was unsure, too, the . . . legality of it now, and maybe the foolishness of it at our age. And then I thought, well, one of us has to make a move so it might as well be me!'

He laughed and got up on his elbow and he was that young man again with the amber eyes bent on her as she lay on the ground. 'Do you remember,' he said, 'long ago, when you were thrown from your horse?'

'You bent over me as you're doing now.'

'It was your hair. It had come loose. Your beautiful hair . . . I wanted to possess you.'

'It was your eyes. River eyes, I thought, like the Sholtie, the same amber depths. I wanted to drown . . .' She heard her voice thicken with a kind of delight. 'I'm feeling a wee bit cold, Alastair. I have to watch chills at my age.'

'And I have to watch my bad leg. The arthritis in it.' His face was solemn. Not the eyes. 'Would you stand up for a second, Lady Crawford, while we turn back the sheets?'

'Of course.'

'And I don't think you'll need that negligée, nice as it is.'

'No.' She let it slip on to the floor.

'We'll decide about the nightgown later.' He got in beside her with remarkable agility considering his bad leg.

'Shouldn't you have come to me, all the same?' She tucked the silk sheets round them in a housewifely fashion, turning the top one back.

'Perhaps you didn't notice but I was on my way . . . if you hadn't been so impatient.' He spoke in her ear.

'Oh, it wasn't impatience, I assure you. I got . . . worried. And in any case I wanted a ribbon for my hair, and once I was up . . .'

'You didn't need a ribbon.' He pulled the piece of velvet and she felt the swish of her hair, felt its redness. Not many women of her age kept their red hair. She felt him bury his face in it. 'Ah, lovely . . .' His voice came to her, muffled, 'Maybe we should have gone back to your bed for the sake of the proprieties. I shouldn't like Mrs Robertson, when she brings the morning tea, to think I've married a forward woman.'

'I'm nicely settled here, Alastair,' she said, turning to him. 'It suits me fine.'

At sixty-two you could still love, and you had a wealth of experience behind you. Indeed, come to think of it, you had reached your peak. Oh, maybe it was downhill all the way from now on, but there was no point in dwelling on that now, when there was such satisfaction in loving, being loved and knowing how to love. Kieran had helped her there. He would not mind, wherever he was, seeing her so happy.

13

The Manse, Sholton, Lanarkshire, Scotland
Easter, 1897

Dear Kieran,

I came back to driech old Scotland to find a different
atmosphere altogether from Paris, constant discussions about
the South African problem in the papers, Mother and Father
full of plans about how I'll buckle down now and help in the
parish, Uncle Patrick and Aunt Maria planning to go to live in
America soon – their new baby, Virginia, is lovely – and, of
course, Grandma is now Lady Crawford.

Maybe they got married to curb the Sholton tongues which
wag like the kirk bell at the slightest opportunity. You can see
how *du monde* I've become! But there are always auld wives
with their heads together when you go to the village, although I
must say they're nice enough to me. Except a half-cracked old
woman called Beenie Drummond who came leering up to me in
the butchers the other day and said, 'So you're losin' twa faithers
noo, ur ye?' She's horrible. She should be shut up in an
institution.

I can't begin to tell you what life was like in Paris, the
elegance of it. Even Gizelle at twelve wore silk stockings and
bows on her slippers – no, it was much more than that, an
ambiance, although Madame Sevigny at the school was very
strict. We had lessons in deportment and all that which I found
boring and rather old-fashioned, not suited for Today's Woman,
as Aunt Maevy likes to say.

'*Ça m'embête,*' the girls say all the time about history lessons,
but I loved them. Mademoiselle Gervais – she looked about fifty
but you can be a mademoiselle there till you die – said I had a
receptive mind and it was a pity I couldn't have gone to the
Sorbonne. 'Here,' she said, 'we only scratch the surface.'

Nigel Crawford was spending a year in Paris, as his father had
done, before going up to Balliol, his college in Oxford, and he

applied for permission to take me out to tea. Of course I had to take a chaperon – you wouldn't get Madame Sevigny risking the reputation of her precious young ladies – so I took Marie-Clare, a big fat pudding of a girl because she never gets invitations. I can hear you say that it was so that I shouldn't have any competition, but, no, truly, it was because I felt sorry for her.

I wish you could meet Nigel now. He's grown very tall and he looks like a younger edition of his father. They aren't brawny men. I mean, if they were in a boxing ring they might get knocked out, but I don't think so because they would be quick and nimble on their feet and so skilful at the moves that they would probably be victors in the end.

He was having a wonderful time sowing his wild oats, he said, and he'd even seen the cancan being danced. I said he just had to walk along the Trongate or the Gallowgate on a Saturday night and he'd see as much high-kicking and petticoat-waving as he liked, and as for famous stars, my Aunt Maevy and Uncle Charlie had heard Patti sing in the St Andrew's Hall. He laughed and said, 'Oh, it's useless trying to impress you, Lizzie Craigie.'

She put down her pen . . . I can't tell him how I couldn't sleep for thinking of Nigel, or how he embarrassed me by looking at me. *What's wrong, Lizzie? Do I make you shy?* Nor how the girls threw pillows at me and said, '*Leezie est amoureuse . . .*'

I was allowed by Madame Sevigny to spend an occasional weekend with your step-sister at their Normandy seat, and that was wonderful. I haven't seen countryside like that ever. Here, although our immediate surroundings are pretty, you only need to travel a mile or two before you run up against Crawford's pits and foundries. What a mess the old laird made of this place!

Oh, I had an idyllic time in Normandy, *la Normandie*. Everything is slow and lazy and lush, the cows stare sleepily at you with great eyes, the grass is long and golden, and when I was there in autumn the trees were almost bent to the ground with the weight of the apples. We helped with *la recolte*, and had picnics in the hay fields, and the sun shone and the butterflies were too lazy to dance or the bees to buzz . . . it's all a golden Normandy haze in my memory, even the milk is golden with cream.

I don't think Emily enjoys country life. She sits in the shuttered drawing-room chatting and drinking tea with ladies in beautiful gowns, then in the evening she and Monsieur Barthe go out and dine at another country seat, or if he's still in Paris earning more money, she goes alone. She says she's dying for the twins to be old enough to escort her. They're a comical pair. They do make me laugh.

She told me how much she'd enjoyed having Grandma and Aunt Maevy in Paris. 'I owe a great deal to your wonderful grandma,' she said. 'Sometime you must ask her about the two bullets embedded high up in the two trees in the *Blois de St Cloud.*' She loves creating mysteries.

But she was very kind to me. She gave me a lovely peacock blue gown which she said was too big for her, but Mother wouldn't let me wear it because it was 'too revealing'. I believe, all the same, you could go out 'bare scuddie' and the Sholton people would hardly notice! Oh, it was a lovely time and coming back to Sholton was like coming down to earth with a bump . . .

She put down her pen again and stared into space. Coming back to Sholton . . . why did that make her think of that old woman, Beenie Drummond, with her grey locks straggling over her face like a witch, her mouthful of rotten teeth, her venom when she spat out those words, 'So you're losin' twa faithers noo, ur ye?'? Her plaid shawl had had spittle on it. Willy, the butcher, had looked embarrassed, sympathetic, and yet there had been some hidden knowledge in his eyes.

She lived in the Row, didn't she, so she must have known Grandma when they were both young. Grandma had never made any secret of having lived there, or that Grandfather had worked down the pit. That was enough to rile a half-cracked bitch like that . . . she got satisfaction from thinking that word.

Because of her sick visiting she knew better than Grandma the amount of malice that went on, the jealousy and the vindictiveness against those who 'got above themselves'. And the kirk was the place where you saw most of it, the sidelong glances, the veiled hints, the smarmy smiles when Father appeared. Oh, Grandma had the right way of it. She did not attend very regularly, even although Lord Crawford occupied the laird's pew when he was feeling up to it, limping in, but still elegant, growing more like a stork as he grew older.

No smoke without fire, she thought now, unease creeping round her heart. Could she ask Father or Mother what the old devil meant, at least, tell them what she had said? The enormity, the impossibility of the idea struck her immediately, the idea of repeating village gossip at the table, their closed faces.

Mother maybe, but then so often now she took her cue from Father, and over the years her prettiness had faded and her physical frailty made her complaining. 'It's the least you can do, Lizzie, after being allowed to go to Paris, to help me with the parish duties.' It was on the tip of her tongue more than once to say she would have been better not to have gone if this was all she was going to do with her life, but she was schooled in obedience . . . She began to write again.

I had a talk with Maevy once. 'I know it's wrong for a minister's daughter to feel like this,' I said, 'especially when everybody has been so good to me but I feel . . . stifled.'
'I don't blame you,' she said. She listens so carefully to what you say, gives it her full attention. 'What would they say to you becoming a nurse? I never regretted it. Even now, if it weren't for Ellie and Charlie I'd be glad to go back. And if there's a war, I'm going to feel badly about not volunteering.' Her eyes lit up. 'Florence Nightingale was my inspiration. I wanted to go all over the world with my lamp tending the sick and wounded.' She laughed. That's the good thing about Aunt Maevy. She has a sense of humour.
I told her I understood her feelings, but never in a thousand years would I want to be a nurse. 'You have to imagine yourself *doing* it,' I said, 'though I wouldn't mind the travelling bit, and

if there was a war I'd rather *manage* it in some way than carry a lamp.' We laughed at that. 'You can see,' I said to her, 'why young girls rush into marriage. But it seems so silly to just sit around and wait.'

'You're not sitting and waiting,' she said, 'you're helping my sister who's frail. But, remember, only marry for love. It's the one good reason.' So I shall have to be content with sick visiting meantime, doing the flowers for the kirk, paying afternoon calls with my mother, and doing Father's accounts.

Write sometime and tell me of all *your* doings. You'll soon have Uncle Patrick and Aunt Maria beside you, Sarah, Gaylord and little Virginia. I'll miss them very much, and I hope they find happiness in their new land . . .

Lizzie

14

Maevy and Charlie were dressing to go to the Hall for dinner. 'Will there be anyone else there?' Charlie said. He came to stand behind her as she lifted her pearl necklace, his birthday present to her. 'Let me.' He fastened the clasp, kissed the nape of her neck. 'My favourite place. I fell in love with it when I stood looking down on you in the Infirmary ward. So many years ago.'

'When Arthur Cranston was in?' She smiled at him in the glass. 'No, we're the only ones. Mother says she has something to tell us.'

'Lady Crawford?' The corner of his mouth went up.

'Can't you get used to it?'

'With not the slightest difficulty. There's only one person I know with the same grace, and that's you.' He put his hands under her elbows, made her rise and turn to him. 'You . . .' He kissed her slowly, with husbandly enjoyment, hands free to roam, no pretences, she thought, no maidenly modesty . . . a waste of time. So satisfying. Such love I've known with him, complete, except for one thing. Now she never mentioned it. Ellie was five, going to school, the prospect had receded. 'Sometimes my love for you quite overwhelms me,' she said. 'It . . . frightens me.'

'Why should it frighten you, my darling?'

'My dependence on you, not for living, but for my happiness. When I imagine life without you, the void is . . . frightening. I don't know what I'd do.'

'You'd live. For Ellie, for your family, for yourself, for

402

being a midwife. Three times you've helped us out now in the practice.'

'Survive, not live. Busy people are the ones who feel loss most keenly. If your life is . . . shapeless, there would be no void.'

'What a philosopher you've become!' He teased her. 'It's all that reading. But what is this discussion about anyhow? We're both fit, happy, not in our dotage, we have a lovely daughter. I accept that gratefully, no ifs or buts.' She saw the shadow in his eyes, knew where his thoughts lay. He grieved for her wish for another child, rather than wished himself, or perhaps he was better at accepting.

'Yes, what's come over us?' She laughed and kissed him quickly, lightly. 'We're off to have dinner with Lord and Lady Crawford, and if we don't go now we'll be late.'

'Doctors are always excused for being late. But you're right, as always.'

She lifted her beaded handbag and long white gloves from the dressing-table. 'I'll just have a last peep at Ellie.'

'We'll both have a last peep.' He put his arm round her waist as they went out of the room.

Her mother and Lord Crawford were in the drawing-room waiting for them. She and Charlie had been in the house recently at the small reception after the wedding, but seeing it emptied of people made Maevy realize its vastness. Space was the essential difference between how the rich lived and the poor. Two people occupying all this space when they were still crowding into Colliers' Row three or four to a bed. Mother knew all about that. Did the thought ever occur to her?

'Come away in, Maevy, Charlie.' She rose to greet them. 'Isn't she a picture, Alastair, my youngest?'

'A delight to the eye.' Lord Crawford came towards

403

Maevy, leaning on his stick. 'Welcome, my dear.' And then to Charlie, 'How are you, Dr McNab? It's good of you to spare an evening from your busy schedule to come and see us.'

'Good of you to ask us. I only hope Biddy doesn't have to send anyone to fetch me. We're into the season of coughs and colds which rapidly get elevated to pneumonia or worse in the minds of my patients.' He laughed. 'Especially in the wee sma' hours.'

'Do you blame the Lowlands climate? I remember your brother-in-law, Patrick, felt it accounted for a lot.'

'Maybe so, but even with the improvements you've made, the men in the pits and foundry don't work in ideal conditions.' Oh, Charlie, *haud your wheesht*, Maevy thought. She glanced at her mother, pulling down her mouth.

'The penalty of the Industrial Revolution, I'm afraid, although we aren't blameless, as landowners. But while on the subject of social conditions, let me congratulate you on your book. I greatly appreciated you letting me have a copy.'

'May I ask your opinion?' There was a butler hovering at Lord Crawford's elbow with a silver tray.

'First let me ask your opinion of this sherry, if you will. And you, too, Maevy.' They both accepted a glass, sipped.

'I like it,' Maevy said. 'You can't buy *this* in Crannoch.'

He laughed appreciatively. 'I tell my wife I'm going to take her to Spain sometime, but she says, "Don't add to my list! There's Ireland, and America . . ."'

'Only when I retire from the firm next spring,' her mother put in.

'Do you still go to the office?' Maevy asked her.

'Twice a week. Fortunately Alastair has banking and business interests as well, so we travel together. Yes, now

404

that Patrick's gone, and we haven't Terence, there's a great deal of reorganization to do. We've increased the staff by quite a few, taken on Tom Johnson's son as manager, and Ernest, Kate's stepson, will be coming over for a year or so. There's plenty to be done.'

'I think I'm almost a member of the staff myself,' Lord Crawford said.

'He's helping us to make some investments in freehold properties. It's a way of increasing our capital.' Maeve looked at him, and Maevy saw the fond glance they exchanged. It's love, she thought complacently. Maybe it's always been there a little. It wouldn't encroach on Father's, she was a generous woman, with love as with everything else. 'But what am I thinking of, getting on to business right away? We were talking about your book, Charlie.'

'Let me know the worst.'

'There's no worst,' Lord Crawford said. 'It's well researched, illuminating, and above all, readable. And you don't moralize. You have my sincere admiration.'

'And mine.' Maeve smiled at him. 'Two writers in the family, you and Honor. You must be proud of him, Maevy.'

'I am.' The sherry had slipped, golden and smooth, down her throat, loosening her tongue. 'Sometimes I wonder if he has a little regret giving up surgery, but this compensates.'

'Maevy's exaggerating.' Charlie waved his hand. 'Besides, a skill learned is never lost. I can excise a boil better than Jim Geddes.' He laughed.

'I hear he has a daughter who wants to do medicine.' Lord Crawford spoke to Charlie.

'Belle. Yes, who would have thought of a woman? I'm all in favour of it.'

Maevy sat down on the sofa beside her mother. 'You

405

look lovely in that.' She touched the grey taffeta skirt of her gown. The shining folds had a hint of copper in them which echoed her hair. She wore topaz earrings. Maeve fingered one of them, looking pleased.

'Do you hear my daughter buttering me up, Alastair?' He was busy talking to Charlie and did not hear her. She spoke softly to Maevy. 'I know I shouldn't wear the neckline as low as this at my age, but he liked it.' She's pleased to be married, to have a man admiring her, Maevy thought. She patted her mother's knee.

'Would you ever go back to France, Mother?' she asked. 'When you've retired, of course. I often think of it. And that duel!' she said to Lord Crawford. 'Have you heard about it?'

'I told you all about it, Alastair,' Maeve said.

'You did.' He laughed. 'Duels are a farce in Paris for the most part. Nigel's back from there now and up at Balliol. I'm hoping he'll be here over Christmas and the New Year. He took Lizzie out. Said getting permission from her headmistress was worse than braving Balmoral Castle with John Brown barring the way.'

'Have you seen her recently?' Maeve asked Maevy.

'Yes, she comes about our house a fair amount. She's pale, not so full of spirits as she used to be. I'm worried about her.'

Maeve spoke sharply. 'Paris was meant to be a spring-board for her life, not to come back to an eternal round of parish duties. I asked Isobel if she would tell Lizzie we'd be glad to make room for her in the firm, but she said John wouldn't countenance it. What's happened to the man?'

'Now, now, my dear.' Her husband was clearly amused. 'Don't you remember that handsome letter he sent us thanking us for our donation to the Diamond Jubilee Fund last year?'

'That was because I made you double your contribution. The Queen won't have another one, I said to you, you'd better make the most of it!'

The door opened. 'Dinner is served,' Redfern announced.

They discussed family matters over the early part of the meal. The food showed her mother's usual flair, although this time she would have had no hand in the cooking. 'I hear your brother is enjoying America,' Lord Crawford said to Maevy. The butler had poured her a white wine with her sole which made her wonder how she had ever eaten fish without it.

'Yes, although I never doubted it. The parting was sad, especially for Mother,' she smiled across the table at her, 'but they promise to come back from time to time.'

'The Atlantic's going to be only a hop, skip and a jump soon,' Charlie said. 'After balloons it will be flying machines. We shan't need the ocean greyhounds before long.'

'I think I'd always prefer to sail,' Maeve said, and to Maevy, 'Have you heard if they have a house yet? In my last letter they were staying at Springhill.'

'They're still there, but I think there's something in the wind.'

'Shall I . . . ?' Maevy saw the question in her mother's eyes as she looked at her husband.

'Later, my dear. I want them to do full justice to your dinner.'

Mother's got something up her sleeve, Maevy thought as she watched her superintending the maids by a glance or two. How right she was in her place there at the other end of the table from Lord Crawford, how fitting. The heavy silver salver bearing the roast pheasants was brought in – they would be shot on the estate – tureens of vegetables, the silver sauceboats, the family crest on all of them. The maids curtseyed, withdrew, Redfern stayed, unobtrusive as ever. She listened to the conversation.

'You're right, sir,' Charlie was saying, 'tottering from one crisis to the other ever since the Jubilee . . .'

'Ever since Majuba Hill, more correctly.'

'Thank you,' Maevy said. One of the fine Worcester plates was before her. She was offered vegetables. She raised her eyes to her mother with her first forkful and saw that she was listening attentively. She had always shown a keen interest in politics, in 'men's talk' as she called it, and had avoided the endless conversations about children and servants which were usual amongst women. She listened again.

'Yes. Do you think Milner's the man?'

'Well, he's from my old college, and Nigel's now, if that's any recommendation. Seriously, I'd say he was the right type to make Kruger see reason, and get equality for the Uitlanders if it hadn't been for this latest incident – I don't think it's too strong a word – calamity.'

'The Boer policeman shooting dead that man?'

'Yes. My guess is he'll be acquitted and the Uitlanders will be incensed and humiliated. They hate the Zarps.'

'The Zarps?' Maeve's eyebrows went up.

'Tough young Boers armed with loaded pistols, my dear. Breaking into houses. We'll see how far diplomacy can take us then.'

'And then ordinary men are thrown into war by the manipulators,' Maevy said.

'My daughter feels strongly about the fate of the common man.' Her mother smiled at her. 'Don't let it put you off your pheasant, Maevy.'

'Who in their right senses would want war?' Lord Crawford said, 'although some people maintain it's only an extension of diplomacy, brought to fruition, so to speak.'

'A defeatist viewpoint, surely,' Charlie put in. 'I think part of the truth is that there's a general feeling about that we're becoming decadent, that we must reassert our importance in the eyes of the world. It's a battle between British paramountcy and Boer obstinacy.'

'But there must be sensible people in the Government, surely,' Maevy said, 'people like Chamberlain.'

'Charlie's right.' Her mother nodded. 'When it comes to the crunch, prestige will be the keyword.'

'Chamberlain believes in Imperialism just as strongly as Milner does, I'm afraid.' Lord Crawford looked at Maevy. 'We're going to be swept over the precipice, mark my words.'

'Oh, Alastair!' Maeve smiled at him, 'must you be so gloomy? We're all right, at least. You're too old to fight, sorry, darling, but it's true, and you've got that leg of yours. Charlie will be exempted, being a doctor. In any case, there will never be conscription. It will be just a little war . . .'

'I have a son. I hope you're right, that it will be just . . . a little war.'

'I'm in the Volunteers,' Charlie said.

'Oh, that doesn't matter. It was long before you became a doctor.' Her mother was quick in seeing the implication, in dismissing it. For my sake, Maevy thought. But she knows as well as I do, once in, always in. The feeling was with her, more like a creeping cancer than a sword thrust, the knowledge that the fear would now be a constant companion. I could go instead of him, she thought, and then again, but there's Ellie. Oh, you're stupid, Maevy, so vulnerable, she thought, look how you tortured yourself over destroying Ethel Mavor's letter. Now you're going to let this thing fester inside you . . .

'You've had to turn up for training, I imagine.' Lord Crawford was speaking.

'More as a joke than anything else.' Charlie shrugged. Now *he*'s at it, playing it down.

'You're needed here,' Maeve said decidedly, 'we'll get up a petition. Look what you've started, Alastair, scaremongering about something which will probably never happen. The Queen would never allow it!' They all laughed as if to relieve the tension.

'She's certainly becoming all powerful and indestructible.' He lifted his hand to Redfern.

'No, thank you.' Charlie and Maevy declined the proffered dishes, praised the bird.

'Terence tells me in his letters he does some rough shooting,' Maeve said. 'Not in Woodlea, unless it's been restocked. But you know Terence. He'll have plenty of friends already. He sounds very happy.'

'You should really go and see them, Mother.' Maevy's own happiness had drained away. This gracious room with its panelled walls and its sconsed lighting, the maids and butler hovering as they changed plates, her mother's smiling face which in its happiness should have been a happiness for her, had become meaningless, as tasteless as the wine she was sipping, bitter on her tongue.

She accepted some pudding, a concoction of hazelnuts and meringue built up in an edifice of spangled sugar, raised her eyes to find Lord Crawford's on her. His look had awareness, kindness, and a sort of sympathy. 'Maeve,' he said, 'perhaps you should make your suggestion now to our young couple.'

'About Braidholme? Of course. I've been waiting for your permission.' She smiled mischievously, then turned to Maevy and Charlie. 'I hate to see it go out of the family. Would you consider living there?'

'But I thought . . .' Maevy said, and then, lamely, 'I don't know what I thought.'

'It was bought with the company's money, and you're

410

still a director. Don't you think you should, Charlie?' She appealed to him.

Maevy could see his surprise. 'Well, of course, it's up to Maevy. She'd be the owner. I'd only be the lodger.'

'No, no,' Maeve waved her hand, 'it would be given to both of you.'

'It's too generous.' He turned to Maevy. 'How do you feel about it?'

'The same. It's too generous. And would *you* mind moving out of Larkhill? It's always been the doctor's house.'

'Braidholme is so near. They'd soon get used to it. And you know we've talked about having a surgery in the village . . .'

Thoughts went flashing through her head. Braidholme, a house of happy memories, a beautiful house, but above all, a McGrath house. It would be a shame to see strangers in it. And if . . . Alastair should die and mother wanted to go back it would be there for her. She would be sad to leave Larkhill, of course, but it had not the special place in her heart which Braidholme had. 'I like the idea, Mother,' she said, 'but if we accept there must be clauses, conditions. We must be trustees only.'

'John Carter will see to all that. Well, that's settled.' She looked pleased. 'It's such a load off my mind. The thought of being unable to visit there quite tore my heart out. And Susan must be kept on, of course. She's there now, caretaking.'

'Now you won't be able to keep your mother away, Maevy,' Lord Crawford said, his glance on her again, astute, sensitive. He understood people.

'I won't try to. This is a lovely pudding, Mother.' Her taste buds were functioning again.

15

John Craigie rustled the pages of the *Glasgow Herald*. 'Chamberlain says the crisis is over. He's a mediator, that man. Kruger isn't to be trusted.'

'Do you think there will be a war, Father?' Lizzie looked up from reading a letter from one of her former school friends in Paris. She was being married soon and wondered if her dear friend would like to come to the wedding. Her dear friend would . . .

'"The wheels of war grind exceeding slow . . ." Who said that? Come on, Lizzie, you're the one who got the expensive education.'

'I haven't any idea. Is it likely, do you think, the war?'

'Who's your letter from, Lizzie?' Isobel asked. She was always paler and if anything more wan in the morning. She had a slow metabolism. She had to be fortified with numerous cups of tea before she could 'get going' as she put it.

'Louise Douenne, a girl at Madame Sevigny's. She's being married in September. She was asking if there was any chance of my coming.' She appealed with her eyes. 'I could stay with Emily Barthe.'

'That's the least of it.' Isobel put several teaspoonfuls of sugar into her cup. 'There would be the fare and the outfit and a hundred and one expenses.'

'If I told Grandma she might help me . . .'

John looked over his paper. 'I think your grandmother made a mistake giving you that year in Paris. Are you saying you would have no compunction in begging from her? I don't think I like your attitude at all, Lizzie.'

'Oh, I wouldn't *beg*. I'd just tell her about it. She's always very keen on parties and gatherings. She would probably offer . . .'

'I think you've forgotten your position,' Isobel said. She had one elbow on the table, her hand supporting her head. She looked at Lizzie from black-ringed eyes, and her conscience smote her. Poor Mother. She was so frail. 'I don't mean to be unkind, but to go to the Hall, to my mother, cap in hand . . .' She liked to dramatize things.

'Oh, forget it!' She smiled to take the sting out of her words. 'I wasn't really thinking of it. Maybe sometime I'll visit the Barthes. I promised.' She drew in her breath. 'What were you saying about South Africa, Father?'

'Oh, South Africa . . .' Isobel said, adding some more tea to her cup from the teapot which always stood beside her, 'I get tired of those Boers . . .'

Her husband looked at her, then addressed Lizzie. 'I'm not like your Uncle Charlie who thinks the Boers are running rings round us and we don't know it. British diplomacy is admired throughout the world. Sir Arthur Milner will keep Kruger in check. And if we do have to fight in the end, the Boers will regret it. You can't tamper with Britain's might and remain unscathed.'

Jingoism, Lizzie thought. It was Uncle Charlie's word. 'You'll see,' he had said one day when she was visiting them, 'we'll muddle along in the same old way. If there's an ultimatum, and there's bound to be, we'll send out ill-equipped armies, poor old generals brought out of moth-balls. And only when a few thousand men have been killed and people begin to protest will they waken up to the fact that they'd better get organized.'

'I'm not feeling up to the mark this morning,' Isobel said pathetically.

'Poor dear,' John said from behind his paper, 'why don't you go back to bed?'

413

'Listen to him, Lizzie.' Her head drooped on her thin neck. 'Back to bed, he says, when the shopping's to be done and this is the day for visiting at Colliers' Row, and the sewing woman is coming to turn the worn sheets.'

'Now, now,' he lowered the paper, spoke playfully, 'you have a beautiful young daughter sitting there ready and willing to help. Isn't that so, Lizzie?'

She deplored the fact that lately, or was it since she came back from Madame Sevigny's establishment, she had become critical of her own father. She looked at him now, at his broad handsome face, the general jolly beneficence of his expression, or was it only an appearance? Was it too . . . practised? Was it a matter of maturity, that you saw the faults as well as the virtues of those dearest to you?

Perhaps, she thought, teachers and ministers shared this common delusion that they were always right. Uncle Charlie, for instance, learned in a way Father would never be, never declaimed. He put forward ideas, was prepared to listen to other people's opinions . . . 'I don't know about being young and beautiful – well, maybe young – ' she felt like a hundred, 'but I'll do anything you like, Mother. Come on,' she got up, went round the table and helped Isobel to rise, 'I'll see you back to bed and you can give me a list . . .'

'I feel so useless.' Isobel leant on Lizzie's shoulder, looking backwards at her husband, 'Should I, John?'

'Now, you do what you're told, my dear.' He was helping himself to more toast. 'Lizzie and I will keep it dark that the minister's wife has had to creep back to bed when she should be up and doing.' He put a large spoonful of marmalade directly on to the toast. 'Manners, John,' her mother would say when she was feeling her own dainty self.

'I feel terrible,' Isobel said, going upstairs with Lizzie.

What a thin waist she had. How was she ever able to have me?

'Don't feel guilty, Mother.' She would write a letter to Louise and say there was no chance of coming to her wedding. She did not mind that so much compared with the opportunity it had presented of going back to Paris. Paris . . . she thought of the Monceau Park and Emily in her startling costumes and *maquillage* for every hour of the day, which always ended up by her looking like a brilliantly plumaged bird, of Marc, Olivier and Gizelle who made her laugh, of that time Nigel Crawford had taken her out to tea and the gaiety of the street café . . .

'Get Cook to slice up the bit of beef that's left and make some gravy to go with it.' Isobel was now in bed and propped up with pillows. 'What would relieve my mind, Lizzie, would be if you'd go to Colliers' Row for me today. There's both a young and an old woman in bed who need visiting. You know how your father regards that side of our ministry as being in the same category as missionary work.' Lizzie remembered that he also came from 'humble beginnings' as he put it. 'I make no bones about it. I was reared in the Glasgow slums. It makes you humble . . .'

'Don't you worry, Mother. Just lie and rest. Would you like your book?'

'No, I'll just lie . . . and think.' She smiled pathetically, and Lizzie thought, tucking her up, she enjoys being an invalid, and then again, this is my day for being critical.

In the first house the young woman was recovering after childbirth and her young husband had taken a day off the pit to tend her. She could hear his harassed voice as she knocked at the door, 'Aggie, pit that doon! A've telt ye a hunner times.' He looked weary when he opened it, and . . . guilty. She knew that look well on the faces of

415

husbands. When they had had a few more it generally disappeared. 'Oh, it's you. Come away in, Miss Craigie.'

'I've brought you some provisions from the Parish Fund.' She put down the basket on the table and went over to the bed. The young wife was asleep. A tiny baby, wrapped up to the eyes in a dirty shawl was in one arm. Better to leave them.

'Can I do anything for you, Mr Kerr?' She turned to the man, 'It's a shame to disturb her.'

'A'm managin' fine. And the neighbour next door will come in the morrow when I go back doon the pit.' He smiled wearily. 'We need the money.'

'Sit down for a minute and let me do that.' He was standing at the kitchen table peeling potatoes in a dirty bucket. She took the knife from him.

'Wull ma Mammy dee?' A dirty-faced child of about three was pulling at her skirt.

'Shoosh, ya wee brat. The cheek o' it.' The man, he was scarcely more than a boy, lifted the child and cuddled her in his arms. Lizzie saw the love in his face.

'Look at that wee lad.' She grabbed at a little boy, surely not more than a year, who was crawling determinedly towards the fire. She set him on the floor, well back from it. 'There isn't much space between them, surely?'

'Not much.'

I sound crabbit and old, she thought, and smiled at him, 'You're lucky to have such a lovely family.'

'Aye, they're no' bad when they get cleaned up.'

'When I finish this I'll wash their hands and faces and give them some soup. I brought it in a can.'

'That's awfy kind o' ye.' He looked over at the sleeping girl with the new infant, 'Jenny would thank ye if . . .'

She got away an hour later. The young wife had woken up and her husband had asked Lizzie if she would mind

416

combing her hair. 'She says a tug it oot o' her pow,' he admitted bashfully.

It's a poverty trap, she thought, walking along the Row. Young love, passion, then children, poor accommodation, constant illness, and yet she knew she was missing something. It could breed in poverty as well as in a palace.

How had Grandma ever lived in a place like that? And was it possible that her frail, dainty mother had spent all her childhood under the same conditions, slept in a bed with Aunt Maevy, walked down the garden to a privy, carried water from a well, ate in a stone-flagged kitchen?

Aunt Maevy was different, hardier. It was such a pity she could not have any more children. 'My, your aunt's a fair hand at the nursing,' the young man had said, 'you should see the way she changed the sheets and washed the wife – a bed-bath she called it. She's a professional . . .'

She had to knock several times at the door of her next port of call, and then all she heard was a hoarse shout, 'Shove the door! It's no' locked!' She obeyed and found herself in a room whose squalor was worse than she had ever seen before.

The fire was dull and choked with ash, the remains of a meal were still on the table, a hacked loaf, a greasy piece of butter half-wrapped in paper, a piece of cold bacon curled yellow-brown at the edges. In the bed there was a woman, at least she thought it was a woman because the head was covered with some sort of grey knitted cap. As she drew near the sour smell made her stomach turn.

'I'm Miss Craigie,' she said, 'my mother . . .'

'Come closer,' the voice croaked, 'it's that daurk in this bluidy kitchen.'

'I've brought some provisions for you from the parish.' She retreated back to the table, swallowing, and began to empty her basket of the scones their cook had baked that morning, some eggs, sugar and a fresh loaf. 'She's no' a mixer,' Ellen had said, 'and half daft into the bargain, but it doesn't excuse her for no' keepin' hersel clean.' Even then she had not thought, or remembered . . .

'You're gey guid at turnin' yer back on me, Miss Craigie, the minister's daughter.' She heard the voice behind her. 'Come ower here, a've somethin' tae tell ye.'

'In a moment.' It was so dark. She looked towards the window and saw it was half-obscured by curtains which were streaked with dirt. She pushed them back, and a thin stream of sunlight shone bleakly through the grime. Now . . .

She turned. She could see the woman more clearly now, the grey locks hanging under the cap, the great nose, remembered her clearly, and shivered. It was Beenie Drummond. What made her more fearsome now were the bare arms lying outside the dirty cover, immense, shiny, red. 'Could . . . could I make you a cup of tea, Mrs . . . ?' she faltered.

'There's nae missus tae ma name.' She was up on one great elbow now, looking at Lizzie. 'A canna get a man tae fancy me at all though I've tried hard enough.' She let out a high cackle, not taking her gaze away. 'It's Miss, Miss Beenie Drummond, a friend of the family, you might say, a friend o' yer granny's.' Her eyes were rheumy, white-lashed, yet with a malevolent gleam.

'I'll fill the kettle . . .' Lizzie began.

'A've had enough tea to float me doon the Clyde, thank ye. Ma belly's like a poosoned pup's. Come and sit beside me and we'll have a wee crack.' The ingratiating tone was even more fearsome than the former menacing one.

She gave in and went and sat down beside the woman. She would hide her fear, speak a few words and then take to her heels, politely, of course. The woman was in bed, after all. She could be out of the door before she could heave her great bulk from beneath the heaped bedclothes. 'What's been your trouble, Miss Drummond?' she asked.

'Trouble? Who said anything about trouble?' The woman looked at her consideringly. 'A dinna think there's onything the matter wi' me. A just dinna want tae get up. A just hae this sore heid aw the time.' She shook it slowly and the grey locks swung. She sounded completely sane and Lizzie relaxed. 'That interferin' bitch next door when she saw ma lum wisnae reekin' asked the doactor to come in and he gaed me a cough mixture. "A day or two in bed won't harm you," he said.' She gave a ridiculous imitation of Charlie's polite tones, '"You're lucky you're able to indulge yourself, Miss Drummond, not having a family." D'ye know what a said to him?' Her wild glance at Lizzie made her fearful again.

'No.'

'"Jump in beside me, doactor, and a'll indulge massel' aw right."' She let out a high cackle again. 'Aye, it's great bein' daft! You can say what you like.' She rumbled and cackled like an engine running down.

'I think I'll go if there's nothing you would like me to do for you. I'll rake the fire and fill the kettle first.' Lizzie made to rise but the woman shot out her hand and gripped her arm. It was like a mailed fist, the strength of it. She subsided into the chair again, her heart beating quickly with fright.

'How do you like being back where your granny used to stay?' Miss Drummond sounded sane again, but this time she was not reassured. The grip was if anything tighter on her arm.

'It's very nice. Do you mind letting go of my arm, Miss Drummond? I'll really have . . .'

'Nice, is it?' She ignored Lizzie's request, 'A stinkin' hole like this? A wee bit different from up at the Hall in the arms of her fancy man, is it no'?'

'I don't care to discuss my grandmother with you.'
Anger came to her, banishing her fear. 'Kindly let go of
me . . .'

'Miss High and Mighty, is it, the minister's daughter?
Aye, you could play these tricks if he *wis* your faither!'
Her grip tightened, viciously. 'That sickly mother of yours
couldn't give birth to a pup! Sit doon. You'll hear me oot
if ye have to drag me doon Colliers' Row after ye.' Her
voice was ugly now, menacing. 'But you're aw right.
You've got plenty o' faithers, hae ye no? Answer, ye
bitch.' She shook Lizzie's arm.

'I don't know what you're talking about!' It must be a
dream. Somewhere outside the sun was shining, men were
working down the pits, the old organist, Scrymsher, was
practising, her father was hanging about the vestry, listening, Aunt Maevy was working in the garden at Braidholme . . . 'By God, they were a randy lot the McGraths!
First your granny stealin' off wi' the laird when your
grandfaither was doon the pit, then that son o' hers layin'
every lass for miles and finishing up wi' landin' Bessie
Haddow wi' a bastard if it hadn't been for his . . . where
are ye gawn tae, Miss Craigie?' By a vicious twist of her
arm she forced Lizzie back on her seat, 'Dae ye no' want
to hear the rest o' it, eh? Eh?'

'Take your hand off my arm.' Lizzie struggled, half-
weeping. What was this filth the woman was pouring out
now? 'Bitch!' she shouted, 'Let me be!'

'Bitch, is it? A like a bit o' spirit.' She cackled, this
time it was a bronchitic rattle, turning into a coughing fit
which went on and on. She ended by spitting a gob of
phlegm onto the floor. 'Aye, a guid bottle, that, the
doactor gave me,' she wiped her mouth with the back of
her hand, 'gets it up. A'll let you go,' she was panting
now, 'after a tell ye aboot the happiest time in my life. It
was when . . . a punched your granny. And kicked her in

the belly forbye. By jove, it was as guid as bein' . . . in bed wi' . . . a man, maybe, stoons o' delight running up ma legs and intae ma . . . aye, it was better.' She was screaming now, sitting bolt upright, and with the movement her grip slackened. Lizzie, seizing her opportunity, twisted away from her, got to her feet and was out of the room, not even stopping to shut the door behind her.

Down Colliers' Row she ran, seeing out of the side of her glance a shawled woman looking at her, amazement on her face, along the road towards the Sholtie Brae, plunging down it, feeling the ground slip away from her because of the steep slope, half-sobbing, panting, hysterical with fear and a terrible half-knowledge, a memory of the woman's voice . . .

'You could play these tricks if he *wis* your faither . . .' 'Oh, no, no,' she sobbed, 'You've got plenty o' faithers . . .' Plenty of fathers. That was too awful to contemplate, her mother, or the woman who had borne her, with plenty of lovers, not knowing which one . . . 'No, no!' she shouted, running, stumbling in the deep dark slope of the Brae, the high stone walls on each side guarding the policies where her grandmother was now Lady Crawford . . . who had been 'punched and kicked in the belly . . .'

She was at the foot now, and running along the towpath beside the Sholtie. Long ago her Uncle John, a boy of six, had drowned here. Grandma, Lady Crawford, had told her, described the sadness in the family, and how they all blamed each other for the tragedy. 'But it came right in the end, my lovely, you have to live through grief, the anguish, the anger . . .'

'And that son of hers laying every lass for miles and finishing up wi' landin' Bessie Haddow wi' a bastard if it hadn't been for his . . .' *Bastard.* The high cackle echoed in her head, making her wince with the throbbing pain of it, causing her to stop, to lean against a tree. *Who was she?* The bitch of a woman had stripped her self from her, Lizzie Craigie, the minister's daughter, made her a nothing, fatherless, or multi-fathered, a tinker's bairn or worse. How would she ever get rid of this terrible anguish which made life not worth living, insupportable . . .

She looked at the river, how it widened into a pool, and felt a longing to walk in, not to swim, only to feel it closing over her head, to float away into nothingness since she was nothing. She stood, hesitating, and then saw the steps cut out in the banking. It was the pool beneath Braidholme. Grandma had had those steps cut out so that Grandpa could come down and fish for trout.

Had he ever done it, that quiet, gentle man? Would it be left to some other fisherman to get his hook entwined in her floating hair, to pull her to the bank, her face pale with death? But would it not be worth it, to have no more of those awful doubts and fears, not having to go back to the manse, to say to Father and Mother, 'Beenie Drummond says you're not . . .' Never to see the horror on their faces?

The fear was going, despair remained, but now a smouldering anger was growing inside her. She turned away from the water. To drown there would solve nothing. She went towards the bank and started to climb. They had all been in it, Grandma, Mother and Father, even Maevy. She would ask *her* to explain what had been happening all those years, why so much had been kept from her. Grandma was Lady Crawford now, not so young, and she had suffered enough if what Beenie Drummond had said was true. Yes, Maevy was more to blame. She had been her friend as well as her aunt . . .

But what if Mother and Father had pleaded with all of them not to tell her? Maevy and Grandma had always been good at minding their own business. 'No tittle-tattle,

422

please.' She had even heard Grandma rebuke Aunt Catherine long ago.

But surely Maevy could have told her, of all people. Oh, those lovely times in America together, the laughter and the confidences. It was good she had them to look back on. She would never laugh again. Life was too terrible, too difficult to understand, how any parents, however loving, could keep their own counsel about something as momentous as *not* being her parents, so that it had to take a half-crazed woman to grip her by the arm and tell her.

Her mounting anger had carried her without realizing it up the steep flight of steps. She was at the top now, her skirt torn with brambles, her hands bleeding where she had fallen, or stumbled, she could not remember, her face stiff with dried tears. Anger was better than despair. The pool down there would not have given her an answer.

She saw she was beside the summer-house, Grandma's summer-house where her early memories began, of gentle voices and laughter, the china noise of tea cups and the feel of a soft rug under her. She looked around, and at the far end near the house she saw Maevy working in the herbaceous border. She had on a pink cotton dress, a straw hat, a basket was beside her where she was kneeling.

'Maevy, Maevy!' She stumbled forward, waving her arms, then began to run, 'Maevy . . . I want you . . .'

16

Maevy looked up as she heard the shout and saw Lizzie, a strange Lizzie, coming stumbling towards her, one arm waving. Something had happened, something terrible.

Thoughts flashed through her mind as she started towards the girl. If it was something at the manse, why on earth would she take the long way round, down the Sholtie Brae, along by the tow-path to climb up the steps in the steep embankment to the garden? No, she must have been walking and somebody had frightened her. That was the likeliest explanation.

She met the girl in the middle of the lawn and saw the face streaked with dirt and tears, the torn skirt. Oh, God, she thought, not that. There had been a case last year of an unemployed miner who had yoked on a girl up the river. 'Lizzie . . .' she began, but she interrupted her. Her voice was harsh.

'Don't touch me. You're as much to blame as the rest of them.' Her arms were flailing. 'Mother and Father started it, but you kept it up. I've been duped . . .' One of the flying hands caught Maevy a swipe on the side of the face and she staggered back, but only for a moment. She caught the hand, then the other one, imprisoned them between her own. She could feel her face smarting under the blow.

'What on earth's wrong, Lizzie?' She tried to speak calmly. 'What's happened?'

'Leave me! Leave me!' She struggled free again, arms going in wide circles round her head, but this time Maevy was ready. Before she received another blow she slapped the girl hard across the cheek. Lizzie's arms stopped flailing, one hand went up as if to cover the rapidly spreading stain of red.

'You hit me . . .' She started to weep.

'So we're quits,' Maevy said. 'Come inside and don't make it more of a field day for Susan than you can help. I saw her face at the window.' She put her arm round Lizzie and directed her towards the house, murmuring anything of comfort which came into her head, 'It's all right . . . You'll have a nice hot cup of tea . . . Don't take on so, my lovely . . .' That was one of Mother's endearments. What would she make of this?

'Oh, Maevy,' the girl said, 'I'm so miserable.' She heard Lizzie's voice interrupting the futile words, 'I think I'm going to die.'

'Not you. You've had a shock, that's all.' What shock, she wondered? Susan was at the door, her gaunt face alight with anticipation. 'Lizzie's had a fall on the tow-path,' she said shortly, 'bring in some tea, Susan. Nice and strong.'

'Some brandy, Maevy?' In times of stress, and this seemed to be one of them, she forgot to say, 'Mrs NcNab.'

'No, no brandy. Just the tea. On you go.' Susan was showing a tendency to linger.

In the drawing-room she settled Lizzie on the sofa, tenderly wiping her face with a handkerchief. She tried a smile but there was no response. The eyes frightened her. 'We'll go upstairs later,' she said, 'and you can bathe that poor face of yours.' And as the girl winced as she wiped, 'Ah, I'm sorry about that slap, Lizzie. It's recognized nursing practice.'

'Is it?' Now there was a ghost of a smile. She had always had a good sense of humour. 'Maevy,' she said, 'today . . .'

'Wait till Susan's been. Whatever it is, I can see you've

425

had a shock. Now rest your head on that cushion and breathe deeply and slowly. Close your eyes. Try deliberately to calm yourself. That's right, nice and slowly. Say to yourself, the worst is over now, that Maevy will help you.' She went on talking, 'And there's Charlie. Don't forget Charlie. Just tell me one thing, my love, have you been . . . molested?'

'Molested?' Lizzie's eyes opened. She did not start. 'Do you mean by a man?'

'Yes. I thought if you'd been walking along . . .'

'No, no . . .' She was impatient, 'I could get over that . . .' She closed her eyes again and Maevy saw how deathly pale she was except for the one red cheek where she had slapped her. Maybe she had the same herself. She was rising to get up and look in the mirror when Susan came in with the tray.

'A good strong cup,' she said. 'Is she feeling better now?'

'Yes, she's fine. Just resting. She was a bit shaken up.'

Susan's eyes were on Lizzie as she put down the tray on a nearby side-table. She peered. 'Is that where she hurt herself?' She sounded unbelieving, 'On her cheek?'

'Yes, I expect so. Thanks, Susan. I want you to go to the manse and tell Mrs Craigie Lizzie will be staying for lunch.'

'If a go it'll no' be ready.'

'What is it?'

'Soup, and . . .'

'Is the soup made?'

'Yes, but . . .'

'Soup and cheese will be fine. Off you go, now.'

'All right.' She backed out of the room, reluctant to leave a situation so fraught with intriguing possibilities. 'A girl of her age falling. I've never heard the like,' she said as she closed the door.

Maevy poured the tea, put two teaspoonfuls of sugar into Lizzie's cup and handed it to her. 'Drink that up. Are you beginning to feel better?'

Lizzie sipped. Her hand trembled. 'Not so murderous.'

'Who do you want to murder?'

'The whole McGrath family, starting with my mother and father, only they're not . . .' She put down the cup and put her face in her hands. Maevy sat down beside her and took her in her arms.

'Tell me,' she said, 'you don't have to look at me. Just tell me what happened, bit by bit. I'll make sense of it.' I have already, she thought, someone's told her.

Lizzie was sobbing now in a heart-broken fashion. 'You'll be lucky if you can make sense of it because I can't. I went to that old woman's house, Beenie Drummond, and she asked me how I knew my father was my father. Am I going mad?'

'No, you're not going mad.' She had been right. It had happened at last. No good saying to Isobel and John, 'I told you so. Terence pleaded with you, Patrick pleaded with you.' I should have gone to Isobel myself, made a direct appeal to her. Oh, this fatal flaw I have of not interfering in other people's affairs. But it *was* my affair . . . 'Go on,' she said almost roughly, 'get it out.'

'*Is* he?'

'Get it all out. Tell me what else she said.' There was no good answering this piecemeal.

'That I had plenty of fathers. I thought she meant my mother was . . . you know,' she smiled faintly, apologetically. 'And that Uncle Terence had an illegitimate child by Bessie Haddow. She put it differently. Coarsely. It's me, isn't it?' She took her hands away from her face and raised it to Maevy. The tears were running down it. 'I'm going . . . out of my mind. Tell me who I am. Tell me!

427

Tell me!' she screamed. It was a good thing Susan was out of the house.

'Stop that, Lizzie,' she said. 'There's no point in it. Sit quietly and listen. Look, I have my arms round you. Yes, you're Bessie Haddow's daughter and Terence's. He was married already, but to the wrong woman. Be sure you were conceived in love. Patrick married Bessie instead. She died after you were born. Listen to me when I tell you this. Patrick also loved Bessie, always had loved her. They had four happy months together.'

'Why didn't one of them take me?'

'Now what could a young man like Patrick do with a baby needing to be breast-fed? A young man in the deepest grief, who'd had happiness snatched away from him?'

'But there was . . .' she stumbled over the words, 'my . . . father?'

'Terence? Catherine wouldn't hear of it. She was difficult, as you know. She died as she lived. You know about that, too. Isobel, your mother . . .'

'But she isn't my mother . . .'

'You can't change the habits of a lifetime in a minute or two, Isobel was ill. She had lost a baby, couldn't have any more. We all agreed at the time it was best they should have you. You saved her life, Lizzie. Doesn't that make a difference to you? And you've been happy, haven't you?'

'I don't know.' She turned her face to Maevy. 'How can I say now when my heart's full of anger and resentment against them, against all of you? I should have been *told* who I was. I shouldn't have been left to find out this way.' Oh, she was right.

'Your parents didn't want you to know,' Maevy said feebly. 'They had definite ideas. Your father, your real father, tried to reason with them several times. Patrick begged them to tell you, or let him tell you before he went to America. They were adamant.'

'They've ruined my life, then. I'll never forgive them for it! And how can I face them? How will they be able to face *me*?' Her tears had dried. She pushed Maevy's arms aside and sat up straight in the sofa, her face set. All the youthfulness had gone from it.

'They've devoted their lives to your welfare, Lizzie. Try and remember that. Oh, try not to blame them too much for how they thought. People are as they are. Perhaps Isobel followed her husband's wishes too closely.' She smiled. 'She puts ministers on a pedestal, always has since she was a little girl.' There was no answering smile in Lizzie's voice.

'Why did Grandma not tell me?'

'How can I say, my lovely, how can I say? People often let sleeping dogs lie, think it's for the best. You were born when Terence and Patrick were young, when Grandma was preoccupied with the firm and Grandpa's health. The boys got married, had other cares and worries, their passions cooled. They saw you well looked after in a loving home. Perhaps it was that Isobel felt she would lose your love if she told you that you didn't belong to them. John had strict ideas, principles of his own. Nobody . . . challenged them.' I was under his spell at one time, too, she thought. She heard a noise at the front door. Susan couldn't be back so quickly, surely, and then there was Charlie's voice.

'Home early, Maevy! Small surgery, thank God!' He came into the room, took a look at both of them sitting on the sofa, saw Maevy's warning glance. 'Well,' he said, 'this is a pleasant surprise, Lizzie.'

'Lizzie's had a shock,' Maevy said.

'What's happened?' He came to stand in front of them. The girl did not look up.

'She's learned Isobel and John aren't her parents.'

'Ah, now.' He bent down, took Lizzie by the hands and gently pulled her to her feet, took her in his arms. 'Do you want my candid opinion for what it's worth?' Her face was against his shoulder. She did not speak. 'Right, then, I'll give it to you whether you want it or not. I'm glad that particular cat's out of its bag.' She gave a muffled snort, then started to weep, sobs which seemed to be dragged from the depths of her. His eyes met Maevy's across her head.

There was little enough chance for serious talk at the lunch table because Ellie came home from school swaggering with her new satchel, and pleased to have Lizzie as audience.

'I need a big bag because I have a lot of books, you see. And homework. I'm top of the class now.'

'Don't boast,' Maevy said.

'It's the truth. I go back in the afternoons. That *proves* I'm a big girl.'

'I may be walking back with Lizzie to the manse after lunch,' Maevy said. 'When you come out I want you to go straight home. Susan will be in.'

'Could I not come to the manse to see everybody?'

'You've just said you have homework to do. No, go straight home.'

'Hoist by your own petard, Ellie,' Charlie said.

'What does that mean?'

'Caught out. You'll have to read Shakespeare. You do what your mother tells you, there's a good girl.' While Lizzie had been upstairs washing he and Maevy had agreed on a hurried plan. He would leave before them, call in at the manse on his way to the surgery and tell Isobel and John that Lizzie knew about her parentage. That way it would not be such a shock for them when, or if, Maevy and Lizzie appeared.

430

When Ellie had been bustled off to school Lizzie spoke. She had been very quiet, and had scarcely eaten. 'I don't want to see them. Couldn't I stay here? I can't face them. It's too difficult.' Her voice trembled.

'I understand that,' Charlie said, 'but believe me, Lizzie, it will only get more difficult the longer you put it off. If you like, I could call in and break the news to them.'

She looked at him, doubtfully. 'It might not be so bad, then.'

'No. And you would have Maevy with you. If you want to come back with her, you're welcome, you know that, but we can't come between you and your parents.'

'They're not my parents.'

'Technically they are. Accept that.'

'They should have told me.'

'Maybe they should but they didn't and you know now. Better late than never. At least you're still a McGrath. Have you thought of that?'

She sat, looking down, and Maevy's heart ached for her. Her first hurdle, she thought, but a bad one. 'I'll go,' she said, 'but you'll see them first, Charlie?' It was significant, Maevy thought, that she had dropped the title of uncle.

They started off about half past two, walking through the village. Lizzie did not utter a word, looking straight ahead, not noticing, or indeed recognizing, the occasional passer-by. Maevy slipped her hand through her arm. 'I know it's a terrible adjustment to make. Not many have to do it. But you'll manage. You're a braw lass.' She smiled.

'Don't butter me up, Aunt Maevy.' The title, resurrected again, put a distance between them.

The door was on the latch, and they went into the

empty hall. An afternoon stillness hung about the place. The table was littered with the usual array of Bible tracts and leaflets. There was a row of chairs. John expected any visitors to employ their time usefully when they were waiting. The sun, shining through the stained glass window on the stair landing, caused coloured lozenges of light to fall on the white paper. From the kitchen came the thin clatter of dishes. Ellen would be washing up after the substantial midday dinner they always had at the manse.

'They'll be in the drawing-room,' Lizzie said. 'Mother . . . probably got up.'

Maevy went to the door, knocked, opened it and stood aside for Lizzie. The girl hesitated and then went in, Maevy following.

John and Isobel were on their feet. The fragility of Isobel made Lizzie look robust in comparison. Her sister's face seemed greenish-white, Maevy thought, or perhaps it was the reflection from the green gown she was wearing.

'Oh, Lizzie,' Isobel said in a heart-broken voice, 'Charlie told us. I'm sorry, that sorry for everything.' She held out her arms and Lizzie went into them. They were both weeping.

John was stern, but not too discomposed. 'Sit down, Maevy.'

'I'm not waiting. I just came . . .'

He broke in, glancing at the weeping women. 'That'll do, Lizzie, my dear. We don't have to get maudlin. Help your mother to sit down. This has been too much for her.' Maevy watched the tenderness with which Lizzie seated Isobel, then sat down beside her.

John took up a position of authority before the fire. 'I understand from your uncle that Beenie Drummond hinted we weren't your real father and mother. Is that so?'

432

'Yes.' Lizzie raised her head. Her face was expressionless.

'It was in your own interest that we kept your real parentage from you.'

'It was in my own *interest*?' Lizzie said, her cheeks were flaming. 'I'd like to know . . .'

'Kindly don't interrupt. You weren't a judge of that at the time. Perhaps it's fitting now that you should know. Indeed, I was just coming round to it, but unfortunately pressure of work prevented my dealing with the matter.'

'You could have told me.'

'So you say now, but a young girl isn't in a position to deal with adult problems . . . scandal shouldn't be encouraged by repeating it.'

'Uncle Patrick wanted to tell me before he went to America. You stopped him.'

'That is so,' he raised his chin, 'and so did your Uncle Terence. He . . . approached me. But I was the best judge of that. You'll thank us later for having given you an untrammelled, happy childhood and girlhood. I'm sorry you have to hear it in this way from a simpleton, but she's always borne malice towards the McGraths. I've cautioned her before. No,' he drew himself up, 'I flatter myself I took the right course.' He adjusted his lapels, straightened his back. Is this the man who filled my life for so long, Maevy thought. How can he have changed so much?

'Would you like some tea, Maevy?' Isobel also drew herself up in her chair, touched her eyes with her handkerchief.

'No, thanks. I just walked round for the air. I'll maybe pick up Ellie at school on the way back.'

'Is she going now after dinner as well?' She had become the lady of the manse again.

'Yes, she's a big girl, as she's never done telling me.'

433

She spoke to Lizzie directly. 'You're very welcome to come to Braidholme for a few days if you like.'

The girl looked up. Her eyes were full. 'Perhaps I will . . .'

'There's no need for that,' John said, 'Lizzie's found out she was adopted, that's the sum of it. I'm sorry she had to hear it from Beenie Drummond, but I know she'll soon come to the conclusion that she was lucky to have been brought up in a God-fearing home, unlike some.'

Maevy bent and kissed the girl. 'Come any time, Lizzie.' I mustn't interfere, she told herself, feeling ashamed at the same time that she did not speak her mind.

'Thank you, Aunt.' Lizzie's face was closed.

'Don't cry, Isobel.' Her sister's handkerchief was once again at her mouth. 'It's out now. That's the main thing.'

'I only wanted to . . . keep it nice for her.'

'Yes, I know that. Good afternoon, John.' She walked out of the room. No one was speaking behind her. She did not care to imagine that first half-hour. It hurt too much. Nothing will ever be the same again in that house, she thought. Lizzie knows that.

17

Coincidentally Maevy's mother called at Braidholme that evening on her way home from Glasgow. It had been a lovely day although Maevy had scarcely noticed it, the late peak of summer, a golden day as far as the weather was concerned.

'You look tired, Mother,' she said, 'let me make you a cup of tea.'

'D'you know,' she sat down, drawing off her gloves, 'I'd like a glass of sherry. I'm afraid Alastair has taught me a few new tricks.'

'Is he at home?' she asked, as she filled out two glasses from the decanter.

'No, he's in London, otherwise I should have gone straight home. I just wanted to see you for some reason. I don't know why.'

'You'll soon know . . .'

'You're feeling wabbit as well? For the first time in my life I'm looking forward to my retirement. Sixty-five in November . . .' She looked at Maevy. 'There's something wrong. I can see it in your face.'

'Beenie Drummond let the cat out of the bag when Lizzie was sick visiting today.'

'Beenie Drummond!' Her mother never paled or flushed, but Maevy watched the life drain out of her face. For the first time she looked her age, the downward lines, the flatness of her eyes which were usually so filled with vitality. 'You mean . . . about who she is?'

'That's it. Who she is. And that's what's floored the poor lass, that she's not who she *thought* she was, that and anger at Isobel and John, at all of us, come to that. She feels she's been tricked, made a fool of.'

'Oh, the poor lamb! She's not far wrong. I blame myself, although you know I never liked the thought of her growing up in ignorance.'

'None of us did. Did you ever suggest to Isobel that she should tell Lizzie?'

'More than once, and to John, but they wouldn't budge, or rather John wouldn't budge, and you know Isobel, she follows him in everything.' She looked at Maevy, shook her head. 'Oh, he wouldn't have done for you at all.'

She turned away, embarrassed. 'So long I dreamt of him. It's *like* a dream now. Isn't it strange, Mother, how some people mellow and mature, like my Charlie, while others harden . . . like tar in the frost?'

She nodded. 'It suits Isobel. She was always rigid, too. But not Lizzie. She's vulnerable, high-spirited, and she's been curbed by their inflexibility.' Her face hardened. 'I wonder what that bitch said to her.'

'Isobel?' She was astonished.

'No. Beenie Drummond. Oh, it wouldn't be pretty! She and two of her friends knocked me down long ago . . . when we lived in Colliers' Row.'

'Knocked you down!' Lizzie had not told her *that*.

'Punched and kicked me for carrying on with Alastair, as they called it. I deserved it. It stopped me in time . . . no, the pit explosion did that. Never mind now. Tell me about Lizzie.'

She told her. It was an effort to take her mind off this latest disclosure. 'Anyhow, she's back home now.'

'How did they face up to it, Isobel and John?'

'He was self-righteous, Isobel weepy. There's a status quo, or at least there seemed to be when I left. That's all I can say.'

'All the skeletons in the McGrath closet are coming out

to dance in my sixty-fifth year.' She smiled faintly over her glass.

'I bet the Crawfords have plenty.'

'No doubt, but they're a smaller family. We're a prolific lot . . .' She bent forward, touched Maevy's hand. 'I'm sorry. I saw that hurt.'

'Goodness no!' She blustered. The sherry must have made her easy-tongued. 'I'll tell you one thing, it's not for want of trying.'

'Oh, the joy of that. Alastair and I . . . we've reached the years of discretion.' She smiled, 'But it's a nice time all the same.'

'You're happy with him?'

'Content. We've always loved each other, although in a different way from Kieran and me. It's a long association . . . stretching back.' She sighed, shook her head. 'It's Lizzie now, her life. What was she like when you left her?'

'Drained, I think. I told her she could come here if she wanted. She'll have to think it out on her own. And adjust.'

'Maybe Emily Barthe would have her this summer. And there's the family celebration looming ahead when I bow out.' She smiled. 'Nigel will be home from Balliol soon. That would be young blood for her. And young Kieran may come with Kate and James. And Patrick writes telling me Ernest wants to come to Glasgow to see this side of the business. My goodness,' Maevy saw the old enthusiasm, not damped yet, 'I can scarcely keep track of it all. The firm's going from strength to strength. We've opened a branch in London now. Can you believe it? And you should come in some day and see the new offices in York Street.'

'I'll do that.'

'It's a pity you couldn't take my place when I go.'

'I haven't your business flair.'

'You've got it all right. Maybe there will be a right time.'

'Maybe.' She had a brief regret that she was only a housewife.

'Well, I must be going. Thomas will be in the kitchen with Susan having a crack.'

'She got a fine helping of drama today with Lizzie coming running in half-deranged.'

Her mother stood up, still beautiful in her blue muslin, the bustle gone now (how well she had worn those bustles), a broad velvet band round her waist instead. But it was the carriage of her, Maevy thought, walking with her to the door. She was in her right place in the Hall.

They talked for a long time in bed that night, but eventually a chance touch of Charlie's hand on her body fired her, and she said, 'Ah, take me, it's the only way to give ease to my mind.' They loved each other passionately and long, the bedclothes thrown on the floor as if it were their first night together, surprising themselves.

'And I thought I was tired,' she said when she lay flushed beside him. 'Love's funny, isn't it? Like the Sholtie in a way, running smoothly sometimes between its soft green banks, other times in spate, throwing itself down its falls in abandon, not to be contained, and then coming again to a quiet pool where it rests. I've hopes tonight.'

'If they're conceived out of passion there would be no doubt, no doubt at all.' He got up on one elbow and kissed her lingeringly.

'Nothing to worry about then,' she said, dizzy from tiredness and from the kiss.

'You still worry?'

'Not all the time. I would have truly liked a son. I

haven't given up hope. It's because a son would be *you* . . . in case I lost you.'

'You're not likely to lose me, dear heart.'

'There's this war . . .'

'It's in a quiet phase just now. Maybe for ever.'

'It's like the Sholtie as well. It will be dashing itself against the rocks any time now . . .' she was half-asleep. 'Nigel's coming home. I wonder what he thinks about it?'

'Young men get carried away . . .' She hardly heard him. She slept.

18

Nigel was there when Lizzie went to stay at the Hall, a fortnight after she had learned about her real parentage. She recognized that her grandmother was trying to ease the situation for her at the manse. She could not adequately explain to her there was no situation, at least as far as her mother and father were concerned . . . she had still to think of them as that since *they* did.

A veil had been drawn over that day when Beenie Drummond had exposed their secret. It was as if it had never happened. She could not understand their lack of sensitivity. It was as if the woman's outpourings had been a kindly act of God which they accepted as their due, as if she was His intermediary. After a few sleepless nights when her pillow was wet with tears, she decided to do as they did, act normally.

Grandma had said she would write a diplomatic letter to Emily Barthe to see if Lizzie could visit them for a time, and she had agreed. Anything to get away from the manse. And she took Maevy's advice because she got none from Isobel and John, and wrote to Terence and Patrick, telling them, simply, that she knew the secret of her birth, but not how she had found out.

Terence's reply came by return, voluble, loving, relieved. 'It's a great load off my mind, Lizzie, the only thing that kept me from being completely happy here with Honor.' He'd often blamed himself, he said, for not insisting that the truth should come out, but then she knew all about poor Catherine and how that had taken over in his mind. 'But, ah, for sure, all's well that ends

440

well.' He was more Irish than the Irish. She would have to visit them often in Ireland and stay as long as she liked since wasn't she his true daughter whom he'd always loved?

There was a short note from Honor which touched her. 'Come and stay with us. We've always thought of you as part of the family. Now even more so.'

Patrick's came a week or so later in the same vein, quieter in tone than Terence's, but as sincere. 'Our life here has been very pleasant since we arrived. Little Virginia thrives and is a great happiness to us. You would add to that happiness if you came, any time. It is your house as well as ours.' They had recently moved to a house not far from Kate and James which he described in glowing terms, 'built entirely of stone, a rarity here. You'd feel you were still at Braidholme.' He did not say 'the manse'.

Nigel was as she remembered, tall and slender, handsome like his father, but why had she not noticed before the golden tint of his skin, a tone lighter than his eyes, and how his hair fell in between the two in colour, a soft dun brown. His father was dark. It was possible to see that despite the grizzled greyness, but they shared the same spare elegance.

'Hello, Lizzie,' he said. 'How grown up you look!' His amber eyes were playful. There was no shyness in him at all, again like his father who never appeared awkward whatever the situation.

'So do you.' They laughed, and she saw how the playfulness in his eyes was repeated in the upward turn of his mouth, the cleft on the right side of it. Very much *du monde*. She was tongue-tied. No one she knew, no young men in the village, Kieran and Ernest in America, had this effect on her, but then they had not his easiness,

441

the way his hands were in the pockets of his light trousers, the way his white shirt was open at the neck. It was inborn. Charles Barthe had it, perhaps, but he was too fussily correct in his dress, and she could not imagine him without his cravat or the black string tie he sometimes wore.

'I think Nigel's overcome by your beauty, Lizzie,' his father said. 'He isn't usually so bereft of speech.'

'She's like you, Stepmother,' Nigel smiled round at Maeve, 'no one told me how like you she was.'

'Well, then, I can understand you being awestruck,' Lord Crawford said.

'Oh, what a family this is for compliments!' Maeve laughed. 'We're not used to it, are we, Lizzie? Away and take a walk outside the two of you. Tea's at half past four.'

'Where would you like to go?' Nigel asked when they were standing on the broad gravelled drive. 'The stables? Father said I had to have a look at his old mount. He's getting past it . . .' he laughed, 'I mean the horse, not Father.'

'Neither of them ride much now. Grandma's offered me hers, if I'd like it.'

'Are you keen?'

'I don't know. She used to have a pony for us at Braidholme. That's the extent of it.' How prosaic I sound, she thought. I'm not used to my new identity. I feel it's written on my forehead, 'Illegitimate child of Terence McGrath and Bessie Haddow . . .'

They walked the quarter of a mile to the stables, not speaking a great deal. Nigel kept his hands in his pockets. Occasionally he took a glancing kick with the side of his foot at a stone. Once he hummed, probably a music hall ditty. They only had hymn music at the manse. She asked

442

him politely about his studies and he asked her if she had been back in Paris.

The word was like an open sesame. The memory came flooding back of how he had taken her to the *Café de la Paix*, and how they had sat at a pavement table watching the passers-by and he had told her he had seen the cancan being danced. 'Sprowsing.' Grandma's word. She remembered lying in bed sleepless, thinking of him, of being teased by the girls at Madame Sevigny's. 'Lizzie's in love.' The shock she had had about her birth had wiped out the past.

'No,' she said, they were at the loose boxes now. An old groom touched his cap to Nigel. 'Welcome home, sir.'

'Thank you, Craig. Just having a look at the horses.' They stood together at the half-door of a stall and stroked the nose of the mare inside, their fingers occasionally touching on its bony head with its soft covering of hair.

'I'm hoping to go to Paris before long,' Lizzie said. 'Grandma's trying to arrange it.'

He looked at her questioningly, said to the groom, 'You keep them in good order, Craig,' and then to her, 'You don't want to ride today?'

'No . . .'

'Come on, then, we'll go over the fields.' They climbed over the stile at the back of the stables and she jumped down disregarding his hand.

'Showing off?' he said, smiling, and as they set themselves to the slope. 'You're different, Lizzie. I didn't remember you looking sad. Nor pale . . .'

'Didn't you?' She found the words pouring out of her as they walked, everything Beenie Drummond had said, how she had felt, how her parents had reacted. 'I have to say "parents",' she said, 'but I don't feel the same about them. Oh, they're kind, but they don't understand the blow it's been. Can you? How would *you* feel if you weren't who you thought you were, if you had to readjust your ideas, how would you feel if you were *adrift*, belonging and not belonging, eating breakfast and dinner and supper with two people who weren't as you thought, but who treated it as if it was a trifling matter, better out but not important . . . how would you feel, Nigel?' They were climbing up the steep fields skirting Brow Farm, but it was not only that which made her breathless. She fell silent, trying to control her breathing, remembering what Maevy had said, 'Breathe long and deeply . . .'

'It frees you of them in a way,' he said. She was glad he did not say, 'Poor Lizzie'. She would have wept.

'Who?' She looked at him.

'Your legal parents. You've got a new identity, the bond tying you to them is cut.'

'I never thought of it that way.'

'Oh, you must. It will have that effect on them, too, maybe not at first. Parents, even the best of them, cling to you. I feel that with my father, for instance. They put a moral pressure on you. They demand allegiance without knowing they do it. I'd go into the Army tomorrow if it weren't that he wants me to get my degree. It's difficult to hurt him.'

'If it ever starts it would be over by the time you were trained.'

'No, it won't be like that. I follow the news carefully. We shan't be ready. We'll blunder along for ages.'

'That's what Uncle Charlie says. He's been going to train every week recently. He's in the Volunteers.'

'He's a doctor. He'll be needed here.'

'That's what Aunt Maevy hopes. But he's a surgeon as well.'

'That's different, then.' They were walking through the woods now, on the ride which ran through it, and it had become dark. Occasionally the low-hanging branches

444

caught her hair, and Nigel had to disentangle it. 'Your lovely red hair,' he said, 'how pale your face is in the gloom.'

'I never had much colour.' She was embarrassed. She tried to pin up some stray locks, then said, 'To the devil with it! Who's to see?'

'That's the Lizzie I remember.' He laughed. The wood was thinning now, and he was able to walk beside her. 'Don't be downcast. That's the main thing. Feel happy that you're a love child, that you've got two other people interested in your welfare now, two places to visit. And there's Paris perhaps. The world's opening out for you. You have to welcome it, not hide from it.'

Her spirits lifted. Oh, it took someone of her own age to cut through all the misery and doubt, to point her the way. 'There's the old monastery,' she said. Ahead of them she could see the standing walls of rough stone, partly covered by moss, a flight of stone steps running round the one remaining tower.

'Is that what it is? I've always meant to read it up. We'll have a rest there when we reach it.'

'All right.' She was at ease now. She had known him for ever and yet this older Nigel was different, stranger, more introspective. Although he had no problems about who *his* parents were, he still had to question who he was. Perhaps everyone had to do that to become mature, 'go through the whins' as Grandma said.

The turf was short and dry because of the long hot summer, and they threw themselves down on it, laughing.

'Oh, lovely, lovely,' she said, 'have you ever known a summer like this one, golden, peaceful . . .'

'The last summer of the century. Don't you feel the melancholy of it?' He was lying stretched out beside her. He reached for and took her hand. 'Dear little Lizzie. You've had a bad time.'

445

'I'm sorry I burdened you with my troubles. But you've helped me . . .'

'It's not a burden and I'm glad you did. Now you must put it behind you and think of all those places you can go to. What a choice you have!'

Yesterday, she thought, I should have cheerfully gone to any one of them, been happy to be away, now the desire's gone. They fell silent, and she lay enjoying the sun beating down on her, the golden warmth of it. Life was different now, she was someone, her own person . . . she half-dozed, she did not know for how long, then waking suddenly, felt a new sadness which made her sit up and look around her, blinking her eyes. Was the melancholy which Nigel had spoken about affecting her, too? He thought there would be a war. So did Uncle Charlie. Women hoped there would not, because they knew it would bring only sorrow.

'What are you thinking of, Lizzie?' She turned to look at him, lying at her side. He has the kind of skin which will never burn, she thought. His amber eyes were on her. They were flecked in the sunlight.

'I don't know. Life, and you, and women and men and the difference between them . . .'

'No, no, you haven't to be sad.' He stretched up a hand and touched her cheek. 'I told you. You've got so much.'

She smiled down at him, feeling older, remote, wiser. She bent down and kissed his lips. They were pale pink-brown, soft. Red lips would have been wrong in the golden tint of his face. 'A kiss from a grateful little Lizzie,' she said.

'That was nice. Lie down beside me.'

She lay in the curve of his arm and they talked for a long time, at peace with each other.

19

A letter came from Emily Barthe in Normandy. They would be there until the middle of September and they would love to have her join them. The twins and Giselle said, tell her to come, Lizzie makes us laugh. 'You loved Normandy,' Maeve said. 'Why don't you go? I would see you all right.' She meant money.

'I'll think of it,' she said, 'but it's so nice here.'

'You mean the weather?' Maeve's blue eyes were very blue.

'Yes, the weather,' she said. She was like Grandma, pale skin. She did not know how to blush. Perhaps her eyes went a deeper blue also.

Nigel absented himself from time to time on trips to Glasgow but for the most part he was at the Hall, playful, *insouciant*, getting on beautifully with 'Lady Crawford' . . . when he addressed her like that his eyes twinkled. He seemed to have a good relationship with his father.

They had carriage trips together up into what Alastair called the wilds of Lanarkshire. Nigel knew a man at Oxford whose father had a Daimler horseless carriage, but Alastair said he was waiting until those new-fangled contraptions could seat more than one person and a coachman. They saw where the Clyde began in the Lowther Hills, further down where its falls were, and they searched for and found where the Sholtie branched off.

Both father and son added an extra dimension to any sightseeing because of their interest in topography and geology, what Nigel called 'the start of things', they could lift a stone and make what he called 'a reasonable 'assumption' as to its origin. He did not understand people who just looked without questioning.

'You're like my Uncle Charlie,' she said, 'how you question.'

'Doesn't everybody?' he said, and she realized how self-centred she was, how in the manse there had only been one assumption and that a heavenly one, which was considered quite enough to be going on with.

They walked endlessly, generally between five and seven when it became slightly cooler, because the beautiful weather still continued. The papers were now beginning to call it 'ominous' rather than 'beautiful'. The walks again were expeditions to some point of interest, never aimless. 'You should have followed in the steps of Livingstone,' she said to him once.

In the evenings they bathed and dressed and met in the drawing-room for sherry, the men in evening dress, Lizzie and her grandmother in their finest fur and feathers. It was a small pleasure Lizzie had never known, accustomed as she was in the manse to treat all interest in dress as frivolous.

'I've never felt narcissistic before,' she said one evening, making them laugh. Alastair had complimented her on her appearance. She was beginning to use words now which were strange and different, but which she had always known. The French learned at Madame Sevigny's came back to her, and she was able to pepper her conversation with allusions to writers like Racine and Balzac, even greatly daring, Rimbaud and Baudelaire. The latter two had *not* been on Madame's curriculum.

Once, the wine and the new intellectual excitement having taken effect, she recited without self-consciousness, '*Car j'ai de chaque chose extrait la quintessence, Tu m'as donné ta boue et j'en ai fait de l'or . . .*' And she found that she was looking at Nigel. There was a silence which Maeve broke.

'It's as good as if I'd read Baudelaire myself. Long ago in Ireland I had an English tutor for a short time. Richard. He opened doors for me . . . that's all you need,' her grandmother looked around, smiling, 'someone to open doors. But I got married and came here, and I was too busy after that.'

'You were using your intellect in a practical sense, dearest,' her husband said, 'McGrath's is the book you never read because you were writing it. But it's there for all to see, a successful publication.'

'Bravo!' Nigel applauded. 'And I shouldn't be surprised if she's working on the second volume. I came home with her on the train the other day and she had a bulging Gladstone bag.'

'That's my last chapter.' She smiled at him. 'But I don't find you quite so forthcoming, Nigel, about *your* ploys.'

'I like to compare Glasgow with Oxford. It's got a rough vitality I don't find there. Life is real, it seems to say to me. Get rid of your Oxford dreams.' He looked away, and Lizzie thought, he's avoiding the question.

There followed a discussion about the personalities of different cities and she sat content, sometimes adding her own contribution, but listening for the most part. It's all good, she thought, but the best part is when Grandma and Alastair are resting in the early afternoon, and sometimes we take the horses and ride up to the ruined monastery. Too hot to walk although they were into September now, and the lovely sinister sun shone on a country seemingly flooded with peace. Not a cloud in the sky . . .

'Father was telling me that he and your grandmother used to come here,' Nigel said to her. They were lying on the

449

short grass, burnt brown now, but at least it was cooler here at the top of the hill. The Hall gardens, deeply shaded by trees, were too much of a sun trap.

'I had a feeling right from the start that it was . . .' she wanted to say 'haunted', but that seemed too dramatic, '. . . different. But when was it? A long time ago?' This is what Beenie Drummond must have meant.

'Yes. When she was young and married to your grandfather. She and my father used to have clandestine meetings here.' She turned to look at him and his eyes were on her.

'You're daring me to be shocked.'

'Am I?' He was laughing now. She was very close to him. She could see the beads of sweat caught in the hairs on his upper lip, the moist white teeth, the two front ones rounded, giving a boyish look to his face.

'Yes you are. I'm only shocked that he told you about his . . . past.'

'You're preening yourself. You're thinking, how could a young woman like me who has not long ago been told the dramatic tale of her birth, all that . . . dark passion and regret, how could she be shocked? Isn't that so?'

'No.' She shook her head. 'I sort of . . . knew. But I'm surprised your father was so frank with you.'

'He's always been like that, in important things. Your grandmother is the love of his life. I wish I could be as frank with him.' He fell silent.

'I'm glad you told me.' He did not reply.

She lay in the sun with her eyes closed, but she was disturbed. On this particular spot all those years ago, had her grandmother and Nigel's father lain, too? What a strong passion there must have been between them to make her forget her marriage vows, even to that extent. Everyone said she was like Grandmother. Had *she* the same passion in her? And yet there had been a strong

450

love between her two grandparents. 'Like two coorie doos' Aunt Maevy had said of them. It was . . . disturbing . . .

'What are you thinking of?' Nigel said.

'Them.'

'So am I. You rationalize things, tell yourself it was a long time ago, two different people, and yet your emotions get in the way and against your will your blood begins to mount and you feel excitement . . . look at me, Lizzie.' She turned slowly.

'Your eyes are strange.'

'So are yours. They're so deeply blue that they're almost black.'

'I blush with my eyes.'

He laughed. 'Dear Lizzie. I have this desire . . . it's nothing to do with them . . . I've had it since the first day when you told me your sad story and I couldn't bear the sadness in your eyes . . . I have this desire . . .' He slipped one arm round her neck, the other went round her waist and he kissed her. She closed her eyes because there was a pain, a pain of delight, sharp like a blade, and when she opened them at last she met his, widely open, as if he had been reading in her face that pain. He released her. 'Are you not going to scream?' he said.

'I don't think she did, do you?' He laughed at her.

'You're so like her.' He took her more strongly in his arms this time, and there was only the heat of the sun, not even the noise of birds. They had been defeated by the heat all summer, and the woods and fields had been silent. Later she was to think of it as a waiting silence . . .

20

John and Isobel came to tea and suggested she might be overstaying her welcome. It was now into September, and the work was piling up at the manse. 'I'm lost without my amanuensis,' John said playfully, but Isobel was more understanding, perhaps, and suggested that Lizzie should 'begin' to think of coming home. Her wan little face touched her. 'Grandma says I can stay as long as I like,' she said, 'but I'll come back next week.' She knew Nigel's vacation was coming to an end. She dared not think of it.

She seemed to be living two separate lives. There were the family sightseeing trips, the visiting and entertaining of friends to tea and dinner, visits to Aunt Maevy and Uncle Charlie. The Transvaal question always cropped up, or as one newspaper euphemistically called it, the Transvaal Difficulty. The position between us and the Boers, she suggested to Alastair, was like one of those stately gavottes where partners advanced and retreated to slow music.

'Apt, Lizzie,' he said, 'but the music's getting quicker all the time.' As the days became shorter and the sun less fierce, the war fever mounted. There were more and more articles by people who purported to be well-informed about the latest news, more and more discussion.

Charlie was more reliable. He told her of a great Liberal rally in Manchester which was declaring against war, and she said she would not mind joining it.

'Are *you* a Liberal?' Nigel asked, astonished.

'If it means being against war, yes, I am. I get tired of "war, war, and rumours of war . . ."'

But there was the other life when she and Nigel absented themselves from the Hall, ostensibly to walk. There was no pretence between them now. They walked in a trance, fingers touching, when they felt they wanted to be free of even the few passers-by on the estate or the tow-path, they would ride to the ruined monastery and fall into each other's arms, mouthing words, 'Oh, I've wanted you . . . it's been so long . . . since yesterday . . .'

They would laugh, because they had the same sense of the ridiculous. Neither of them could quite comprehend this overwhelming feeling which possessed them both. 'It must be love,' Nigel once said, solemnly, and she mimicked him, also solemn, round-eyed, 'It must be love.'

But at times he was distant, silent, and she could not reach him. He would shut himself away from her in his room. She walked with him to post letters in the village, and teased him about his correspondence. He muttered something about having a lot of clearing up to do for Oxford.

The day before she was due to go back to the manse she went to Glasgow in the afternoon. She met him when he was getting into the carriage to be driven to the station. 'Fancy wasting your last afternoon like this,' she spoke gaily because Thomas was within earshot. She felt a keen sense of loss.

'I'm terribly sorry, Lizzie,' he looked tense, 'I've an urgent appointment. I couldn't find you to tell you.'

'I was in my room packing.' She could see by the slant of Thomas' head that he was listening. 'Never mind, I'll see you at dinner.' And there might be time for a last stroll by the Sholtie. There was a harvest moon.

She stood watching the retreating carriage. It was over, the wonderful summer. He had not 'said' anything, except that he loved her, once that he would die for her. But he

453

had to finish his studies, she thought, and again that he was not as impetuous as she was by nature.

Grandmother eloped, she thought. But there was no need for that in their case. If it should come to that stage, there would be no objection. Lord Crawford seemed to like her. Grandmother would be pleased. She believed in love . . . oh, give it up, she told herself. She stood in the driveway, undecided as to how to occupy herself.

The weather did not help. The storm clouds were gathering above the high elms, she could hear the rooks chattering angrily in their branches. She would go in and do some sewing, she decided, in preparation for going back to the manse. That would bring her down to reality. She met Lord Crawford as she was going through the hall.

'Hello,' he said, 'are you and I the only two left? Your grandmother's at the Gallowgate office today.'

'Everybody's busy except us.' She smiled at him to combat the quaver in her voice.

'I imagine you'll be busy enough when you go back home. Never mind, we've had the best of the weather, a summer to remember.'

'A summer to remember . . .' She repeated his words. 'I think I heard thunder as I came in.'

'I shouldn't be surprised. It's oppressive. Where's Nigel?'

'He's gone to Glasgow.'

'Really?' His brows drew together. Nigel has not told him and he resents it, she thought. 'Ah, well, I suppose he has things to buy before going up. Yes, that'll be it.' Surprisingly he laid his hand on her arm. His eyes were tender. 'Nigel isn't the only one who's going to miss you, Lizzie. Your grandmother has always sung your praises. Now she's got me singing them, too.'

She felt touched, and ashamed. They had absented themselves so much, possessed with each other. There

454

had been no criticism, but Grandmother and Lord Crawford were not naïve. They had been through the whins . . . 'I've enjoyed myself so much here,' she said, 'coming when it did, after . . .' She felt her eyes fill. 'I can't thank you enough. I'll miss . . . everything and . . . everybody . . . excuse me, I'll have to go and pack.' She ran up the broad staircase, stumbling because of her tears.

He was there in the evening, freshly bathed, but quieter than usual, and she thought, paler, but then the heat was oppressive. During the meal he did not tease her as usual, and they all seemed to be subdued, only speaking of local matters, the state of the gardens because of the prolonged dry spell, the good hay crop, the necessity to get new mounts and put the old horses out to grass. 'I think your stepmother and I have lost our keenness nowadays,' Alastair said.

'Yes, I prefer the comfort of the carriage,' Maeve smiled at him. 'Those little jaunts of ours have been grand. I shan't soon forget them.'

'I'll never forget them,' Nigel said. He looked across the table at Lizzie.

When Redfern had gone away for the last time Alastair said, 'I've had this claret brought up.' He touched the bottle's silver coaster. 'My father laid it down twenty years ago.' He looked at his wife, 'We're going to have to say *au revoir* to our two young people soon. We should toast them.'

'At least Lizzie will be near.' She smiled at Nigel. 'And Oxford isn't so far either. You'll be driving here in your horseless carriage before long.'

'Perhaps.' His mouth was taut for a second then he was smiling and saying to her grandmother, 'When are you thinking of having your grand celebration?'

'My retirement party? Oh, dear, oh, dear . . .' She looked blooming. 'Around the middle of October, I think.

455

It seems the most suitable date for everyone, and the travellers would be home before the really bad weather starts. I hope they'll release you from your studies, Nigel. I want everyone there, all my family.' She smiled at him, turned to her husband, and Lizzie thought, she's happy. This party will be the high point of her life, not the end of it.

'Wild horses wouldn't keep me away,' Nigel said.

'I wonder if it's Lizzie who's the bigger attraction?'

'Lizzie!' He joked with her. 'It's you who'll be the belle of the ball, won't she, Lizzie?' The expression in his eyes alarmed her, as if he was begging for forgiveness.

He doesn't love me, she thought. The summer's over and our affair's over. I've been a dalliance for him merely, he hasn't meant any of those things he said, those caresses, the things he didn't say but which were in his eyes.

'Let's drink at least to our young people.' Alastair filled the glasses and passed them round. Lizzie sipped hers, then sipped again, feeling the effect of the smooth rich potency of the wine almost immediately. Anything to dull the pain of parting, and worse still the pain of not knowing, or did she know and was it rejection? She closed her eyes momentarily against that, a keener pain.

'Very fine,' Nigel said to his father, turning his glass in his hand, 'a good year.'

'Yes, indeed.' He savoured his own, two connoisseurs more interested in an old dusty bottle Nigel's grandfather had tucked away (he who had sold cheap whisky to the miners at a profit), than in her pain, her rejection. 'Have you seen the papers today?'

'No, I've been too busy.'

'Yes, Lizzie told me you were in Glasgow. Mr Chamberlain has authorized the despatch of ten thousand men to Natal.'

Nigel's face seemed to clear of its sternness. 'I'm not surprised. The Boer forces are collecting near the border. It's as good as started.' She tried to read his expression. His head seemed to go up. He looked . . . vindicated. Yes, that was the word. It couldn't be . . . no, she told herself, don't think anything like that. He wouldn't, without telling you. 'Instead of waiting for Sir George White's arrival they should get on with ordering reinforcements. It's too late for prevarications now. Too late . . .' He looked at Lizzie as he was speaking and yet she felt cut off from him.

'It's never too late, surely,' Maeve said. 'This is a lovely claret, Alastair.'

He seldom ignored her. 'Chamberlain missed his opportunity as far back as May.' He nodded to Nigel.

'When he authorized Milner to meet Kruger at Bloemfontein?'

'Yes. That's when the government should have thought out the course to be taken in case he turned down our proposals.' There was a roll of thunder as he spoke and the candles on the table flickered in a sudden gust of wind from the open french windows. Nigel got up and closed them.

'It's very sultry,' Maeve said. 'It makes me feel rather headachy.' She smiled her rich smile, 'and that's an unusual thing for *me* to say. But there's an . . . atmosphere.'

'Try some more claret,' Alastair lifted the decanter, 'guaranteed to banish headaches. You, Lizzie?'

'Yes, please.' She was wearing a thin silk dress, but the tight velvet cummerbund made her feel hot, and she felt as if a similar band was round her forehead. She had a headache, too. What was the difference between a headache and a dull presentiment? It had been there all day. She sipped and said, her voice sounding hysterical in her ears, 'It's all this talk about war, it's menacing . . . oh, how I've come to hate it!'

'Who doesn't?' Alastair's voice was drowned by a terrific clap of thunder. The room was brilliantly lit for a moment and then the rain was drumming, battering on the windows, fierce angry squalls which threatened to shatter them or blow them into the room.

'No walking tonight,' Nigel said.

'Let's go into the study. It's more . . .' Alastair was half on his feet when there was a blue-white bolt of lightning which lit up the room, followed by a loud, groaning crash and the sound of glass splintering near at hand. 'My God, it's a tree down!' she heard him say. Silhouetted against the shattered window was a great branch shining blackly in the teeming rain and the almost constant sheets of lightning. Glass lay all round the floor near the broken window, the gauze curtains with no protection now streaked out like pennants.

'Is anyone hurt?' They were all on their feet. 'Maeve? Lizzie?'

'Are you all right?' Nigel was beside her.

'Yes.' She was dazed. Her head was heavy, aching. She could not think clearly. 'Are you sure *you*'re all right, Grandma?' She looked shaken.

'Of course I am. What a good thing we have the table at this end of the room.'

'We'd better get out of here before something else happens.' Nigel put his arm round her. She saw Lord Crawford was shepherding her grandmother. They went into the hall where a frightened group of servants stood.

'The dining-room window's smashed, Redfern,' Lord Crawford said. 'What other damage?'

'It's the conservatory, sir. It took the full force of the elm. Praise be! Otherwise it would have been the front rooms. I always thought it was too near the house . . .'

'Were any of the gardeners there?'

Mrs Robertson spoke, her voice trembling, 'They were having their supper downstairs, sir, all of them . . . well, I think . . .'

'Drewie wasn't,' one of the maids said. 'He went to water the plants . . .' She put her hand to her mouth.

'Get downstairs again all of you,' Alastair said. 'Make sure it's only Drewie. Redfern, Thomas, come with master Nigel and me. We'll need . . .' Lizzie stood listening as he gave instructions. If only her brain would clear. It was not real . . .

She heard her grandmother's voice, the Irish lilt in it which always came back if she was disturbed. 'You and I are going, too. Jessie, get cloaks for us. And do what his lordship says after that. Get downstairs and send the other lads up.'

Lizzie felt a cloak put round her shoulders, automatically lifted the hood over her head and hurried out with her grandmother. The first shock of the rain and wind was like a benison. It cleared her head as if it blew through it. She was herself again, hurrying after the retreating figures of Nigel and his father going towards the conservatory, or what remained of it.

It led off the drawing-room. She had often admired its elegance, its wrought iron work from Walter MacFarlane of Saracen Street, Lord Crawford had told her, which was repainted pristine white each winter by one of the gardener's boys. She remembered Drewie, an awkward freckled lad with buck teeth and an anxious expression. His mother was a widow woman. She would have impressed upon him his good fortune to be working up at the Hall.

The trunk of the tree had fallen directly over the centre of the conservatory where it curved out in a graceful domed section. Here the tables and chairs of wrought iron were set and where they had tea, mostly in wet weather, but there had been so little this summer. 'It brings the garden into the house,' she remembered Grandma saying once.

'If anyone was in the middle of that they wouldn't stand a chance,' she heard her say. 'Will you look at that mess?'

The rain was drumming steadily, bouncing off the broken mass. In the occasional flash of lightning she could make out the bent girders, some sheets of glass clinging precariously to them, and on the ground, broken urns, their flowers and plants spilling out of them. The scarlet of the geraniums hurt her eyes. There was twisted iron, broken glass everywhere, making it difficult to walk.

'Watch your feet,' her grandmother said.

She could see Nigel and his father and the two men moving about in what remained of the interior, bending down from time to time to pull the wreckage aside. 'Can you manage, Grandma?'

'Of course I can.' They stepped over the low stone wall which had formed the base for the elegant windows with their cathedral arches. There were two of the gardener's boys standing respectfully behind them now, waiting their turn. 'On you go, lads.' And when they had jumped over, 'Do you know Drewie's mother? Mrs Morrison? She makes gey heavy work of her misfortunes. I hope this isn't going to be another one.'

The rain had soaked them to the skin long ago. Lizzie had let her hood fall back. It was good to feel clear-headed again, to be able to bend and search carefully (her eyes and ears were keener than her grandmother's although she wouldn't dare say that), sometimes crawling under shelves if she thought she saw a figure, a dark shadow. She put all her concentration to the task.

She found herself at the end nearest the lily pool where there had been staging for the orchids. Most of it was intact except one place where it had fallen in, a great, jagged plank rearing up diagonally. Orchids . . . didn't they take a lot of attention? Grandma had had the habit of going into her greenhouse sometimes in the evening at Braidholme. Maybe Drewie . . . she heard a low moan and then a voice like a child's although it had a rough adolescent timbre, 'Mammy, Mammy, get me oot . . .'

'Nigel!' she screamed, 'I've found him. He's here.'

They were all around her, Nigel first, even Grandmother was helping to tear away the planking to release the boy and then to lift him gently onto a bare piece of earth. Lizzie took off her cloak and laid it over him. She knelt down with her grandmother to tuck it round, to soothe him. He was moaning softly, 'Mammy, Mammy . . .' He would hardly be fourteen.

'Oh, I wish we had Maevy here,' her grandmother said, 'she would know . . .'

'Drewie,' Lizzy said, 'it's Miss Craigie from the manse. You're all right, don't worry.' She saw the boy's eyes flicker with recognition.

'Oh, Miss Craigie, ma leg's awfy sore . . .'

'Don't move. You'll soon be all right.' Nigel and Thomas had disappeared. Lord Crawford spoke. 'They're getting the carriage out. It's quicker than sending for Charlie.' He bent down and put his hand on one of the boy's.

'We'll take you to Dr McNab, Drewie. And we'll tell your mother. Don't worry. We'll soon fix you up. You're a brave lad.'

'Thankye, your lordship.' His hand went to his forelock, fell back again.

Two of the girls from the house were there with blankets, there was the sound of the carriage wheels on the gravel and Thomas saying, 'Whoa there, my beauties,' and then they were helping to lift the boy gently into the back seat of the carriage.

461

'I'll go with him,' Nigel said. 'If Dr McNab thinks it necessary, we'll drive him on to Crannoch Hospital.'

'Good,' his father said. When the carriage had rolled away he turned to Lizzie and her grandmother. 'You've lost your cloak, Lizzie.'

'It doesn't matter. D'you think he'll be all right?'

'It depends on his injuries. What do you think?' He turned to his wife.

'The right leg, maybe, There's nothing on his face . . .'

'The shelves were across his stomach when I saw him,' Lizzie said, 'they're heavy. And all those plant pots . . .'

'Well, let us hope there are no internal injuries. It was fortunate you found him so quickly. I should go back to the house now with your grandmother or you'll catch your death.'

'Aren't you coming?' Maeve asked him.

'No, there's a lot for me to do yet. On you go and both of you have a hot bath right away. It's an order.' He put his arm round Maeve for a moment and then he was picking his way over the broken pieces of staging towards the men. Lizzie noticed how badly he limped. 'It's worse when he's tired,' Grandmother had once said.

She said to Lizzie when they were back in the house, 'We're not going to sit down. It's men's work now. For once we'll do what we're told and get upstairs.' Mrs Robertson was hovering in the hall.

'Oh, you're baith fair drookit, your ladyship,' she said, coming forward.

'Water never hurt anyone. Get the girls to prepare baths for us, if you please. And tell one of them to bring up some hot milk. And, oh, Mrs Robertson, see that Mrs Morrison has company. She'll be right worried.'

'I'd rather wait till Nigel comes back,' Lizzie said when the housekeeper went scurrying downstairs.

'You'll do nothing of the kind. I don't want to send you

back to Isobel and John with pneumonia. Do what your grandmother tells you.' She put her arms round her, patted her back. 'Oh, lass, I can see how it is. I've been young, too.' She released her to look at her. 'Well, I tell you what, have your bath and get into bed with your hot milk and I'll do the same. Then when we hear them coming in we can slip down, maybe . . .'

'Oh, Grandma,' she said, 'I'm so miserable . . . he's going away.'

'He'll be back, my lovely. And who wouldn't be miserable if they'd been soaked to the skin? Off you go, now.'

She did as she had been told. She lay in the warm water, the tears running constantly down her face as she sponged it, sponged it again to mop them, got into the clean warm nightgown that had been left by the fire for her, got into bed and lay in the firelight, sipping the warm milk, the tears gone now except for a quivering sob or two. It was quiet now with the storm gone, a greater quietness than usual on those summer nights. There was no sound from the front of the house where the men would still be working. It was too far away. Poor Drewie, she thought, I hope he has got his Mammy beside him.

There would be no walk by the Sholtie tonight, maybe any night, maybe never. But she would listen very carefully, lie quietly and strain her ears. It would take ten minutes to drive to Uncle Charlie's, then if they had to drive to Crannoch Hospital, another twenty minutes at least. Ten minutes there arranging for poor Drewie . . . it would all take at least an hour and a half. There was consolation in realizing that half an hour had been spent in bathing. She would lie quietly imagining Nigel driving through the night, having seen to Drewie, maybe saying to Thomas, 'Faster!', the dark countryside, soaking black with rain, sleeping . . . she would listen for the sound of the carriage coming rolling up the drive, the crackling noise as the wheels spun over the gravel, slower, slower, wheels over the gravel, wheels over the gravel, wheels over the . . . she slept.

When she went hurrying downstairs in the morning, he had gone. There was a note at her place, a thick cream envelope of the Hall stationery. She tore it open, read the few words. 'I had to go early. Love you, always will, Nigel.'

She looked up. Lord Crawford was steadily reading his morning paper. Grandmother was as usual beautifully turned out in her morning gown, the ribbons fresh, her hair still like a flame. Lizzie was aware of her own hastily-brushed head . . . 'you have to take care when you get to my age,' she had once said.

'Are you both all right after last night?' she asked them, love in her voice.

21

Braidholme was full, the way Maeve would have liked to see it had she still been there. Kate, James and Kieran had arrived two days ago, the docking of their ship hardly noticed in all the excitement of Sir Redver Buller's triumphant departure from Southampton Docks in the *Dunottar Castle*.

Kruger had sent his reckless ultimatum and Chamberlain had landed his fish, as Charlie said. Talk about the War took precedence even over the forthcoming ball at the Hall to celebrate Maeve's retirement from the McGrath Carting Company.

'We've certainly chosen an exciting time to come,' Kieran said, 'as well as being my birthday month.' He was now twenty-one.

'Don't tell me you're more excited about the War than your grandmother's ball?' Maevy teased him. She was glad of their visit if only that it kept her from dwelling on what to her was a disaster.

She had taken to this true son of Kate and James on her visit to America, so like her memory of her own father with his curls and gentle smile. Now as a young man he had more assurance, but the same charm was there. He had followed his step-brothers to Yale, and now he would probably spend a year abroad before settling in to a job.

He was different from Nigel with an easiness which was possibly the result of his American schooling and his parents' attitude. Nigel tended to be formal in company like his father. You had to pierce his shell.

Lizzie had done that. She would know a different Nigel from any of them. It was easy to see she was in love. When she and Maevy had gone to buy their gowns for the ball to 'dear old Walter Wilson's', she had noticed a new maturity in the girl. She had always been young for her age. They had kept her young at the manse, perhaps deliberately. And a new reticence. She never spoke about Nigel, but when Maevy asked her if he would be home, she was surprised at her intensity. 'Oh, he'll be there. I know it!'

Charlie called him a dark young man, saying that Kieran was an open, Nigel a closed, book, but that some of his reserve had rubbed off on Lizzie, and perhaps a maturity.

If so it had certainly helped her when she had gone back to the manse. She had thrown herself into the parochial work and spoke kindly of her adoptive parents as if the fact of her parentage had ceased to trouble her. 'Father needs some help, he's so hard-working,' and, 'Mother isn't strong enough to go to Glasgow now, Maevy. She's having her gown made by Miss Thomson at Crannoch. She comes and fits her at the house.'

Braidholme was bursting at the seams with children. Honor and Terence's five, no less. There was to be a party for the young ones from five to eight o'clock on the night of the ball, but the older children could stay on. Robert and Moira would be eligible for that.

Robert and Kieran hit it off immediately, and were soon away for long walks together along the tow-path of the Sholtie, no doubt discussing life and its perplexities, as Honor said. 'He's a serious lad, Robert, not at all like his father,' she laughed at Terence, 'and he's anxious to get to Trinity now he's eighteen. He'll be picking Kieran's brains.'

'Sure and he does a lot of tapping yours, too,' Terence said. His eyes rested fondly on her.

'If ever there was a happy marriage,' Maevy said to Charlie later, 'there it is. Honor is right for Terence, strong-willed but womanly.'

'And passionate,' Charlie added. 'That dark Irish beauty and those full red lips hold promises for a man. Now, don't flash those eyes at me, my sweetheart, it's an academic observation only.'

She laughed. 'He's so proud of her writing, and how she's beginning to be noticed. He sees she gets time to go to her study every day. And in between he's building up a nice little stable, he tells me.'

'The picture of a man who's made safe harbour before he's too old to appreciate it,' Charlie said. 'And since he's always been a ladies' man, what could be nicer than to have three admiring young ladies running to ask his advice, teasing, seducing him with their glances . . . haven't you noticed?'

She laughed. 'Moira's only fifteen, for goodness sake, Dymphna two years younger and that adorable Clare a year younger than that!'

'They're never too young. Didn't you capture my heart at sixteen?'

Maevy, Honor and Kate had time for some womanly talk in spite of the children who went careering about the house all day. Susan, given an extra girl from the village to do the washing up, spent a lot of her time dashing in and out of the kitchen. 'Will ye haud your wheesht? Your folks need some peace!' The whole thing took years off her age.

'You like your writing?' Maevy asked Honor when they were having tea the day before the ball.

'Yes, to be sure. Something of my own, you see. We

467

come together at night, Terence and I, bringing new ideas to each other.'

'"Something for yourself," my mother once said. I loved nursing, but that finishes with marriage. I should have had half a dozen children to rear instead.'

'Children aren't everything. Never feel deprived. It's a temporary happiness as far as they're concerned.'

'I wouldn't say that.' Calm Kate, Maevy thought, with her serene, beautiful face and the wing of grey new in her dark, still abundant hair.

'The caring, I mean. They break away soon enough. They slough you off.'

'Not altogether,' Kate said, smiling.

'Ah, you're a stickler for accuracy! Physically, then. And then what? Husband? What if he's away all day? Lover? Well, that's not to everybody's taste. Don't despair, Maevy. Something extra will come along for you, if you feel you need it.'

'What if your husband's away more than all day?' She voiced her fear. 'Goes to the War, for instance?'

'Ah, I never had that problem, sure enough, but I'll tell you one thing, for any full-blooded intelligent woman, children are never enough, even when like me you couldn't pretend to be sorry when your husband died.'

Kate said, 'I've never had the slightest notion to do anything else than look after my family. Like Maevy, I should have liked more. But now that George and Ernest have left home, the girls before that, and Kieran soon, it only brings James and me closer, gives us more time together.'

'Ah, but you're an angel come down from heaven!' Honor said laughing.

'Not me. Just a contented woman. James is getting on now. Sometimes he has a longing to come back to Scotland. Maybe being here will intensify it.'

'He's got as many Scottish relatives over there,' Maevy said. She laughed, 'Can you see Aunt Caroline fluttering round Lord Crawford like a butterfly?'

Kate laughed. 'It would have been worse if he'd had Emily to cope with. Mother always says she's like a bright little humming-bird.'

'I'm only sorry George and his wife and Ernest couldn't have been here.'

'Abigail thought it was too far to bring the children, and Ernest will be coming to McGraths here in January. It would have been too close.'

'Isobel was willing to take last-minute guests. Even Victoria and Jason.'

'They'd never travel with their brood, nor would they leave them at home. Perhaps it's as well. Isobel looks very frail. It must have been difficult for Lizzie when she found out they were her aunt and uncle . . .' They fell to talking about Lizzie.

But at the dinner table that night the talk was all about the war, as was to be expected.

'I suppose it's always the way,' Charlie said, 'when something which has been hanging over us for ages eventually happens, we can't believe it. "There's no difference," we say, and we go on saying it until we hear of the casualties and the loss of lives and the poor hospital equipment, and the lack of doctors and the general unpreparedness . . .' Maevy listened to him. Now that it's here, she thought, how long will he be able to keep out of it?

'They tell me doctors are in short supply,' Terence said, 'like everything else.' He had begun to resemble his uncle, which was the same as saying, his mother, except that he had his uncle's florid complexion, not his mother's paleness.

'When was it ever anything else?' Charlie said. 'It

469

breaks one's heart to think of young lads sorely wounded, or with enteric fever, lying waiting for attention in some forward base.'

'Surely amongst all that paraphernalia on the troopship there would be plenty of room for some hospital equipment,' James said, 'or doctors, for that matter.' His voice had a definite American twang now, his hair was lint-white at the front, his face long and lined. He spoke and looked like an elder statesman. 'War correspondents. That young Winston Churchill with his polo sticks. Can you ever fathom the English, Charlie, polo sticks at a war? I can understand Sir Redver's war horses, but not his piano. His piano!' He looked round the table at the laughing faces, his own wry with amusement.

'There was a picture of him in the *Glasgow Herald*,' Charlie said, 'standing on the gang-plank of the *Dunottar Castle*. Dressed in dark coat and felt hat. No, it's not a laughing matter. He'll be a very worried man, even in his mufti. He'll have to pay the price, like so many. And Chamberlain will have to paper over the cracks.'

Terence, Maevy noticed, sat silent, neutral, as indeed he was. Oh, my lucky brother, you moved to Ireland at the right time, she thought.

22

Lizzie went with her parents to the ball in fear and trembling, the trembling of delight. She would see Nigel. He had written twice from Oxford, short letters saying he was very busy but that she was never out of his thoughts. He could hardly wait till he saw her again.

In the last one he had said, 'I've been reading quite a lot of poetry, strange for me. I came across one with these lines, "I would not love thee, dear, so much, loved I not honour more." It has stayed with me. Some day I'll copy all of it out and send it to you, and instead of calling you Lizzie, I'll call you "Lucasta".'

She had never heard of the poem. It was useless to search in her father's study for a copy of it. There was nothing secular there, only heavy tomes, Howeis' *Testament for the use of Families and Private Christians*, Carlyle's *Essays*, several famous sermons by doughty ministers of bygone eras.

'I hope the dinner doesn't go on too long,' Isobel said. 'The food and the talk can be tiring . . .'

'The table will be groaning, my dear, and there will be lots of talk.' John was sitting across from them in the carriage, spruced up in his best frock-coat which was beginning to look a bit rusty through yeoman service. He liked 'affairs' as he called them.

He's looking forward to taking part in it, Lizzie thought. Her mother's frailty seemed to have made him more rumbustious, rosy-cheeked, large-framed. He seemed to swell and fill his frame as she shrunk in hers.

'It will be mostly about the War, I imagine,' Isobel said.

'Ah, well, I can lend my support to that in no uncertain terms,' he drew himself up, 'and that of the Church. We have to show those natives who is supreme. We can't allow ourselves to be bullied by an old Dutch farmer, "Oom Paul", as they call him. The might of the British Empire cannot be tampered with.'

'He's tweaked the lion's tail at least,' Lizzie said.

'Now, that's in poor taste, Lizzie.' He looked reproving. 'I trust you won't make remarks of that kind at the dinner table.'

'Lizzie knows hows to conduct herself as well as the rest of them although she'll be with the highest in the land.' Isobel had an exaggerated idea of aristocracy, and never forgot to mention to callers that her mother was Lady Crawford of the Hall. It was her one small vice, and Lizzie was touched by it.

Her animosity, and even her resentment towards her adoptive parents had gone. What did it matter now that they had shielded her from the truth for so long? They had had their own good reasons. She would be going away from the manse soon. She would be with Nigel. This was just a waiting time.

And, as well, there would be the meeting with her real father and Uncle Patrick tonight. The thought did not embarrass her. When she and Nigel were married, when he had finished at Oxford and had found himself a good job, perhaps managing his father's estate, they would visit together in Ireland and America. The future opened out in front of her, full of interest, full of love. She turned to Isobel in the fulness of that love, 'You look beautiful tonight, Mother. You and Miss Thomson made a wise choice with that shot silk.'

'Do you think so?' Isobel smiled her pale smile, touched

472

her pale hair. She had chosen silver-grey taffeta. With her pearls and her wan face she looked like a sad grey ghost. 'I thought it would be very serviceable afterwards with a lace fichu to cover the low neckline. For best, of course.' Where was the tart mother she used to know as a young child in this pale subservient creature?

'I was hoping you weren't thinking of wearing it as it is,' John said, 'you'd shock my parishioners.'

'Oh, John,' Isobel said, 'as if I would.'

'How do you like *my* gown, Father?' Lizzie asked him, deliberately daring. It was of violet mousseline-de-soie, her shoulders bare, the skirt caught up at intervals with velvet bunches of violets to reveal a lace frilled underskirt.

He gave her a reproving but wholly masculine look. 'I imagine your Aunt Maevy and your grandmother had quite a hand in the choice. The colour's vastly becoming with your hair, I will say that, but the bare shoulders . . . of course, I'm no judge of what's what, a poor country parson.'

'She will be amongst the richest and smartest in the land and you know the standard Lady Crawford sets as regards dress.' Isobel spoke as if her mother had become a stranger.

'I've known that since I was a young man,' her husband said. 'My congregation took more notice of Mrs McGrath coming down the aisle than they did of my sermons.'

'That might have been a reflection on your sermons,' Isobel said. There was a dead silence in the carriage for a second and then she was saying, supplicatingly, 'I'm only teasing, John. It's because of my nerves.'

'I should hope so.' He looked out of the window. It would be a few minutes before his *amour propre* was restored.

As they were rolling up the long drive another carriage came towards them. The two coachmen slowed down to pass each other. There were balloons flying from the open window of the other one, and Lizzie could see the excited face of Ellie at the window. 'There's Ellie!' she said. 'Oh, she'll be mad at having to go home early.'

'Lizzie!' Ellie was hanging half-out. 'Look, my Irish cousins.' She gesticulated backwards. Lizzie could see two pretty faces behind her. They would be Dymphna and Clare. Moira was old enough to stay on. 'Fourteen upwards,' Grandma had said firmly.

'Did you have a good time?' she called. The coachman had obligingly stopped to permit the interchange.

'Oh, the trifle and meringues!' Ellie looked ecstatic. 'And a puppet man! And balloons! This is Gaylord from America!' She saw a thin young boy hanging back shyly. No longer Uncle Patrick's and Aunt Maria's youngest, she thought, now that Virginia had taken the place of Mary.

'Drive on, coachman,' John said. 'We're blocking the driveway.'

'Good-bye, good-bye!' The children waved enthusiastically, following Ellie's example, their hands fluttering until they were out of sight round the bend.

'Susan will have her hands full tonight,' Isobel said.

'Oh, I think she's quite capable of handling them.' Lizzie sat back in her seat, laughing, 'What a lass Ellie is!'

'I sometimes think Charlie and Maevy are a sight too lenient with her,' John said. 'Spare the rod and spoil the child.' Maybe it's as well I wasn't a boy, Lizzie thought.

'Susan will watch that,' Isobel said. 'Even when Lady Crawford was at Braidholme, she ran the show.'

'The McGraths are Susan's life,' Lizzie agreed. 'She's like the chorus at the feast.' Sometimes she wondered where her thoughts came from, or her words.

* * *

474

Lord and Lady Crawford were standing to receive their dinner guests in the drawing-room. How truly regal Grandma was in her bronze gown and those golden orchids on her low corsage . . . *cataylas*, the French word came to her. There would be no complaints from *her* husband about its lowness, nor her bare shoulders. And how handsome he was in his spare elegance, leaning on his silver-knobbed stick, black frock-coat, dazzling white linen, white-gloved, his smart grey moustache and side-whiskers. Lizzie had eyes for no one else but them for the first minute or two, only knew that there were others standing about in groups, talking, that Redfern and Jessie and Cathy were circulating with silver trays of glasses.

'Grandma,' she said, kissing her, 'you look beautiful . . . like a queen.'

'Dear wee Lizzie.' Maeve hugged her, her eyes brightly blue, her pale skin luminous. And that delicious scent she wore. Lord Crawford sent specially to France for it.

'Lizzie, my dear.' He bent to greet her. 'You'll turn her head. But much as I admire our dear queen, I won't have your grandmother compared with her. Shall we say that they are both in their way unique?'

'She's a dumpy wee wife,' Lizzie whispered in his ear, and he laughed delightedly.

'Mother . . .' Isobel was saying beside her. Her voice trembled. She was already wilting. Lizzie put an arm comfortingly round her.

'I feel I could crush you to bits.' Maeve kissed her fondly. 'Doesn't she look lovely, John? She was always my prettiest girl. You must be proud of her.' She offered him her cheek.

'Indeed I am. And glad when the gown was finished. Two parish meetings had to be cancelled last week because the dining-room was occupied by Miss Thomson cutting and pingling all day long . . .'

'Lizzie!' She turned and it was Uncle Terence, no, not Uncle Terence, her real father. His eyes were shining with love, he was handsome, boyish. 'Lizzie . . .' he said again, and took her in his arms, hugged her as a father would, or should. How natural, she thought. And now it was his wife's turn, beautiful, as if she had brought Ireland with her, laughing, exclaiming, their eyes moist. She basked in their love.

'We could hardly wait to see you,' Terence said, passing his hand over his eyes, but smiling. 'We think of you as part of our family. Isn't that so, Honor?'

'Sure, it is so, but maybe the girl doesn't want to be part of any family,' Honor said. They helped themselves to the sherry which Redfern was offering them. She would sip slowly this time, she wanted to be fully in command of her senses when she met Nigel, not like on the night of the storm when she had fallen asleep instead of staying awake for him coming back. 'Indeed,' Honor was saying, 'the revelation, if that was what it was, came at the right time. She's now herself, isn't that the way of it, Lizzie?'

Lizzie met the girl's dark eyes, thinking how wise she was. Maybe that was why she wrote books.

'Yes,' she said, 'it released me,' and looking around, 'Don't tell me this is just our family!'

'Nearly all,' Terence said, smiling, 'we've certainly spread a bit since my mother and father came from Ireland. There are twenty-six for dinner, I believe, only one on Lord Crawford's side, and that by marriage, too, his unmarried sister-in-law from Wiltshire, Miss Sinclair. Over there . . .' She half-turned to see a stick of a woman talking to two couples, recognized them as Tom Johnson and his wife, Bob Carter with his, both men probably the same age as Grandma but looking years older. They must be on the point of retirement as well if they had not already gone. 'You know who she's talking to, the two stalwarts of McGraths, bless them.'

'I used to call them my uncles when I was small.'

'And Lord Crawford's son is here. I spoke to him earlier.'

'Did you?' She tried to be non-committal as she searched the room for him.

'That's Dan Johnson,' Terence was saying, 'Tom's son, he's in the business now. A grand young man. Talking to two young girls, yes, there, the Carters' only unmarried ones . . . And that little beauty talking to Robert is Moira, Honor's eldest. Did you ever see the like of that?' He turned to Honor. 'Comes all the way from Ireland to meet strange folks and ends up talking to her step-brother.'

'They're both a bit nervous, bless them. Now if it had been Clare . . .'

'Don't you think Moira has the look of her mother all the same, Lizzie?' Terence asked.

'Just as beautiful,' she said, smiling at Honor.

'Oh, we're ten a penny in Ireland, us dark ones. You come and see for yourself and you'll knock them all sideways. The men there get tired of dark eyes and dark hair.'

She had seen him. Oh, the joy of it, tall, spare, the dashing brown moustache where his father's was grey, the same narrow head, the same way of bending slightly forward as he listened, my Nigel . . . 'Who's that Nigel's talking to in the blue dress?' She tried to sound casual.

'It's Sarah, Patrick's girl. I'm not surprised you didn't recognize her. She's sixteen and a young lady now. A serious girl, but sweet with it . . . oh, there you are, Patrick.' His brother had joined them, 'We're just admiring your Sarah, a lovely young lady she's become.'

'Yes, she's opened out in America. We've been looking

477

for you, Lizzie.' He kissed her, almost shyly. My serious uncle who was my father for a short time . . . it all seemed remote, unimportant now. 'And here's your aunt.'

Maria embraced her fondly. How well she looked now compared with the drawn woman she had known when Mary was alive. But there was the same straight glance and the love in it. 'I've longed for this meeting, Lizzie. We've talked and talked about you. Oh, it was such a relief to us when we knew that you knew . . .' She laughed. She wasn't going to say anything against Isobel and John. 'How like Aunt Maeve you've grown, hasn't she, Patrick?'

'Darker in the hair a bit, more copper, maybe, but despite the likeness, her own self.'

Terence and Honor had moved on. She looked through the space they had left towards Nigel and Sarah, and this time he turned and saw her. Their eyes held, he smiled, half-raising his hand, and then he was bending towards Sarah again. Was he making his excuses? Her heart beat rapidly, 'Come, come . . .'

The space was filled by Grandma's brother and his wife, one jolly, the other fluttery in her white organdie with white satin bows and rosebuds sewn in their centres *and* a corsage of rosebuds, and no, no, it *could*n't be, a rose in her hair from which ascended a tall osprey feather which waved as she talked . . .

'Dear wee Lizzie! How you've grown! Oh, the joy to see you again. Do you remember that day we went to Wanapeake Point? You on bicycles. Isn't she the image of your sister, Terence, but there's something else, something . . .' she pursed her little rouged mouth.

'Something of Lizzie herself, dear heart. Now isn't this a great day for us, a great day to be sure, except that it's evening?' He threw back his head and laughed.

478

'It's wonderful that you were able to make the trip, Great-aunt. I know you rather dreaded sea-travel.'

'I can't *tell* you the agonies I suffered!' Her face crumpled at the thought and Lizzie saw the powder lying thickly in the folds round her mouth and eyes, 'and then the joy and delight when I found I was seaborne and actually sailing on the Atlantic! The captain couldn't have been kinder. He placed us at his table.'

'He practically held her hand the whole voyage,' Terence said with another roar of laughter, 'and I was madly jealous . . .'

'Good evening, Lizzie.' He was there, standing politely beside them, bowing, kissing Aunt Caroline's hand. He kissed her formally and his nearness made her feel faint.

'We were just saying how like Lizzie is to your step-mother,' Terence said, shaking Nigel vigorously by the hand, 'Do you agree?'

'Yes and no,' he said. His amber eyes were on her, smiling, seeing further than they. I know a different Lizzie, one who has lain in my arms . . .

'Just my words, Nigel. She's Lizzie, first and foremost.'

'Oh, do stop talking about me!' she said laughing, full of happiness now. 'When did you arrive, Nigel?'

'An hour or so ago. Just time to have a chat with Father then get bathed and dressed for the great occasion.'

'Did you have a good journey?' She wanted to keep him at her side, to look at him, to refresh her memory of his features. Was it her imagination or were there marks of fatigue round his eyes? They seemed more deeply set and the golden skin was muddy under them. Had he been burning the midnight oil? He would want good results in his examination before he left Balliol.

'Yes. I scarcely noticed it. My mind was full . . .' He looked deliberately at her and she could have gone into

479

his arms, been enclosed in them, forgotten the rest of the world.

Redfern was at the door with a gong. She heard his voice above the hubbub of people talking, laughing. 'Dinner is served.'

'Ah, good,' Terence said. 'I thought they'd never announce it.' He laughed. 'May I escort you, Lizzie, and there you are, Nigel, my wife's dying to have a young man from Oxford, England, do the same for her.'

'It's my pleasure.' He held out his arm and Caroline took it, fluttery, opening and shutting her fan, laughing with that nervous little laugh of hers which always ended by her seeking her husband's eyes as if for reassurance. What would she do if he died? Lizzie thought. She put her hand through Great-uncle Terence's arm and they went in to dinner.

The table was beautiful, complementing the panelled room, the tall golden candlesticks, the golden épergne piled high with fruit. The flowers were gold-coloured, orchids like those worn by Maeve, the napkins of golden damask. Lizzie noticed people's heads nodding together in admiration. 'Grandma's taste shows in everything,' she said to Terence.

'Ah, yes, it's a natural thing with her. Some have it, some haven't.' His eyes rested fondly on his wife sitting directly opposite him in her white organdie and her white satin bows, the osprey feather nodding as she spoke to Nigel. Beauty is in the eye of the beholder. As it is in mine.

She turned at a touch on her arm, exclaimed, 'It's Kieran! I hadn't noticed you.'

'I thought you were cutting me dead . . .' He put a finger to his lips, 'Shh . . .' Lord Crawford was saying grace.

She was genuinely glad to see him. 'How are you?

480

You've changed. Remember all those letters I wrote to you? You must have got tired of them.'

'No, I kept them. I hope you kept mine.' They teased each other but her eyes rarely left Nigel.

'Lord Crawford's son and I are roughly the same age, I believe,' he said, and she knew she had been indiscreet.

'You were just twelve when I last saw you and absolutely disgusted at Ernest's swank. How is he? Oh, he made me laugh so much.' She had loved him a little, she thought, a passing love.

'He's the same, very man-about-town, a real city gent, but still great fun. You'll see him when he arrives next year. He's doing a great job for McGraths already, Patrick says.' His gentle gaze was on her. 'Why did you stop writing to me, Lizzie?'

'I expect I grew up. Life became . . . real.' Her eyes strayed again.

'Do you still admire Nigel Crawford? You once wrote that he looked like a musical comedy star.'

'Did I? What do you think?' She was shameless. Nigel's head was bent as he listened politely to Great-aunt Caroline. The difference between her fluttering and her pouting and Kieran's mother on his other side was striking. How *complete* she was as she listened to Bob Carter, how he expanded in her presence. 'Kate was always the success of the family,' Grandma had once said. I'm so lucky to be a McGrath, she thought, her eyes going to Nigel again.

This time he had turned his head and was looking straight at her. She had seen that look before at the ruined monastery when sometimes he got up on one elbow to gaze down at her, not speaking, as if he was . . . committing her to memory? Why should she think that?

'Yes, he's very handsome,' Kieran said. She turned and saw the wryness in his smile. Not so gentle.

She realized people had stopped talking, that Lord Crawford was on his feet at the head of the table.

'May I presume on your patience for a few moments on this auspicious occasion?' he was saying, totally at ease as he looked smilingly round the table. Grandma sat at his side, composed, her head high with that beautiful flame-coloured hair in a long shining wave above her brow, its bulk dressed high round her head like an aureole, her topaz earrings glittering as she turned this way and that to include everyone in her rich curving smile.

23

'I would like to welcome you all to our table tonight.' Alastair looked round his guests, smiling. 'With her usual sense of the dramatic, my dear wife has chosen the outbreak of hostilities against the Boers to celebrate her retirement from the McGrath Carting Company, but maybe that's a good augury, and the war will be of short duration.' He hesitated, 'I've a special reason for hoping that.' He's worried about Crawfords, Lizzie told herself, but surely iron and steel would be needed?

'I'm a comparative newcomer to the family, so to speak,' he was smiling again, 'but over the years I've watched McGrath's prosper, thanks to my wife and her late husband, Kieran, a man beloved by all. It has become a world-wide name. There are branches in Scotland and in London, and her son, Patrick, is extending the company on the other side of the world. But I think he and the rest of the family would be the first to admit that the success of the firm is due largely to their mother's efforts.'

Everyone clapped enthusiastically. Lizzie looked at her grandmother. She was not the type to hang her head meekly. She sat, smiling, self-composed, but without arrogance. Only someone who knew her own worth could look like that.

'Here, here!' That was her brother.

'Many of you have come from far afield to join us tonight, and I bid you a special welcome. There's my sister-in-law from Wiltshire,' he smiled at the thin spinster who bowed frostily – did she feel she was amongst the heathen here, Lizzie wondered . . . 'my wife's brother

and his wife from America' – Caroline fluttered her fan
. . . oh, those huge gigot sleeves above her bony arms –
'also Patrick and his wife whom most of you know, and of
course, Kate with her husband and son. Then we have
Terence and Honor from Ireland and their combined
families. Honor is a distant relative, and she and Terence
live in my wife's childhood home which seems to me . . .
fitting.' He smiled round at Maeve.

'But I haven't finished yet. Nearer home we have some
of the valued senior members of the firm, Tom Johnson
and Bob Carter, both with their wives and families. I had
strict instructions that they had on no account to be left
out because my wife has always regarded them as members of the family and says the firm could never have
prospered without them.'

'Here, here!' That was Patrick, possibly emboldened by
Terence. Lizzie looked at the grey heads of Tom and
Bob, so long her honorary uncles, bent modestly.

'Indeed, it seems my son, Nigel, my sister-in-law, Miss
Sinclair, and my humble self, are the only incomers here
tonight. I hope we'll not be labelled as gate-crashers and
shown the door!' There was a roar of laughter.

'But should I have to give a reason for being included
tonight, I'm certainly in a position to speak of the
managing director's qualities as I know them, her strength
of character, her grace, her sense of fun, and not least of
all, her beauty. You've all heard of the expression,
"beauty and brains". Ladies and gentlemen, sitting beside
me tonight is the living embodiment of that saying.'

'Oh, Alastair, that's too much!' Maeve waved her hand
deprecatingly.

'I'm embarrassing her, but there's one further attribute
I must pay her. She has brought happiness to my life
when I'd told myself it was too late to expect it.' Lizzie
saw the look which passed between them. How wise

Grandma had been to marry him. She could well have remained at Braidholme, a devoted grandmother to an ever-increasing family, but she's always wanted to go on. What will we do when she goes? She felt the imagined pain of her loss for a second, swift and keen.

'Who, then,' Lord Crawford was saying, 'is best able to express all that's in our hearts? Many of you could, I'm sure, but there's someone here who's known her longer than anyone else, someone who's travelled a long way to be here tonight, and I'm hoping to ask him to propose a toast to her. Her brother, Mr Terence Muldoon of Springhill, Wallace Point, New York State, America!'

He sat down to vigorous applause and immediately Terence was on his feet beside Lizzie, florid, jolly, hair still the colour of his sister's, even if it was only a circlet of sparse curls round his bald pate.

'I won't pretend,' he looked around, 'to be bowled over at finding myself on my own two legs. When Lord Crawford wrote to Caroline, my dear wife, and myself, inviting us to be present on this grand occasion, he warned me. "I shall expect a speech from you," he said, "so don't say I haven't given you due notice."' He smiled. 'You see how truthful I am.' There was a ripple of laughter.

'Well, I took the task very seriously at first. Wonderful eulogies were composed by the midnight oil, and torn up. They just didn't suit my sister, Maeve, at all. She's no plaster saint, never has been, she's warm, lovely, alive, so I decided just to speak from the heart and sure enough it's a full heart I have here tonight.' He looked across at Maeve and there were murmurs of understanding all round.

'My memory of Maeve Muldoon is of a harum-scarum little girl in Ireland with long red plaits who was mad about horses, like our father. You can see something of her in Lizzie here beside me.' She moved shyly in her seat

...nd met Nigel's eyes. He was smiling at her. 'And also in young Ellie who's been packed off to bed, maybe tied down, because she was dying to come tonight. That capacity for living life to its full, for meeting it head on, for belief in her opinions and herself – that's my sister.

'I left home early to seek my fortune in America, my sister a few years later with Kieran McGrath, one of the finest men who ever breathed, and that's with no disrespect to our host. I know best Kate who has lived beside us for many years with her husband and family, and it resides in her in full abundance.' Kate looked at her plate and Lizzie saw James put his hand over hers.

'Maeve, my sister, gave up a lot when she eloped to Scotland with young Kieran McGrath – there, your secret's out, mavourneen,' he smiled at her across the table, 'maybe not money for we were a penurious lot, but position. She stepped out of her class, one of the oldest families in the west of Ireland.' He looked towards the head of the table, put that in your pipe and smoke it, Lord Crawford, Lizzie thought.

'For the first part of her life she had to bring up a family on little money, she had to perform all the mundane tasks we accept willingly, and maybe wrongly, from our servants. But as soon as she could, her fertile brain was looking for a way to get her husband up from the mine which was slowly killing him, and find it she did with the inception of the McGrath Carting Company.

'You all know the rest of the story. She has not become a dragon although she has had to compete with men on their own territory. She's kept her femininity although she was a pioneer. Her beauty and her humour despite the many sadnesses in her life, kept her the same high-spirited girl who left Woodlea in Ireland so long ago. And isn't it fitting that her son, Terence, today occupies that self-same house with his wife and children?

'Charge your glasses, if you please.' He lifted his own with a flourish, 'I ask you to be upstanding and drink a toast to Lady Crawford, and the young girl who's still there, Maeve Muldoon.'

Everyone was on their feet. 'Maeve Muldoon!' Lizzie raised her own glass, saw Lord Crawford toasting his wife as she sat smiling and bowing. I'll keep that picture in my mind for ever, she thought. 'Maeve Muldoon!' She clinked glasses with Kieran, then with her great-uncle. 'Maeve Muldoon!' She sought Nigel's eyes and they were on her. She did not know if she said the word, or shaped it with her lips, 'Soon . . .'

Her grandmother had risen. She stood erect, waiting until the talk and the laughter had subsided, smiling in her gold-coloured gown, the dark fur trimming showing up the whiteness of her shoulders, her face pale but seeming to be lit from within. 'This is . . . the grandest day in my life.' Her voice broke. 'Thank you, thank you all.' Everyone clapped, went on clapping. She made to sit down but her husband stopped her, whispered in her ear. She said, laughing, 'He says I'm not getting off so easily.'

'Quite right, too,' someone shouted.

Her eyes searched. 'A long time ago I stood up at my brother's table. Do you remember, Terence? It was Isobel's twenty-first dance . . . where are you, Isobel?'

'Here, Mother!' She looked more animated than she had been when she came.

'What a picture she was that night, still is. But I regret to say I got carried away by the sound of my own voice.'

'Never!' Terence called.

'Oh, yes. Well, I'm not going to make that mistake tonight and blot my copybook, not after I've been made out to be such a paragon of virtue by my dear husband,' she looked down at him, and then across the table to Terence, 'and my very dear brother. In any case my heart is too full for words. I can only repeat what I said at the beginning, thank you all sincerely for coming here.' She paused for a second. 'I felt when I left Ireland with Kieran I was doing the right thing. Now when I look around the table I'm sure of it. And I was sure of it this afternoon watching the children play. My progeny, I thought. What a grand word that is for something which was started by that young couple long ago who stole down a dark drive in the middle of the night . . . yes, Terence told the truth.' She smiled at him.

'But McGraths, as was said earlier, is always expanding, and now we've made inroads on the Crawford family!' There was a burst of laughter. 'I've acquired in the process a dear husband and an upright young stepson I'm proud of. I count myself a fortunate woman, ill-deserved, but I'm not going to quarrel with that. Providence has been very kind to give me a companion for the latter part of my journey. I'm grateful, and we both thank you for being with us to share our joy tonight.' She sat down to applause which went on for several minutes.

'She's wonderful,' Kieran said. He was still clapping enthusiastically. 'Now I see what Mother means. There's an . . . enchantment which you rarely see in people.' He looked at Lizzie. 'You have it.'

'Oh, away with you!' She was pleased.

Lord Crawford was on his feet again, holding up his hand for silence. 'I think they may be waiting for us to start the Grand March. I believe I can even hear the strains of the Crannoch Ensemble from here. The ball goes on until four in the morning which may surprise some of you from across the water, but here in Sholton we've had stamina drummed into us as well as deportment. We know how to "lift oor pairtners" politely, not as one old man is supposed to have said "as if ye were drawin' a hog oot o' a ditch"!' There was a roar of laughter, as much at the capacity of Lord Crawford to speak the vernacular as at the quality of the joke. 'By God, that's a good one,' Lizzie heard Terence say. Nigel bent forward to her, signalling with his eyes. She could hear him clearly with the noise around them. 'May I *lift* you for the Grand March?' She nodded, happiness flooding through her.

She noticed Lord Crawford was still on his feet. His face had changed. People fell silent, looking at him. 'My wife says since we're all one family, it's right that I should make this announcement.' He looked around the table. 'Even on happy occasions like this, the War which has come upon us so suddenly and yet not so suddenly if we think of it, pushes to the forefront. My son, Nigel, brought me news today which didn't surprise me as much as he thought it would. I was proud, but sad. He has just heard that he is to join his regiment tomorrow morning.' There was rustling and murmuring all round. 'I'd like you all to drink a toast to him.' He raised his glass, 'God speed to you, Nigel, and safe homecoming.'

Lizzie found herself on her feet with the others, not believing what she had heard. Her head was spinning. Was it to test her strength, to see if she was really like her grandmother, a horrible joke? But, of course, she had known, just as his father had known or guessed. She tried to make Nigel look at her, but he was bowing, smiling, saying 'Thank you', pale, but composed.

'That was a surprise.' It was Kieran. 'Did you know, Lizzie?' She shook her head. 'It almost makes me wish I could do the same, but it's so remote from us, the whole thing . . .' She scarcely listened to him.

Great-uncle Terence was speaking to her now. 'I can see Kate signalling to you. On you go.' When she met his eyes they were full of understanding.

She was in the centre of the rush and bustle, pushed

his way and that as if she were a leaf. Someone with a loud voice was assembling them for the Grand March. 'Lord and Lady Crawford first. Then you, sir. Miss?' Nigel had her hand. She was mute, too overcome to speak.

Behind them were Patrick and Maria, Terence and Honor, and so on through the McGrath family, followed by friends and workers on the estate. Everything was clear and yet like a dream. She noticed the three chandeliers down the centre of the room, the handsome painted walls of dancing nymphs with their swains – old Lord Crawford's choice, no doubt – the gallery divided into boxes above, in one of which was the Crannoch Ensemble. She remembered Lord Crawford saying that the ballroom had rarely been used in his father's time, that he had preferred prayer meetings.

Far down the line she saw Arthur Cranston with his intense gaze and high brow, accompanied by his discontented-looking wife. Maevy had told her she had nursed him at the Royal when his leg was injured at a strike march, and that it was through him that she and Charlie had come together. How happy they looked, Maevy in a flounced green dress with her hair done up in curls and a green bow buried in them. They had never known this dread in their hearts, surely, this fear coupled with the deep disappointment of not having been warned. Maevy would agree that it was cruel, coming from someone who had said so often that he loved her.

'We're starting,' Nigel said. She looked up at the minstrel's gallery, saw the fiddlers poised, saw the older heads of the spectators looking down from the boxes. She curtseyed to Nigel, he bowed deeply to her, gave her his hand, and they were away to the strains of the Brig o' Perth. They must have put chalk on the floor. Her thin slippers slid easily on it like glass.

'You're annoyed with me, Lizzie.' His voice was low.

'No,' she said, 'not annoyed, hurt.' She lowered her own, 'Why didn't you tell me?' It was safe to talk, the noise of the Ensemble, the scuffing of feet and the chatter all round them, drowned their voices.

'I wanted to, believe me, but to begin with I didn't know if they'd take me. I hadn't told Father either. It seemed foolish to distress everybody.'

'You should have told me, warned me.' But she *had* known, there had been that presentiment . . . 'over', 'over', the word echoed in her head as they proceeded round the room to the music. It would never be the same again, that hot summer, those walks and rides to the ruined monastery, all that loving. They were marching away from their youth.

She saw her grandmother and Lord Crawford leaving the line, having done their duty in opening the ball. It must have been difficult for him because of his lameness. She saw that Grandmother's gold brocade gown was edged at the hem with fur, like the deep wide neckline, and there was an embroidered silver and gold flower spray spiralling up the skirt. So sumptuous. Typically Grandma. She was surprised that her mind could wander so, as if it refused to be tethered to the one thought above all others. It was over.

'I was tortured,' he was saying, 'consumed with desire to fight for my country, consumed with love of you. And yet I knew I could never live with myself if I didn't offer my services.'

She turned to him and saw the suffering in his eyes. Her anger began to leave her. Why should she find it so difficult to understand him, considering her strict moral upbringing? She remembered her father's many sermons during the last year about right being might, and his constant haranguing of those 'upstarts' on the other side of the world who did not have the Lord on their side. That should have made it easy. Was it that Maevy and Charlie, with their more liberal attitude, had influenced her more? Charlie would never do as Nigel had done. Or would he? What if his services were needed? Wouldn't he have to choose?

'Can you understand, my love?' Nigel's arm tightened round her.

'I'm beginning to,' she said, 'all your upbringing . . . but it's the thought of losing you. I can't see beyond that.' Someone lifted his hand as they passed, shyly. 'That's Drewie, did you notice? Remember the night of the storm when he was trapped?' How strange that she should talk like this when her heart ached so badly.

'Try and put yourself in my place, brought up to put my country first since my schooldays. I could see Father was secretly proud of me when I told him. He would have done the same, he said. He appreciated how incarcerated I'd felt at Balliol.' His arm tightened on her waist again. 'I'll miss you, my darling, believe me. You're my life.' They proceeded in step to the March. They smiled when someone smiled at them.

'Do you remember,' she said, 'that line from the poem?'

'The Lovelace one?'

'I think so. What was it called?'

'"To Lucasta on Going to the Wars." Lizzie, I love you . . .'

'That's why you called me that?'

'Yes. I came across it . . . at the right time for me.'

'Will you send me a copy of it, to keep?'

'Surely. I'll send you a letter every day. I won't be out of the country for ages.' He was boyish, lovable. 'And there will be leaves before they send me there . . .'

The music stopped to clapping from all over the ball-

room. He still held her. 'You'll be inundated with partners. Save some dances for me.'

'Take your partners for the Polka.' It was the Master of
Ceremonies, Mr Sharp, the Crannoch grocer (Delicates-
sen and Fine Wines). She held out her arms to Nigel,
smiling, and he swept her into his. They were first on the
floor. 'I love you, love you.' He was breathless with the
speed of the dance. 'Love me . . . always.'

'Always . . .' Her violet skirts swung out, her silver
slippers scarcely touched the floor. She would not think
ahead, she would dance and forget about wars and
partings, and love which was heart-breaking . . .

It became a dizzy whirl of delight. She danced the
Petronella with Kieran, Strip the Willow with Terence
(how natural to be in her father's arms and what a fine,
sprightly dancer he was), a staider waltz with Uncle
Patrick, and reels upon reels as the Crannoch Ensemble
warmed to their task.

She took part in a Foursome Reel with Kieran and
Moira, and an Eightsome Reel with most of the McGrath
family – Nigel was the exception – Kieran and Sarah,
Aunt Kate and her brother (my handsome father), Honor
and her stepson, Robert. She danced as she had never
danced before, feeling weightless in her violet voile.

Terence, *heuching* and snapping his finger and thumb
with fine abandon, lifted her from the floor when he
swung her, and Kieran and Nigel, not to be outdone, did
the same. She floated and spun in a dream. The only
sedate one was Robert who was still learning the steps
and who when he was in the centre was all arms and legs
in the wrong places. She ached with laughter at him.
Tears ran down her cheeks.

'Best set in the hall!' Terence called, and Robert,
having pointed his toe in the right direction for once
called out triumphantly, 'Easy!' The clapping from the

rey-heads in the minstrel's gallery was loud and long when the dance finished.

'Ladies and gentlemen!' Mr Sharp announced, his face red and his gloves very white. 'Refreshments will now be served!' His waxed moustache had gone limp with the heat, but his face was as sonsy as one of his own mealie puddings.

'Let's all go together,' Kieran said, flushed, his curls falling over his brow. He had his arm round Sarah. 'They have to get to know their American cousins, haven't they?' The girl smiled at him. At sixteen she was as quiet as Lizzie remembered her at six when she had lived at Claremont Terrace.

'We'll join you when we've had some fresh air,' Nigel said, 'Lizzie's almost fainting with the heat.' He led her away through the double-doors into the long corridor and from there to the drawing-room. 'It has its advantages living in the place.' He smiled as he unlatched the french windows. 'We'll go into the walled garden. It's quieter there.'

'You were a bit rude to Kieran,' she said as they went round the back of the house and down the narrow drive towards the gardens.

'Was I? I don't regret it.' He opened the tall wrought-iron gate in the wall and they walked between the rows of flowers for cutting. A mingled flower smell came to her, the cinnamon smell of clove pinks predominating. 'Here's a bench. I've something to give you.'

She sat down, then jumped up again, laughing, holding her skirts. 'Oh, it's cold.'

'How stupid of me.' He took off his evening coat and spread it on the bench. 'There. Is that better?' He sat down beside her. How dark his face looked against the white of his shirt and waistcoat. She watched him take a small box out of his waistcoat pocket and hold it out her. His hand closed round her hand. 'Open it, Lizzie.'

Her heart was beating rapidly. She guessed what it was before she opened it, but she pretended surprise. That was how girls were expected to behave. But her delight overcame her pretence, suffusing her with love, filling her eyes with tears as she looked at the ring. It must be a ruby although it was black in the moonlight, the twinkling circlet of diamonds. 'Nigel . . .' She raised her eyes to his.

'Father gave it to me for you. It was my grandmother's, Annabel.' Grandma had liked her, Lizzie remembered, had called her, 'her dearest friend'. 'Let me put it on your finger.' He slid it on. 'Does it fit?'

'Yes, it's just right. It's lovely, Nigel. Thank you.' They kissed, their lips cool, like the night.

'He knew about us.'

'I'm sure Grandma does, too. I suppose it was obvious.'

'It must have been. We were so absorbed . . . He asked me if I'd like to announce our engagement tonight, but I said I'd have to ask you first, and besides, it was your grandmother's day.'

'That was right.' She turned the ring on her finger. What a sense of belonging it gave her. And yet it was only the beginning . . . 'You've forgotten one thing.'

'What's that?'

'You haven't proposed.'

He put his arms round her, his face against hers. There was laughter in his voice. 'It's been understood from the beginning. You know that.'

'Ask me all the same.'

'I love you. I'll always love you. Will you marry me?'

'I will.' She breathed deeply. 'There, that's that. I'm sad in a way.'

'Why?'

495

We seem to have become more circumspect now. You know, proper.'

'You improper girl!' He laughed. 'Only for a short time and then when I come back from the Transvaal we'll get married.' He kissed her, then again and again. His kisses were not so cool now. His hands went to her shoulders, to her breasts, and she thought, what does it matter? I'm Lucasta. He's going to the Wars . . . she was trembling when she forced herself to say, 'We'll have to go back.'

'I suppose so.' A lock of hair had fallen over his brow. He looked pale.

She took off the ring and put it in the beaded reticule over her wrist. 'We'll keep it a secret. I'll wear it on a chain round my neck and only you and I will know about it.'

'And my father and your grandmother.'

'And perhaps I'll tell Maevy and Charlie.'

'And your mother and father?'

'My real father? No, of course, you mean . . . I had a talk with him, and Honor. They were so nice to me. I've another home now if I wanted it.'

'I told you. I meant the Reverend.'

'No, he'd want to announce it from the pulpit. Besides, it won't be for long.' She stood up. 'Here's your coat.' She helped him into it. 'Will it?'

'No, my darling, it won't be for long.' In his evening coat he seemed to go a little from her, become the Honourable Nigel Garston Crawford, off to the Wars . . .

She saw her grandmother's eyes on her when they were dancing and she knew she had noticed they had been away for a long time. She smiled and waved. She said to Nigel, as befitted a newly-engaged young woman, that they must not slip out again, Grandmother would not like it, and she made him dance what he called duty dances

with Moira and Sarah, a slow waltz with Isobel, and eve
a Lancers and Pas de Quatre with the two unmarried
daughters of Bob Carter, which he said was a penance
indeed. He even took part in a Circassian Circle with his
Aunt Selina.

When he was dancing she went and sat beside her
grandmother. Her heart was too full to speak at first.
'You're like that little candle, Lizzie,' she said, 'burning
in the night.'

'You know, Grandma.' She met the brilliance of the
still blue eyes. 'Oh, I'm so happy, but so sad at the
thought of losing him.'

'You show him a smiling face when he goes. You don't
want a gloomy one left in his memory, now, do you?'

'No. It's been a lovely evening for me. You know why.
Has it been lovely for you, too? Are you happy?'

'Like you, happy and sad. Happy for you and Nigel,
and for all my good fortune, sad because it's the end of
an era. I feel it in my bones. This War, and soon the end
of the century, and maybe the end of me before long.'

'Don't talk such nonsense,' she said. A coldness crept
round her heart.

The dancing went on until four in the morning, as Lord
Crawford had said, and he and his wife stayed until the
end, gracious, smiling, bidding farewell to each couple as
they began to take their leave. Isobel and John had gone
long ago, she like a wraith hanging on to his arm, but
Charlie and Maevy were taking Lizzie to Braidholme for
the remainder of the night.

'We'd better go,' he said, 'I've to be up in an hour to
drive to Glasgow to get some essential medicaments for
the morning surgery.' He yawned hugely.

'Never mind.' Maevy laughed at him. 'Half the folks

re getting into working clothes as soon as they get home, as you well know.'

She said goodbye to Nigel in full view of everybody in the ballroom. He kissed her hand, and when he straightened he held her eyes with his until she felt the silence round them and walked away. She smiled and went on smiling until she was in the carriage with Maevy and Charlie and rolling towards Braidholme. 'Oh, Maevy,' she said, 'I'm engaged!' and burst into tears. Maevy took her in her arms.

'Hush, hush. You're the first lass I've ever known who cried about that. What do you say, Charlie?'

'Crying and laughing are not far apart, that's what I say.'

'But he's going to the War . . .' she sobbed on.

'He's not the only one. You're tired out, my lamb. You'll be proud of him in the morning, won't she, Charlie?'

'I hope so. Yes, maybe you're right,' his voice sounded weary.

24

Maevy sat waiting for the Crawford carriage to take her
to the docks. Only Ellie kept her from breaking down,
and Susan, who in her eagerness to be in on every detail
of this exciting day kept coming in and out of the room.

'Do you want me to take Ellie out of your way, Mrs
McNab?' she asked.

'No, it'll soon be here. She's as good as gold, aren't
you, Ellie?'

'I'm going to the Queen's Dock in Glasgow to see my
daddy sail away in a big boat,' Ellie said, her chin high.
'He's going to make all the poor soldiers better.'

'You don't have to be so chirpy about it, Miss,' Susan
said, 'your poor mother . . .'

'Mammy said we've not to be sad. The War's nearly
over and he'll bring Uncle Nigel back with him, and look,
Susan, I've got my hair out of plaits and into ringlets! We
tied it up in rags last night because Mammy says we've to
look our best . . .'

'Have you got that clean white hankie I gave you to
wave? Your daddy might not spot you in the crowd.'

'Yes, it's in my muff.' She produced a folded handkerchief from the astrakhan muff she wore on a chain round
her neck. Her waisted coat was green with a collar of the
same fur.

'Come away ben to the kitchen and I'll give your boots a
final lick. You've scuffed the toecaps already. Didn't I tell
you not to rin oot in the gairden . . . ?' There was a ring
at the bell. 'Oh, dearie me, here's your granny and Lizzie,
I mean, the Honourable Mrs Garston Crawford, to give

499

er her right title, oh, dearie, dearie me, everything's happening today.' She looked delighted as she went to open the door.

'She'll be in at our deaths that one,' Maevy said under her breath.

'What did you say, Mammy?' Ellie was restoring her handkerchief to its secure place in her muff.

'Nothing for your ears. Come over here and get your bonnet on.' Maevy lifted it from the sofa. 'It'll be cold at the Clydeside today. There, now, you're a lovely little girl.'

'Your eyes are all wet, Mammy.'

'Nonsense.' She hugged Ellie, longed to burst into loud, even ugly sobs, but Charlie had said in bed last night, 'Don't make heavy weather of it with the wee lass. She'll take her cue from you.'

Susan came back. 'They won't get out of the carriage, missus. They don't want to be late.'

'Right. Come on, Ellie, give me your hand. Expect us when you see us, Susan. We might have a bite to eat in Argyle Street when we're close.'

'Making a day of it, are you? Well, so would I in your shoes. Three generations of you all the gether, so to speak, and Lizzie as well, I mean, the Honourable Mrs Garston Crawford.'

'You'll get tired saying that,' Maevy said, smiling at the woman.

'I'm tired saying it already. I always think of her as Lizzie. Now, tell that doactor man o' yours to hurry back.' She wiped her eyes with her apron and dashed out of the room.

Lizzie was sitting beside her grandmother, both dressed in velveteen walking costumes edged with fur, Lizzie wearing a small black toque, Maeve a brimmed hat with a curling ostrich feather. Since Lizzie had been staying at

the Hall some of her grandmother's flair for dress
seemed to have rubbed off on her, even some of he
mannerisms. Her back was straight, but her paleness had
not the luminous quality of her grandmother's.

'How are you this morning, Mother?' she said, getting
in with Ellie. Thomas placed a rug over them. It was a
raw day, mid-winter at its worst.

'I'm fine, Maevy. It's Alastair that's not so good. The
dampness gets into his bad leg. He couldn't put it under
him this morning.'

'Poor soul. You should both go off to Spain and get
some of that sun on it. He knows Spain well, doesn't he?'

'Yes, he went there for the foundry often, but he's not
so keen on travelling nowadays. Besides, Lizzie keeps
him cheerful.'

Lizzie smiled. 'I read to him, that's all.'

'I could bring him some of my books,' Ellie said. She
had been left out of the conversation too long. 'They've
got some grand pictures in them.'

'You come with your mother tomorrow and spend the
day,' Maeve said. 'Now, that's a promise, Maevy.' Her
eyes held her daughter's. She knows how I'm feeling, she
thought, she's been through it with Lizzie.

When the War news had rapidly worsened, first the
disaster of Kissieburg and then Kimberley, Nigel and
Lizzie had got married. There was no question of waiting
until the War was over now. The wedding had been a
quiet affair because he was on embarkation leave, and
they had spent their honeymoon at the Hall. 'It's where
we've been happiest,' Lizzie had said to Maevy, 'and we
don't want to waste any time travelling. It's big enough to
get lost in.'

She had been brave when he had left. 'A stalwart,'
Maeve had said, 'and strangely enough, it's Alastair who's
able to give her the most comfort. He tells her about

...l when he was a little boy, and they spend hours
...ether discussing the War. I'm only the light relief.'
Maevy doubted that. Her mother's gaiety of spirit would
be an extra support to the girl.

But then had come that terrible Black Week in December when the total British casualties from the three battles
was three thousand, and the knowledge that Nigel would
have arrived and would possibly be in the thick of it.

'I've never known the daily agony of that girl,' Maeve
had said. 'We tried to keep the papers away from her but
it was no good. She seemed to feel as well the general
agony, the sense of humiliation. The world's turning
against us. It's no good the old Queen saying, "I will tell
you one thing, I will have no depression in our house."'

Maevy had nodded. 'Charlie says it will be a good thing
in the end. Our belief in our superiority and our sentimentality are better finished with.' She remembered him
reading aloud to her a piece of sanctimonious verse
supposedly written by a fourteen-year-old bugler. 'Give
me another that I may go, to the Front and return them
blow for blow.' He had thrown the paper away from him
in disgust.

'Have you any word from Nigel?' she asked Lizzie as
the carriage bowled through Sholton between the stone
walls of the estate and on to the Glasgow Road. The high
elms were bare. A few deserted nests showed where the
rooks had been. 'In the bleak mid-winter . . .' Maevy
thought of the words of the hymn, except that there was
no snow. It's almost too cold for snow, dead, like my
heart.

It had been the many reverses which had decided
Charlie, as well as the appeal for volunteers during the
first days of January. Had it been a straightforward short
war as everyone had thought, he would have gone on
working in the practice, feeling that he was more needed

there, but as the papers filled up with one setback·after another, she had seen him quieten, sit brooding at the fire, scan the papers anxiously every day, even get up at night to sit by the window.

One night, when she discovered he was no longer at her side, she had got up, wrapped herself in a woollen dressing-gown and gone downstairs. He was sitting at the window of the drawing-room, gazing into the black garden. There was nothing to be seen.

She sat beside him, put her arm round his shoulders. 'Are you wrestling with that conscience of yours?' she asked.

He looked round at her. 'You shouldn't have got up.'

'I wanted to be beside you.'

'It was that description in the *Herald* today of the Scots Guards caught in a vice at the Hodder River. A hundred and eight degrees, unable to retreat or advance, heads blown off if they lifted them . . . I couldn't get it out of my mind all day.'

'I know. I read it.'

'Belle Geddes would come in as an assistant to her father. She's dying for some experience in general practice.'

'You mean you've been talking it over?' She tried to keep the fear out of her voice.

'Just finding out the lie of the land.' He sounded shame-faced.

'Be honest with me, Charlie. You feel you should go. What's stopping you?'

'You know damn well. The great dilemma of every man who has loved ones.'

'But if you stayed put here wouldn't you begin to resent those loved ones?'

'No . . . never that.' His voice was low. She sighed deeply.

…t wouldn't be as bad for me as for Lizzie. You'd be a
…on-combatant. Maybe you . . . should . . . lend your
skills.'

'Oh, Maevy . . .' He touched her cheek. 'You're too
good. It's surgeons they need badly. Such injuries. The
Boers' artillery is far superior to ours. When I was at the
Royal the other day visiting a patient, I read a notice
asking for volunteers. D'you know who'd signed it?'

'No.' Nor cared.

'Mr Wilcox. He's retired now, but he'd lent his name
to the appeal.'

'I wonder what happened to his daughter?'

'I wonder . . .' He looked away.

He volunteered, as she had known he would. The
dullness she felt in her heart would not leave her until he
came back, but she smiled and said she was glad, and he
was not to worry. She would never reproach him . . .

They were glad to get to the Queen's Dock. Even with
the warm plaid rug and the foot warmers Thomas had put
in the carriage, they were cold. 'We'll have a cup of tea in
Cranstons afterwards,' Maeve said, 'and maybe a cream
cookie or two, eh, Ellie? Would you like that?'

'I'd rather have a scone and butter, Grandma, and one
of those wee pots of jam to myself.'

'You shall have whatever you like, my lovely. We'll all
have a treat.' Grandma and her treats, her sense of
occasion, but there was nothing to celebrate today . . .

Queen's Dock was crowded with soldiers and soldiers'
wives and families. There was the rattle of hooves of
frightened and neighing horses as they were loaded, the
cries of children, the shouting of officers as the men
marched in from Maryhill Barracks. Maevy, possibly for
the first time in her life, realized that the average working-
class Glaswegian was not much over five feet in height.
Poverty and malnutrition, she thought.

504

The McGrath family were all tall and erect, Nigel his father also. The lordly ones. Some of those wee shilp creatures looked hardly able to fight a war. But they were cannon fodder. That was the important thing. And she remembered they had a reputation for fierceness in battle. Maybe the battle for survival in the streets of Glasgow had taught them that.

She saw Charlie from afar off in his khaki, but no quicker than her mother. 'There's your husband, Maevy. On you go and have a word with him. Lizzie and I will stand here.'

'Come on, Ellie. Are you sure, Mother?' She hesitated. 'You come, too.'

'Don't waste time,' Lizzie said. 'It's short.' How pale she was. 'I'll watch Grandma doesn't get off with one of the officers.' Maevy went, half-running, Ellie by the hand, to where Charlie was standing.

He kissed her, put his arm round her and bent to kiss Ellie. He looked fit and happy. His mind was at peace at least, he had said last night. 'Have you been looking after your Mammy for me?' he said.

'I don't know what to do to look after her,' Ellie looked up at him, 'but maybe when you go away I'll see something.' Maevy and Charlie laughed at each other, and he hugged her against him.

'Grandma and Lizzie are standing over there.' She pointed. 'They're being tactful. They don't want to intrude.'

'They'd never intrude. Come along and we'll go over to them.' They walked back, with Ellie skipping between them.

Talk flowed between them for the first few minutes. They outdid each other in cheerfulness. Charlie cheered up Lizzie about Ladysmith and said they were all in good heart and would soon be relieved.

ou keep your eyes open for him, Charlie, won't you?'
 asked. 'I've had a feeling, I've had it ever since I
new you were going, that if he got hurt, you'd be at
hand to cure him.' She smiled. It would have been better
if she had wept.

'I'll make it my special mission.'

'I'm glad Isobel didn't come,' her mother said. 'It would
have been too cold for her.'

'Yes, she feels the cold badly.'

'And Alastair sends his apologies and his best wishes,
Charlie. He had to stay in bed today.'

'John said I was to be sure and tell you he'd pray for
you.' Maevy had noticed that since Lizzie had married,
she sometimes referred to him by his Christian name.

'He has quite a list on Sundays . . .' They were talking
for the sake of talking. There was nothing more to say.

'I'm cold,' Ellie said, whimpering. 'When are we going
for our tea, Grandma?'

'We're off!' Charlie said. There was relief in his voice.
He had been keeping his eye on the soldiers who were
milling around. Now they were forming in twos to march
on to the ship. The band struck up again, a rollicking tune
as if it was a festive occasion. A Sunday School Picnic . . .

This was it, then, suddenly, like that. When the colonel
said 'Go', they went. But Charlie was all right, he was
non-combatant, remember to smile. She put her hands on
his shoulders, 'Come back soon, my darling.' They kissed
briefly. She wished afterwards it had been for a longer
time, but in both of them there had been a shyness and
an impatience to get it over with.

He swung Ellie off her feet and kissed her, then
embraced his mother-in-law and Lizzie. 'I'm lucky. I've
four lovely girls to wave to me.' His smile was stiff.

'I've got my hankie,' Ellie said, excited now that things
were happening. 'I'll wave when you're on the big boat.'

506

'Write its name in your jotter when you get home. Y
mother will spell it out for you. The *Carthaginian.*'

'It's a big name for a little girl.' She took Ellie's hand,
her eyes fixed on him. Black hair, thin, no longer in his
first youth, why had she let him go . . . ?

Now his eyes were on her, only for a moment, those
brilliant intelligent, deeply dark eyes which were not black
but indigo, he was looking at her. He did not touch her.
'It'll soon be over. Everybody says it. We're on the
straight road to victory.' It was not the kind of words he
used. They were meant for comfort. He said to Lizzie,
'I'll remember.'

He was gone. Lizzie and her mother were on either
side of her, she had Ellie by the hand. She smiled a
general kind of smile, looking away from them. 'There's
a wee corner that's more sheltered, look, by that shed.
We'll stand there till he goes.'

They stood and watched the men marching up the
gangways to the jolly music – who wrote all those cheerful
marching songs which were a snare and a delusion – stood
while all the things were done on the dock which were
necessary to set the men off on their journey, put their
hands to their ears at the loud hooting which was meant
as farewell but was like a banshee wailing. Ellie laughed,
Maevy smiled, and smiled.

They spotted Charlie, waved and kept on waving till he
was a blur, till the troopship which looked top-heavy from
the weight of men had become an indistinct shape. One
minute it was filling the Clyde, the next it had gone. They
waited until the bands had stopped playing their jolly
tunes as a mark of respect and people began to slowly
turn on their heels and drift away. Better to be one of the
crowd. She was luckier than most, married to a non-
combatant.

'He saw us waving, didn't he?' Ellie was tearful now as

folded her handkerchief and put it carefully back in
her muff. It was to be kept for 'best'. 'I want my Daddy
. .' Her lip trembled.

'Of course he saw us. Now you've to be a big brave girl
the way you promised.' She stooped down and gave her a
hug, straightened her bonnet. How had they looked to
Charlie, standing against that rail in a sea of khaki figures?
Three generations of the McGraths, the distaff side,
wasn't it called?

Had he been proud of them? Sad? Of course he'd been
sad. But it was good for him to know that he had a family
behind him. He'd often said he'd felt one of them ever
since they'd been married. And that her mother was very
special . . .

'Can we go to that tearoom now, Grandma?' Ellie said,
'and get that wee pot of jam to myself?'

Outstanding fiction in paperback from Grafton Books

Nicola Thorne

Yesterday's Promises	£3.50	☐
A Woman Like Us	£1.25	☐
The Perfect Wife and Mother	£1.50	☐
The Daughters of the House	£2.50	☐
Where the Rivers Meet	£2.50	☐
Affairs of Love	£2.50	☐
The Enchantress Saga	£3.95	☐
Never Such Innocence	£2.95	☐

Jacqueline Briskin

Paloverde	£3.50	☐
Rich Friends	£2.95	☐
Decade	£2.50	☐
The Onyx	£3.50	☐
Everything and More	£2.50	☐

Barbara Taylor Bradford

A Woman of Substance	£3.95	☐
Voice of the Heart	£3.95	☐
Hold the Dream	£3.50	☐

Alan Ebert and Janice Rotchstein

Traditions	£3.95	☐
The Long Way Home	£2.95	☐

Marcelle Bernstein

Sadie	£2.95	☐

order direct from the publisher just tick the titles you want
in the order form.

Outstanding women's fiction in paperback from Grafton Books

Mary E Pearce

The Land Endures	£1.95	☐
Apple Tree Saga	£3.50	☐
Polsinney Harbour	£1.95	☐

Kathleen Winsor

Wanderers Eastward, Wanderers West (omnibus)	£3.95	☐

Margaret Thomson Davis

The Breadmakers Saga	£2.95	☐
A Baby Might Be Crying	£1.50	☐
A Sort of Peace	£1.50	☐

Rebecca Brandewyne

Love, Cherish Me	£2.95	☐
Rose of Rapture	£2.95	☐
And Gold was Ours	£2.95	☐

Pamela Jekel

Sea Star	£2.50	☐

Chloe Gartner

The Image and the Dream	£2.95	☐
Greenleaf	£2.95	☐
Still Falls the Rain	£2.50	☐

Gloria Keverne

A Man Cannot Cry	£3.50	☐

To order direct from the publisher just tick the titles you want and fill in the order form.

All these books are available at your local bookshop or newsagent, or can be ordered direct from the publisher.

To order direct from the publishers just tick the titles you want and fill in the form below.

Name _____

Address _____

_____

Send to:
Grafton Cash Sales
PO Box 11, Falmouth, Cornwall TR10 9EN.

Please enclose remittance to the value of the cover price plus:

UK 60p for the first book, 25p for the second book plus 15p per copy for each additional book ordered to a maximum charge of £1.90.

BFPO 60p for the first book, 25p for the second book plus 15p per copy for the next 7 books, thereafter 9p per book.

Overseas including Eire £1.25 for the first book, 75p for second book and 28p for each additional book.

Grafton Books reserve the right to show new retail prices on covers, which may differ from those previously advertised in the text or elsewhere.